DOCTOR WHO

THE INFINITY DOCTORS

LANCE PARKIN

BBC

Published by BBC Worldwide Ltd
Woodlands, 80 Wood Lane
London W12 0TT

First published 1998
Reprinted 1999

Copyright © Lance Parkin 1998
The moral right of the author has been asserted

Original series broadcast on the BBC
Format © BBC 1963
Doctor Who and TARDIS are trademarks of the BBC

ISBN 0 563 40591 0
Imaging by Black Sheep, copyright © BBC 1998

Printed and bound in Great Britain by Mackays of Chatham
Cover printed by Belmont Press Ltd, Northampton

For Cassandra May, always.

This book and its author owe a great deal to Cassandra May, Mark Jones, Mike Evans, Mark Clapham, Kate Orman, Jon Blum and Rebecca Levene.

Thanks also to Donald Gillikin, Patricia Gillikin, Elsa Frohman, Lawrence Miles, Henry Potts, Benjamin Elliott and Gavin Standen.

Prologue
The Old Days

Each snowflake melted as it batted into the thick walls of the Citadel, but still they came, like an invading army.

Eighty-five storeys below, everything was black or white. Only the tallest of the ruins were visible now, the snows covered the rest. Not that there had been much to see before the ice had come, merely the ancient temples and amphitheatres, the last evidence of a race that had ruled by the sword and built an empire planet by planet until it had spread across the universe.

When the temples had been built, the future had been an open sea. Gallifrey had been ruled by seers who remembered the future as they remembered the past. Destiny was manifest, the bountiful cargo that filled the holds of a thousand thousand starships. The prophecies had been bound and bound up to be the charts used to circumnavigate infinity. Explorers travelled ever outward, apprised of the marvels they would find, aware of the dangers. Prospectors rushed to the stars, knowing where to look for gold. Heroes took great risks, certain of the outcome. The future had shone as bright as the moon, and had been just as incorruptible.

Those times had gone, swept away in a few short years. The statues and towers had toppled and the fleets had been scuttled. The heroes had died, blind and alone, as all true heroes must. And as the temples and libraries had burned, the Books of Prophecy had been lost to the fire, along with all the other books. Only one fragment had been salvaged from the rubble. Now there were only memories of those definitive, intricate maps of what was to come. But the memory cheats, it steals, it lies, it tells you what you want to hear.

Today was a day to live in the memory.

The ships were a dream come true, and looked the part. Just from the vivid coloration of their hulls it was obvious that they didn't belong here – they hung like vast tropical fish amongst the half-submerged clock towers and minarets, light like the planet hadn't seen for a generation pouring from their portholes and hatches and into the evening. No wonder that the crowds of Newborn thronged around the observation levels of the quays. The older generation were more sceptical, seeing the whole enterprise as wasteful, potentially catastrophic. The ships hadn't been in the prophecy, they insisted. This was a betrayal, a calculated attempt to sever all links with the future they knew: it hadn't been foretold that the Gallifreyan race would become sterile, there was nothing in the Fragment about Looms, Houses, Cousins, this, that or the other.

Only a handful of the Elders had ventured out here from the shelters, obvious from their stature, let alone their robes of office. Many of them still begrudged the decision that the ships would be crewed by the young, that only a handful of crew members would be over ten years old. But the announcement came as no surprise. Those born since the darkness had fallen were a race apart from their ancestors. The young were eager, enthusiastic and their best days were still ahead of them. They didn't dwell on the glories of the past, they wanted to live in the future, shape it, rather than merely remember. The new order was no longer shocking, indeed it was becoming comfortable, familiar. The Old harboured a new resentment: the New should have been temporary, they had been meant as a substitute while things settled down, a poor substitute at that. But now they were the only future. And with the wisdom of the ages, some of the Elders knew it would only be a matter of time before the younger generation began to see the past as a dead weight, one holding them back, preventing them from reaching their potential.

Teams of the young were loading the last supplies aboard the ships, passing boxes and modules along in carefully orchestrated lines. In their designated dome, the flight crews would be putting on their uniforms, with the help of the necessary attendants and helpers. A phalanx of the Watch stood guard over proceedings. An army of engineers in protective garments swarmed around and inside the ships, checking every last detail. A small band of musicians had started playing a tune, and the Newborn had taken up the chant.

'Sing about the past again, and sing that same old song.
Tell me what you know, so I can tell you that you're wrong.
Just sing about the past, and the past's where you belong.

Let's travel to tomorrow, and learn a brand new song.'

Their voices drifted up on the wind. Two robed figures, a man and a woman, watched proceedings from their own balcony on the highest level of the Citadel. It was open to the elements, but the snows and the winds circled around them, not daring to intrude.

'They are magnificent,' Omega declared without needing to speak.

'A dream come true,' his wife agreed silently. She was slender, with green eyes. Beneath her fur cloak she wore a close-fitting bodice and leggings.

He towered over her, he seemed to be twice her size at least, an effect only magnified by his immense armour. It was bronze, studded with aluminium, with a lead breastplate. 'I must go to my ship. We have to embark before nightfall.'

'Good luck,' she said wordlessly.

'We have prophecy, so who needs luck?' he laughed, hugging her.

She nodded, and they parted. He strode away, leaving the woman alone on the observation balcony with her thoughts and memories.

Or so she had thought.

'Who indeed?' the little man said, breaking the silence.

She turned to face him.

'How long have you been here?' He stood in the middle of the tiled floor as though he always had been there.

'Time is relative.' He checked his pocket watch. 'Or at least it might be from lunch time tomorrow.'

'We know from the last line of the Fragment that the expedition will succeed. It is written.' She turned back to face the ships. 'It is what comes afterwards that is uncertain. But soon we will not just know the future, soon we will walk amongst it.'

'The Fragment,' he said, walking over to her, placing his hand easily on her shoulder. 'I thought you must have guessed.'

She knew what he was about to say.

He spoke softly, deep sadness in his voice. 'Rassilon needed to rally his people, he needed to justify his insane plan. You remember what it was like a decade ago, after the Curse. The Elders were looking to the past, they were giving up. All we had was our memory. All those golden ages and legendary adventures, all that infighting over which past glory was the best past glory. Gallifrey had died.'

'Even without Rassilon, we would have lived for many millions of years. We are very difficult to kill.'

'Oh yes. We're immortal, barring accidents. But accidents happen, my Lady. We would have died in the end without Rassilon and his plan. Didn't it ever occur to you how contrived the situation was? A workman clearing away the rubble of some fallen temple just happened to find a page from the Book of Prophecy. A single page, a little charred around the edges. Didn't you think that was odd? Didn't you wonder what had happened to the rest of the book? And it was such a useful page – the very one that told of the coming decade, showed the whole of Gallifrey that we would become the first of the Lords of Time. Even Rassilon's enemies conceded that the future seemed to be quoting word-for-word from Rassilon's manifesto half the time. An interesting coincidence, wouldn't you say?'

'The discovery of the Fragment was the clearest possible indication of our destiny,' she said firmly. 'The universe moves in mysterious ways.'

'The Fragment!' the little man snorted. 'Rassilon wrote it himself, placed the paper under a stone during one of his walkabouts. He doesn't want to see the future, he wants to shape it. The Scrolls are what *might* happen, what he *wants* to happen, not what *will*. Without the Fragment, Rassilon and the Consortium would not have been allowed to continue the time travel experiments, we'd have squandered the planet's resources just trying to stay alive, rather than investing them.'

And it made sense, but it made the future an abyss.

She shrugged his hand from her shoulder, turned to face him. The little man didn't speak for a moment. Finally, in that soft voice of his, he said, 'There are many races across the universe who have never remembered the future.'

She shuddered. 'It has been bad enough not knowing what would happen this last nine years. To be blind for ever... is that how you want to live?'

'You would be surprised how easy they find ways to explain away what happens. They have many beliefs that we would find strange. They talk of "cause and effect", "quantum mechanics", "prediction". Mostly they put their trust in their gods. They believe that the gods can directly influence the mortal sphere, rewarding their followers, punishing the unbelievers. The laws of physics bend to the will of the gods. They call it "divine intervention".'

She stared at him.

'A curious notion,' she said finally.

'Yes,' he replied. 'Without it, we are forced to create our own miracles.'

He pointed back at the ships and she turned. The sun was behind her, and barely above the horizon. The shadows were long, matt black, beginning to flow together, like droplets of mercury. The ships hung above the ruined Capitol, inviolate. The gangways and docking tubes had withdrawn, the ground crews were retreating back to the safety of the Citadel. The singing had stopped some time ago.

Without further ceremony, the air filled with an unearthly wheezing, groaning sound and the massive ships faded away like memories. Then there was nothing there except the ruins of the Capitol, the shadows of the past, and a winter's evening.

'Shouldn't you have been with your ship?' she asked.

But he had gone.

Part One
Intervention

Chapter One
Night Beneath the Dome

He'd never seen the rain, but he'd heard it.

It clattered against the lead and concrete of the Dome, sloshed into the gutters and heaved its way along until it was sucked down the drainpipes or thrown from the spouts. Whenever it was raining there was a hiss that filled the air, and a pulsating, chaotic pattering. It sounded like an animal clawing away at the shell of a tortoise; edging around, testing defences, quickly withdrawing when it found any opposition. You could only hear the rain if you were this close to the Dome, and that meant that you had to be at the highest points of the Citadel, the parts in the East Towers where it reached right to the apex. In fact, here the masonry of the Citadel's roof formed the skin of the Dome, and some of the lofts and attics actually lay between the inner and outer layers of the Dome walls. Although the Time Lords had an infinite amount of energy at their disposal, these areas were kept dark, and weren't heated. Few people ventured this far from the splendour of the main chambers, only the occasional Technician and the semi-regular patrols of Watchmen. A few tafelshrews had lived here once, but they'd long since turned into fossils, and their descendants had probably scurried off, evolved into spacefarers and left Gallifrey altogether.

From time to time, Captain Raimor had wondered what rainfall looked like. He'd never been carried away by this curiosity, never been so moved as to venture to one of the derelict observation attics or to look up the subject in one of the Archive Libraries. He had never had the desire to accompany one of the maintenance teams that - once a century or so - would go Outside, clambering up the side of the Dome to check the state of the tiles and guttering. Someone had told him once that rain was nothing more than falling droplets of water, and how interesting could they be?

The clock tower in the Old Harbour was tolling Four Point Five Bells, he could hear it even through the Citadel walls. It was the mid-point of the night, traditionally the time when the vampires and the other ghosts of dead immortals walked in the lands of the mortal men.

Over the sound of the rain he could hear footsteps.

'Who goes there?' Raimor intoned wearily.

'It is me, Peltroc,' an eager voice called out. Peltroc was a youngster, not even eighty years old. Raimor envied him his lined face and greying hair. Complications with his last regeneration meant that Raimor's physical form was a great deal younger in appearance than he would have liked. Most members of the Chancellery Watch wore younger bodies than the Gallifreyan norm, but Raimor's new body was barely past puberty. There were promising signs: a receding hairline, the first traces of worry lines developing on his forehead, but it would almost certainly be a century before he'd be comfortable with his appearance. The way you look shouldn't matter, but it did, and no one took him seriously any more. He was wondering whether he could fill the intervening decades before this body matured with a spell in Traffic Control.

Peltroc always joined him at this point. Those who weren't in the Watch might have questioned why it was that some sections of the weekly patrol required one Watchman, yet others required two or three. But each route had its own tradition, and tradition had served Gallifrey well. There had been the Watch long before there had been Time Lords, and there were ten million years' worth of history coded in the traditional routes. Some reminded of great disasters: the storerooms of the Endless Library were searched every night, ensuring that there would never be another Biblioclasm. The chambers of the High and Supreme Councils were ritually sterilised before each session, even a quarter of a million years after the Blank Plague had been eradicated. Triumphs were remembered, too: ceremonial marches every month retraced the victory parades that had followed the wars against Rigel, Gosolus and the dozen or so other worlds that had launched attacks on Gallifrey since the time of Rassilon and Omega. Then there was the wreath-laying at the tombs, cenotaphs, memorials and monuments all around the Capitol, to remind that the present had not been built without casualties.

As they set off on their patrol Peltroc was full of his boyish enthusiasm, as ever. 'It's raining again.'

Raimor affected a surprised expression. 'Is it? I didn't notice.'

'It's rained a lot recently.'

Raimor saw a whole night of similar banter yawning in front of him.
'And what do you put that down to?' he asked dolefully.

Peltroc considered the question. 'Could be the aliens,' he offered. He wasn't rewarded with a reply, so he spent a couple of seconds refining the answer. 'It didn't rain so much before they came on the scene. Perhaps it's Rassilon's way of telling us to keep ourselves to ourselves, let them sort out their own problems.'

The boy wasn't right, Raimor knew that, but his theory certainly had its attractions.

'Rassilon's Rain,' he snorted. 'I like the thought of that. Just think, Peltroc, up there are two battlefleets, heading this way. A hundred warships on each side. It's madness. It's sure to lead to trouble. There's the paperwork more than anything else.'

'I heard that there's a fair few on the High Council that would agree with that. You talk to a Time Lord, he'll tell you that he's not happy.' Peltroc sniffed.

'The President used his casting vote, though. So the alien fleet will arrive at dawn.'

'But the aliens themselves won't be on Gallifrey until tomorrow night, will they?'

'Didn't you read the briefing? The aliens arrive at dusk. Nine Bells precisely. They'll spend the day before that in orbit sorting out some last-minute details.'

Raimor held up his lantern. The guard light probed the darkness, creeping into the nooks and crannies, but there was nothing there and the light quickly shuffled back into its cage. It was quiet here, and this part of the Capitol was always kept cooler than the occupied quarters. He knew every inch of it, and nothing ever changed, no one ever came here. Night after night he would go about this beat, pacing his way from the Watch quarters, through the Archives, to the edge of the Dome. He'd follow the dome around for three or four hundred yards, weaving through the honeycomb of cell-like rooms and long-deserted galleries until he found himself here. Then together with his partner they would trudge back to their dormitories.

Their wrist communicators chirped.

Peltroc was looking as shocked as Raimor felt.

They had never chirped before.

Raimor held it up, angling his wrist experimentally, wondering what do to next.

It chirped again, and a text message flashed across its face.

FOUR POINT SIX BELLS. BREAK-IN AT ARCHIVE CHAMBER FOUR ZERO THREE. INVESTIGATE AND ADVISE.

Raimor frowned.

'So what do we do?' Peltroc asked.

'Investigate and advise, I suppose.'

He had been past Archive Chamber 403 just a few minutes ago. Idly, as they made their way back there, Raimor wondered if he had managed to trip the alarm himself. Some of the security systems dated back to the Old Times, but whatever their pedigree, they were notoriously sensitive.

Notoriously erratic, too. As Raimor and Peltroc arrived at Chamber 403, they saw that at least one thing hadn't worked. Iron security shutters were meant to have slammed down when the alarm was activated, sealing the chamber until the guards arrived.

Raimor hesitated at the open archway into the chamber. He couldn't hear anything or anyone in there. He realised that he was resting his hand on the butt of his staser. It was a peculiar instinct, and – rather ashamed that Peltroc might notice – he withdrew it, placing his arm back at his side.

Peltroc stepped in first, and Raimor was happy to let him.

The room, like many in this part of the Capitol, was filled with dusty display cases and ancient lacquered cabinets. Raimor knew that this was part of the Citadel that dated back to the time of Rassilon. It was still possible to see that from the angle of the roof, the quality of the masonry, the shape of the room. The brickwork and panelling along one wall was recent, a partition perhaps only ten millennia old, but it couldn't hide the room's heritage: in former times this had been an open balcony which had overlooked the old starharbour. Since then this room must have been a hundred things, from the office of a high-ranking Ordinal to student lodgings. Nowadays no one ever came here, except the patrol.

Peltroc and Raimor crossed the room, light from their lanterns nervously scouting the way.

There was a giant stuffed bird in one case, trapped aloft in a suspensor field along with a millennium's worth of dust. It glared down at the two guards, three of its wings drawn back as if ready to lash out at them. A pile of oily cogwheels lay next to it – presumably they were discarded components of a giant clock mechanism. A battered wardrobe sat at an angle to the rest of the room. One corner was dominated by a vast suit of armour. A rusty plaque informed anyone who read it that it had once belonged to Tegorak, although the name meant nothing to Captain Raimor. Vast cupboards loomed along the walls, not giving away anything about their contents.

One of the clear-fronted cabinets lining the back wall had been disturbed. Glass lay in shards over the tiled floor. There had been a simple lock on the case, but the thief had bludgeoned it off. Raimor glanced around, and found the remains of the scanner alongside the brick that had been used to smash first it, then the glass. Rather a clumsy way to go about things.

Peltroc was occupying himself with the cabinet door, so Raimor began a quick search of the room.

Raimor grimaced. 'What's in there?'

Peltroc peered into the gloomy cupboard and shrugged. 'Just boxes. Nothing special.' He pulled out one of the caskets and waved it around by way of demonstration.

'Some mischief-makers from Low Town.'

'They don't usually come up this far.'

'There's not much farther up for them to go unless they fancy a stint walking around on the Dome.'

'Could be the aliens.'

Raimor nodded thoughtfully. 'Aliens might not realise that there's nothing important in this room. Either way, we need to report this. Remember? "Investigate and Advise". We've investigated.'

Peltroc held up the casket. 'Who do we advise about all this, then?'

Raimor looked around, as if the answer to the question might emerge from the gloom. 'This part of the building is owned by Prydon College. We need to tell a senior Prydonian.'

Peltroc grinned. '*He's* a Prydonian, isn't he?'

'He consorts with aliens, too. He practically *is* an alien. That settles it. Bring the box and the brick.'

The cloaked figure heard the two guards leaving the room, heard their footsteps receding.

Alone once again, he edged around the cabinet, found the hole he had made. He reached in, carefully, to avoid the jagged glass. His hands ran across the tops of the caskets, sitting in their rows, letters and numbers embossed on them.

The one casket he was looking for wasn't there.

His hand probed the gap on the shelf where it should have been.

He remembered the Watchman saying that he would take a casket with him.

'No,' he hissed. 'No!'

The red eyes were upon him, staring at him, not saying a word or needing to.

Raimor and Peltroc made their way to the elevators and down fifty storeys.

This time of night, the Citadel was virtually deserted. There were a couple of other patrols on duty, a handful of Time Lords in Temporal Monitoring and the night porters at the Colleges, but that was it. Tonight, they passed about half a dozen Time Lords. More than usual, probably preparing for the arrival of the aliens.

As a member of the High Council, *his* rooms were right at the heart of the Citadel. Although it was a little distance from the Council chambers, they had to cut across one of the galleries that overlooked the Panopticon to get there. There was no chance of hearing the rain this far under the Dome.

Few Time Lords ever saw the public areas of the Citadel at night. The fountains still ran, there was still the ever-present humming of machinery, but the lighting was lower, shadows were cast from every transept and alcove. Everything became unfamiliar.

Perhaps the best example was the Panopticon itself, the enormous hexagonal hall that occupied the entire central area of the Citadel. During the day, even on a minor feast day like Harrenenmas, colourful banners would be waving from every column. The centre of the floor was inlaid with the omniscate, the Seal of Rassilon, an ancient, swirling, circular design that symbolised infinity and eternity. Far, far, beneath there was the Eye of Harmony, the black hole that the ancient Time Lords had harnessed. The power from that was infinite, to all intents and purposes, providing every erg of Gallifrey's energy, and plenty to spare. Around this focal point would be a couple of dozen Time Lords in their robes, along with their attendants and pupils. A choir might be singing, there would certainly be music or chanting of some kind. One group would be making an offering, there would be ten serious philosophical discussions underway and twice as many games of chess. By any right, the Gallifreyans should have been dwarfed by the architecture, but instead they filled the vast space. The Panopticon would be alive.

By night, the Panopticon was the largest tomb in the universe. Silence hung like cobwebs, the slightest scrape or clatter echoing guiltily around forever. The same places that seemed gay and airy at day seemed murky and stagnant by night. The floor, an expanse of marble large enough to land aircraft on, was the colour of bone. A vast statue of one of the Gallifreyan Founders stood in each corner of the Panopticon. At night they looked like giant ghosts, frozen in time. Raimor found it difficult to walk past them without paying his respects.

Raimor always took a minute to stare down at the Panopticon at night. He could hear Peltroc shuffling impatiently at his side. The lad would have to wait.

A Time Lord in a violet robe was walking down the gallery, his head bowed. He almost collided with the two Watchmen.

'I'm sorry, my Lord,' they both muttered.

'I couldn't sleep,' the Time Lord said, almost apologetically. 'I say, Captain, there isn't anything the matter, is there?' The Time Lord automatically addressed Peltroc, because Peltroc looked the right age. Raimor recognised the man as Lord Wratfac, an expert on cosmic radiation who'd been lecturing at Patrex College since the decoupling era. He was probably taking a short cut on his way to one of the Infinity Chambers.

'Don't worry, my Lord, it's nothing we can't handle.'

Lord Wratfac had bushy eyebrows and a rasping voice. 'It's not something to do with the aliens, is it?'

'That's what we are trying to establish,' Raimor said.

'You're going to see *him*, are you? The troublemaker?'

'That's right, my Lord.'

'It's very late, he'll probably be asleep.' But before Raimor could respond, Wratfac gave a cackling laugh. He jabbed a finger into Raimor's chest. 'Serve the young fool right! Carry on the good work.' He walked off, still chuckling to himself.

* * *

A short walk later, they had reached their destination.

Raimor rapped at the door. There was no reply. He tapped his foot.

'His servant's a bit slow,' Raimor remarked.

'Doesn't have one,' Peltroc sniffed. 'Doesn't believe in them.'

'Doing some poor bloke out a job, then, isn't he? Not that anyone would work for him.'

The door still hadn't opened.

'He's asleep,' Peltroc said. 'We should leave our cards and wait till morning.'

'We'll do no such thing,' Raimor replied stubbornly. 'You heard what Old Ratface said.'

He knocked again. This time, the door unbolted itself.

Warily, trying to show the appropriate respect, they stepped into the anteroom. The door closed itself behind them. They made their way through into the main part of the lodgings, all too conscious of their boots squeaking against the varnished floor. It was a rare privilege for ordinary Gallifreyans to be allowed into the chambers of a Council member. In nine centuries' service, Captain Raimor had only been in such a place three times. From the look on Peltroc's face, this was the first time he'd had such an honour, but it was clear that he had been expecting something elaborate: peristyles and fountains. But this room was only a little larger than a guard's berth. All six walls were lined with bookcases, making it seem even smaller. A staircase led up to the upper level.

Raimor stepped past a large wooden globe. He didn't recognise the planet it represented, and the globe itself looked like the product of a non-Gallifreyan civilisation. It was typical of this particular Councillor that he would have a map of an alien planet as such a prominent feature of his room. An odd world, too, with the landmasses broken up into colourful jigsaw pieces.

'He's not here,' Raimor snorted, careful not to raise his voice. He turned back to his companion. 'Look at this place. It's all wrong.'

Peltroc was examining himself in an ornately framed mirror. 'How do you mean, Captain?'

Raimor fished for the right words. 'A room like this... it should strive for *mathematical simplicity*.'

Peltroc frowned at his own reflection. 'I never got the hang of maths,' he said softly. 'All that adding and subtracting. Never got the hang of it. Maths is anything but simple in my book.'

'What it means,' Raimor sighed, 'is that a room such as this should have clean, straight lines. It should look like it was designed by a computer. If there absolutely has to be a curve it ought to be a parabola, or an arc. There's no excuse whatsoever for *colour*. This room is gloomy, it's cluttered.'

'I see what you mean now,' Peltroc whispered. He'd turned his attention away from the mirror and towards the shelves. 'Does this bloke really need so many books?'

'I'd remind you, son, that this "bloke", whatever we might think of him, is still a member of the High Council. Show some respect.'

To his credit, Peltroc straightened. 'Sir.'

There was a large fireplace on one wall, the light from it filled half the room. Two pictures in heavy frames hung above the mantel. The smaller painting was of a couple: the man was powerfully built with rugged features, a weathered face with dark eyes; the woman was a redhead, a little plump. Pride of place, though, was a large informal portrait of a beautiful lady with short black hair and a straight golden gown. Her shoulders were bare, she wore a necklace with a blue gem pendant and held a scroll in her hand. Facing the fire – and the pictures – was a large, high-backed chair.

'Who?' Peltroc grunted, gazing across at the pictures.

Raimor nudged Peltroc and indicated the chair. 'Never mind that,' he whispered. 'I think we've tracked him down.'

Raimor stepped across the room and over to the fireside. It was warmer over here, comfortable. Next to the chair was an occasional table. On it rested a wooden tray, and on that was a neatly arranged collection of silver jugs and pots. There were also three bone china cups.

'My Lord?' Raimor asked, bending over the chair. A rather bemused grey cat stared up at him. It blinked and stretched, in a calculated effort to appear unconcerned, even bored, with the guard.

A second later Raimor was upright again.

'He's not here.'

At the other end of the room, Peltroc tried to help by checking behind a tapestry, but all he found was the alcove containing the food machine. Tutting to himself, Raimor turned his attention back to the table. Steam was rising from the spout of the tallest jug. He could only have been gone a moment or so.

'Good evening, gentlemen. How can I help you?'

Raimor started, and turned.

He was standing between them, square in the middle of the room. He wore a thick cotton night-gown. His long face was oval, with an aristocratic nose and a full mouth. He had a high forehead, emphasised by his close-cropped hair. He had sad blue eyes, and he was clutching an old book.

The Doctor.

'Sorry to wake you, sir.'

The Doctor was staring at him as he walked over. Raimor could almost feel him looking into his soul, but all the old Watchman could think was that the Doctor wasn't as tall as he looked. He stopped inches away from Raimor.

Then he smiled. 'No, no, no, you didn't disturb me. I was finding it difficult to sleep. I was just reading. The *Iliad*. Have you ever read it?'

'No, sir.' Peltroc had made his way to Raimor's side.

'You should, you should.' An wave of realisation passed over his face. 'Here,' he said, pressing the book into the Captain's hand. 'Take it. I've not finished it, but I can work out how it ends. And take a seat. Shoo, Wycliff.'

The Doctor carefully placed the cat in his box and took his place in the chair. As it dragged itself around to face the room rather than the fire, the Captain made a show of examining his gift. This edition was recent, perhaps a millennia old. From the crest on the spine it was clear that it had been commissioned by one of the minor college libraries. If he had been addressing anyone other than a member of the High Council, the Captain might well have asked how it had ended up in private hands. Instead he merely thanked the Doctor.

'It's Captain Raimor and Constable Peltroc, isn't it?' the Doctor asked softly. Peltroc had found a rather rickety wooden chair, and it quickly transpired that this was the only other seat. Raimor declined the Doctor's suggestion that he sit on the rocking horse, choosing to remain standing.

'Tea?' the Doctor offered.

The two Watchmen nodded, although neither was sure what they had just been asked. As they took their places, the Doctor leant over the table, selecting the smaller of the two jugs. Deftly he splashed a little white liquid - nothing more exotic than milk, by the look of it - into each china cup. Pausing to smile up at his guests, he replaced the small jug with the larger one, filling each cup almost to the brim. Finally, he took a spoon and swirled the contents of each cup in turn. The operation complete, the Doctor passed a cup over to both of the guards, taking the third for himself.

Raimor took his cup, and almost immediately he'd managed to slop a little of the drink into the saucer. The liquid was brown, grey vapour was drifting up from it. Raimor sniffed it and took a swig. It was bitter, almost acidic, but that was counterpointed by the milk. Probably a plant extract of some kind. Pleasant enough.

'A display cabinet was smashed open in the Archives,' he explained. 'We don't know why.'

The Doctor sipped at his tea. 'Who says there has to be a reason?'

'Well, sir, that's what we thought: it was probably just vandals.'

The Doctor smiled. 'You misunderstand me.' He pointed at the pocket watch that nestled between the teapot and milk jug. 'How did that get there?'

Raimor hadn't noticed the watch on the table before. 'You must have just put it there,' he concluded.

'Must I?'

'It doesn't have to have been you,' Peltroc offered. 'It could have been someone else.'

'Why?'

'Things don't just happen,' Peltroc explained. 'If I find a coin in the street, then that's because someone has dropped it.'

The Doctor raised an eyebrow. 'And that's the only possible explanation?'

Peltroc screwed his face up. 'The owner of the coin... might... have put it there deliberately.'

'But this watch wasn't here a moment ago, and now it is.' He paused. 'What if there were two watches?'

The Doctor glanced down, and feigned amazement at the two identical watches he saw there. 'Two watches. Or perhaps the same watch, twice over. Time and space are elegantly inter-related, you know. Time is relative, as they say.'

'A trick, my Lord,' Raimor said, a little impatiently. 'You are trying to make a philosophical point, sir, using the watch.'

The Doctor grinned. 'And now both the watches have vanished, anyway.'

'My Lord, if we could return to the crime.'

'What has it got to do with me?' The Doctor scowled. His face fell. 'I'm not a suspect, am I, Captain?'

Raimor chuckled politely. 'No, sir. The room is owned by the Prydonian College and as the most senior member of the chapter –'

'Apart from the Magistrate,' the Doctor pointed out.

'Well, yes, sir...'

'We thought it might be the aliens, my Lord,' Peltroc stammered from his seat.

The Doctor cocked his head to one side. 'Why do you think that?'

'No Gallifreyan would do that sort of thing.'

'But the aliens don't actually arrive here until tomorrow night, do they?'

The two guards looked at each other. That hadn't occurred to them.

'They did it with this brick,' Peltroc said helpfully, holding out the offending article.

The Doctor smiled forgivingly as he examined it. 'I don't suppose you brought the lock up?'

'Er, no, sir.'

'What sort of lock was it?'

'Retinal.'

The Doctor pursed his lips. 'Why smash it open? They are straightforward enough to bypass.'

'If you've got Gallifreyan eyes,' Peltroc murmured to himself.

'Even if you haven't, it's still quite easy,' the Doctor assured him.

Raimor continued his story. 'The alarm went off, but the iron shutters and bell were both jammed somehow.'

'It would only take a couple of blocks of wood and a cushion or two,' the Doctor mused to himself. 'Was it the nearest cabinet to the door?'

Raimor tried to remember. 'No, there was a stuffed bird and... the smashed cabinet was right at the back of the room.'

The Doctor smiled. 'So what was taken?'

'Taken?' they said simultaneously.

'We don't think anything was taken,' Peltroc explained. 'Just vandalised.'

The Doctor rolled his eyes. 'Someone walked into a room, disabled the alarm, walked up to the back wall, smashed off a lock and broke into a single case, leaving everything else intact. Hardly the actions of a mindless vandal.' He narrowed his eyes. 'Although he's clever, he's not very well informed. He managed to pick the only day of the week that your patrol is up there. He's lucky you didn't walk straight in on him.'

'We don't know if anything was stolen, sir,' Peltroc piped up. 'You might be able to tell us.'

'Me? Which chamber was it?'

'403.'

The Doctor pursed his lips and shook his head. 'Off the beaten path. Despite that, I don't ever recall going there. Not for centuries, anyway.'

'I brought you this casket,' Peltroc said smugly. 'It came from the cabinet.'

The Doctor eagerly set about opening it and examining the contents.

'There wasn't anything special in there,' Raimor observed.

'Well no. If there had been anything special in there it wouldn't have been in there, would it? Now, the key to the mystery must be in here somewhere.' The Doctor opened the box, fished out what he found, laying everything on the table beside him. 'Interspatial protractors. The last time I saw one of these was at school.' He turned one over and over in his hand, rotating it through its five dimensions. Next he found a couple of translucent discs.

'Are those data cards?' Raimor asked.

'Yes,' the Doctor sighed. 'But you can tell just by looking at them that they've been corrupted for centuries. Only a hard burst of radiation could do that. Which means they were wiped *before* they were put away in this box.'

Right at the bottom of the casket was the hilt of a knife.

'Careful with that,' Raimor warned.

'What is it?' the Doctor asked. Peltroc looked equally blank.

'A force knife. Works on the same principle as a forcefield, creates a blade.'

The Doctor flicked it on. The blade shimmered into existence, solid as metal. The Doctor examined it. 'Why not just use a proper knife?'

'Try it,' Raimor suggested.

The Doctor weighed the knife in his hand and then stabbed it down at the table. He was clearly surprised when it went straight through the tray and the tabletop. It had slid through the silver and wood as if they weren't there, right up to the hilt. Now it looked as though it had always been there, and no force in the galaxy could remove it.

'That's a sharp knife,' Peltroc observed.

'The blade can be anything from a quark to a metre long. It adjusts itself so it can cut through anything, even at the molecular level. If you've got a death wish, you can split an atom with it. It was designed as an all-purpose tool.'

The Doctor glanced down at it. 'I'll stick with the sonic screwdriver, I think. It's more my style.'

He rummaged around in the box for a minute, producing a bunch of keys, a handful of treazants and a couple of cracked exitonic circuits before he looked up sadly. 'It's all junk. Nothing valuable. There's no reason why we couldn't have just thrown it all out millennia ago. There are no clues here. I...' his voice tailed off, as he had just found a slip of paper, one that was brown with age and folded in half.

There was a single word on the paper, hand-written, in capitals.

WHO

The Doctor was wincing, screwing up his eyes as though someone was shining a bright light at him.

Raimor and Peltroc glanced at each other. 'Are you all right, my Lord?'

'Can't you hear it?' he said. 'It's coming towards us, but all around us.' The Doctor shook his head, as though he was trying to dislodge something. Then he looked up, fixing Raimor in his sights.

'I'm fine,' he assured them. 'A headache, that's all. Not enough sleep.' He straightened. 'There's nothing more that you can do here. Return to your patrols, I will make the necessary arrangements.'

The guards snapped to attention saying, 'Sir!', before marching from the room.

It was Seven Bells, two hours to dawn, and there had been enough excitement for one night, so Raimor and Peltroc skipped the last part of their patrol. They returned to barracks, changed out of their uniforms into their day-tunics, checked in their weapons and communicators and released their lights into the luxquarium.

Tonight had been eventful, and tomorrow would be a long day. Both men were going to be on duty when the aliens arrived, and would be spending most of the day beforehand in the Panopticon, practising their drill. Raimor grumbled about this before heading to his berth. Before he went, the Captain handed Peltroc the copy of the *Iliad*, saying that he had no use for it. Peltroc watched him go, flicked through the book to the frontispiece, looked at the first colour plates and then dialled up a meal on the food machine: nothing fancy, just basic nutrition. He'd eat the food, start the book and then get some sleep.

Peltroc thought about elephants, and wondered how they could possibly play four-dimensional snooker.

He shook his head. What was that all about?

Holding the cues would present a particular challenge, and they'd probably object on moral grounds if the balls were made of ivory.

As he moved to sit down, his chair was kicked away from him. There was something sharp at his throat before he'd hit the ground.

'This is a force knife. It can cut through anything. In the right hands it can split an –'

'– an atom,' Peltroc stammered. 'I know. I've just had this conversation.'

The knife blade pressed into his skin, drawing blood. 'Then you should know to treat whoever is holding one with respect.' The voice was calm, too calm to be natural. 'Release the mental blocks.'

The hand holding the knife drew back a little, giving Peltroc his first glimpse of his attacker. Black cotton gloves, loose sleeves in heavy grey material. The hum of the knife filled the air, hovering like a wasp over his neck.

Realisation dawned over Peltroc. 'Oh, now I get it. You were trying to read my mind, and you couldn't. You just saw gibberish. Elephants, was it?'

The man stepped back. He was wearing a thick grey cloak that swamped his body. His head was concealed beneath a heavy hood. 'All the Chancellery Watch are trained to resist the mind probe,' the voice said calmly. 'But there are ways to break through your conditioning, if you know how. Chamber 403. I was there.'

The room had been so dark, Peltroc realised. There could have been an army hiding in there. Why hadn't it occurred to them to look? He was thinking about it again... remembering everything and a particularly surly-looking bull elephant potted the black, and gathered up the row of coins stacked up along the side of the table, grinning smugly at his mates. His hypnotic conditioning was kicking in again.

'Show me your face, and we'll talk,' Peltroc replied.

There was a sound something like a roar, something like a cry of anguish.

The knife swept through the air, slicing the leather-bound *Iliad* in two.

'*Everything* is at stake, Constable Peltroc, and your life is unimportant. You will tell me what I want to know, one way or the other.'

The guard whispered something. The hooded man leant closer to catch it.

Peltroc grabbed the cowl. 'Let's see who you are.' He tugged down.

The head was blank, an egg of smoothly polished chrome. Peltroc took a step back, his terror reflected back at him. Whatever it was gave a gurgling laugh and began advancing towards him, arm raised.

Before Peltroc could scream or call for help, everything went black.

The fire was dying down, the teapot had grown cold, the night was nearly over and the Doctor hadn't slept. Wycliff wasn't having any such problem, and was still fast asleep on his rug.

Something was wrong.

Water was seeping into the Doctor's shoes. He scolded himself for standing right at the edge of the shore, with the sea lapping around him. The Doctor looked down at his feet for a moment, before turning to gaze around his surroundings.

The landscape here was timeless. It was Earth, of course, unmistakably Earth. No other planet had the same light, the same smells or sounds. There was no confusing the Sun that hung in this clear winter's sky with another sun, and there was literally nothing quite like this sea breeze anywhere else in the universe. The Doctor guessed that it was the English coast. A couple of hundred yards away, seagulls circled the cliffs, their cries drifting across the beach.

And then there was something else here, something fearful. The Doctor could sense it closing in on him, surrounding him. It was watching him with ancient eyes.

The world was blood-red, the Sun was swollen, twice as old as it should be. Red light filled the sky, filled the sea, but there was little warmth. The beach had grown dark, and was darkening further.

A grey shape was moving across the face of the Sun. The Doctor relaxed a little, recognising it as an eclipse. The Moon was passing between the Sun and the Earth. But... the sun was larger now, bloated with age, so how could the Moon be blotting it out? The Chinese used to think that eclipses were caused by dragons taking bites from the Sun. It would have to be a vast creature, with eyes the size of the Earth, a tail longer than any comet's. The Doctor imagined the creature's mouth opening, the sun in its claw like a fruit. If he could see it, the Doctor realised, then there was nothing he could do. It was in the past. The Sun had died long ago, and now its light was catching up with it.

There were howling winds in the distance, although the air felt warm. The Earth was lost.

Black columns were sweeping the earth like searchlight beams. Pillars made from the opposite of light, angling, snapping on and off, dancing over the sea and the cliff tops. The Doctor scanned the heavens for their source, but they were like sunbeams poking through the clouds.

Laughter surrounded him, mocking laughter that drowned out every other sound. He could hear it calling his name. Something from the past and future, something infinitely bigger than him. Everything was at stake. Everything.

There was someone alongside him, staring out to sea. A man his age, his height, but with flowing, shoulder-length hair. All his children were dead, and the seas were dry. The stars were coming out, now. Night was falling.

The Doctor's eyes snapped open.

It had all been a terrible dream.

Chapter Two
Total Perspective

The Main Temporal Monitoring Chamber appeared larger than it was, but as its central feature was the whole of infinity and eternity this was hardly surprising.

The room was a torus, a ring the size of a stadium, and it encircled an Infinity Chamber, one of the ultimate expressions of Time Lord technological achievement, beyond the dreams of even the founders of Gallifreyan civilisation. It wasn't simply a device that monitored or observed the known universe, it *encapsulated* it. To all intents and purposes, the Time Lords gathering here weren't watching an image of Gallifrey's moon, Pazithi, they were watching Pazithi itself, in full scale. The Time Lords entered, moved clockwise around the colonnade that marked the perimeter of the room until they found their place and shuffled out onto the floor of the Chamber. In all, a little over five hundred Time Lords were present, all bathed in the holographic moonlight. More than half the total number, which was almost unprecedented, especially as it wasn't even quite dawn yet. This must have been the first time that some of these people had ventured out of their room for decades. The public galleries weren't quite so busy, but there was still a respectable turnout. The Chamber hummed with conversation and expectation.

Larna hesitated, removing herself from the shuffling crowd. Everyone already knew precisely which part of the amphitheatre they should be standing in. They clustered in the usual groups determined by elaborate equations of seniority, office, family ties, college allegiance and personal acquaintance. Everyone knew where to stand except for Larna. Her robes flapped and blocked her feet and hands, the high-backed ceremonial collarpiece was digging down into her shoulders.

'Are you lost, my dear?'

She turned. It was Lord Hedin. He had a thin face, kindly and shrewd. He was an historian, a mainstay of the High Council, as his father had been before him. Larna had attended some of his lectures about the Old

Time. He was usually to be found in the Endless Library compiling the bibliography for his life's work, the three-hundred-volume *Life of Omega*.

'This is the first time I've been here, my Lord,' she explained. 'On the floor of the Chamber, I mean. I've spent most of the last few years in the public galleries or operating the machines.'

Lord Hedin smiled. 'You're Larna, aren't you? One of the Doctor's pupils?'

'That is right, my Lord.'

'You are a Time Lord, now, my Lady. You may call me Hedin.'

She acknowledged him by bowing her head.

He pointed out a space on the floor. 'As a recent graduate of Prydon and a full citizen of the Capitol, you should stand there.'

Had she seen the Lord Ghene and the Lady Thlau earlier, she would have been able to work out for herself that she should stand close to them.

'You'll be within earshot of the High Council themselves,' Hedin said. The prospect pleased Larna, although the tone of Hedin's voice suggested that this was a mixed blessing. 'You recognise the Councillors?'

'Of course,' she said. She knew the names of everyone standing around the President: the Magistrate and the other Ministers, the Castellan, the Co-ordinator of the Matrix, half a dozen Cardinals and a couple of cowled representatives from the religious orders. Larna found it difficult to believe that now she was a cog in the same intricate clockwork as these people, that she was beginning to acquire titles and duties of her own.

Hedin pointed out a neatly bearded Councillor in jade green robes. 'Who's that?'

'Councillor Norval, the Chief Scientific Adviser.'

Hedin nodded. 'Have you noticed that he's not used to his robes yet, either?'

He did look a little overwhelmed.

'But the Lord Norval has been a Time Lord for four thousand years,' she said.

Hedin smiled. 'Look around, my dear. See how virtually everyone here is in the same predicament as yourself. What was that word you used? Overwhelmed. All your fellow Time Lords, even very senior ones, are still overwhelmed by the folds and flows of the material or the weight of the collarpiece.'

Larna brightened. 'Thank you... Hedin.'

Hedin smiled.

'The alien fleets are in position,' a Technician proclaimed.

'It's not long since you did that job, is it?' Hedin asked her. 'Last time you were here you would have been wearing that monochrome tabard.'

It was impossible to become a Time Lord without at least a short stint as a Technician, although Larna had never been on duty on such a momentous occasion. 'The last time I served as a Technician was for the conjunction of the planets Tarva and Alambil.'

'I missed that,' Hedin said sadly.

'Full records were archived within the Matrix, my Lord. You could replay them whenever you wanted.'

Hedin nodded. 'Yes, but it's not the same as being there, is it?'

'Archiving causes no degradation of pattern –' she paused, her mind catching up with her mouth. 'You are right. There is a qualitative difference between watching the data being collected and watching a recording.'

He was smiling. 'Do you know the Duty Technician today?'

She looked across. 'He was in one of my study groups. His name is Waym of Olyesti.' She found herself envious of Waym, but also glad that she wasn't at the controls. Few of the Time Lords had noticed the Technician as they had shuffled into the chamber. Not that many had noticed him now, even after he had spoken, but a single mistake on his part might mean shame, disgrace, even an end to his academic career. There had been a hint of nervousness in Waym's voice, and he seemed dwarfed by his surroundings.

'Olyesti is one of the Three Minute Cities in the East.'

'That is right.'

'Despite his family connections you graduated before him.'

'Probably because his tutor seemed more interested in kaons than students,' she said, before she could stop herself.

Hedin chuckled. 'Wratfac?'

'That's right, my Lord.' She looked around, worried he might have overheard, but couldn't see him anywhere.

'A fool. Worse than that, an old fool.' The ushers began calling for silence. 'I had better get into place. It has been good to talk to you, my Lady Larna.'

She bowed her head and took her place.

Larna didn't have to strain too hard to pick up on the topic of conversation. The assembled Time Lords might not have noticed Waym's presence, but they had noticed an important absence. Beneath the normal conversations, Time Lords were beginning to mutter about the gap in the ranks of the High Council. Where was the architect of today's proceedings?

'There is still time to call this off,' one of the backbenchers insisted from behind the President.

The President's current body was tiny, withered, his face was even more pale than his ivory robes or the white of his beard. He barely seemed to have the strength to stand and wear the ceremonial Sash of Rassilon at the same time. He didn't turn to face the man who had addressed him. 'I have consulted the Matrix,' he said, indicating the metal circlet that hovered above his head like a halo. 'This is to be a momentous day.'

There was more muttering.

A Council member stepped forwards, Lord Norval, who Larna had just been talking about to Hedin. 'Lord President, as there is a delay here, perhaps we might use this opportunity to turn our attention to the temporal flicker in –'

'Oh no you don't,' called another, taller, Dromeian Councillor as he pushed his way to the front of the crowd. Larna realised that it was Castellan Voran, who had just arrived with his fat little assistant, Pendrel. 'Before we worry about that, we really must look into the latest disturbances on Tyler's Folly. Certain of the other higher powers are recommending that their people withdraw from the area. The planet is a major temporal nexus and the events there –'

'Are of limited and local interest, Voran, as well you –'

The Castellan waved his hand dismissively. 'And a temporal flicker isn't? Unlike your little problem, Tyler's Folly is actually on the agenda for the next Council Meeting.'

The President raised his hand. 'Enough!'

The two Time Lords fell silent. The President nodded, grateful. 'Magistrate? Where *is* the Doctor?'

The Magistrate moved forwards. He was a man of medium height, dressed in the thick black robes of office. His face was sallow, with a small, pointed beard, but that wasn't what you remembered about him.

You remembered his dark, burning eyes. The Magistrate was one of the President's most trusted advisers, and the Doctor's oldest friend.

'I shall look for him, Excellency.'

The President shook his head. 'I need you here.' He asked one of the Cardinals to locate the Doctor and then turned out to the throng of Time Lords. 'Open the gates of the Time Vortex.'

They hadn't even tied him up.

He was in Low Town, Peltroc knew that even as he opened his eyes. The air was full of the smell of wet carpet and roast grockleroots, the sound of crowds outside bustling along cobbled alleyways. He was sitting on a chair, which in turn was sitting in the middle of a bare room, a first-floor one judging from what he could see out of the grimy window. There wasn't a carpet, the room was lit by a chemical lantern hung from the ceiling, and the only items of furniture were a battered, ancient wardrobe and a chest that looked as if it had once spent a century underwater. There was only one door.

Peltroc stood, flexing and stretching. There didn't seem to be any lasting effects of being knocked out, not even grogginess. Whatever the masked figure had planned for him hadn't been done yet. Every mind probe that Peltroc was aware of required the subject to be conscious.

Low Town was a shanty town that had grown up around the columns that kept the Capitol Dome level. Even on Gallifrey, there were the poor. Many people in Low Town came to the Capitol looking for work in the Guard, or the Civil Service. Perhaps some had tried to apply for the Academy. Others might have left the life in the Capitol, disillusioned with the rule of the Time Lords. Peltroc sometimes felt that way, and he could see that this was a very different way to live from the disciplined, ordered world above, but he could see no benefit in coming down here. The truth was that people lived here because this was a halfway house with many of the advantages of the Capitol, such as energy sources, fresh water and the rule of law, but with none of the social obligations to the 'Timeys', no loomgeld or tithes. The authorities tolerated Low Town because it allowed them to monitor and control lawlessness, keeping it confined to Low Town where they could see it. More than a few Time Lords, particularly the younger ones, had ventured down here to the bars and the brothels to see how the other half lived. They were hypocrites: aristocrats playing at being commoners for the night.

Invariably the Capitol Guard had to venture down to extricate them from the clutches of some criminal or other, but at least those Time Lords acknowledged the existence of places like this. The sad truth was that the poor lived in Low Town because most of the elite didn't care one way or the other what the poor did.

He went over to the window, wiped away a finger's length of dust and peered out, trying to see if he recognised the area.

Some parts of Low Town were almost respectable. In places rich merchants had found and refurbished the ruins of old villas, and restored the old roads, parts of the ancient city that the Dome hadn't enclosed when it had been erected by the generation after Rassilon. There was genuine civic pride there, not to mention a flourishing economy. Other parts of Low Town were filthy, temporary structures made from packing materials and wreckage. There was no disease, of course, no starvation, and the lifespans here were as long as the Time Lords' – once you'd taken into account that the accident rate was several orders higher than the controlled environment of the Capitol and Citadel. But in Low Town the gift of immortality simply meant that the poor lived in squalor for ten thousand years more than they otherwise would.

This was an area somewhere between the two extremes, like most places were. It was dark outside, so this was either a subterranean part of the Town, or it was night outside. No way of telling which from in here. No way of telling exactly which street it was.

There was a creak on the stair. Someone was coming. Peltroc tensed, unable to get into a better position. Another few seconds and he could have been behind the door, ready to attack. The door unbolted and a man and a woman stepped in.

They wore the cloth smocks preferred by the Outsiders, those Gallifreyans who had rejected the civilised life in favour of the wilderness beyond the walls and domes. Their tanned faces and the muscles of their arms suggested that they were genuine outcasts, and that they would know how to use the metal blades sheathed at their waists. The modern-looking communicators and utility capsules clipped to their belts suggested that they hadn't abandoned all technology. The male was a bear of a man, she was lithe, her hair tied in braids.

'Huran, he's up!' the woman cried out.

'Of course he's up,' a calm voice said from behind Peltroc. 'Hurry! It is nearly dawn.'

He had been standing behind him the whole time. Still wearing the hooded robes, and still with that blank, metal face. Peltroc wondered whether it might be a robot, or an artificially generated form of some kind. Perhaps even something as sophisticated as a shayde. But the more he thought about it, the more Peltroc became certain that there was a man under all that. A man wearing a mask and a voice distorter. There was an unsteadiness there that would have been programmed out of a robot. But it was impossible to guess what he looked like, or even his physical build. The male Outsider was preparing a syringe that he'd produced from his belt.

'Now, Constable Peltroc, you will tell me what I want to know,' the masked man said. The Outsider handed the syringe to his master, who brandished it like a knife.

The blank face loomed a little closer. 'Ask me politely,' Peltroc told him. 'I might tell you anyway without the need for any of this.'

The masked man lunged at him, stabbing the syringe clumsily but brutally into Peltroc's side.

Peltroc cried out with pain, and in that moment of weakness he felt a mind brush against his. It felt as if he was trapped in a room with a tiger. Asking about the box. Whatever had been in the syringe was eating its way through his mental defences. He could feel it, warm in his veins, spreading like acid. He wouldn't be able to rely on his conditioning now, but he had willpower of his own, he wasn't without some resources.

Peltroc slumped, grasping the back of the chair to stay upright. 'Why are you so interested? There was nothing. Just a knife, some discs and some keys,' he heard himself say.

Peltroc was watching the two Outsiders out of the corner of his eye. After all that trouble taken to conceal his face, the masked figure had made an obvious mistake: he'd hired two people whose expressions could be read like a book. No reaction to the first two words, but when he'd said 'keys'... the way they had looked at each other, they might as well have shouted that it was the keys they were after.

'I won't tell you,' Peltroc said, tensing, straightening.

The man in the mask hadn't noticed. It occurred to Peltroc that the mask might be quite restrictive – his opponent might not have much peripheral vision. The figure reached into the folds of his cloak, producing the force knife. 'You will tell me, Constable, one way or the other.'

He aimed the device, making a rather clumsy show of adjusting the settings.

Peltroc lifted the chair up, swung it around, smashed it into the side of the masked man. Caught unawares and off-balance, he collapsed with a gurgling gasp, the knife rolling from his hand.

The female Outsider was running for him, screeching.

Peltroc scooped up the knife and brought it to bear on her.

The power setting dial must have been twisted as it rolled along the floor. The blade that shot from the hilt was the length of a lance, enough not only to impale the Outsider's chest, but to lift her off her feet and slam her into the rear wall with such violence that the plaster cracked. Her body slid down, legs and neck twisted, eyes rolled up.

Both Peltroc and the remaining Outsider were too shocked to react for a moment. Then the man – Huran – bore down on him. It was easy enough to dodge him, let him crash into the floorboards. Peltroc knew that his priority was the leader, not the hired muscle.

The masked figure had run to the door. Now he smashed it down with a single kick. He was wearing heavy boots that looked almost metallic.

Peltroc aimed the sword at the doorway, but the masked figure was already out of sight, and he could be heard clambering down a flight of stairs.

Huran punched Peltroc, bringing him to his knees. A couple of kicks in the ribs and he was sagging on the floor. The knife was still in his hand, still set to hit someone with the force of a moving train.

'Don't make me do this,' Peltroc whimpered.

'You killed Yiri. Do you know how long we've been together?' Each word was punctuated with a flailing punch or a jabbing knee.

'I don't want to kill you,' Peltroc said.

But Huran couldn't hear him, he was pinning Peltroc down, pounding away at him, not caring whether he was hitting his face, his chest, his genitals. Peltroc felt a rib break, he wanted to be sick. The Outsider wasn't thinking, he wasn't combat trained. If he was, Peltroc would be dead by now. That was something to hold onto as blow after blow connected with him. Something to hold on to. The knife. Mustn't lose hold of the knife.

And then the Outsider was on the other side of the room, cradling the body of his lover. She was so small next to him, she looked like his doll.

Peltroc must have blacked out, just for a moment. The Outsider had left him for dead. The world was... muddier... its sounds and sights less well defined than they should be. He was deaf, and blind in one eye. He cried out in shock, but didn't hear it. It was just the blood in his eyes and ears, he told himself after a moment of panic. And he was so weak now that what Peltroc had thought was a scream to wake the dead hadn't even reached the other side of the room. Huran didn't know he was awake... alive.

There was one thing he could do, except let himself die. He pulled himself up, lunged at Huran, the blade sword-sized, stabbed him in the back, through his heart, twisted the blade and pulled it to the left and through the other heart. It was the way he'd been trained to kill a Gallifreyan with a sword, but the first time he had ever had cause to use his training. The Outsider jerked once, then slumped forwards, collapsing into a broken heap with his lover. His blood slid frictionless from the blade, dripping down the hilt.

Peltroc's knees buckled and he blacked out again.

Three floors below the Infinity Chamber level, the Great Panopticon Bell had begun to chime Nine. It could be heard through the floor of the Main Temporal Monitoring room.

The Cardinal sent to fetch the Doctor was barely away from the President's side when there was a commotion at one end of the Chamber. The crowd of Time Lords was parting, with considerable reluctance and grumbling. At the centre of the disturbance was the Doctor, his skullcap in one hand, the other waving in front of him, trying to clear the way.

'Sorry I'm late,' he told anyone that would listen. He bustled past Larna's group and reached the President's side.

'Have I missed much?' he said breathlessly, grinning as he pulled the skullcap onto his head, adjusting it until it was right.

This was the man who had invited the aliens to Gallifrey, and Larna's ex-tutor. Now he stood less than ten feet from her, at the President's side. While everyone else's attention returned to the vast display in the centre of the room, Larna kept her eye on the Doctor. He was alongside a handful of his High Council colleagues, men who were his friends, like Hedin and the Magistrate. He was perfectly at home in his scarlet robes, wearing them as though they were day clothes. But despite the gleam in his eyes and the smile, Larna sensed a sadness there. It was not difficult to guess why. Unlike almost everyone else, everyone apart from poor Savar, the Doctor had travelled. This was a man who had looked up at other skies, left footprints in alien soil. To have such freedom, only to be denied it... surely that must be infinitely worse than never tasting it at all.

Condemned to watch the universe on monitor screens, rather than to walk in it.

'The fleets are in the Vortex,' Hedin informed the Doctor.

'They are about to arrive,' the President corrected him. The Bell struck for the ninth time.

'There you go,' the Doctor smiled. 'I'm not late at all, I'm bang on time.'

Space and time unfolded gracefully and the two space fleets faded into view in their allotted positions, one over each pole of Pazithi Gallifreya.

Just from the most superficial observation it was clear that the fleets had been built by races which had evolved along fundamentally different lines, on opposite sides of the galaxy.

One was composed of huge, brutal structures in dark metal. For a number of practical reasons, such as ease of production and battlefield repair, everything that poured from the robot production lines and space docks was modular, prefabricated, standardised, and every ship looked much the same. The only difference was the scale: the smallest fighters were barely three metres across, the flagship was over three miles in diameter. They had all the defensive screens, shields and fields that you'd expect of a fighting vessel, but as well as that they had thick armour, compartmentalisation, back-ups and redundancies that would appear ludicrously cautious in any other context. Some warrior races took pride in ornamentation – decoration on sword hilts, or space armour. There was no evidence of that here. Everything was starkly functional, and while the ships were beautiful in the way that piston engines or suspension bridges can be beautiful, there was no art there, just mass-production. The fleet hung over the north pole of Pazithi Gallifreya: solid, immovable.

The other fleet was more pleasing to the eye. Each ship was perfectly symmetrical, and radiant. They looked like snowflakes and were lit from within, sparkling against the night sky like captured stars. And like snowflakes, each one was different. But this had nothing to do with aesthetics. Their technology was based on crystalline structures, optic information passing and spreading and diffracting through complex prismatic forms. The ship's builders could grow diamonds in vats and cultivate them at the atomic level while they were forming. It was an ideal building material if you could use it: light, hard, virtually impossible to cut or distort. Diamond ships that shone like crystal chandeliers were just as functional as the metal of their enemies. Although the mothership was vast, the other ships tended to be smaller than their opponent's counterparts. They swirled and flurried around their mothership, in carefully orchestrated patterns that nevertheless seemed chaotic to an outside observer.

The logistics of battle, the logic of force and counterforce, meant that the evolution of the two races' weapons technology had converged over the course of their long war. Allowing for the differences in biology and technology, the fleets were of roughly the same size – about a hundred capital ships and around ten times as many support vessels. In most circumstances, tacticians agreed that a couple of capital ships were enough to subdue a planet.

The fleets had been segregated, but only symbolically. At their closest point, they were about two thousand five hundred miles apart, well within firing range. The moon wasn't even a physical barrier and the fleets could have conducted a war without moving. Guided missiles were quite capable of flying around Pazithi, gravitational lenses could bend energy rays around the moon's thick atmosphere. Or, if that proved too subtle, just about any ship over the average size from either fleet contained ordnance that could crack apart the moon, and the larger ships could have used gravitron beams to direct the radioactive rubble at key strategic points in the enemy fleet.

Both sides would now know the strengths and weaknesses of their enemy. During the course of the war, both sides had collected more than enough data to be able to model probable outcomes. Like chess computers, or grandmasters, the battle computers would be able to think a million moves ahead. Like a chain of dominoes falling, there was an inevitability to events. Very early on, within ten or twenty seconds, both sides would know whether they were destined to win or lose the day.

In the early stages of the war, prisoners had been taken, enemy vessels captured for scientific analysis or simply to strip down for raw materials. Virtually all that the two sides knew of each other came from this source. Databases, mind probes, sealed orders, analysis of scientific achievement, communications ciphers. All of it had been recovered by the victors from the battlefield. The winner would gain an advantage in all future struggles. It had quickly become a standard tactic, when all was lost, to set all remaining weapons, every reactor and every battery to self-destruct. All that power unleashed at once in a massive explosion that prevented even the smallest item of your technology from falling into the clutches of the enemy. Naturally, if timed correctly, the blast often destroyed most of the other fleet, too. Over the course of the war it had become a fine art calculating the optimum moment to commit mass suicide – letting the enemy getting close, but not so close that they'd get suspicious and escape into hyperspace. Now, virtually any combat ship that self-destructed could take a mass the size of a small planetoid with it, and in a few notable cases the 'self'-destruction of a warfleet had resulted in the devastation of planetary systems.

All of which meant, in practical terms, that when the two races encountered each other a few shots would be fired and then one fleet would realise it had lost, self-destruct, and take the other with it. Few battles lasted for more than a minute nowadays, and generally less than one percent of the combatants on either side survived.

The fleets over Pazithi began scanning each other, picking out anything even potentially hostile, assessing every threat from the exact configuration of armament and manning levels on the largest ships to broad sweeps for nanoweapons. Within seconds, battlelines and plans had been drawn, targeting solution after targeting solution found, missiles armed, energy cannons aimed.

But neither side fired first. Today, for the first time in recorded history, Sontaran and Rutan fleets were sharing the same star system without instantly trying to annihilate one another.

The commanders of the two fleets realised that the other wasn't going to attack at around the same time. Keeping a careful watch on their enemies, the battle computers started looking around for other targets. This was a five-planet star system, with a star that showed signs of extensive re-engineering to keep it within the main sequence. Only one world showed any significant habitation, Gallifrey itself. The largest population concentration was a large domed city in the Northern hemisphere.

As one, every gun, missile and other weapon in both fleets trained themselves on the Capitol.

The Doctor breathed a sigh of relief, hoping that no one had seen him. He looked around to check, but all eyes were on the image of the fleets. All eyes except Larna's. She'd always been one of his more perceptive pupils. Paradoxically, the way she had carefully braided her long blonde hair to look older simply emphasised how very young she was. But now she was a Time Lord, and one of only a handful in the room who genuinely wanted this initiative to succeed. He grinned over at her, she rewarded him by smiling back. Larna had only just graduated so this must be the first time she had worn her cranberry robes, but she looked quite at home here.

'Temporal transfer is now complete,' the Technician announced.

'A magnificent display,' Hedin admitted. 'But are so many ships really necessary?'

'They are trying to impress us,' the Magistrate chuckled. 'This is intended as a demonstration of their strength.'

Hedin turned away from him, gazing back down at infinity. 'Surely not... it's quite impressive, I suppose, but –'

'They betray their insecurity,' a female voice blurted.

The Doctor and his colleagues turned around at the sound. The people around Larna seemed to edge away, leaving her exposed. The Doctor fancied that he could actually hear the sound of so many eyebrows being raised.

'What are you teaching your students these days, Doctor?' Voran asked. He was a long, thin man, a professor nine times over, a member of the Council, but no one liked him.

'That their elders *can* be their betters. That every teacher is still a student. Larna was one of my very best pupils. You could learn a lot from her.' Baiting such a man wasn't satisfying, the Doctor noted. He wouldn't change his opinions, he'd go out of his way not to.

'Come and join us, Larna,' the President said. She stepped a little closer, her face flushing. 'Closer, child,' the President said, delighted with her. Although he was amongst the oldest of all the Time Lords, the

39

President loved the company of the young. That, the Doctor reflected, was one of the reasons his own activities were tolerated and encouraged. He and the Magistrate were the only members of the Council less than two thousand years old.

'Go on,' the Doctor prompted gently.

Larna stepped a little closer to them, clearly trying to collect her thoughts. 'These are warrior races. Their cultures are based on power, military superiority. But they must know that Gallifreyan technology is far superior to theirs. They know that if they fire their weapons then they'll just bounce off the quantum forcefields and transduction barriers. We could dematerialise every weapon, we could make it so that their home planet never existed.'

One corner of the Magistrate's mouth rose, a sure sign that he was enjoying himself. 'So why aim all their weapons at us? Who are they trying to impress?'

A rhetorical question, but one that Larna was happy to answer. 'Not us. The Time Lords aren't warriors, they know that. They are trying to reassure themselves. They think of themselves as... not our equals... but they want to be able to think that they have *power*. Why else would they send a hundred ships? We can guarantee safe passage far better than a fleet of their warships. The Sontaran delegation and all their provisions could fit in one shuttlecraft, the Rutan emissary only needs something the size of a lifepod.'

The Magistrate had his head back and a broad grin on his face. 'They are impotent. Better to send one ship, with one crewman. If it is the right ship and the right man.'

'Yes, my Lord,' she agreed hurriedly.

The Doctor placed his hand on her shoulder. 'Well done,' he whispered. Hedin also had a wry smile on his face.

The President was still watching the fleets. 'There are many warlike races in the universe,' he said sadly, 'many skilled in creating and using the most terrible weapons.'

'The ability to wipe out your rivals has proved a highly effective method of ensuring your own survival,' the Magistrate said, almost admiringly.

'There are other methods of thriving, of course,' the Doctor said. He looked around, challenging those near him to come up with suggestions. He tried to phrase the invitation so that it would include not just his pupils, but the High Councillors. Perhaps even the President.

'Becoming traders,' one Lord suggested.

The Doctor nodded. 'Or just sell your expertise – the Vegans are miners, the Schlangi build spacecraft. Both sell their services to anyone that will pay, and their customers protect them.'

'Become parasitic, serve or feed on a successful race,' a young student added.

'Simply hiding, not drawing attention to oneself...' Voran suggested.

'Becoming energy beings of pure intelligence,' Pendrel said, giggling. No doubt he was pleased that he'd come up with a more noble example than his master, Voran.

'Swarming across the universe in such numbers that no one could kill you all,' Hedin added, with a hint of distaste. 'I believe that both the Sontarans and Rutans evolved along those lines originally.'

The Doctor nodded. 'It is the only reason the war between them has gone on so long. In the right conditions a breeding Sontaran individual is capable of producing a million offspring a minute. They are full grown and ready for combat in six days. The Rutans are essentially giant amoebae, each cell is capable of becoming a fully formed individual, part of the group mind.'

'I'm surprised that they didn't wipe themselves out long before discovering space travel,' the President said. 'Most uncivilised.'

Lord Norval shook his head. 'As an evolutionary strategy, there are many advantages to being war-like. An effective military is single-minded, organised. As well as the best weapons, it needs the best communications, the best supply lines.'

'The strategy is risky, though. Live by the sword, die by the sword,' the Doctor told them.

'On the other hand,' Larna piped up, 'some civilisations discover that during a war, or living under the threat of war, there is a period of technological advancement. Often a development on one side will force a new advance on the other. When the Sontarans developed spectronic drive, the Rutans suddenly needed better sensors or they'd be wiped out in sneak attacks. So they invented better sensors.'

The Doctor looked wistfully at the fleets. 'The Sontaran/Rutan Wars are not so much an arms race as an arms marathon, an arms decathlon. Think of what they could have achieved if their scientists had spent the time building ploughshares instead of swords.'

A number of the assembled Time Lords ventured the opinion that all aliens were savages.

'It is a normal stage that most civilisations go through,' the Doctor reminded them all. 'Gallifrey itself went through a phase of galactic conquest and warfare, many millions of years ago.'

Voran objected. 'I am aware of that. We grew out of it. The Sontarans and the Rutans have been fighting since the time of Rassilon and Omega. It's in their blood, their genes, their memes... they don't know any better. Might I ask what is next on the Doctor's agenda? Perhaps he might try to negotiate a settlement between the cats and the dogs!'

There was laughter, and enough for the Doctor to feel disappointed. He put a brave face on it. 'I don't have an agenda, Lord Voran.'

'Live by the agenda, die by the agenda,' Larna said, more than a hint of anger in her voice. There was a little more laughter, including chuckles from the President and the Magistrate. That silenced the Doctor's critics.

The Sontarans and the Rutans had been run-of-the-mill militaristic societies when the universe was young. Each had built up an empire in the usual way, emerging from their homeworlds, subjugating local planets, expanding their sphere of influence. Nothing unusual up to that point. Rapid population growth meant that colony worlds could swiftly be populated, converted into mines and factories, added to the expansion effort. Other races were run by the military, they had warriors' codes, they had evolved whole societies from honour, chivalry and espionage. Life was a series of glorious battles, of magnificent conquests and terrible defeats, of heroes and traitors, kings and lords and knights and armies. There were stories, legends, sagas about wars and warriors. But the Sontarans and Rutans were different. In a way, Voran was right. These were two races that *existed* for war, that had forgotten everything else. But surely, surely, some part of the Sontaran and Rutan mind longed for peace. Why else would they fight except for the hope of a better time once the war was over?

'When are these fleets from?' asked Lord Hedin.

The Magistrate stepped forward, a holographic Penrose diagram annotated with unreadable runes appearing behind him. 'To minimise disruption to known history we selected a period in the far future. Three hundred thousand years before the Last of Man.'

'And such a very great time after the fall of our own people,' Hedin noted.

'Everything has its time,' the President replied sombrely. 'As its Lords, we above all others must know that.'

The Time Lords watched over the timelines, observing and recording everything from the beginning: Event One, the Big Bang that marked the creation of the universe from a naked singularity, to the end, Event Two: when the universe would collapse back into singularity. Although they could survey the entire universe from the lofty heights of Gallifrey, it was impossible for the Time Lords to travel into their own future and they couldn't change their own past. That was the fealty paid for their title. But as they amassed information, as they prepared projections, they couldn't help but glean something of their own destiny. They couldn't see their future, but they could snatch the *reflection* of what was to come, extrapolate from the ripples and shadows in Time. A legend recounted on the wall of a ruin here, a footnote in a textbook in a forgotten library there. They knew some of the names that would appear in the history books of the future: Varnax, Faction Paradox, Catavolcus, the Timewyrm. Threats to the entire Time Lord race, but quantifiable ones, ones that the Time Lords were destined to survive.

There was another.

Details were vague. There was to be a conflict, a war fought at some point against an implacable force. It wouldn't be the first time that the rumour of the destruction of Gallifrey had spread. But then only one of the rumours had to be true. The High Council were uncertain what to do. Were they to command the Matrix to scour the universe looking for threats of the magnitude the legends seemed to talk of, or would that just be the first event in a chain that would inevitably lead to contact and conflict with the enemy? The sub-committee dealing with the issue, to everyone's relief, had not yet come to any conclusions, after several millennia of deliberations.

The President was staring out at the fleets again.

'This is the last chance that we have to change our minds,' the Doctor warned. 'Invite the delegations down and we will have committed ourselves.'

'You are having doubts?' the Magistrate asked.

'No,' the Doctor said. 'No, but *others* here have always had their doubts. They'll dress it up with sarcasm, they'll talk behind our backs. But when this was discussed in Council, they filed through the lobbies, they backed their President like they always do. I just want them all to know that I'll give it up. I'll stop now, send the fleets home. It took a year of negotiation and TARDIS diplomacy just to agree which fleet would appear over which pole of Pazithi. But I'll abandon it all. I'll do it if my fellow Time Lords agree that is the best course of action. Speak now, or hold your peace. If we proceed, we'll proceed to the bitter end, whatever the cost, whatever the consequence.'

'Well, I for one object,' Voran said after a pause. 'This is nonsensical. This mere *Doctor* is a halfwit if he thinks he can change anything.'

'He is a Time Lord,' the Magistrate warned. 'A member of the Supreme Council.'

'He barely scraped his PhD, as I recall. Not one college wanted him for post-doctoral work. Yet he wears that badge of academic failure as his name. Do you really feel the need to parade your ignorance, Doctor?'

The Doctor smiled. 'No. But nor do I need to quantify it, Senior Lecturer Professor-nine-times-over Voran.'

Pendrel clapped his hands together. 'This Doctor has my vote!' he squeaked. The look that Voran flashed him stopped him dead.

'During the course of the war, how many have died?' another Councillor asked.

'We could ask the Matrix to compute the death toll,' the Co-ordinator informed them. 'An immense task, even for us. I estimate it would take a day or so to get the precise casualty figure.'

'And would it bring back a single one of the dead?' the Doctor asked.

'You know that it would not.'

'Then we don't need to count them. Let us change the future.'

A number of Time Lords murmured their assent.

The President turned to him. 'You really think that we can end this war?'

'Yes.'

'These races have nothing in common.'

'Wrong. Wrong. There's a rule of combat that not even the Time Lords have forgotten. Know your enemy. The strategists and scientists on both sides have come to understand each other. At the moment they only use this knowledge to kill, but it is a common bond. It is a place we can start to look for solutions.'

The President laughed. 'Only you could see an opportunity amongst such total war, old friend. Very well.' He turned to the assembled Time Lords.

'Do any of you have a reason or the courage to object?'

None spoke.

The President raised his hand. 'Then in the name of Rassilon and Omega: proceed.'

Chapter Three
The Enemy Within

Larna still wasn't used to having a maidservant, and was surprised every time she returned to her chambers to find her there, in the middle of some domestic task.

Vrayto was an old woman, quiet and wizened. They had known each other only for a matter of weeks, and neither was yet comfortable with the other. Vrayto had been in service for a long time, and knew better than anyone how to remove the ceremonial collarpiece, placing it to one side so that she could help her mistress out of her robes. Larna didn't even need to unbraid her hair, untie her shirt, pull down her petticoats or unbutton her breeches, that was done for her as well. She drew the line at the undergarment, removing it herself behind the shower screen and handing it over. Through the crack in the panels, Larna could see Vrayto standing patiently with the robes over her arm.

'Thank you,' Larna said, 'you may go now.'

Vrayto's head was bowed a little as she left the washroom, the maid was apparently embarrassed by something. Larna wondered what she had done to offend her this time. Perhaps there had been an arcane breach of etiquette. Was it not the done thing to thank your servant?

Vrayto would be stowing the robes away in their locker, ready for the next ceremony. That would be next week: the Feast of Rassilon the Lamp. The robes were millennia-old, and although they had been altered for her, they had originally been tailored for a man. It was the same with all the ritual garments. There were only a handful of female Time Lords, and the petty considerations of the flesh were felt to be unimportant. No concessions were made for her. It was one of the paradoxes of society here within the Citadel. Everyone knew that women were the equal of men – such a statement bordered on the facile. But no one ever questioned why women rarely applied to the Academy, or why so few of the applications were accepted. Over ten percent of the Gallifreyan population was female, but no more than a dozen of the thousand Time Lords were women. In ten centuries of service, it was entirely possible that Vrayto had never served a woman before. Perhaps Vrayto was jealous of Larna's youth, her vigour, her success.

More likely, she was ashamed that her mistress reeked of sweat, dust and anointing incense in roughly equal measure. Vrayto hadn't given any sign that she had noticed, but how could she not have? The dirt offended Larna. The oil and water shower responded to her presence, now, activating automatically. It was embarrassing that she enjoyed such a purely sensual pleasure, but she lingered, let the thousand tiny jets of hot water pummel her, kneading the muscle oil into her skin and caressing shampoo into her scalp. The thought that Vrayto would disapprove of such hedonism made it all the more appealing. The shower had a limited degree of sentience, but Larna's hair was too long for it to wash, so she worked the foam down using her hands. That done, she straightened, her eyes closed, her arms by her sides, emptying her mind of anything and everything except the whoosh of the water and the feel of it as it swept away the grime that had come away from her robes to cover her skin.

The Doctor was right to try to end the war, Larna knew that. No: more than that, she *felt* it, at the base of each heart. The alternative was to do what the other Time Lords would do: observe the war, quantify it. Many of the students believed as the Doctor did. Perhaps hers would be the generation with ambitions that reached further than the roof of the Dome. They could be men and women who went out into the universe in an attempt to find the truth, make contact and spread science and light. Larna had her doubts. Each generation felt this way, each thought that they would usher in an age of revolution and a better way of doing things. Somehow, somewhere along the way, the dust and cobwebs and routines got into the blood, the desire always cooled. What had been energetic had always become ossified. Worse still, those who retained their fervour into adult life had become tyrants, intent on power whatever the cost. There were those who placed the Doctor in that category, as no better than Pengallia, Marnal or Morbius.

She gasped in frustration, before remembering where she was or that Vrayto might have heard her. The mere idea that the Doctor could be thought of as a tyrant made Larna burn inside, it provoked an anger that she felt ashamed she couldn't control. They knew the Doctor, they'd heard the sincerity in his voice as he argued his case at Council, at fringe meetings and in his lectures. Hadn't they looked into those sad eyes, seen his soul laid bare?

The water massaged her shoulders like strong hands, it played over her face and chest. The things she had said today in front of the High Council... if she had given them a moment's consideration she couldn't have said them. But all those acolytes around her had thought the same. In the safety of their common rooms and dorms, she'd heard them all denounce the Public Record broadcasts that mocked the Doctor's plans and misrepresented his aims. If she was to be damned, then at least it would be for something in which she believed. She saw the Doctor smiling at her. His gratitude meant more than anything else to her, that smile was worth a hundred professorships.

Larna could sense the shower's impatience, and set it to dry and powder her. That done, she stepped out. Vrayto should have been waiting for her. Instead Larna was alone, her nightshirt over the back of a chair, the hairbrush still in its case.

She wriggled into the crisp cotton shirt, found some slippers and pushed on her hairband. Her hair needed cutting again: her fringe was barely above her eyes.

Vrayto came into the room, carrying a card.

'Have we got guests?' Larna asked, wondering who it could be.

Vrayto looked down at her shoes, disapprovingly, offering the card. 'Technician First Class Waymivrudimqwe wishes to talk to you,' she announced. 'Despite the hour.'

Larna nodded, unaware of any problems with the eighth hour of the day. 'Waym,' she said, buttoning herself up. 'I'll see him.'

'Like that?' Vrayto asked.

Larna looked down at herself. 'This night-gown covers parts of my body I didn't even realise that I had, Vrayto.'

'You're a Time Lady, now, ma'am. There are standards.'

Larna sighed, and walked out the door.

Waym was standing by her sofa, still in his Technician's uniform. Vrayto hadn't offered him a seat. Larna corrected that, and sat next to him, both feet firmly on the floor. Thanks to Vrayto she felt absurdly self-conscious. Her housemaid hovered at the edge of the room, chaperoning them carefully.

'I'm sorry to come round unannounced, but you're the best-qualified person I know.'

'You've not dragged me out of the shower to help you with an essay?'

'No, no.'

'Relax, Waym. Look. I know I'm a Time Lord now, but it's still me.'

That seemed to put him at his ease. 'Larna, I noticed a problem when I was running the Chamber this morning. I think the aliens might have infiltrated it.'

Larna frowned. 'What sort of problem?'

'I noticed it just before the fleets arrived. Look, it's going to be easier if I show you. I'll meet you in Chamber Epsilon in a couple of minutes.'

Larna stood. 'Why can't I come now?'

Waym pointed vaguely towards her. 'You're in your nightshirt.'

She was already on her feet. 'It's ankle length. Epsilon is only up on the next level. Come on.'

There was barely time to aim a triumphant smile at Vrayto before she strode out of the room –

– and straight into the Doctor, who had been running past her doorway. He steadied her, and himself. He had found the time to change into his normal clothes, or rather the clothes he normally wore. The Doctor was the only person on Gallifrey to wear a battered cashmere jacket, pressed silk shirt and tailored tan trousers. He peered down at her over his glasses. She began apologising.

He didn't seem to notice what she was wearing. 'Like I just said, Larna, we'll need to discuss it, but I'm busy with the alien delegations. Come to my room at Nine Point Five Bells.'

The Doctor hurried away, his jacket flapping behind him. Her hearts sank. He needed to discuss her behaviour. Conduct was very important to the Time Lords. She would not have been able to graduate from the Academy without knowing that. Some Time Lords were still best-known for minor transgressions of decorum they had performed centuries before. Lord Glebun would be Glebun the Flatulent until the day he died, despite his groundbreaking research into fluid dynamics. Such actions could blight careers, exclude you from the best circles and societies. What she found most disappointing was that Vrayto had been proved right. She could picture her servant now, a smug grin on her face.

'That's hardly fair,' Larna scowled at Waym. 'It was *him* running, not me.'

The Doctor sat on Rassilon's foot, legs dangling, wriggling as he tried to get comfortable.

In his own day, Rassilon had been thought of as an architect. That was difficult for some modern Time Lords to believe. Nowadays Rassilon was the greatest of the founders, the Father of Gallifrey, the man who not only saved the planet but gave it the gift of time travel and the wisdom to use that gift wisely. His achievements went far beyond designing some pretty buildings. Modern Time Lords knew the Panopticon, took it for granted. They barely used the elaborate exitonic landscapes of the Matrix any more. The Citadel had been there for so long that there was no power in the way it both dominated and blended into the enclosed cityscape of the Capitol. And so it was that some of the most awe-inspiring buildings in the known universe became everyday experiences, places you had to walk through to get to or from lectures.

The Doctor envied the Sontarans and the Rutans the experience they would have this evening as they saw Gallifrey for the first time.

Few Time Lords stopped to consider the thought that had gone into the design of the Panopticon. The statues that stood in each corner were a clever trick of perspective. When you entered the Panopticon, passing under an impossibly high archway, you were immediately faced with the statue of one of the legendary Founders of Gallifrey, the six individuals credited with the creation of modern civilisation. Enter the hall from the north, for example, and you'd see a statue of Omega in the southern corner, a big bearded man, resplendent in a somewhat romanticised version of the hydraulic space suit he'd worn at Qqaba, his helmet under his arm. Your mind would sketch in an idea of scale, and guess that the statue was perhaps three times actual size. You'd walk towards the raised area at the centre of the room. The statue wouldn't move. Only as you walked out underneath the canopy of the Panopticon Dome would you realise how big this place was, that it would take an hour to cross. And only when you turned around to see how far you'd come did you realise that the arch you had originally come through was formed by the legs of another statue, and that Omega must be the size of a tower block.

If you'd come in from the north, you'd have walked between the Legs of Rassilon, between sculpted feet the size of houses. There was a way of remembering the names of the statues and what they had done for Gallifrey. It was an old nursery riddle, a six-line rhyming logic puzzle that every Gallifreyan learned off by hearts. The Doctor could only remember the first half:

'Neath Panopticon Dome
Rassilon faces Omega
But who is the other?'

At that point the Doctor's memory got a bit hazy. The last word of the next line was 'brother', he remembered that much. The Doctor had never been impressed: solving the riddle was rather easy, and even the bits he could remember didn't scan or rhyme properly.

Regeneration had caused all sorts of problems with Gallifreyan figural sculpture and iconography, but fortunately there was a consensus about what Rassilon looked like. For some reason, lost in the mists of time, the founder of Gallifreyan society was always depicted wearing leather sandals. That made Rassilon the best bet if you fancied a sit down, far better than Omega's industrial footwear or the spiny combat boots of Apeiron.

'There were giants in those days.' It was the Magistrate, emerging from the evening shadows.

The Doctor looked down at him from his vantage point on Rassilon's big toenail. 'They weren't really this big, you know,' he called down.

'I was speaking metaphorically.'

'I know. So was I.'

'An hour to go.'

'Yes. But *where* will it go?' the Doctor wondered as the Magistrate clambered up to join him. He pulled himself up hand over hand with little effort, not even his knee-length cloak could slow him down. It was the first time they'd been up here since their college days, and it had taken the Doctor five or six minutes to make the climb. Still, the Magistrate did need his help. The Doctor reached down, took his hand, pulled him up.

'You're looking smart,' the Doctor observed as the Magistrate took his place alongside him. 'Black suits you.'

Underneath his cloak was a collarless tunic. The Magistrate brushed some dust from it. 'What are you going to wear?'

'This,' the Doctor said, flicking his old college scarf over his shoulder. 'Don't you think?'

The Magistrate raised an eyebrow. 'Not very formal. Scruffy, in fact. Won't our guests be offended?'

'Sontarans and Rutans have different sartorial standards,' he shrugged. 'I'd dress to impress them, but my suit of armour's at the cleaner's.' The Doctor yawned, looking out over the Panopticon. 'I'm sure they'll like the soldiers, though.'

A phalanx of the Chancellery Watch was practising the drill for the morning. They were in full ceremonial uniform, crimson, striped fur, breastplates and cloaks. They'd formed a neat square, and were marching up and down, boots clacking against the marble floor as regular as the tick of a clock. They'd done these drills for thousands of years – literally in the case of many of the soldiers. Long ago they must have exhausted every creative possibility there. That was the point, wasn't it? They weren't thinking, they were doing something that came as naturally and easily to them as breathing. But all they were doing was marching, not fighting. It had been a while since the Watch had seen action, longer still since they'd faced an external threat.

The Magistrate smiled thinly, as if reading the Doctor's thoughts. 'Don't underestimate them, Doctor. After a thousand years of target practice and battle meditation they'd be able to show the Sontarans a thing or two about hand-to-hand combat.'

The Doctor cocked his head. 'Think so? My money would still be on the genetically re-engineered guy from the high gravity world.'

'I have no doubt that Lord Voran would agree with you. But the President was on your side, "old friend",' laughed the Magistrate, imitating the President's plummy voice.

The Doctor chuckled, and then looked thoughtful for a moment. 'I have never needed to tell anyone that they are an old friend.'

'Why would you need to? You have so many *new* friends, after all. Larna is a credit to you.'

'Thank you. My brightest pupil.'

'You'll raise a generation of revolutionaries, yet, Doctor.'

The Doctor nodded. 'One way or the other.'

The Magistrate smiled. 'How big is the Sontaran delegation?'

'We got it down to ten in the end.'

'Is everything arranged now?'

'Down to the last detail. Crossed every "i", dotted every "t". They'll be Scooped down at Nine Bells tonight. To avoid any complications, the Sontarans will arrive at the Western Materialisation Zone, the Rutans will go to the Eastern one. They'll be welcomed, and then a squad of Watchmen will escort them along the walkway through the Capitol and into the Citadel until they meet here, in the middle of the Panopticon. The Public Record cameras will capture the first meeting. This will be their first face-to-face encounter for a fair while. It could be a little awkward, so all we'll do is say "hello" to each other. After that, they'll be taken to their respective xenodochia by the Guard. The conditions in their rooms exactly match their homeworlds.'

'I see a problem.'

'Just the one?'

'You're the chief negotiator, the one who has brought the two sides here, the only individual in the universe that both races will talk to.'

'That's not too much of a problem, I hope,' the Doctor laughed.

'If the Sontarans and Rutans are arriving at the same time at different ends of the city, then who's going to meet them? You'll be in here, I presume. If you were to favour either of the races with your company, the other might be offended. But they are also going to be deeply offended if they are met by some minor official.'

The Doctor rubbed his chin. 'Good point.'

'It's a shame I can't be in two places at once,' said the Doctor.

'Yes,' the Doctor called over from Rassilon's little toe, 'that would solve everything.'

Both Doctors grinned.

Larna entered the Infinity Chamber in front of Waym.

This was a smaller chamber than the main one, just a balcony that looked down on the universe. Larna would have made her way to the control console, but there was someone there already.

'It's Savàr,' Waym said. 'Sorry, Larna, he wasn't here before.'

'That's OK. I don't mind him.'

'No? I think he's creepy.'

Savar was hunched over the console, tapping away at the controls. He wore vivid blue robes. He seemed obsessed with the buttons, mesmerised by the way they flashed and winked. He might look perfectly ordinary, but Savar wasn't a healthy man.

'Lord Savar,' Larna said. 'Are you all right?'

'Larna!' he cried out. '*Lady* Larna,' he corrected himself, before returning to the controls. He hadn't acknowledged Waym's existence.

She moved over to him.

'They took my eyes, you know,' he told them thoughtfully. 'It was after I found God, and before I came back here.'

Larna nodded, and looked over to Waym, a sad smile on her face. Long ago, long before they had been born, field trips out into the universe had been a little more common. The High Council had relaxed their non-intervention codes by a degree or two and allowed a limited degree of observer-only travel to intergalactic scientific conferences, or sites of special interest. Once again the TARDIS time capsules travelled the universe on official Time Lord business. Savar had set out on such an expedition.

A decade later, they'd found him.

The rematerialisation of his escape pod had been detected in the depths of space. A TARDIS rescue crew had been dispatched straight away. What they had found was horrifying – a capsule stripped bare of virtually everything but its pilot, left squatting alone in darkness. Savar had been mutilated, *his eyes had been removed*. Both eyeballs, every millimetre of optic nerve, even the lobes of the brain that dealt with vision had all been taken. However it had happened, the experience had driven Savar mad. He'd been returned to Gallifrey and his body had been healed, a new pair of eyes had been spun for him. But his mind, some even said his *soul*, had gone. He'd babbled about his eyes, how his eyes had taken his eyes, how he'd fallen off the edge of the universe and that he'd seen the face of god. The surgeons couldn't repair his soul. Even a couple of regenerations later, Savar was a broken man, a once-great scientist and traveller reduced to a harmless distraction. Most Time Lords ignored him. Those that didn't, like Larna and the Doctor, tended to treat him like a small child. Neither fate appealed to Waym.

'I think I've found God again,' Savar concluded sadly.

Larna smiled at him. 'Do you mind if I take the controls?'

'Not at all, my dear.' He stepped back, to let Larna through, and Waym took his place alongside her.

Waym checked the settings. Savar had reprogrammed it, knocked it off all the carefully selected co-ordinates that Waym had been trying to monitor.

'We need to see the arrival of the alien fleet,' he told Savar.

Savar chuckled, pointing at the display.

Space and time unfolded gracefully and the two space fleets faded into view in their allotted positions, one over each pole of Pazithi Gallifreya.

This time, the display was awash with annotations, added by Savar's hand. Larna froze the image and began leafing through the notes. Waym already knew where to look, and could see that there really was something unusual there.

'There's a wall of... something,' Larna concluded. 'Like a ripple in spacetime.' She pointed it out on the display. There was an almost imperceptible disturbance, across the whole picture, originating behind Pazithi, sweeping towards and through Gallifrey in as much time as it took the Vortex gates to open. It was like the image on a viewscreen being a pixel out, nothing more.

'You did well to spot this,' Larna concluded.

'What is it?' Waym asked.

'It is the end of the universe,' Savar said simply, 'and there is nothing we can do about it.'

The other Doctor had clambered over to them and they stood next to each other, like twins.

'Doesn't this violate the Laws of Time?' the Magistrate asked, unsure which of the Doctors he should be addressing.

'Not all of them,' the Doctor replied, laughing at his own joke.

'I wish I'd said that,' whispered the Doctor.

'You will, you will,' the Doctor mumbled back.

The Magistrate looked at the newer arrival. 'You are from the future?'

'I'm him from an hour and a half in the future. I've just popped back here after greeting the Rutan delegation.'

'Did everything go smoothly with them?' the Doctor asked himself.

'You know I couldn't possibly answer that without serious implications to the Web of Time. It went fine, and judging from the grin that'll be on my face in an hour's time, the Sontarans were no trouble either.'

Both Doctors checked their wristwatch. 'We'd better get into place,' they concluded.

'No need to synchronise watches,' the Magistrate observed. 'Or Doctors.'

The earlier Doctor slapped his counterpart on the shoulder. 'I'm off to the Western Platform. Don't do anything I wouldn't do,' he advised, before he began clambering down.

'I knew he'd say that,' the Doctor muttered.

'It could be a malfunction with the chamber,' Larna suggested. 'I'll need to see the fault locator records.'

'Do these things ever go wrong?' Waym wondered.

Savar nodded sagely. 'Oh yes, from time to time.'

Waym scowled at him. 'I wasn't talking to you. Larna?'

She was trying to release the controls from Savar's program, but with no success. 'Could you let me have a look?'

Savar shook his head, grinning like an idiot. 'I've not finished yet.'

Larna tried again.

'What could it be?'

Larna frowned. 'Well, Infinity Chambers draw their information from the Matrix. They don't observe the real universe, just a very, very elaborate computer model of the universe. One that's accurate to the last quark. There could be a glitch in the data.'

'Caused by?'

'Intervention,' Savar said suddenly. 'Divine intervention.'

'No alien race has access to the Matrix. Well, not any more. Over the years, a number of races have tried and...' She broke off, staring at the two fleets hovering over Gallifrey.

'If this image of the universe has been interfered with, then the fleets might not be there at all. Something else could have come through the vortex gate instead, something that we just can't see. The Doctor could be walking right into a trap...'

She checked the chronometer set in the console. Eight Point Eight Nine Bells. 'It's nearly nightfall. He'll be in the Panopticon. I haven't got much time...'

She bolted out of the room, the hem of her night-gown in her hands.

* * *

A squad of Watchmen ringed the materialisation zone, the Doctor stood a little way off-centre. Behind him, the hourglass-shape of the Time Lord Citadel was dominating the skyline of the Capitol. Aircar traffic had been diverted away from this part of the city, but it was still bustling.

As one, the clocks began chiming Nine Bells.

The centre of the platform began to shimmer. An ebony pyramid rotated into three-dimensional space, and continued to hang there, spinning slowly. The Doctor held a blue control pad in his hand. He pressed the green button.

The pyramid faded away as it stopped swirling, and in its place was a single Rutan, if such a term meant anything. It was a churning mass of various slimy, viscous substances, like a giant oyster swimming in thick vegetable soup. It glowed and pulsed from within. And then, as quickly and instinctively as a pupil dilating in bright light, the Rutan began to adapt to its new environment. Its outer layers grew thicker, the way that skin forms on cooling cocoa. Tendrils began to sprout from its underside, the diffuse glowing began to concentrate into three points, deep within the body. This had the effect of backlighting the creature's nascent internal organs and muscle structures. Within a matter of seconds, the Rutan had transformed itself into a creature that resembled a translucent squid. Electricity crackled around it.

It sat there, not acknowledging its surroundings.

The Doctor licked his lips. 'Hello?' he called over.

No response, not even a flickering tentacle. The Doctor walked over to the Rutan. Without anything like an eye, an ear or a nose, how did it perceive the world? Obviously not from sight, sound or smell. To a Rutan, the world must be made up of temperature fluctuations or variations in the local electrical or magnetic fields. Or, perhaps, they didn't even make that distinction. To a telepathic group mind of metamorphic amoebae, the universe probably existed in a binary state: Rutan and Not-Rutan.

The Doctor bent over the Rutan, not even sure that it knew he was there.

A slit had just appeared in the Rutan's flank. It would be about wide enough for the Doctor to put his hand in, not that he had the slightest intention of doing so. It parted, the sides of the slit thickening up. Inside it was black.

The Doctor knew he was staring, but doubted that the Rutan could blame him for that, or even distinguish one humanoid facial expression from another.

As the crack opened wider, the Doctor saw teeth. A row of white teeth, like a baby's, and behind them a fat red tongue.

'Greetings, Time Lord,' the mouth – the Rutan – said in a woman's voice. 'The humanoid larynx is not capable of recreating the sound, nor is the humanoid mind of sufficient sophistication to appreciate the complexity of the vocabulary, grammar nor syntax, nor is the humanoid nervous system adequate to fully experience the language of the Rutan. For convenience, we have reluctantly adopted your primitive method of communication.'

'That is most considerate,' the Doctor replied in Rutan.

The mouth dropped open.

'Shall we go in?' the Doctor said sweetly.

The only elevator from the Infinity Chamber floor down to the Panopticon was restricted to Time Lords, to prevent public access to the TARDIS Cradles in between. Larna had been forced to use the emergency staircase that swept around the lift shaft. There were literally thousands of steps down from the Infinity Chambers to the floor of the Panopticon. Hard, grey, stone steps. Halfway down, it had occurred to Larna that there was no reason why the stairs couldn't be dimensionally transcendental. It would be a straightforward engineering job to arrange the staircases so that you never needed to go up or down more than one flight of stairs to get to whichever level you wanted. She began to model the neatest solution in her head. The mathematics kept her mind from the cramp, her aching hips and sore feet. By the time she had reached the bottom of the stairs she had it all planned, and she vowed to raise the matter to Council as soon as possible.

Not that it helped her now.

As soon as she had finished her descent, it all caught up with her, and she found herself doubled up, desperately unable to suck enough air into her lungs. Sweat was pouring from her forehead, and her back. She was dizzy, her bare feet simultaneously icy cold and stinging with heat. She was too tired to even acknowledge the Doctor's presence.

'Have you just run down all these stairs in your nightie?' the Doctor asked.

Larna nodded, almost managing to straighten herself up.

He was bent over her, unsure whether to put his arm around her shoulders or to give her enough space to recover. Wisely, he chose the latter.

'What's the matter?' he asked gently. 'Did you have a bad dream?'

'You noticed what I'm wearing this time,' she replied hoarsely. 'And this time it *was* me running.'

The Doctor looked blankly at her.

'Terrible danger!' she blurted, remembering the reason that she had been running in the first place.

'Calm down. What about it?'

Larna caught her breath. 'We're in it. I don't think that the aliens are all that they seem –'

'But I've just welcomed the Rutan. Everything went swimmingly.'

'Just the Rutan?' Larna asked, puzzled. 'I thought that the Sontarans were due at the same time.'

The Doctor checked his watch and slapped his forehead. 'Look, Larna, we'll talk about this. Go to my room, get yourself a drink, make yourself at home. I'll be there soon. I've not quite finished yet, and I don't like to leave a job only half done. If a job's worth doing blah blah, and all that.'

With a smile, the Doctor tapped in his access code and opened up the elevator. The door slid smoothly shut behind him.

And, around two thousand steps too late, it occurred to Larna that she was allowed in the Time-Lord-only elevators these days.

A little later and earlier, the Doctor stood at the Western Materialisation Zone. Behind him, the hourglass-shape of the Time Lord Citadel was dominating the skyline of the Capitol. Aircar traffic had been diverted away from this part of the city, but it was still bustling.

As one, the clocks began chiming Nine Bells.

The centre of the platform began to shimmer. An ebony pyramid rotated into three-dimensional space, and continued to hang there, spinning slowly. The Doctor held a blue control pad in his hand. He pressed the green button.

The pyramid faded away as it stopped swirling, and in its place were ten Sontaran warriors, in full space armour. They were identical – squat humanoids, with rounded shoulders and torsos. Their limbs were bodybuilder-powerful. The armour was made from a soft, almost-leathery silver material that covered every square inch of their skin. They wore vast dome-shaped helmets. The Doctor wondered how they told each other apart. They must be able to, as combat was almost impossible without the ability to distinguish rank and position. They were all exactly the same height and build, the only distinguishing features at this stage being insignia on their collars and regimental motifs on their helmets. They didn't wear medals, or other marks of past glory, but there were certain electronic devices clipped to their belts. No weapons, though, as had been agreed. All but three of the Sontarans stood in a rough circle, around – presumably – their leader. They were scanning their surroundings, looking for traps, fearful of ambush. The remaining two were hoisting crates on their shoulders. The boxes were almost as big as they were, and presumably contained provisions and other equipment. Deep within the Citadel, a monitoring team would have scanned the contents, using techniques so subtle that the Sontarans weren't even aware of the scientific principles involved, let alone the scan itself. If there were weapons in those crates, they would already have been quietly disarmed or removed.

'Welcome,' the Doctor said. 'I am the Doctor.'

The Sontaran at the centre of the circle stepped forwards, his protective circle closing up behind him. He reached up to his helmet, removing it. As he did so, the others, except the two carrying the crates, did the same. All Sontarans shared the same toady face, smeared on a domed head the colour and texture of clay. There were traces of individuality there, though: facial hair, scars from past battles, even tattoos and traces of sunburn.

But behind the cosmetic differences, the face that every Sontaran wore was that of their leader. And the Doctor was astonished to discover that this was the man standing in front of him now. This Sontaran was wrinkled, the skin loose and fading into a sickly orange colour, the piggy eyes seemed even closer together. Tufts of crudely manicured hair sprouted from his ears, nose and chin.

'General Sontar,' the Doctor gasped.

He was the only old Sontaran. The history of the Sontaran race was obscured by the passing of time, and the rigorous reworking of propaganda, but most versions of events mentioned General Sontar. At some point around the declaration of war with the Rutans – no one could agree whether it had been just before or just after – the Supreme Council of the urSontaran Warburg realised that there was military advantage in cloning their finest warriors. Most renowned of all was Sontar, the mastermind behind the victory in the two-thousand-year war with the Isari. He had been such a perfect warrior that before long every new soldier was a clone of Sontar. Shortly after that there had been a military coup, and the population had been purged of all non-Sontarans. Either that had happened, or something completely different. The authorities couldn't agree, and there was little point asking either the Sontarans or Rutans for an objective discussion of the matter.

This wasn't the original General Sontar, of course, he had died millions of years ago. The natural Sontaran lifespan was about fifty years – but thanks to the war none reached that age except Sontar, safe on his Throneworld, surrounded by medics, bodyguards and energytasters. As Sontar drew the last breath into his dry, withered body, his consciousness was downloaded into a custom-made clone, and his immortality was assured. To an outsider, his perpetual cycle might resemble the way Time Lords regenerated. But there was every difference. With each regeneration, a Gallifreyan gained an entirely new body, with a new nervous system, a new appearance and a new personality. All but the most basic experiences had to be discovered anew. Regeneration brought fresh perspectives, removed the stagnation that developed with old age and staying the same for too long. The process that General Sontar went through kept in place all the blinkers, clinkers and cankers.

'Your presence is an unexpected honour,' the Doctor said. He'd been expecting a Cabinet member, but not its head. He recognised a Sontaran handful of the others: Admiral Krax of the Three Millionth Fleet, Chancellor Stroc, Chief of Staff Grol. All with enough firepower at their command to level a galaxy. But Sontar had the power to level *them*.

'My presence is a clear demonstration of the priority the Sontaran race assigns to the campaign for peace,' Sontar bellowed.

If things went wrong, then no doubt there would be another General Sontar on the Sontaran Throne by this evening, the Doctor mused. In the early days there had been civil wars and schisms as rival General Sontars vied for supremacy, each convinced – and each of them correct in the assertion by every definition – that they were the rightful heir. Nowadays, the Sontaran War Cabinet simply declared which of them was the one, true General Sontar, and all Sontarans followed that order, that Sontar, without question. Life was less complicated that way.

'General, I appreciate exactly the significance of your presence.'

'Good,' Sontar barked. He looked around. 'So this is the fabled city of the Time Lords.'

The materialisation platform was thirty-five storeys above ground level, and allowed excellent vistas of the Capitol. It must have been difficult for an outsider to distinguish the larger computer banks and machines from the tower blocks. Everything under the Dome was carefully harmonised, joined with a delicate network of walkways and roadways. There were terraced gardens, sculpture parks, clock towers and ornamental lakes. Architecture without any limitations on the architect's imagination, lit perfectly by the holographic lamps fixed to the roof of the Dome, preserved in this weatherless, controlled environment.

'The Capitol has stood for millions of years. It was Rassilon's capital, although of course in those days it looked very different and the Dome had not yet been built. The Time Lord Citadel dates from the time of Rassilon and Omega, although many parts are much older. Negotiations will be held in there.'

The Doctor indicated the Citadel, although he didn't need to – it was the largest building, set right underneath the apex of the Dome.

'Proceed,' Sontar ordered. Before the Doctor could react, the Sontarans began marching as one along the walkway that led to the Citadel. The Doctor kept pace, and although the Capitol Guard were caught unawares, they quickly closed ranks to escort the alien delegation.

Sontar had fixed his gaze on the dark structure, but gave no sign of an emotional response. 'Military Intelligence informs me that not all Gallifreyans are Time Lords.'

'Quite correct. And not all Time Lords are Gallifreyans, although the vast majority are.'

'All the Time Lords are in that Citadel?'

'Correct. All the colleges, living quarters, control rooms and scientific research facilities.'

'It seems too small for that.'

'The Citadel, like many of the Capitol's buildings, is larger on the inside than the outside.'

'Who lives out here?' Sontar asked, indicating the city with a sweep of his claw.

'Ancillary staff and their families. Technicians, artisans, cleaners, artists, engineers, cooks, musicians. Everyone the Time Lords need to support them and their Citadel. Although truth be told the Citadel is probably self-sufficient.'

'It was once a fortress,' Sontar stated.

The Doctor turned to him, puzzled. 'I don't think so.'

'Of course it was,' the General laughed. 'Look at the thickness of the walls, the buttresses and battlements. I should say it was a stronghold built to withstand a siege. No need to be coy about your race's past with me, Doctor.'

'I'm not. You are clearly right, it's just that it never occurred to me before.'

'There are no great legends of those battles? Does every Time Lord not sing praise of that day?'

'No.'

There was a gleam in Sontar's eye. 'I wonder who it was that the Time Lords fought? It must have been a glorious conflict, and a magnificent victory. Yet you choose to honour those that died by forgetting them. You should remember, Time Lord, that all your power, and this beautiful city, were not built without sacrifice.'

The Doctor nodded. 'Oh, no. Gallifrey honours its dead, as you will see. When we reach the Panopticon you will see the Flowers of Remembrance of the Lost Dead. There –' he pointed across the city to an unassuming geodesic structure – 'is the Tomb of the Uncertain Soldier.'

'You value a lack of decisiveness in your military? This man died because he hesitated?'

'No, no, no. This was a Gallifreyan body recovered from an alternate reality. We couldn't identify him because that soldier, and many like him who fought in the Time Wars, *didn't* hesitate at the critical moment, they chose to cancel out their own timelines for the greater good of Gallifrey.'

'An impressive sacrifice. It would please me to hope that my own men would destroy the universe rather than let it fall into enemy hands.'

The Doctor smiled forgivingly, and didn't correct the old General. 'Later, I will show you some of the surviving buildings that never existed or ever will, and we'll tour the Omega Memorial. Our entire civilisation was built from his sacrifice. It is thanks to Omega that we became Time Lords. Many Gallifreyans still worship him, including the current President, who has written a number of volumes on the subject.'

'I would like to learn of how your race acquired time travel.'

I bet you would, you old fox, the Doctor thought.

'No doubt we'll have that opportunity,' he said.

The Past
Eldest Sun

They had turned their backs on one hundred billion stars.

The Gallifreyan fleet had left its home galaxy and was deep in intergalactic space. Now the ships slowed down as they approached their destination, dropping out of vworp drive and proceeding at near-light speed towards the target co-ordinates. Omega had no need to look back. The galaxy behind him was a vast spiral, a hundred thousand light years from one side to the other. It was too far away now to make out any but the crudest of features. Within that mass was Gallifrey's sun, along with every star that could be seen in the night's sky of his homeworld.

There were two generations of stars. The spiral arms were filled with the youngest suns, which scientists designated Population I. Gallifrey's sun was a typical example, hot, rich in elements heavier than helium and hydrogen, surrounded by a planetary system. Towards the galactic core were clusters of older, larger, redder stars, those of Population II. They had formed before the heavy elements, indeed they were the nuclear factories in which the heavy elements had been forged. As Population II stars died they exploded, seeding the galaxy with heavier elements, the process that had brought the Population I stars into being many billions of years ago.

But even the Population II stars contained traces of metals and other complex molecules that could only have been created in the hearts of stars. Long ago, long before even the first galaxy had formed, there must have been another type of star. These Population III stars were supermassive, far brighter and hotter than their modern equivalents. Gallifrey's sun had been shining for around three billion years, and – even without the assistance of a solar engineer – would do so for twice as long again. The processes within a Population III star were so intense that they would have burned out three or four hundred times faster. The typical Population III star lived for ten million years before going supernova. In the early days of the universe these short-lived, vast stars had been the fuel for the newborn galaxies, filling them with riches. All the Population III stars were long dead, either vanished altogether or become vast black holes.

All but one.

Qqaba was the last in the universe, of that Omega was certain. It had barely survived this long, sustained by a drip feed of interstellar matter from the intergalactic nebula that partially obscured it. Even so, it had been teetering on the brink of death for aeons when Omega had found it. He had reconfigured the star, kept it alive. If he had discovered the star a week later, it would have been too late. Qqaba would have died, and so would have Gallifrey.

Now they had returned to Qqaba to destroy it.

A dying star.

No doubt there were writers capable of capturing the waning majesty of such a thing, or its sheer scale. A poet might be able to sum up a man's feelings as he saw such a spectacle, find words for the new emotions that welled up in its presence. Perhaps he would fall back on physical description of the mundane surroundings of the observation bay, and note that everything was transformed by the evening starlight, becoming either harsh crimson light or sharp black shadows. There might be room for philosophical or moral instruction in that imagery, Omega thought. He didn't know. He was an engineer, not a poet, and he was here to do a job.

He ran his gloved hand over each casket in turn. Their clasps and buckles rattled with expectation and impatience. He could feel them in there, radiant. They were so beautiful, so intricate. They were children in a womb, twins, with many possible futures. Omega had brought them into existence, built boxes that were larger on the inside than the outside, filled them with basic programming and operational parameters and opportunities, let them feed on energy and data. Unobserved, the Hands had slipped the bonds of technology. Even Omega didn't know what they were any longer, he couldn't know without collapsing their potential. Whatever was in the boxes might be infinite, it could be anything.

Their thoughts touched his, the link of parents, children and lovers through the ages. They had always felt cold, they told him in unison, they had always known their destiny.

'Today was a day to live in history,' Omega thought.

'What about tomorrow?' they asked. 'This wasn't an ending, this was a beginning.'

'Who knows where it will all end?' Omega asked out loud, the words echoing around the room.

They knew. Should they tell?

'It is time.'

His mind linked with the captains of the other ships in the fleet. They were on the control decks of their own starbreakers, they would follow him in. There was no room for hesitation or hubris. There was no doubt. There was only the Plan, and that began with a single word.

'Open,' he said.

The caskets cracked open, the merest chinks of light filling the room.

'Go.'

And they were gone, spiralling round each other, singing like dolphins.

Others could track them, others could monitor their progress. Omega was content to watch through the dark windows and the shaded visor of his helmet. Two points of light, brilliant even against the surface of a star. Then they were gone, plunging into the photosphere, the convection zone, the vast radiation zone, onwards to the core.

There was a burst of static in his earpiece. 'The computer indicates that the star has reached the point of collapse.'

'Activate the stasis halo,' Omega responded automatically. He could feel the halo activating, the protective field granting the ship temporal grace, swathing it from the rest of time and space.

When new, Qqaba had been twenty times more massive than Gallifrey's sun. The huge weight of the star had pressed down on the centre, and it should have collapsed – except that the sheer pressure squeezed energy from the hydrogen in the core, energy that pushed outwards, holding the star up. In its heyday, this star shone fifty thousand times brighter than Gallifrey's sun. But it burned so fiercely that within ten million years it had converted all the hydrogen fuel into helium. It cooled, lost energy, and the inner parts began to shrink. This only intensified the pressures once more, helium burned, the star swelled and darkened. Helium burning took place for a million years, and once the helium at the core had gone, the star ran through increasingly desperate alternatives. Converting its carbon into neon, magnesium and oxygen sustained it for ten thousand years, and then burning the neon had kept the star alive for a dozen years. The oxygen lasted for four. There was only one fuel source left – the traces of silicon. Qqaba had been creating energy using nuclear fusion of silicon for just a week when Omega had discovered it, and it had already run dry. Since then, the nuclear processes were only kept going by Gallifreyan technology. By the Hands of Omega.

Omega had already sensed it. Was that intuition, or was it the Hands telling him? He could hear the spacedrive of his ship powering up.

All was going to plan.

For the whole of its life, the energy radiating outwards from the core had balanced out the gravitational force pulling inwards. There had been equilibrium, stability. Now there was nothing left in the core that the star could use as fuel. The only elements left were iron, cobalt, nickel – all too stable to break down with any ease. As the last molecules of silicon were converted into iron, the star died. Over a million years, the core had burned away most of its mass, and it was now a vestige of its former self, only around one and a half million kilometres across.

Three tenths of a second later, the core was ten kilometres in diameter.

The energy involved in the compression was incomprehensible. Most of it was shed as heat and light, enough of it to disintegrate atomic nuclei. The chains locking protons, electrons and neutrons together as atoms and molecules were shattered. These fundamental building blocks of the universe began behaving differently in their strange new environment. Tiny electrons were pressed together to form neutrons by sheer force of gravity. Neutrons normally formed the nucleus of atoms. Here, as the core reached a new equilibrium, all that was left of the core was a sphere of densely packed neutrons, a hundred kilometres across but with twice the mass of the Sun.

The haloes are malfunctioning.

The news came from all around. He heard it via the telepathic link to the others, the shouts of his crew over the intercom, his instincts.

The pressures at the heart of the star were so intense that the neutron material was squeezed harder than it could bear. It sprang out, sending a shock wave out into the rest of the star.

He would not be denied this moment, he would watch. He would survive, he knew this from the Fragment. The others would find a way to restore the shields.

With no energy radiating from the core, there was nothing supporting the outer layers of the star. Although Qqaba was a mere shadow of its former self, there was still enough material there to build a dozen Gallifreyan suns. All of that matter, weighing down on the core. The outer shell began falling down the gravity well to the core, at a quarter of the speed of light.

'Neutrino flood detected,' the helmsman called.

It was half a minute since the star had died.

The haloes had not been restored.

Omega knew that he would die. That glorious dying star was suddenly a maw that he was staring into. He knew his destiny. He heard the first sparks and muffled explosions as radiation began to blast apart his ship.

A shock wave had formed in the core. Even now it surged outwards. It was immensely powerful, easily enough to reverse the infall of the outer layers. Suddenly there were fifteen solar masses heading outwards, an expanding spherical shock front. The instruments were registering the neutrinos now because neutrinos have no mass, and they were so small that they were passing through all but the densest matter at the speed of light. They were created after the shock front, but they outran it. The shock front was already on its way, it had already happened.

But the Fragment...

He heard one of their voices, then the other.

'No!'

'The Fragment's a forgery. Rassilon's work.'

'No!'

'You deny it even now?'

'I thought *you* had forged it.'

Omega wasn't listening to their squabbling any longer. He stood, hands behind his back, facing the shock front. Around him his crew betrayed their animal instincts, they flinched, they cowered, they tried to run or shield themselves. The Gallifreyan fleet was right in the path of the destruction, facing towards it, unprotected. Omega's ship was the closest. It had about ten seconds. The other ships had a quarter of a minute more.

Every piece of matter in the star was becoming compressed and energetic. Very heavy elements rapidly formed from this neutron soup.

The core was now a neutron star, barely twenty kilometres across.

There was a great deal of material in the shock front. Two-with-twenty-eight-noughts tonnes. It took energy to force that amount of matter outwards and even the death-throes of the heart of a star can't generate enough.

The shock wave slowed, almost to a halt. It was still a hundred kilometres from Omega's ship. There must have been members of his crew that thought they had been saved, that there had been a miracle.

There was a tear in Omega's eye.

Remember the neutrinos? Remember how they travel at the speed of light? Remember how they can travel through all but the densest matter?

As the shockwave slowed, the layers of stellar material started piling into one another, jamming, solidifying. The outer layers of the star formed a shell, compressed to a density of three hundred trillion neutrons in every cubic centimetre.

Thick enough to stop just a few of the neutrinos.

Remember the neutrinos? Remember how they travel at the speed of light?

They hit the outer layers with literally infinite force. The dense material absorbed the energy, ablated it, spread it out. But it was too much.

The neutrino impacts blasted the shock front outwards again, away from the core, faster than ever. The shock front was now travelling at two percent light speed.

Omega's crew saw it coming.

Hard radiation evaporated the outer skin of the hull. The ship popped, burst and blistered like a fruit on a fire. Below him, Omega heard the screams of his crew, but he couldn't see them through the thick black smoke and the red pall of the emergency lighting. Emergency lighting here, when the light outside was melting the hull! He could smell his own flesh, he stared at the shock front as it swamped his ship, annihilating it.

The shock front passed through him.

If the Fragment was a forgery, then why was he still alive?

'This is my destiny,' Omega objected over the terrible noise of the deckplates and bulkheads obliterating. He had fulfilled that destiny. 'Feel the Energy around us!' Gravitational forces, raw matter, the stuff that universes are made of. Space and time and matter are linked. 'These are the reins, seize them!' Why wasn't he dead? He could hear the other two in his mind, talking to each other, but not to him. Their voices were fading.

'We can power the stasis haloes with our minds. The ships will be saved.'

'Not Omega's, the machinery has gone.'

'We can't save his ship or his crew.'

'We can save him.'

Their minds had gone, his ship had gone, but Omega was still there, truly immortal in his stasis halo. Gravity had taken a hold, he plunged towards the dawning neutron star at the heart of the destruction at a third the speed of light. Time began to slow around him. This wasn't just his imagination: the intense gravity had dilated space and time, rendered them plastic. He could feel Time washing through him, altering him, even through his protective shield.

The surviving starbreakers would be bathed in the Time Energy within the next few seconds. They would collect a fraction of that power, siphon it, store it in vast batteries. That was the Plan – that would be the fuel for the timeships. But what Rassilon hadn't foreseen was that the crews themselves would be exposed, they would be anointed in the energies. Omega saw it all now, he saw Time laid out in front of him as plain as the stars in the night's sky. He could feel the harmonies there.

He saw the future, he felt the time winds at his back.

There was one last process taking place at the heart of the star.

If any object is squeezed small enough – the exact size depends on the mass of the object, but is easy to calculate – then space closes up around it. The object drops out of spacetime. All that remained was a perfect matte black sphere, a hole in the universe. But the object would have a gravitational pull, it could still draw matter and energy towards it. The very centre of the hole would have infinite density in an infinitely small radius. None of the laws of physics would apply there, space and time would be uncoupled. Anything might exist there, a man might be a god.

Omega smiled, opened his arms, ready to embrace the singularity.

He could hear their voices again, infinitesimally faint, over the roar of the dying star.

They could see the effect the singularity was having on space and time. It was like a hammer smashing against thick glass, or a block of ice. Cracks developing, growing together into a network of lines. The universe was a block of stone before, now it was being chipped away to reveal the sculpture that had always lain within it. Spacetime is shattering, the laws of physics have been repealed.

Rassilon was panicking. Rassilon would not let it happen.

Omega could feel Rassilon's mind once again. He lifted his head, strained to hear the voice far above him.

But the mind wasn't speaking to him, it was speaking to the black hole, encompassing it, manipulating it. By sheer force of will, Rassilon passed a new law of physics. He struck up equilibrium, established beautifully elaborate equations. A surface appeared upon the darkness, a surface from which the escape velocity was exactly the speed of light. The naked singularity was covered, the hole in the universe was sealed over, and outside the storm was subsiding.

The universe was safe. Nothing can ever be allowed to escape from the darkness.

The crewmen of the surviving ships were the Lords of Time.

Omega stared up. He couldn't see anything, but he heard the event horizon slamming shut far above him.

There was no force in the universe that could reach him now, no form of contact. There was only him, immortal in his stasis halo, protected from his infernal surroundings.

He fell, an impossible, anomalous streak of light against the darkness.

Omega fell forever.

Chapter Four
Sleep in My Mind

The door to the Doctor's room recognised Larna and opened for her, even though she was a little early and she hadn't brought a card.

She had spent a great deal of time with the Doctor over the last few years, but most of it had been in his office at college, and she had never been invited to his private rooms before. They were configured in a different way to her own chambers. She had only just moved in, and had yet to settle. The Doctor had lived here for many, many years and every brick and floorboard was infused with his own personality. Larna knew that the Doctor wasn't here. This was a chance to look around.

There was a full-length mirror by the door, and Larna stopped to look at herself in it. She had got used to walking around in nothing but her nightshirt by now, but this was the first sight of herself as others would see her. She had recovered from the exertions of running down the stairs, and the nanoweave of the cotton had worked its magic on the sweat, also keeping the garment clean and crisp. The shift had a high collar and fitted cuffs, and swathed every inch of her skin apart from her head and her hands. Larna had worn day robes less decent than this nightshirt. Besides, the love of formality and decorum shared by all Time Lords might disapprove of her being in another's chambers in one's night wear but would also prevent anyone from finding her here, or from enquiring about it if they did. After this morning Larna had realised that there was only one Time Lord's approval that she sought, and the rest could be damned. She ran her fingers through her hair, tightening the braids.

The main room was of an average size, and was full of books and artefacts from every planet in the universe. On the floor as she walked through the door was an intricately woven rug. Larna found herself stepping round, as it felt disrespectful to place her bare feet on it. She moved down into the main area, past a wooden globe of Sol Three. The most cursory examination of the room revealed that there were many objects from the Earth here, from every period in its history. Time Lords had long been fascinated by a planet so similar to their own – same length of day and year, same gravity, same distance from the same type of sun. The Earthlings also strongly resembled Gallifreyans. A significant number of Time Lords felt a special affinity with Earth, and none more so than the Doctor. Earth was an important cornerstone of galactic cosmology, its history underpinning much of established time. Earth had a vibrancy that Gallifrey had lost, or which had degenerated into cheap Low Town thrills.

She remembered the words of a human writer: 'We are all in the gutter, but some of us are looking at the stars.' When an Earthman looked up at the stars, it wasn't simply to measure the flow of electrically charged particles or variation between the absolute and apparent magnitudes.

The Doctor's cat, Wycliff, was brushing around her legs. She knelt down to stroke him. That was another similarity between Gallifrey and Earth: the demanding nature of the local cats. Locating a bowl near the food machine, she dispensed some food and milk for him. He munched away at his meal, tail quivering. Larna dispensed a drink for herself and began to sip at it as she explored the room. A variety of coats and hats hung from a wooden hat stand. His robes of office lay in a heap at its base. Either they had fallen off or he'd simply thrown them there in the first place. A dozen of the galaxy's finest wines lay in their rack, the dust gathering.

Larna found the Doctor's chair, facing the fireplace. Guiltily, she wondered whether she could sit there, rather than the guest chair. He wouldn't be here for a few minutes yet, so she moved the book she found there – *Four Quartets* – and settled down, tucking her legs up rather than use the footrest. Over time, the cushions had become moulded to his body, used to his presence. The chair was upholstered in a velvet material like the coat the Doctor used to wear. It was still warm from where Wycliff had been dozing. She finished her drink, seeing the Doctor's room from his perspective. She realised that there wasn't a video screen in here, so she would be unable to watch the Doctor and the alien delegations arriving in the Panopticon.

The chair faced the fireplace, framed by a heavy marble mantel, with a number of ornaments. There was only one timepiece in the whole room, an ormolu clock from Earth that sat on the mantelpiece, its day divided up into twelve hours of equal length. The longer of the two hands was between the two and the three, the shorter sat about a quarter of the way between the five and the six. At the side of the chair was an occasional table, and it was littered with junk. A tea service was surrounded by bric-a-brac: computer cards, a bunch of keys. There was a slip of brown paper. Instinctively glancing around to confirm that she was alone, Larna opened it.

There was a single word, hand-written, in capitals.

OHM

Larna recognised the word from somewhere. It was an Earth word signifying the SI unit for electrical resistance, named after one of their scientists, but there was some other meaning that eluded her. She put the paper away guiltily, sure someone had just seen her. But she was still alone, apart from Wycliff.

There was an empty wooden box there, too, presumably where all the stuff had come from. Sticking right through the table was a knife. Larna plucked it out, surprised how easily it came free. The knife couldn't be metal, it must be a field of some kind. She tapped at the tip of the blade to see how sharp it was, and was rewarded by it pricking her thumb. She yelped, dropping the knife.

Larna sucked a drop of blood from her finger.

Two pictures hung over the mantelpiece. The first was a computer painting of a couple. The man wore a body in late middle age, with white hair and a clipped beard. The woman was smiling. Their eyes were extraordinary: his were dark and knowing, those of an ancient warrior. Hers were grey, young. Larna didn't recognise either of them, but somehow knew that the painting represented a moment in time that had now been lost. They were dead, now, or separated by the tides of time and deserts of space.

The second picture was so beautiful that as Larna looked up at it she felt a tear form. This wasn't drawn by a computer, it had been hand-painted. The woman in the painting was almost feline, with hair in a black bob and eyes such a vivid green that they would seem unnatural if only they weren't so *right*. She was slender, with bare, freckled shoulders. This woman was so much older and wiser than she appeared. This picture was just a shadow of her, it only captured one facet of a passionate, intellectual, lovely person. The gown she wore was archaic, made from a flowing gold material that no Gallifreyan woman had worn for generations.

There was a scroll in her hand, bearing an inscription. Larna strained to read it. It was in High Gallifreyan.

'"Death is but a door",' she whispered.

And then there was a door in the wall in front of her that hadn't been there before.

The Doctor stood between the Sontaran delegation and the Rutan. His past self had nipped away before either the delegates or the Public Record cameras had noticed him and would now be on his way up to the TARDIS cradles. The rest, as they say, was history. Now he could turn his full attention to the conference without worrying that the universe was going to unravel because of the time paradoxes he had created.

The delegates were face to face for the first time. It was impossible to tell what the Rutan was thinking. Its tentacles were quivering and patterns of colour flushed across its skin, but the Doctor couldn't be sure whether that was a sign of its emotional state, or just how its body reacted in these conditions. He knew that he would have to be careful not to favour the Sontarans simply because they were humanoid, with expressions and emotions that he could relate to. That said, the Sontarans were no better at the moment: they'd all put their helmets back on as they entered the Citadel, and only their eyes were visible, glaring through the narrow eye-slits. Their stance suggested grim resolution, but it always did.

A word out of place here, and the Doctor knew that the delegates would storm away, return to their ships and resume hostilities.

'Welcome, once again,' the Doctor said, careful to turn to both delegations as he said it. 'Thank you both for coming. We will convene at First Bells tomorrow. We have prepared quarters for you, as per your specifications. You will find the conditions of your homeworlds perfectly recreated there. Are there any further issues before the Chancellery Watch escort you to your rooms?'

The column of soldiers split into two groups, saluting the aliens, and began to form into ranks of escort.

'There is the matter of security,' the Rutan said. 'Do we have your total assurance that the Sontarans will be confined to their rooms, preventing them from assassinating the Rutan?'

'Neither yourself nor the Sontarans will be confined to quarters, but if you choose to leave the xenodochia, you will be escorted by the Watch and carefully monitored. Both delegations have the freedom of the Citadel, except, of course, you will not be allowed into your opponent's quarters. Neither side is permitted weapons of any kind, and both have agreed to be continually monitored to prevent the acquisition of any weapons.'

The Doctor paused. 'You are all perfectly safe here, the safest that any of you have ever been. I hope that in this atmosphere of tranquillity, without the constant threat of assassination or attack, you may learn that there is common ground between your two races.'

The Sontarans and Rutans remained unmoved.

The Doctor's smile flickered.

The Doctor's empty words had drifted up like convection currents. Now the roof vault echoed with the sound of marching boots, as the Chancellery Watch led the alien delegates away. They thought they were safe, that the Time Lords could guarantee their security. They were wrong, and so utterly complacent.

A masked figure perched on one of the roof-beams that supported the Panopticon Dome. Beneath its mask, it smiled. They would see how wrong they had been.

Huran woke up dead.

He screamed, drawing air into phantom lungs and hurling it out of his ghost-throat. It was like being alive, *like* it. He was only breathing because he chose to, there was no blood in his veins or food in his stomach.

The Time Lord stood watching him the whole time. He was a senior member of the High Council, one of the Ministers. He wore a black robe that absorbed every photon of light that fell on it. There was no sympathy in the man's eyes, no feeling at all. Behind him were two of the Watch: a young one and the man that had been held hostage. The man who had killed him. They were sifting through a tray of Huran's belongings.

'I'm dead. Aren't I?' Huran asked.

'Yes,' the Magistrate said simply. 'We found your body above the shop in Fish Street. Your current form is a computer simulation, reconstructed from your brain patterns.' He indicated a glowing datacube slotted into his hand terminal.

Thoughts spiralled around Huran's head, not quite connecting with each other. 'You're going to fix me up, aren't you, though? Force a regeneration by remote.'

'No.'

A digital shiver ran down Huran's spine. 'You could do it,' he insisted. 'You brought that guard back.'

'We found Constable Peltroc in time. Despite the injuries that you had inflicted on him, the surgeons were able to effect a full recovery.'

'If you found *him* in time, you found *me* in time!' Huran shouted.

The Magistrate didn't deny it. 'Your body has already been recycled,' the Time Lord calmly informed him.

'Then weave me a new one!'

The Magistrate shook his head.

Huran closed his eyes, never more aware of the skin on his face and the weight of his skull. 'Yiri,' he said.

'The female has also been matriculated.'

'Could we be together when this is over?'

'It is already over.'

'But we both still exist, even if it is only as simulations. This is still me. We could be downloaded into the same program, we could be together.'

'Whyever would you want to do that?'

'You'd never understand, you motherless dried-up Timey –' The rest of the words didn't come out, however much Huran wanted them to.

The Magistrate yawned, then released one of the controls. 'Constable Peltroc is a hero, injured in the course of his duties. You were a criminal, Huran, and so was your mate. There is no reason why we should extend any privileges to you. However, we are not inhumane and have no wish to annihilate you. Both your biodata records will be archived and preserved.'

'Show me Yiri, promise that we can be together. If you don't, then I won't tell you anything.'

The Magistrate sighed, tapping at his hand terminal. 'You were assisting a masked man in the abduction of a Capitol Guard. Who was this man?'

Huran smiled, ready to stand his ground, but then found himself answering. 'I don't know his name. He was a Timey, never gave us his name.' It was him speaking, but he wasn't Huran any more. Just a computer model, a push-button copy. The Time Lords knew everything about him, now, even more than he'd told Yiri. They knew about every lie, every false boast, every excuse, every private thought and moment. All they had to do was ask.

The interrogation continued without his needing to think. 'A Time Lord? Why do you say that?'

'You all speak and act the same way, you all act as if you own the place. And only Timeys have telepathy, you've made sure of that.'

The Magistrate nodded thoughtfully. 'When did you first meet?'

'Ten days ago, Outside. Said he needed some work doing and that he'd pay us in components.'

The Magistrate raised an eyebrow.

'Spare circuits and gears, other parts for machines. Hard to come by normally, unless you've got contacts Inside. Always valuable, especially new ones.'

'What sort of work?'

'We rented that room for him, helped him find stuff.'

'Did you help him break into Chamber 403?'

'Where?'

'An archive storeroom in the Citadel. Immediately before Constable Peltroc was abducted, certain items were stolen from there.'

'Not by me or Yiri.'

'Are you suggesting that your employer was able to carry Peltroc's unconscious body from the barracks to Low Town without help?'

'I never said that, I just said that it wasn't me. I was with Yiri in Low Town. The boss called, said he needed some drolminathol.'

The young guard stepped forward and whispered into the Magistrate's ear. 'A chemical relaxant designed to weaken telepathic defences. Street name: intermace. The physician found traces of it in the Constable's bloodstream.'

'Yeah,' Huran agreed. 'Common enough if you know where to look. Whores use it when they have Timey customers and they want to get really friendly.'

'Your employer, the renegade, was after knowledge, and he felt that Constable Peltroc had that knowledge. What did he want to know?'

'I've no idea. Something about some keys, that's all I know.'

'Keys to what?'

'I don't know which keys.'

'The Great Key? The Key to Time?'

Huran laughed. 'Those are out of his league. I think it was more personal than that.'

'Let's talk about your employer.'

Constable Peltroc moved forward. 'When you came into the room, he said, "We have to be quick, it's nearly dawn." What was so important about the dawn?'

'Dunno. We only ever saw him at night. Yiri reckons he works early shifts back at the Dome and that someone would miss him.'

'You never saw him during the day?'

'No. Never got a message from him either except after dark.'

'Did you ever see him without the mask or cloak?'

'Never. You know the question you should be asking? Why does he wear a mask, eh? Only one reason. We'd recognise his face. Why wear a voicebox unless we'd recognise his voice?'

The Magistrate nodded, mulling over the question. Then, without ceremony, he unplugged the datacube and placed it in its rack with the others.

It was as if Larna was walking amongst the stars.

It was impossible to judge perspective, the room could be the size of a bedchamber or an arena or both. A field of candles against a black background. The room was warmed by them, awash with golden light, and filled with their fragrance.

There was a small glass bowl in front of her on a little plinth. She knelt down, and found a necklace nesting amongst a few flower blossoms. A silver chain with a sapphire pendant. Larna had seen it somewhere before, she was sure, but couldn't say where. She put the necklace on. Everything felt so right. In this room nothing else existed, it was like the best meditation. This was peace, she thought. Larna didn't know how long it had been since she had stepped out of the Doctor's room and into this place. Time had ceased to matter. She turned, to see how far away the door was.

The Doctor was a silhouette in the doorway.

'I-I'm sorry,' she said.

Her hand had moved to cover her chest. It had known before she had that this was a private place, and that she was intruding. Suddenly the room was an empty, vast void. She was an alien here.

The Doctor stepped down into the room. Warm light fell over his face as he walked towards her.

'I'll leave.' But she would have to get past him.

'No,' the Doctor said, as the door began to slide shut behind him. He was standing over her now, the traces of a smile on his face. 'I have no secrets from you.'

They were almost touching, and Larna's hand was by her side. She had lowered her head, out of respect.

The Doctor touched the pendant lightly with his index finger, then pulled it away. He wore a ring on the middle finger of his right hand which had the same blue gem set in it.

'It suits you,' he concluded softly.

Larna had just remembered where she had seen the necklace. 'The woman in the picture died, didn't she?'

There was no need for the Doctor to say anything.

'I didn't know.'

'It was a long time ago,' he said matter-of-factly. 'A year for each candle, and so long ago that everyone else has forgotten.' There was a tear in the corner of his eye. 'I've forgotten her. I only remember now when I want to. You can't change the past.'

'Yet you have this zero room for her.'

'This place is for me. I have many other places, too.'

'You've travelled,' Larna whispered. 'I've never left the Dome. I've never even been to Low Town. I want to. You had the chance to leave. Why did you come back?'

'This is home.'

'Tell me about her. Where did you meet?'

'We didn't.' The Doctor paused.

'You painted that picture of her,' Larna said.

The Doctor nodded. 'She taught me to dance.'

Larna smiled, and so did the Doctor. Their eyes and thoughts met.

And they had the floor to themselves and they were dancing beneath a sky the colour of amber. He was dressed formally, a neat row of gold buttons running down his chest, matching the silk of her gown. The harpists were playing a pavane. It was a celebration of some kind, a festival, it didn't matter which one. The entire household and their friends were all around. There were a number of aliens, too – Mr Saldaamir, a pair from Althrace, and a fat yellow-skinned man with red fins around the crown of his head. Everyone was smiling, spellbound, watching their choreography. Anywhere else this would be unspeakably decadent, but even here it was scandalous. The young son and the older woman. What would his father think?

It didn't matter to them. The dance was everything, all that existed at that moment. Elaborate equations of form and sound were expressed through their slow, stately movements. He led, not merely remembering what she had taught him that afternoon, but developing it, elaborating upon it. Now, for the very first time, she was learning from him. And they knew, they remembered, that she still had much to teach him, and that she would learn from him in turn.

The music stopped and every single guest began to applaud them, even the harpists. This was the first time that they had ever been so happy, but the night was still young.

She reached out to stroke his face, daring to do it and damn the consequences.

Larna was going to pull her hand away, but the Doctor held it there, sliding his fingers between hers, placing his other hand on her waist, never taking his eyes from her. His touch was warm, and as they drew together she could feel the velvet of his jacket against her, even through the cotton of her shift.

They began to dance.

Gallifrey's nameless sun rose over the Capitol Dome, as it had done since the first days of the universe.

No sunlight penetrated the Dome itself, but the Oldharbour Clock that stood in the Eastern parts of the Capitol marked the occasion by chiming Nine Bells. On the ledge beneath the vast clock face, an intricate mechanical ballet began, as life-sized animated figures emerged from their positions and set about their daily routine. They were gaily painted and beautifully dressed, certainly symbolic of something, although even the few Gallifreyans that had noticed them couldn't agree what it might be. One of the problems was that the clock had never been built. Not in this timeline, anyway. It was a paradoxical survivor from the Time Wars, probably the only vestige of its parallel Gallifrey still in existence. It had just appeared one day, no one remembered when.

The analogue Time Lords that had built the Tower had imbued the clockwork figurines with a degree of sentience and the capacity for self-development. Now, unknown to anyone, the clock people were the most intelligent beings on Gallifrey. Their social interactions were complex, if perfectly regulated, and they had developed a complex framework of philosophy and etiquette to explain their world and their actions. It would be some time yet before they realised that they were just characters on a long-forgotten clock face, but the discovery would come. When it did there would be dissension, schism and war. But still they would circle each other in perfect orbits, moving their limbs in perfect arcs.

The chimes from the Clock Tower could be heard on the Eastern side of the Citadel. Raimor and Peltroc heard it as they walked through one of the common hexangles around the Panopticon galleries. All around them, Time Lords and Technicians began to emerge from their quarters and glide smoothly to their work and their leisure. Life in the Citadel normally ran like clockwork, everything in harmony, the same every day. Today, though, there were notes of discord. Lord Henspring almost bumped into Captain Jomdek as they passed the living fountain. Lady Gehammer was nowhere to be seen, Lord Norval took her place. Tiny things, unimportant things, but Raimor noticed them. The guards themselves were late trudging back to barracks. It had been an eventful eighteen hours. The damn aliens were already a chaotic influence.

The Magistrate swept past them, giving them the faintest acknowledgement. His black cloak swirled behind him like a living thing.

Peltroc's shoulders were sagging, he'd had something on his mind for the last few hours.

'What's the matter, son?' Raimor asked. 'The surgeons fixed you up, didn't they? You're probably healthier than you were this time yesterday.'

Peltroc still didn't smile. 'Probably.'

'What is it?'

'When he was talking to Huran,' Peltroc began, indicating the Magistrate, 'he called me a hero. I'm not a hero.'

'You acted bravely. Got two dangerous criminals, and you nearly caught the ringleader. You've certainly given us a lot to go on. That's heroism.'

'I killed two people. One of them was a woman.'

'That was an accident.'

'The other one wasn't. I stabbed him in the back. That's not heroic.'

'He'd have killed you. And –'

The Doctor hurried between them, in those ridiculous clothes of his. He greeted them as he passed.

'– and you never gave up, you never gave that masked lunatic what he wanted.'

Peltroc shook his head. 'So why don't I feel like a hero? Why am I still shaking?'

A Technician was running towards them. A young lad with blond hair. Naturally, he took one look at them and concluded that Peltroc was the senior officer.

'You have to come quickly!' he blurted.

Raimor stepped forwards, tried to reassert any authority that he had.

'Calm down, sir. I'm sure we can help you.'

'I've just found a body,' the Technician blurted. 'In Chamber Epsilon. It's Technician First Class Waymivrudimqwe. I think he's been stabbed.'

The Doctor could have sworn that for a moment the guards on the Conference Room door weren't going to let him in. Just as the Doctor was on the threshold, Lord Nulquemper, a minor official with an obscure function, interposed himself.

'Good morning, Doctor. Late again, I see.'

'I am, Nulquemper, so if you could just –' the Doctor tried bobbing around him, but the little man ducked across to block him.

'The alien delegations arrived some ten minutes ago, a few minutes earlier than scheduled.'

'Yes well, I'll –' the Doctor stared at the door. 'Where are they?'

'In the Conference Room.'

'Who's in there with them?'

'*With* them, my Lord Doctor?'

'With. Them.'

'No one, my Lord.'

The Doctor opened his mouth to say something, but it took a couple of seconds for the words to arrive. 'For ten million years, the Sontarans and the Rutans have killed each other on sight. To prevent that from happening here, they were supposed to convene in different antechambers and only to enter the Conference Room itself when I had arrived.'

'Were they?' Nulquemper said, his face the picture of innocence. 'Oh, but you were late, weren't you?'

'There's probably a war underway in there!'

The Doctor shoved him out of the way, much to Nulquemper's alarm. He flung open the doors, not knowing what he would find.

The Rutan and the Sontarans were sitting at the triangular negotiating table. As there were ten Sontarans but only one Rutan, the arrangement looked a little unbalanced. General Sontar sat with his knees beneath the table, two advisers at either side. The remaining five Sontarans sat in a neat row near the back wall.

The Rutan just sat there, its underside half-draped, half-perched on the chair.

To a rather frosty silence, the Doctor took his seat. They had been sitting here like this for the last ten minutes. It was like a playground game, staring at each other, hoping the other child would blink first. Neither race had eyelids.

'I am a few minutes late,' he began. 'I apologise.'

No response from either party, they didn't even turn to face him. They sat watching each other suspiciously across the table. There were no weapons here, both sides knew that, but they still suspected that this was a trap of some kind.

For another ten, agonising, seconds no one spoke.

'What language are we to use?' one of the Sontarans growled.

'Whichever you want to hear,' the Doctor explained, grateful. 'One of the advantages of holding a conference here on Gallifrey is that there will be no difficulties with translation. Your races have different names for planets and units of measurements. The planet the Sontarans call New Quentar, the Rutans call Sisswurgplok. We classify it as Procyon. You will always hear a name you understand, you will not be forced to use the name coined by your enemy.'

The Rutan gurgled. 'It is not as straightforward as that in all cases, as our units of time are based on the rotational period of our homeworlds and a Rutan year is three times the length of a Sontaran year and a Gallifreyan year is different again.'

'Oh yes,' the Doctor said, brightening. 'Take the way that Gallifrey measures an hour. In the ancient days, we used sundials, divided up into nine periods. We called those "hours", after an ancient sun god. There were also nine hours of darkness, measured by candle, or hourglass.

Nine Bells is always dawn in the morning and dusk in the evening. A very simple system, but also very complicated. Our planet is slightly tilted on its axis, so there is more daylight in the summer than in winter. But whatever the time of year, the sundial would divide the daylight period into nine hours. So hours vary in length from forty-five minutes in the depths of midwinter to one hundred and ten at midsummer. At the moment, this being towards the end of the eleventh month of the year, each daylight hour is about fifty-five minutes long, each hour of the night is about one hundred and five.'

The Rutan snorted, which was a rather extraordinary sight. 'Illogical, unscientific.'

The Doctor nodded. 'Oh yes, especially now that we live under the Dome, and never see the sun anyway. But that's still the way we do it, for the most part. Some Time Lords operate their own systems, based on their own body clock or the needs of their job. My point is that the phrase "one Gallifreyan hour" is pretty meaningless at the best of times, and would take the best part of a day to explain to non-Gallifreyans. But everything is translated for you. If I say "one hour", the Sontarans would hear it as 'Four subLunar cycles' and you would hear it as "Sixty-Three Million Beats". We would all understand which period of time was meant.'

'We would expect the Time Lords of all the universal races to understand that time is relative,' the Rutan said.

General Sontar gave a gruff laugh. 'It would be irony indeed if they did not.' Either out of etiquette, or because they were slower on the uptake, the other Sontarans waited for Sontar to finish before chuckling themselves. It was an odd sound, like the revving of a motorbike engine, and not without a hint of malice.

The Doctor smiled broadly.

The Rutan had cracked a joke and the Sontarans had laughed. There was hope for them all yet.

Larna was dreaming, she knew that because sunlight didn't stream over the Capitol's roof gardens and it wasn't Outside either, it wasn't wild enough to be the place that she'd read about. She knew she was dreaming because really she was safe in the Doctor's bed.

There were no paths here, no carefully laid out flower-beds or mazes or hedgerows. But the purple grass was neatly manicured, and there was a bench by the side of the pool. There was a delicate mist in the air, one that hid the rest of the world from her, and her from the rest of the world. But the sky was blue, cloudless, and the air was warm. She wondered whose garden it was, and how she had got here. She wondered what she was wearing, and noticed that she wasn't wearing anything at all. But there were no Time Lords here to disapprove, only butterflies, and this was just a dream.

Her feet were still sore from climbing so many steps. Because she could, she stepped into the water. The pool wasn't quite bath-warm. She walked further in, letting the water lap around her toes, her thighs, her waist, her breasts, her neck. The water began to take her weight, lift her. Lazily, she let herself drift until she was horizontal, on her back, facing up into the perfect sky, unable to see anything else. Her hair had unwound, and floated around her. Her head was far enough in the water now to cover her ears and block out the sound of the birdsong. She closed her eyes.

For dream-like minutes, there was just her, with the water and the sun different kinds of warm against her skin.

And then there was something else, something fearful. Larna could sense it closing in on her, surrounding her, watching her, and the water was freezing cold, cramping her limbs, making her gasp for air, locking her muscles. Her eyes were open, but she couldn't move. She was sinking, she wasn't going to drown, but the sky hanging over her was blood-red. The garden had grown dark, and was darkening further. The trees and grass were trembling in the breeze. The water had become gelid, a pane of glass was forming between her and the air.

Her ears were immersed, this was all happening silently. Despite that, laughter surrounded her, mocking laughter that drowned out every other sound. Everything was at stake. Everything.

There was urgent knocking, gloved fists against wood.

The sky had cooled to black iron, and Larna was staring down at her own body from it. She looked calm, and seemed to be shining because everything around her body was so dark. Her hair and eyes were golden, and if her teeth were ivory then her skin must have been pearl. Petal blossom blew over her from the garden, and into the black water. She was dead, she realised. There was a clean wound, just beneath her left breast.

Her death didn't alarm her, why should it? This was just a dream, and everyone else was dead, too.

But it wasn't a dream, and she was naked. There were few stars, but she could see herself, feel herself, freezing over. As she watched, she began to unravel, strands of DNA and hair unfurling. And there was something peeling her away until there was nothing left. It didn't hurt, but she was dead and so she couldn't stop it, she couldn't even move. Behind her, all around her, the garden was unravelling, too. The butterflies vanished like untying knots, the bench and grass dissolved into strands of cotton.

She screamed.

The Magistrate flung open the door, to find the Lady Larna tangled in the bed sheets. She was alone, screaming. Her waist-length hair was bedraggled. The Magistrate crossed the room in three paces, clamped one hand over her mouth, held her down with the other. She struggled, and she was strong, almost managing to throw him off the narrow bed, but finally she calmed down.

Finally, he withdrew the hand, let her sit upright.

Her eyes were wild, her chest was heaving, the pendant hanging from her neck was leaping about like a jumping bean. Despite that, she bowed her head. 'Magistrate...' she said reverentially.

'Never mind that,' he snapped.

Whether it was his tone of voice or the look on his face, she had regained her composure. 'I had a nightmare,' she told him. 'I was unravelling, just coming apart.'

'What have you done with the Doctor?' he asked.

She stared around, aware of her surroundings for the first time. 'Nothing,' she said guiltily, far too quickly. 'It isn't what it looks like, we didn't do –'

She pulled her cotton shift back into place, but still didn't look comfortable. 'He was here,' she admitted. 'I didn't hear him leave.'

The Magistrate shifted around, ready to stand.

Larna grabbed his arm. 'We have to get to an Infinity Chamber. I'd forgotten – we have to get to Chamber Epsilon. I left a program running. I'll explain when we get there.'

Something about her voice made him agree to the request without thinking.

His wrist communicator bleeped. The Magistrate pulled back his glove to uncover it.

'This is Nulquemper. The Doctor arrived a few moments ago. He is now –'

'Priority over-ride. Magistrate, this is Constable Peltroc. There's been a –'

'I'm not alone, Constable. Please give me a moment.' The communicator went dead and the Magistrate turned to Larna. 'I will talk to the Constable in the main room. Please join me there, once you are dressed.'

He swept from the bedchamber, closing the door carefully behind him.

The Doctor's room seemed the same as always, just a little too cluttered for the Magistrate's liking. However many times he came here, there would always be some new artefact or treasure to see. He smiled. This was the first time that he had found a woman in amongst the bric-a-brac. He was unsure whether to feel elated or disappointed. Glancing up at the portrait that hung over the fire, the answer came to him. Larna was so young, but she was no longer the Doctor's student, and she was one of the few things on Gallifrey that he was completely happy with. It was a matter for them, and them alone.

There was no sign of Wycliff. The Magistrate checked the cat's box.

'Are you alive or dead in there, puss?' he asked the box solemnly. There was no reply.

The guest's chair was where it always was. The Magistrate sat there and called Peltroc.

'There's been a murder, sir. A Technician.' The agitation was evident in the man's voice. Death was unusual here.

'The renegade?'

'Could well be, your lordship. He was stabbed, and, as you know, the masked man carried a force knife. The body's still here, in Infinity Chamber Epsilon. I called you before I called anyone else.'

'Epsilon...' the Magistrate murmured.

There was something in the corner of his eye. Amongst the small heap of junk – keys, coins, datacards – on the table was a force knife. There were a couple of drops of blood on its hilt.

'That's right, my Lord, Epsilon.'

The Magistrate steepled his hands. This complicated matters. 'How tall was the renegade, did you say?'

'Average size, I'd say. Difficult to say what was inside the cloak.'

'Could it have been a woman?' the Magistrate asked.

There was a pause. 'No reason why not. Damn strong one, though. Is something the matter?'

Lady Larna had come through the door. She had dressed herself in some of the Doctor's clothes. The Magistrate recognised the brocade waistcoat, he wondered if she did. Larna and the Doctor were around the same height, and so she carried the outfit well. She was also wearing a collarless white shirt with baggy sleeves and gabardine trousers that she'd had to find a belt for. She had brushed out her blonde hair, and left it loose. She was barefoot. Putting on the Doctor's clothes had given her some of his confidence, and she stood poised, alert.

'I'm ready,' she said.

The Magistrate nodded. 'Thank you, Constable,' he told his communicator. 'Please don't let anyone in. I will be there shortly.'

Part Two
The End of the Universe

Chapter Five
Cause and Effect

The Doctor had turned his hand to many things over the years, but he hadn't the first idea how to conduct an interstellar peace conference, he'd known that all along. He had hoped for a degree of informality, and knew that he didn't want to get bogged down with procedural matters – leaving the room after the second day, elated that they'd finally decided what shape the negotiating table should be, but in reality not one step closer to real achievement, or making a real decision.

However, the first thing he did was a terrible mistake: he asked the Sontarans and the Rutans why they had started fighting.

The origins of The War were a genuine historical mystery, and the subject of academic and popular debate across the galaxy. To prepare for the Conference, the Doctor had tried to lay his hands on as many as possible of the books on the subject. There were thirty or forty distinct theories attempting to account for the start of The War, and each theory branched off in a thousand different directions. It was like studying an evolutionary chart, seeing ideas developing, evolving, refining themselves. Research and themes cross-pollinated, sparking new and frequently bizarre explanations. It was fascinating, and the Doctor could have written any number of monographs on the subject, but it was absolutely no use if you wanted the answer to the question. By hearing the reason the war started from the horses' mouths, the Doctor wasn't just hoping to solve an academic puzzle, he thought it would help the two sides to settle their differences. If they realised that it had all been a terrible misunderstanding, the Sontarans and Rutans could shake hands and agree to differ.

The Rutan spoke first. The War had started when a Sontaran armada had invaded Rutan space. Eight hundred warships had emerged from hyperspace in the Constellation of Zyt, and systematically destroyed all evidence of Rutan colonisation in the area, from planetary capitals to remote deep space observatories. There had been no warning, no attempt at diplomacy or even communication. No prisoners had been taken, there were no survivors. When scoutships arrived to respond to the emergency broadcasts, they found twenty-seven Rutan colonies in ruins, the destroyers long gone.

The Doctor listened to every word of the Rutan, but he watched Sontar. The ancient General's wide mouth was curled into what would have been a smirk on a human face. He was leaning back, clearly enjoying every moment as his ancient enemy was forced to recount details of a Sontaran victory. The other Sontarans mirrored his actions, either because of genetics or good Sontaran manners.

'You glory in this, General,' the Doctor stated.

The Sontaran grunted. 'That was a good day, I was on the flagship as we burned the Rutan from threetimes threetimes three worlds. But the Rutan is not telling you the whole story. We were on a mission of vengeance. Two days before, a Rutan raiding squadron had devastated the world of Holfactur, on the edge of the Established Space, and killed many millions of civilians.'

'Established Space?' the Doctor asked.

Krax glared at the Doctor from across the wide table. 'It is a self-evident fact of nature that the Sontaran Empire spreads across the three edges of the universe, containing galaxies and clusters of galaxies beyond number. However, the Sontaran race has yet to establish its presence in the whole of its domain. The area currently under the direct control of the Sontaran race and its dominions is Established Space, the rest of the universe is Soon-to-be-Established Space.'

'Thank you for the clarification,' the Doctor said.

'There are no civilians,' the Rutan shrieked.

The Doctor was about to ask whether it meant generally, or amongst the Sontaran population, but the Rutan didn't let him get a word in edgeways.

'This so-called civilian planet of Holfactur was a military training camp. We know this because the Sontarans had deployed forces trained on Holfactur in the Purple Areas of Rutan Space.'

'The home of your biological warfare programme,' Grol snapped. 'An area devastated, with native populations sacrificed in your quest to create a virus that would wipe out the Sontaran race.'

Krax was leaning forwards, hands clasping the edge of the table as though he was about to tip it over. 'We sent our men in to prevent another Mancastovon.'

General Sontar stared straight at the Rutan. 'While I sit on my throne there will never be another Mancastovon!'

'You are powerless to prevent it, mud-creature!'

'As you were powerless to prevent our victory in the Battle of Hwyx,' Sontar bawled. 'One Sontaran ship wiping out ten thousand Rutan warcasters. No wonder you shifted your research efforts to underhand methods of combat.'

'The Battle of Hwyx was a freak, a fluke, a luckiness.'

The Doctor clutched his head in his hands. This wasn't working out the way he had expected.

The Magistrate had chatted to Larna as they'd walked up to the Infinity Chamber. He was very senior, with a reputation as a rather forbidding, humourless figure – 'his hearts as black as his robes'. His job, as enforcer of laws from the Citadel bylaws to the First Law of Time, left him no time for lecturing at the Academy, so she barely knew him except from the Public Record broadcasts. They talked about the Doctor. Larna had started with a couple of discreet observations. The Magistrate had known the Doctor all his life, and although they'd had their differences in the past, it was clear that they loved one another. He commended Larna on her insight. Then he had proceeded to recount an anecdote from the Doctor's and his murky past, a ribald incident that had taken place during a trip to Low Town. He and Larna had laughed, and for the first time she realised why the Doctor and the Magistrate were such friends.

She had walked into the Chamber – puzzled by the guard on the door, and the Magistrate's need to exchange whispered words with him – and she had found herself staring at the corpse of one of her friends.

Waym was slumped over the control console. They hadn't covered the body, they hadn't even moved him or closed his eyes. He lay in a pool of his own blood. Waym's clothes had self-repaired and self-cleaned and so the tabard didn't bear a single hint of the stab wound that had killed him. All around them the Infinity Chamber was still running its programme, panning and zooming in, zooming out and panning, over and over. Perhaps it was that making her dizzy.

The Magistrate was hovering behind her.

'And what exactly was it that you wanted me to see in here?' he asked, his voice still containing some levity. Talking to her, joking about the

Doctor, it had all been a ploy to put her at her ease. He hoped to lull her into false security, he hadn't wanted to give her time to prepare. The result was that Larna felt cut adrift, as though her mind and body were in two places.

'I didn't do this,' she said, aware that the words sounded slightly hysterical.

'I didn't suggest that you had,' the Magistrate said calmly.

'Oh yes you did,' Larna said, finally finding something to latch on to, something that wasn't Waym's corpse. Composure and control. She had to be rational. 'Why hasn't he regenerated?' she asked.

'Did you think that he would when you stabbed him? It could be construed as mitigating circumstances.'

'I didn't... do you really think that I am capable of such an act?'

He smiled. 'We are all *capable*. The attacker inserted the knife through the left heart, then brought the blade through the spinal column and the second heart. Surgically precise. Death was instantaneous.'

All it would have needed was a thought. If Waym had managed to think a single word before he died, he'd have triggered the regeneration. His body would have done the rest for him. It needn't have been *his* thought. If she had been here, she could have thought it for him, inserted the keyword telepathically. 'Can't the surgeons do anything?'

The Magistrate's eyes were boring into hers, he was almost certainly reading her thoughts. 'No. It's too late for that. The murderer knew what... he or she was doing. But, my dear, you wouldn't have known how to do it, even if you wanted to, would you?'

Larna turned to him, tried to convey her sincerity. 'No. I was here last night, he asked me to check something for him.'

'What time last night?'

'Just before I went to the Doctor's room – about the time the aliens arrived. Savar's program is still running.'

'Savar?'

'He was here when we arrived. There's some sort of freak effect that he and Waym noticed. Can I show you?'

The Magistrate allowed her over to the console, lifting Waym's body off and dumping it down on the floor. Larna tried not to think about it, she concentrated on the console, blanking the bloodstains from her mind.

'Here,' she said, pulling a couple of levers. 'A disturbance in spacetime that passed over Gallifrey as the fleets arrived.'

'A fault with the system,' the Magistrate concluded. He used Infinity Chambers every day as part of his job, he knew that they weren't infallible.

'That was what I thought. I ran a check.' She located the relevant display panel.

The Magistrate bent over it, confirmed that there wasn't a malfunction. Then he returned to the image of the universe.

'I thought it might be interference, perhaps using the arrival of the aliens as cover. I tried to find the Doctor to warn him.'

'So the Doctor knows about this?'

She shook her head. 'I didn't have time to tell him. He was just about to meet the aliens. He seemed distracted.'

The Magistrate was smiling at something. 'And didn't you have time afterwards, in his room?'

But there was gentleness in his words. Larna didn't answer, knowing that he wouldn't press the point.

'What's it doing now?' The Magistrate was more interested in the image than her now he'd eliminated her as a suspect.

'It's running a program of Lord Savar's. Trying to locate something, by the look of it.'

The Magistrate nodded. 'We need to establish the scale of the interference. I need to see the Council. We also need to find whoever killed your friend. You had better leave your statement with Captain Raimor.'

He swept from the room, leaving Larna alone with Waym.

'You deliberately avoided our fleet to provoke such a response from us.'

'And was that the reason that you detonated nuclear weapons in the atmospheres of Halran II, Gwel and Kalla?'

Negotiations had been continuing like this for an hour or so when the Doctor slammed his fist down on the table.

Both sides stopped dead.

'Gentlemen,' the Doctor said. 'This is getting us nowhere. It's time to change tack.'

The Sontarans and the Rutan both turned their full attention to him. The Rutan had withdrawn some of the tentacles it had been flailing about, all ten of the Sontarans sat on their haunches, nineteen eyes glowering at him.

The Doctor smiled weakly. 'Er... we can't change the past, and so we shouldn't dwell on it. If there is to be any progress... we will have to abandon the old rivalries, and strive towards understanding one another. If the war is to end, we must cast aside some of the bitterness. Both sides have seen casualties and made the most terrible sacri-' He stopped. The Sontarans and Rutan hadn't moved.

'Do you really think that a feeble string of Time Lord clichés will end a war that has lasted since the universe was young?' Sontar snarled.

The Rutan had screwed itself up small, its green skin was flecked with reds and purples. 'Your words are as meaningless as Sontaran defences, as empty as a Sontaran head, rivalling only dust for worthlessness.'

'Well,' the Doctor said through clenched teeth. 'At least you agree on something.'

'Wait,' Stroc said. 'You say that you cannot change the past?'

The Doctor was glad that the subject had changed. 'Well, no.'

Sontar was nodding thoughtfully, a bizarre sight. 'You are a Time Lord. Surely you can change history?'

'No, no,' the Doctor grinned, 'it doesn't work like that. It's difficult to explain to non-Time Lords. It's something that we know instinctively. Like asking a bird how it flies. Time runs a set course, to a pattern. Or – yes, this is a better analogy – like a song. We can hear the tune, and we notice if any of the notes are wrong.' *Get them off the subject, get them talking about something else.*

The Rutan was quivering, eager to join in. 'How can history not be altered? If you can travel into the past then you must be able to affect it. You would know the gaps in your enemy's lines and you would have technical capabilities far in advance of those of your enemy. Just having foreknowledge would put you at a forewarned advantage.'

The Doctor leant back, steepling his hands. 'That's why you have to be so careful.'

'So it is possible?' Stroc insisted, his piggy eyes even narrower than was usual.

He had caught the Doctor off guard. 'Er, well, yes. In theory. But it's far, far too dangerous. That's why Time Lords are sworn to protect established history.'

'From what?' General Krax asked. That man was always identifying threats, finding enemies, locating targets. More brutal than Grol, less of a tactician. Grol sat in command centres, co-ordinating fleets. Krax was a front-line troop.

Speak to him in a language he understands. 'Well, we want to minimise disruptive influences. If, say, the Cybermen were to destroy the Earth before the human race had reached their full potential, then the consequences to universal history would be catastrophic.'

'So you take sides!' the Rutan gurgled. 'We are but aphids in your garden? Time is a weapon! How is your Established History really that different from the arrogant, misguided Sontaran assertion that they have Established Space?'

'Long ago,' began the Doctor, 'a generation or so after Rassilon, around the time that your War was hitting its stride, there were those that thought as you did. They tried to use Time to destroy and subdue their enemies. For thirty thousand years, on a thousand planets, we fought the Time Wars. The devastation would have destroyed the universe had it not been for the intervention of certain higher powers. Since that time, Time has been stabilised. It is impossible to change Gallifrey's past, or to know its future. That is the price that we must pay as its guardians.'

'But you know the future,' Stroc said. He was the most thoughtful Sontaran here, although there wasn't exactly much in the way of competition. 'You can monitor our future. You can observe the universe, this Conference is history from your perspective. Are you telling us that you know its outcome?'

'No. We have selected you from a point in time about which little is known.'

'Little is known *by the Time Lords*,' said Sontar slowly. 'Again we dance to the Time Lord's agenda.'

'No!'

'You can alter history,' the Rutan stated curtly. 'You say it is difficult to explain, we say it is difficult to justify. You have a version of history that is beneficial to your race, and you prevent all other outcomes with your knowledge of what is to come. You alter history.' They were directing their fire at him, not at each other.

'Yes, if necessary. As you know. In the past, we Time Lords have used our powers to remove forces from the universe that threatened all life. The –'

'Are the Sontarans and the Rutan now such a threat that this is why the Time Lords show sudden interest in our military-political situation?'

'No, no. That's not what I meant at all.'

'There is a way to end this war,' Sontar said.

'Yes?' said the Doctor quietly.

Sontar clenched his fist, waved it at the Rutan. 'Wipe it out. Prevent it from ever evolving. It is a parasite, a creature of nothing. This war has lasted millions of years and the Sontarans have lost so much. The Rutan is an obscenity against nature, a half-formed thing that looks like biological waste products, not a life-form.'

The Sontaran leader slumped back in his seat, perhaps realising that he had overstepped the mark. When he looked up again, it was straight at the Doctor. Sontar's eyes were red-rimmed, but beneath the folds of skin and the bloodshot, they looked like Time Lord eyes. Tired Gallifreyan eyes that had seen no peace for geological ages, that could never be allowed the luxury of sleep.

'I remember how it was before The War,' Sontar said wearily. 'There was fighting then, the suppression of local populations, even wars between rival urSontaran factions. But there was more than war.' Sontar paused. 'I remember a hunting trip in the forests of Sontara with a party of friends. All those different faces. I remember women, and childhood, growing up, sex, ambition, feasts, old age, laughter. This Rutan creature has known none of that. But neither have my men. We have lost so much, and if the Rutan win, then all of that will be lost forever.'

The great Sontaran sighed, or growled, the Doctor couldn't be sure which. 'Erase them from the universe.'

The Doctor couldn't look him in the eye. 'No, you must come to an agreement.'

'But you could do it?' Sontar grunted.

'The technologies and abilities of the Time Lords are without limit, not even we fully understand the powers at our command. The capability exists to wipe out both the Sontarans and the Rutans at the touch of a single button. I will not do so. I want the universe to benefit from your existence, not your destruction.'

'I have a counteroffer,' the Rutan announced. 'An alliance between the Rutan and the Gallifreyan Time Lords. We will restore order to the universe, we shall unify the universe outside for you, pacify it. We shall be your army. We shall swear allegiance to your race for all eternity in return for the annihilation of the Sontaran hordes.'

The shrill words hung in the air for a moment or two.

'You have nothing to offer Gallifrey, nothing that we couldn't take from you anyway. But that is not our way. I am not here to choose between you. I am here to help you to talk, to find grounds for co-operation. General Sontar, you say you want to end the war, and I believe you. So end it. Rutan, you want to be a force for good, a galactic policeman. You do that. It is as easy as that.'

'No. The Sontaran plans to escalate this conflict, kill the galaxy rather than admit defeat.'

'You are sitting at a conference table, here to discuss peace. You have heard Sontar's words. Whatever makes you think that the Sontarans want to escalate the war?'

The Rutan formed a throat and cleared it.

There were very few in the Capitol who looked younger than Larna, but Captain Raimor was one of them. His helmet almost came over his eyes. His voice had barely broken. He and his cohort, a constable called Peltroc, had led her to a nearby alcove to question her.

There was only one chair, and they offered it to her. They stood over her, maladroitly, apparently unsure how to proceed. After a minute or so, the Captain clumsily unclipped a headset from his belt and handed it to her. Larna handed it straight back.

'It is your right, my Lady, of course,' Raimor began in a voice that was meant to be worldly-wise, but merely sounded braying, 'but could I ask why you refuse to let us use the mind probe? It would quickly establish your innocence.'

Because my mind is a private place, Larna thought, *because it doesn't just have my own secrets in there any more.*

'I have my reasons,' she said coldly.

Raimor pulled out an old-fashioned computer notepad and stylus. 'You were the last person seen with the murdered man.'

'May I remind you that I am a witness, Captain, not a suspect.'

'I'm sure the evidence will speak for itself,' Raimor told her pompously.

The other one, Peltroc, spoke. 'According to your housemaid, Technician Waymivrudimqwe visited you yesterday evening.'

'That is correct. He had been using the Infinity Chamber, and sought my advice about a problem he had encountered.'

Peltroc, the junior one, didn't really know where to look when he asked her a question. 'Unusual that, a Technician visiting a Time Lord.'

'We were in the same class at the Academy. I have only just graduated. We were friends.'

Raimor bent over her, put his face in front of her own. 'More than friends? *Lovers?*' he asked, breathing over her. She and Waym hadn't been lovers, she had never even considered it, but she wouldn't give this Captain any answer to such an impertinent question. The general population of the Capitol loved to hear stories of hypocrisy and decadence amongst the Time Lords. They liked to think that for all their principles and powers, that their betters were just like them: obsessed with their baser desires.

'That is no concern of yours,' she told him. It was hard to take the smooth-faced boy's threats seriously. Whatever the case, as a noblewoman she outranked him, whatever he thought of her. Raimor had got the message. He pulled back.

Larna was unsure what jurisdiction the Watch had over Time Lords. She had a feeling that any formal enquiry about something as important as this should have to be conducted by a tribunal of her peers, not merely the nearest couple of guards.

'What time was this?'

'I arrived back at my room at around eight and had a shower. Waym arrived shortly afterwards.'

'So you went up to the Chamber with him?'

'Yes.'

Raimor checked his notes carefully. 'And he was still alive at this point?'

'Evidently.'

'Any witnesses?'

'My housekeeper.'

'And witnesses after you left your room?'

'My room is only one floor below us here, a couple of minutes away.'

'So, no witnesses.' Raimor noted that down on his pad, his manner suggesting that he'd just won some crucial point.

'Wait... yes, we saw the Doctor just as we left.'

Raimor and Peltroc looked at each other.

'In chambers, gone Eight Bells?' Peltroc asked.

'Yes. He was in a hurry.'

'Were you?'

'We didn't have to be. I just told you: it is only a couple of minutes from my door to Epsilon.'

'Constable Peltroc here was kidnapped the night before last, held against his will.'

'Such a crime is unknown here!' Larna was genuinely shocked. What was happening here? Murder and kidnap were things that happened in stories, not in the ordered world of the modern Capitol. 'You think that it was the same man that killed Waym?'

'The same person, yes,' Raimor said levelly. 'Naturally, you'll do anything you can to apprehend this criminal.'

Larna shrugged. 'If there is anything I can do.'

'Would you mind putting this on?' Raimor asked. He offered her a tiny black dot.

Larna took it from Raimor. 'What is it?' she asked, suspecting it to be some lie detector.

'A voice distorter, like the one that Constable Peltroc's kidnapper wore.'

'How do I wear this?' she asked.

'Top lip,' Peltroc prompted.

Raimor scowled at him. Larna suddenly realised what was happening. If she had known how to use a voice distorter, that would be evidence against her. 'You think that *I'm* the kidnapper?'

Peltroc grabbed her wrist, Raimor helped to force her hand up to her face.

'It's for the best. Don't struggle and you won't get hurt.'

'Get your hands off me!' Larna pulled her wrist down between Peltroc's thumb and forefinger, lurching back and away from the guards. The two men almost fell over each other.

'You're stronger than you look,' Peltroc observed, nursing his wrist.

'I am a Time Lord, Captain Raimor, don't forget that. Now, watch.' She placed the black dot on her fingertip and pressed it to her face. It must have looked like a beauty spot. 'What would you like me to say?' she asked. A calm, male, voice said the words.

'She's him!' Peltroc blurted. 'It's the voice.'

Larna tore the voice distorter off and flung it over at the Constable. 'It's a voice distorter, you idiot,' she shouted. 'It distorts voices. The whole point is that it makes me sound like him. You wear it. Go on, put the damn thing on yourself. You will sound exactly the same.'

Raimor sneered. 'Is that your best defence? That Peltroc kidnapped himself?'

'I'm sure you could find the evidence to prove it,' she informed him. 'After all, he was at the scene of the crime.'

She turned to Peltroc, who was still cringing from her. 'You saw your kidnapper, I presume. So you saw her face.'

'My attacker wore a face mask and cloak,' he stammered.

'As well you know,' Raimor added.

Larna ignored him. 'A mask, a cloak and a voice distorter? So what makes you think it was me? What makes you even think that it was a woman?'

Raimor held up a metal tube. 'The Magistrate found this force knife in the Doctor's room. You were in the room at the time.' The captain was careful to keep his tone of voice neutral, but just as careful to imply that she and the Doctor had been colluding in some way.

'I didn't put it there,' Larna told them.

'Your fingerprints are all over it,' Raimor noted, passing the knife over. 'And you've never seen this before.'

'I was in the Doctor's room, I never denied that. I saw the knife there.'

'You did more than see it.'

'I touched it.' She held out her thumb, which still bore the scar. 'I pricked my finger on the blasted thing.'

'That's your thumb,' Raimor said, his face twitching with the excitement that he'd discovered an inconsistency, however small, in her story.

Larna rolled her eyes. 'I didn't take that knife into the Doctor's room, it was there when I arrived. I left it on the table.'

'Ah,' said Peltroc triumphantly. 'That's where you're wrong. We put that knife there.'

'What?'

'We went to the Doctor's room the night before last, just before I was kidnapped.'

'The night *before* last?' Larna repeated quietly.

'Yes.'

'So the knife was placed there just *before* you were kidnapped and a full day *before* Waym was killed? It was still there this morning, afterwards.'

'Er... yes,' Raimor said, after a moment or so trying to work it out on his fingers.

'Can I go now?' she asked.

'Maybe it's the same knife, twice over,' Peltroc said suddenly.

Raimor and Larna broke off to look at him.

'Time and space are elephantly inflated,' Peltroc informed them knowledgeably. 'That's what the Doctor says. Remember, Raimor, all that business with the watches.'

Larna stood. 'I'm leaving,' she announced. She was halfway down the corridor before she realised that she still had the knife in her hand.

The Rutan could barely contain its anger, excitement and glee. It quivered, colour changes flashing across its skin. Its voice was surprisingly level in comparison. 'We have many spies within the Sontaran ranks, know that our enemy are developing the most terrible weapons, and that the Sontaran race is not a race dedicated to peace.'

'What sort of weapons?' the Doctor asked calmly.

'The Sontarans have developed a device, a device that infects a star with a self-replicating form of dark matter, a device the purpose of which is clear to all.'

The Doctor was horrified. 'Baxterium?' he whispered, turning to General Sontar. 'The only purpose of a baxteriological device is to kill a star by inhibiting the fusion processes at its heart.'

The Rutan held some sort of computerised report in its tentacle, presumably all the evidence.

General Sontar licked the edges of his lipless mouth. 'The process is irreversible, a disease with no cure.'

The Doctor was trying to work out the implications of such a weapon. Photons are manufactured in the cores of stars, and because they *are* light, they travel at the speed of light. But they don't pass straight out, they claw and zigzag and spiral their way up the gravity well and they do it forever. The journey from the surface of the sun to the surface of Gallifrey took eight minutes; the photon's journey from the core of the sun to the surface took six hundred billion times longer. The light hitting Gallifrey was as old as civilisation on the planet.

'Without the right preparation it would take ten million years at least to snuff out a star.'

'It is a strategic weapon, not for battlefield use,' Sontar conceded.

'Hear the voice of the Sontaran warmonger!' the Rutan cried shrilly. 'This is not a creature of peace! This flesh-creature plans to double the warspan, not to end it!'

The Doctor let the monologue die down. 'I'm afraid I rather agree with the Rutan. You seem ready to fight for millions of years more.'

The old Sontaran snorted and twisted himself to address one of his subordinates. 'Show him the case,' he ordered. General Grol opened up the metal box, pushing it across the negotiating table until it came to a halt in front of the Rutan. With a hiss of hydraulics, the case opened itself.

'Unlike the *peaceful* Rutans, we don't have cowards whose job it is to skulk amongst the ranks of the enemy,' Stroc said. 'We collect our intelligence the honourable way. One of our most brave agents found this at a Rutan research facility, and – after an heroic and inspiring escape – brought it to Sontar. Its true purpose is so foul that it took our scientists a year to comprehend it.'

'You recognise the device?' Sontar grunted.

The Rutan was a neutral shade of green. 'It is called a Converter and is used to swap electrons for positrons, used to reverse certain other of the fundamental interactions, within a precisely designated area, used as a scientific instrument. The Converter is based on metamorphic technology, technology beyond the understanding of creatures made from replicated meat, and many scientists were killed by the Sontaran butcher-trespasser-thief that stole it from us.'

'Gentlemen, if we could keep it civil.' The Doctor held up the metal cylinder, examining it. It was the size of a flask with a far-too intricate control mechanism at one end. 'General Sontar, it's a scientific instrument. A particle accelerator of some kind, by the sound of it.'

Sontar grunted, letting Stroc answer. 'It is used to create anti-matter. You will note that this device has a Rutan timing mechanism and is set to influence a sphere one thousand miles in diameter. All matter within that area becomes anti-matter within a second. That anti-matter then annihilates matter over a much greater area. This device could destroy Gallifrey, its moon and the two fleets. It is capable of seriously harming a star. Our own star-killer technology was developed as a direct result of this provocation, and is primitive compared to our enemy's.'

'You concede your inferiority, yet only a Sontaran, with a heart made of war, could think of such an application for a scientific tool,' the Rutan objected.

The Doctor realised that he was holding the device a little more gingerly than before. 'You will admit that it can be used for such a purpose.'

'That much is obvious.'

Sontar leant back in his chair. 'Doctor, if you were to monitor the star system of Huwyma, three months ago, you will see the "scientific applications" this Converter is put to by the Rutans. Huwyma was a Sontaran colony, now it has been completely destroyed in an anti-matter annihilation.'

The Doctor prompted the desk and a holographic image of the planet faded up over the tabletop. It was as if someone had taken a bite out of the world. Lava was still pouring out from the vast, fresh crater, but the seas had long hissed away, and surely every living thing on the planet must have been dead before that happened. The surface was charcoal, the atmosphere layer upon layer of soot, ash, steam and tektites.

'Huwyma is a Rutan world, conquered by the foul Sontarans, who used it to create primitive neutron weapons.'

The Doctor looked levelly at the Rutan. 'That's not the issue here. Was a Converter used to destroy the colony?'

Krax stood, grasping the edge of the table. 'Use your eyes, Time Lord! That is the Rutan Converter operating at a mere ten percent of its potential yield.'

The Doctor stayed seated. 'Sit down!' he snarled.

Krax found himself sitting.

'Was a Converter used to destroy the colony?' he asked again.

'It was,' the Rutan stated.

The Doctor took a deep breath. 'I thought we were here to talk of peace, of ending the war. Instead I discover that you are both trying to escalate the conflict. I am very disappointed.'

He pressed a button on his desk. Both sides became agitated.

'I'm summoning the Watch. They will escort you back to your quarters. We have said enough for one day. Tomorrow, I hope... you know what I hope.'

The Doctor left the room.

As the Magistrate bowed his head, the rest of the Supreme Councillors watched him, a little suspiciously. They had been about their business when he had summoned them to Temporal Monitoring, he could tell that by what they were wearing. The President, Norval and the Keeper of the Matrix all wore ceremonial robes, so they had been about some official matter. There were a couple in the stark black and white duty robes – they had probably already been here in Temporal Monitoring, or hereabouts. A couple were still in dayclothes. They were all milling around the antechamber to the Monitoring Hall – hadn't any of them the wit to go in?

'Why have you have called us, Magistrate?' Castellan Voran asked. He was one of those in a simple starched toga. He had probably been in his rooms, reading, when his message had come through.

'I have an important announcement,' Hedin declared.

The Magistrate's eyes narrowed. This was not a time for distractions. 'Lord Hedin, if it could wait –'

Hedin ignored him. 'After nearly four centuries' work, my biography of Omega is complete.'

There was a polite round of applause.

The President stepped forwards, patted him on the shoulder. 'Congratulations, Lord Hedin. I have proofread the book. I feel that it is the very last word on its subject. As you know I have more than a passing interest myself and –'

'Lord President,' the Magistrate interrupted. 'There have been a number of incidents in the last day.'

'Incidents?' a couple of the monks murmured.

'Are they to do with the aliens?' Norval mused.

'Or the Doctor? Is that why he isn't here?' Castellan Voran wondered hopefully.

The Magistrate finally had their attention. 'I have no reason to believe that it has anything to do with the aliens. The Doctor is currently chairing the Conference, and there is no need to interrupt his important work there. If I may make my report.'

He stepped through the door that led to Temporal Monitoring. A dozen Technicians and Junior Grade Time Lords sat in their high-backed chairs, monitoring energy levels, scanning the Time Vortex. The Magistrate crossed the roundelled floor, keeping to the left of the room to allow the rest of the Councillors to see the infinity chamber, like a vast arena sunk into the floor. A holographic image of the universe. Everyone here would recognise the familiar fractal shape, rotating imperceptibly slowly.

He folded his hands behind his back, and began to speak before everyone had quite finished getting into their places. 'During routine work yesterday, Technician First Class Waymivrudimqwe observed anomalous behaviour within the Infinity Chamber.'

He nodded to the Duty Technician. None of the staff here knew about Waym's death yet, there was no need for them to be distracted by the knowledge. The young lad who had found the body had been sent back to his dorm for the day. The picture zoomed in on Pazithi Gallifreya, it showed them the fleet and the distortion of the image.

It zoomed in again, and the flaw became more obvious.

A zoom to the molecular level, and the disturbance looked catastrophic.

Everyone in the room understood the importance of it, no one had ever seen anything like it before. They huddled around their nearest control panels.

The President stood in the middle of the room, resting his hands on his walking stick. 'It's a breach in spacetime.'

The image zoomed out again, to show the whole of Gallifrey's galactic sector. The time reference at the bottom of the picture showed that these were live pictures. There was a line of distortion, moving slowly bluewards, away from the direction of universal expansion. It was a filament crack that bisected spacetime, moving through it like a cheesewire. It had at least eleven dimensions, meaning that it was travelling through time as well as space, not to mention in a number of directions that didn't have common names.

'It appears to be spreading. How fast?'

The Keeper of the Matrix looked up from his display. 'It would be able to cross the universe within a matter of weeks.' Not as fast as a TARDIS, then, the Magistrate thought, but an incomprehensible velocity by any other standard, so many more times faster than the speed of light that the calculation was meaningless.

'Can we see the ends of the phenomenon?' one of the Councillors asked.

The scale increased to galactic level, the line still started above the top of the picture and ended below it. Another zoom out revealed that the line bisected the entire Local Group of galaxies. It took another twelve zooms before they had established that the effect was longer than the universe was wide.

The Time Lords watched the image, but couldn't believe it. To a man, they had broken away from their own screens to stare at the main display, ignoring the protocols of where they should be standing.

'It is the largest phenomenon ever observed,' the Keeper of the Matrix told them, after consultation.

The assembled Time Lords began babbling amongst themselves. The Magistrate scowled. There needed to be some order here, clarity of purpose, not the usual bickering. He looked over to the President, whose job it was to impose such order, but he was staring up at the screen, deep in thought. The President was the master of a dozen disciplines, including astronomy, temporal physics and history, but decisive leadership was not one of them.

The Magistrate was about to say something when the President spoke.

'Is there curvature?' he asked.

The other Time Lords fell silent and turned to the screen.

At this scale, the curve in the effect was noticeable.

'Any curve when viewed from close up enough looks like a perfectly straight line,' the President reminded them. 'Take a step back and it's clear that the effect is an arc. Take enough steps back and it may even be a circle, with a centre.'

'Like a ripple in a pond,' the Magistrate said.

The President grasped the Magistrate's arm. 'Indeed. But where's the centre, hmm? What sort of pebble could possibly do that to the entire universe?'

'Show me Hindmost,' the Magistrate ordered.

The scale increased again, and again, and again.

Viewed in its entirety, the universe was a beautiful fractal form. But the same laws that gave it that precisely chaotic shape also smudged its edges Traces and wisps of matter and energy could be found beyond the mathematical boundaries of the cosmos. Hindmost was the most distant significant piece of baryonic matter known to Time Lords. Space and time had been formed from the Big Bang, and the universe was still expanding out from that central point. Hindmost was a clump of matter that a fluke of physics had left trailing behind the rest of the universe. That meant that it was the back marker of the expanding universe, for ever plunging forwards with the rest of the cosmos but destined never to catch up. Behind it was nothing. Hindmost was a tiny planetoid, barely big enough for a man to stand on. Not that anyone had ever been there. Only the Time Lords had the ability to detect it, and they could think of no reason to visit. Apart from its location, Hindmost was unremarkable and it was so far away that a TARDIS would have to be specifically re-engineered for the journey.

A red dot marked the position of the asteroid in relation to the universe. Viewed from this distance, it was clear that the line of distortion was curved, but even at this scale, there was probably only a twentieth of the radius visible.

It was impossibly large. The pebble that had cast this ripple was further away than was physically possible.

Larna wasn't quite crying.

She was sitting on her own, right in the middle of the deserted refectory. She was hunching up, but at the same time desperately trying to keep her back straight. The Doctor made his way towards her, through the rows and rows of empty benches and trestle tables.

'I never knew you had such a sense of style,' he beamed approvingly when he saw what she was wearing. 'Did you sleep well?' He placed his tray on the table, and sat opposite her. Larna's bowl of suet was untouched, she hadn't so much as picked up her goblet of wine. More worrying, she was toying with a force knife exactly like the one Raimor and Peltroc had shown him a couple of nights ago.

'Waym's dead,' she told him, almost choking on the words. The Doctor stared at her for a moment, finding it difficult to believe. Waym was a promising Technician, one of Wratfac's pupils. Larna had been with him yesterday evening, he remembered. They'd all bumped into each other outside her room.

She looked up. 'I'm sorry, this isn't the done thing. I shouldn't be crying in public.'

Larna thought he was horrified with *her*, the Doctor realised, not at the death of her friend. Her face was so pale.

He looked around. Table after table, bench after bench were empty. There were a handful of kitchen staff around the edge of the room, rearranging cutlery and platewarmers, but no Time Lords. 'This is hardly public.'

'Where is everyone?' Larna wondered.

The Doctor took her hand. 'How did it happen?' he asked.

She looked up at him. As he had thought, sharing the news was making it easier to cope with. 'Stabbed, last night while he was working in Infinity Chamber Epsilon. I was the last person to see him alive. They thought I did it...' her voice trailed off. She realised that she was brandishing the knife, and handed over to the Doctor, who pocketed it.

'Who thought that?' the Doctor asked.

'A couple of the Watch. They've been trying to get a confession out of me all day. In the end they had to let me go.'

The Doctor nodded.

Larna fell silent again, looked down at her plate.

The Doctor leant forward. 'The death of a loved one is –'

'I didn't *love* him,' she said quickly. 'I liked him, he was a friend.'

'That's all I meant,' the Doctor said.

She was watching him. 'You've been through this before, haven't you?' she asked.

The Doctor let the memories wash over him. 'Many times.'

Larna was still watching him carefully. 'If you could change the past, would you bring *her* back?'

'You can't change the past,' he said automatically.

'That's not what I asked.'

'I've found that it's better to look to the future than live in the past.' He paused, a feeling of elation sweeping over him. 'Of course!' he was on his feet, grabbing Larna, kissing her forehead. 'I have to get back to the Sontarans and the Rutan.' He was halfway across the refectory before he'd finished the sentence. 'I'll see you later.'

A small army of Time Lord scientists and specialists jostled for places around their monitor screens, scrutinising the data they had collected. And as they checked and rechecked their observations, they had discovered that the breach was widening, propagating across almost half the known universe, spreading ever outwards. It was as if the universe was a sheet of ice, and this was a crack developing in it, spreading, branching out, growing wider.

'Is it as dangerous as it looks?' the Castellan asked finally. As an administrator rather than a scientist, he was standing a little way back from the monitors.

The Magistrate broke away from the pack to face him. 'That, of course, is the question. There were no effects whatsoever when the breach passed through Gallifrey last night, not even at the subatomic level.'

'No effect?' Voran echoed.

Lord Norval joined them. 'It is rather the opposite. It is as if it has picked up every single particle, looked at it and then put it carefully back where it was found.'

The President was watching over them all. 'Can we be sure that history hasn't changed?'

'Yes.' The Magistrate indicated the image of the universe on the main viewer. 'The effect has passed through roughly half of the known cosmos. So, this half of the universe has yet to be affected – it is the "before", if you like. We are in this half, the "after". Both are identical.'

Norval shook his head. 'They can't be completely identical. There will have been changes at the quantum level, and that must have had some effect at the macro scale.'

The Magistrate scowled. 'Of course. I meant no *significant* change, obviously.'

'But the potential is there for catastrophic change?' the President asked.

Lord Norval was gazing at the image of the universe. 'If the effect could be controlled, then literally everything in the universe could be manipulated. Judging by the shape and nature of the effect, this alteration could be retroactive.'

'It has the power to change established time?'

'Nothing can change the established past,' the Keeper of the Matrix insisted. 'Our entire science, all our knowledge, is based on that one principle. History cannot change.'

The Magistrate sighed. 'My Lord President, this breach is so large, so powerful, that the most surprising thing about it is that the past hasn't already been affected.'

'Gallifrey is under threat?' a monk muttered.

The Magistrate nodded. 'It is like a fire or a cancer, spreading unchecked through the structure of the universe.'

The President rubbed his beard. 'Can we stop it?'

Lord Hedin nodded. 'Whatever it is, once we identify the source and understand the processes at its heart, it should be possible to seal it off. It will require intervention on our part.'

Norval was busy calculating something. 'Better than that, we might be able to harness the power in some way.'

The Magistrate raised an eyebrow. 'Take control of it?'

Norval nodded. 'Oh yes. No reason why we couldn't. You say it's like a fire – well, our ancestors found fire rather useful once they understood it. Something like this that can make quantum observations without affecting what is being observed. It's pretty close to an Agathon Engine, a holy grail of Gallifreyan science. It would allow us to observe both position and velocity of quantum particles.'

Voran scowled. 'So what?'

'If we could do that, Castellan, then with our time travel technology it would allow complete observation of the universe at the quantum level. We'd know everything. Until now, no one has been able to solve the Agathon Equations that would allow this, although strictly speaking such a solution is not ruled out by Time Theory.'

The Magistrate tried to remain calm. 'If the breach can be controlled in that way…'

'Oh, controlling the source would be relatively easy,' Norval said. 'The controller would need to be sentient, but that's all. A sentience in control of the observer effect on a universal level. A fascinating thought experiment. They'd be omniscient. Come to think of it, they'd be omnipotent, too. Whatever they observed would exist – the universe would literally bend to their will.'

The Magistrate almost choked. 'A *thought experiment*? Whoever harnesses the Effect will control the universe, and there will be no way of defending ourselves from them.'

Norval nodded. 'In theory,' he agreed, before returning to his monitor.

'Fellow Time Lords, this is the greatest threat to Gallifreyan security that we have ever encountered,' the Magistrate insisted.

The President smiled. 'In theory, Magistrate. But there is no evidence that the Effect is under anyone's control, yet.'

Could they not see?

The Magistrate's eyes narrowed. 'It is only a matter of time. The answer is simple: *we* must locate the source of the Effect, *we* must travel there and prevent access to it.'

'Can we do so?'

'We must,' the Magistrate told them. 'Until we do, the entire universe is under threat, Gallifrey included. Nothing is safe.'

Chapter Six
Grey Universe

The Castellan's office was spartan, all arches and airy light. Unusually for the Citadel, the room had a window, looking down over the Panopticon.

It was a large room, but needn't have been. Business was conducted in the three-sided alcove at the far end. The Doctor crossed the marble floor, his footsteps echoing guiltily around.

'Anyone home?' he called, trying not to say it too loud in case there was. Unusually, none of Castellan Voran's assistants had been in the outer offices either. Perhaps it was their tea-break.

The control panel he needed was hidden somewhere in the room, probably at the far end. The Castellan's chair was a ludicrous high-backed plastic construction. The Doctor did a quick search, but couldn't find any concealed panels. The desk, an immense ebony slab, was now the prime suspect. One side was piled high with papers, dockets and plastic sheets. The other was empty, apart from a sculpture that resembled a molecular model – coloured resin balls linked by white struts.

The chair was half-facing the only painting in the room, a sepia portrait of Castellan Fordfarding, an old man with a high forehead, an aquiline nose and thin white hair. He had lived around the time of Rassilon, and was still seen as the greatest holder of the office of Castellan, mainly because of his obduracy and complete lack of imagination. The Doctor made a quick examination of the picture, and found slight pixellation where the painting met the frame. The portrait concealed a scanner screen, one that the current Castellan sat at his desk and studied. So the controls should be on the desk.

It would be easy for anyone to prove he had been here. He was leaving skin cells, fingerprints, strands of hair, telepathic traces – everything you'd need to identify him but his calling card. The key to this, the Doctor mused as he headed back to the desk, was not to tip anyone off that he had been here. If no one asks the question, then they wouldn't find the answer. So, he needed to be quick, and he had to be careful not to do anything to arouse any suspicion.

The molecular model was bothering him. It was the only dash of colour in the room.

On a hunch, the Doctor plucked off the top ball, the orange one.

The entire model collapsed, showering bits all over the surface of the desk. The balls began rolling away, bouncing off the desk, leaving the little struts lying in a heap.

The Doctor was left holding the orange ball between his finger and thumb, and feeling rather foolish. Now it was in his hand he recognised it as an encoded key – if he held this up to the right sort of reader, then the Chancellery Watch would receive the signal to go to Orange Alert. This would happen if an unauthorised intruder entered an area he shouldn't have. Say, for example, that they discovered someone in the Castellan's office, tampering with sensitive security equipment.

The Doctor quickly collected up all the balls he could find and slotted them back together with the struts. Once he finished, he looked at his handiwork. There was something wrong with it, the shape was somewhat irregular. The Doctor realised he was still holding the orange ball, and so a strut must have been missing. Gingerly, he pocketed the orange ball and left the display well alone.

He sat down on the Castellan's chair, the servos adjusting for his weight and height before he could stop them. He looked over to the portrait again.

The control panel for the scanner must be on the desk somewhere. He ran his fingers along, trying to feel for the seam. After a few seconds he gave up and pulled out the sonic screwdriver. A quick squirt from that, and a section of the desk parted and a retinal scanner flipped out.

With its pantograph and pivots it looked like a shaving mirror. It began extending, swivelling itself, looking for something. The Doctor leant forward, letting it find his face. The round lens duly located itself over his right eye. The Doctor screwed up his left eye and stared into the blue light. This was an eyeboard, a control panel that automatically ran a security check every time you gave a command by checking your retina print. Like a keyboard that scanned your fingerprints. There was a knack to fooling these things, and the Doctor had it. He stared deep into the scanner, tried to focus on something in the morass of faint blue. And then there was the illusion of movement, his eye trying to tell him that he was zooming forwards. Instinctively he grabbed the arms of the chair. Information was squirting straight down his optic nerve to his brain, and it wasn't a very pleasant sensation. He blinked, activating a new subset of options. He blinked again. He started humming to himself. It started out as a Gounod aria, but soon drifted off into Lennon.

There was a click, and he heard the keyboard plopping out of the surface of the desk. He broke away from the retinal scanner to check, then returned, squinting at the scanner until the keyboard morphed, changed to a configuration the Doctor was happier with. One final correction to the layout of the keys and the Doctor was ready. He dismissed the eyeboard, which slid back into the depths of the desk, and tapped at a couple of the keys.

The picture of Castellan Fordfarding vanished, replaced by a series of menus and status displays. The Doctor hesitated over the keyboard for a moment before punching in a short code sequence. A number of the menu entries erased themselves, a couple of the status displays switched places. Transferring a handful of command functions and over-rides took a couple more seconds.

The door at the far end of the room swung open.

It would be a few seconds before the new arrival found him. The Doctor's work was done. He typed one last instruction and the keyboard reset to its default configuration before slipping back into the desk. The images on the scanner faded out, the picture of Fordfarding reappearing in their place.

The Doctor leant back in the chair, his hands behind his head, to welcome the new arrival.

It was Castellan Voran, the Magistrate close behind him.

'I took that promotion I was offered,' the Doctor joked.

The Castellan didn't smile. 'Is the Conference over?'

'For the day,' the Doctor said warily. 'I was looking for you, but you weren't around. What's going on?'

'We have a problem,' the Magistrate told him, folding his arms.

'A big one?'

The Magistrate smiled. 'Oh yes.'

The Castellan squeezed around the Doctor, bent over the desk, let the eyeboard emerge. He frowned at the displays. The Doctor smiled at him, trying to look casual.

The scanner activated, showing an image of the universe.

'Nice trick,' the Doctor observed. 'I'll have to get one of those pictures for my room.'

Castellan Voran tutted. The Magistrate nodded towards the screen. 'Look closely.'

The Doctor peered at the picture, unsure what he was looking for. 'Is that a flaw in spacetime?' he asked finally.

The Castellan didn't speak, he simply readjusted the angle of the viewer.

The Doctor watched a succession of images, all telling him the same thing.

'Have you tracked the source of the disturbance?' he asked.

'No,' said Voran.

The Magistrate was more forthcoming. 'Whatever the Effect is, it is well beyond the boundaries of the universe. We need to locate the source to repair the Effect, seal it off from the rest of time.'

Finally, the picture showed them the entire universe, from some 'distance'. The Effect was a curved line.

'You think that the Effect is a circle, with the source at the centre.' A statement, not a question.

'Yes,' said the Magistrate, 'don't you?'

The Doctor drummed his fingers against the top of the desk while he considered the other options. 'Yes.'

'But you see the problem with that theory?'

'Well, yes. The centre is a very long way away.'

The Magistrate shook his head. 'The centre is outside the boundaries of the universe. It can't exist, so the source can't exist.'

The Doctor stood up, smiling. 'Beyond the current boundaries. But the Effect is moving through time as well as space. Boundaries change.' From the macroscopic perspective of the scanner's image it was clear that the universe was roughly spherical and expanding. It resembled a balloon, with the whole of spacetime on its skin. That analogy was the one that Gallifreyan tutors used in schoolrooms, the problem with it being that there was nothing inside the balloon, and nothing outside. The Effect originated somewhere towards the centre of the balloon, literally in the middle of nowhere. 'Take the Effect's eleven-dimensional nature into effect,' the Doctor suggested.

'The universe has expanded since its creation,' the Castellan said impatiently, 'the arc of the Effect suggests that its point of origin is right at the dawn of time, when the universe was a great deal smaller. We did think to look in the far past.'

'I'm sure you did,' the Doctor said sincerely. He turned to the Magistrate. 'What effect is the Effect having?'

The Magistrate was looking thoughtful. 'None whatsoever at the moment, although the potential is there.'

'And who do you think is behind it all?'

The Castellan and the Magistrate looked at each other, bewildered.

'It's a natural phenomenon,' the Castellan answered.

'Possibly...' the Magistrate responded, his voice trailing off. 'No sentience that we know of is capable of producing anything as powerful.'

'Centro is,' the Doctor replied without hesitation. 'True, none of Centro's spacewarps have ever reached anything like this level, but they could if he found a large enough power source. He certainly has the persistence.'

The Castellan scowled, and gestured towards the picture. The cracked display of the universe vanished. In its place appeared an image of a metal skull with camera eyes, its jaw slack, as if it was screaming. Brilliant white shards of light transfixed it.

'Centro is where you left him,' the Castellan assured them.

'For now,' the Doctor agreed, relieved. 'But if it isn't Centro, then who is it? The Klade? The Tractites? The Ongoing? It could be the Nibblepibblies.'

'It could be them,' the Castellan agreed, unaware that the Doctor had just made them up. 'But it is much more likely that this is a natural phenomenon. We've prepared a report.' He handed over a wad of notes.

The Doctor nodded, made a show of reading the first couple of paragraphs. 'Good. Right, I'll run a check on the Effect from my TARDIS, try locate the Source from there.' He got up and started to make for the door.

The Magistrate caught his arm. 'You can use Main Temporal Monitoring.'

The Doctor shook his head. 'No. Much easier working from familiar surroundings.' The Magistrate didn't seemed convinced. 'My notes are all in the TARDIS.' Still no response. 'I work better on my own.'

'Whatever you say,' the Magistrate said grimly.

'There are good people there: Hedin, Norval, the President. You're not exactly the class dunce.'

'I hope you know what you are doing.'

The Doctor nodded. 'So do I.'

Larna bumped into the Doctor as she left her room.

'We must stop meeting like this,' he said lightly.

She smiled. 'I thought you were on your way to the Conference.'

'Yes, yes, I am.'

'So why have you got a Time Regulator under your arm?'

'I haven't... it's...' he faltered. 'How did you know? It's in a case.'

'It's in a Time Regulator case,' she giggled. 'Nothing else is that shape. Look, it's OK. I'm not going to tell anyone.'

'Right, right. Thank you.' He hurried away.

Larna watched him go, then set off in the opposite direction.

If the Watch weren't going to talk to Savar, then she was going to have to. Lord Savar's rooms were a few levels below hers - she'd checked with one of the porters exactly which one. Despite his experiences in space, and his erratic behaviour since, he was still a Time Lord, and no one had the hearts to evict him from chambers.

She knocked on the door.

After a moment, it opened. Savar stood there, smiling at her, the way he always did.

'Can I come in?' she asked, once she'd realised that he wasn't going to offer.

He checked his pocket watch. 'You will have to be quick, I was just about to go to sleep.'

Larna apologised, but wasn't about to let that stop her. It wasn't even Nine Bells yet. She pushed her way in before Savar could change his mind.

The room was bland, disappointing. Larna hadn't known what to expect, but Savar was unique, and she thought his room would be too. But these resembled the guest quarters of a family Home - neutral colour scheme, a couple of decorative objects that wouldn't offend anyone or make any form of statement. The bookshelf was virtually empty, the battered wardrobe was out of place. The only thing of any note was the huge freestanding clock, ticking its way relentlessly to Nine Bells.

'Would you like a drink?' Savar offered, but he had already sat down. The table in front of him had a scattering of charts and notebooks on it. There was also a small hand terminal, which bleeped every couple of seconds. It reminded Larna of a dripping tap.

Savar was cross-legged on his chair, examining a time chart.

'You know what it is, don't you?' she asked. 'The distortion we noticed.'

'Yes.' He looked up at her with eyes full of sadness. 'The end of the universe.'

'What do you mean by that?'

Savar coughed. 'I didn't realise that the concept was ambiguous.' He glanced up at the clock. 'My dear, you really ought to run along, it is getting late.'

'Waym was murdered,' she insisted.

'Yes, yes, I know,' he returned to his charts, embarrassed.

'You were the last person that saw him alive.'

He didn't look up. 'Yes.'

'They thought that I did it. Some of them still do.'

'Well, we both know that isn't the case.' He looked up, his eyes were pleading with her. 'We can discuss this in the morning.'

The clock began to chime.

Larna stood her ground. 'One of my friends died, one of the guards was kidnapped. This man is vicious.'

Savar looked agitated. 'Please leave,' he said.

'I'm not leaving until I get some answers. This is serious.'

'Leave,' Savar said softly.

The Clock chimed for the ninth time.

A shadow fell over Savar, and when it had passed his blue robes had become a heavy grey cloak and his face had become younger, bearded, more distinguished. But there was nothing where his eyes should have been, the sockets were empty, surgically clean, full of shadow.

Larna backed away.

He gave a thin smile, and glanced over at the door. The lock rattled, bolts slammed. Telekinesis.

'Savar...' she pleaded. This was the Savar who was found in space without his eyes. The insane one. Somehow the timestreams had become crossed. It was possible – against the Laws of Time, of course, but allowed by laws of physics. Or perhaps this Savar had transferred from a parallel universe, one where he hadn't been cured, or... This was the man who had killed Waym, stabbed him through the hearts. He'd kidnapped a guard at knife point, stolen property.

He took a step towards her. There was nowhere to run.

'My name is Larna,' she said.

'I know.' He was her height, with slim build.

There were a dozen folds in his thick cloak to hide a knife, it could be concealed in either boot. She glanced down. The shoes were part of a spacesuit, she recognised the heavy silvery material.

'Are you going to kill me?' she asked.

'Only if you try to stop me,' he said. His voice was deep, with an edge of panic.

'I may even help you,' she replied, trying to keep him calm. 'What are you planning to do?'

'The key.'

Larna felt Savar's mind brush against her. She readied her mental defences, then saw the expression on his face. Block his thoughts and she would be killed, she knew that. She let Savar remember for her. It took him a moment to find what he was looking for. A couple of memories from her childhood; familiar images of landmarks from the Capitol; a few abstract principles of Infinity Chamber operation; the faces of some of her tutors.

The image of the Doctor lingered for a moment.

The Doctor's chair faced the fireplace, framed by a heavy marble mantel, with a number of ornaments. There was only one timepiece in the whole room, an ormolu clock from Earth that sat on the mantelpiece, its day divided up into twelve hours of equal length. The longer of the two hands was between the two and the three, the shorter sat about a quarter of the way between five and six. At the side of the chair was an occasional table, and it was littered with junk. A tea service was surrounded by bric-a-brac: computer cards, a bunch of keys.

Savar smiled.

Nifcol looked around the TARDIS cradle he was guarding. This was one of the most secure areas of the Citadel, and only the oldest and wiliest of the Watch were given duties here. A dozen TARDISes were dotted around the room, each in their own pool of light. Nifcol wasn't a Time Lord, but even he could sense the power that each of these machines contained. They hummed to themselves, and Nifcol caught a faint telepathic buzz out of the corner of his mind.

One of the TARDISes in particular. Nifcol stepped over, running his hand down its side. It was warm, there was a very slight vibration. At that moment, the pitch changed.

There was someone else in the room. A Time Lord. The Doctor. This was his TARDIS.

'My Lord,' Nifcol began. 'Entry to this area is only allowed with approval from the Castellan's office.'

The Doctor smiled. 'If you'll check your screen, you'll see that I have that authorisation.'

'I checked earlier, sir, no one has that clearance tonight.'

'If you could just check again.'

Nifcol nodded, and took his hand terminal from his belt. Sure enough, the Doctor had been granted the authority by the Castellan himself.

He looked up. The Doctor was beaming sweetly at him. But there was something odd here. Nifcol looked him up and down. The Doctor had short hair, which wasn't covered, and he was wearing odd clothes, but he always did.

'What's that under your arm?' he asked him finally.

'This arm?' the Doctor said, holding up a carry case.

'No sir, the other one.'

'Oh, nothing.'

'It looks unusual, sir.'

'Well, yes.' The Doctor held it out. It was a large toy tafelshrew, a big blue fluffy thing with goggly eyes and a big red smile. It was about a foot long.

Nifcol took it from him, examined it. 'Why are you taking this with you?'

The Doctor looked down at his boots, then back up, but he wasn't able to look Nifcol in the eye. 'No reason,' he said.

Nifcol tucked the tafelshrew under his arm. 'With respect, sir, I really think that I should look after this, don't you?'

'I need it... for my research,' the Doctor said quickly.

Nifcol shook his head, moving the stuffed tafelshrew out of the Doctor's reach. 'No you don't, sir.' He found his clipboard. 'If you could just sign the requisition form, I'll let you into your TARDIS, but I'm afraid I can't let you take this in with you.'

The Doctor looked crestfallen, but he nodded. He stepped up to the threshold of the TARDIS, slipping the key from his pocket and into the lock.

'Are you sure I can't take that?' he asked.

'Quite sure, sir,' Nifcol said firmly. 'The regulations are very strict about what one can and can't take into a time capsule.'

The Doctor opened the door to his TARDIS and stepped inside.

The control room looked the same as always. The Doctor moved up to the console in the centre, pulling the lever that closed the doors, pressing the control that locked them. He turned on the scanner. The guard, Nifcol, was examining the toy tafelshrew, prodding its middle. The Doctor chuckled, shaking his head and rested the Time Regulator on one side of the console. Simple psychology: Nifcol hadn't been remotely interested in the dull-looking carry case tucked under the Doctor's left arm, not with such an oddity under his right.

The Doctor set to work isolating the recall circuits. The readouts confirmed the new directives that he had programmed in at the Castellan's office. The displays adjusted to the new instructions. This TARDIS was now completely independent of Citadel Traffic Control, but no one in the Citadel would be informed of this – the Doctor had been very careful to make sure that the scanners in the Capitol wouldn't be watching his activities. He switched on the power circuits, let them warm up while he worked.

He bent underneath the console, unfastening a couple of access panels. Then he opened up the case he'd been carrying and took out the Time Regulator. It was straightforward enough to interface one with the other – the Doctor simply clipped a couple of wires together. That done, he moved around the console, adjusting a setting here, flicking a switch there. He reached the navigation panel. He'd never really got the hang of it, but he knew the basics. He operated a slide control, twisted a dial, jabbed at a couple of over-rides. A tiny warning bell was chiming somewhere in the console. The Doctor found the switch that silenced it.

He crossed back to the Regulator that he had installed. He fiddled with the scanner controls, using the instruments on the Regulator to adjust the image. The rather baffled Nifcol vanished, replaced by a series of scenes from the Citadel: a triad of students checking each others' lecture notes; the kitchen staff in one of the refectories preparing for dinner; two of the Watch at their posts in the Archive.

General Sontar, reclining on a couch. The Doctor tapped the control, keeping that image on the display.

The Sontarans' room was suffused with red light and high gravity. One of the nameless Sontarans was attending to his leader, checking that the energy cables plugged into the back of the General's neck were connected correctly. This was how Sontarans fed – electricity was sent directly down the vent at the back of their necks, stored in bioelectric cells in the abdominal cavity. The other senior Sontarans sat in a huddle, awaiting their turn. They all looked so tired. In the privacy of their own room, they slumped, they sagged. None of the Sontarans were speaking to each other, or doing anything other than wait for their energy feed. The Doctor hadn't expected to see them singing, or knitting, or watching soap operas, but they weren't doing *anything*. They looked like patients in a military hospital, half-exhausted, half-shell-shocked.

He saved the co-ordinates and then fed a couple of commands into the Regulator. The image refocused to the Rutan chamber.

The screen filled with a picture of blue-grey water that made the Doctor feel cold just looking at it. It was murky, too – rich in metallic and organic compounds. The Rutan sat in the centre, in something very similar to its natural form. It was dormant, inscrutable.

The Doctor repeated the instruction to the Regulator to save the co-ordinates before returning to the TARDIS console. The power circuits were fully charged up now.

It was time. Sontar had finished feeding, and was standing up. The other Sontarans were entering their dormancy phase – a dreamless sleep during which their bodies repaired themselves.

The Doctor patched the TARDIS console into the Citadel's architectural configuration. Holographic plans of the xenodochia level appeared in the air in front of him. A couple of minor adjustments and his work was done.

He pulled the big slide control on the Regulator. The hum of power started to build up all around him. He slipped a blue control pad from his coat pocket. There were two buttons, one red, one green.

The Doctor had just built a primitive Time Scoop, taking a few short cuts by feeding it through the TARDIS computer. He turned away from the console. Two ebony pyramids rotated into three-dimensional space by the back wall of the control room, and continued to hang there, spinning slowly. The Doctor pressed the green button twice.

The pyramids faded away as they stopped swirling, and in their place were General Sontar and the Rutan. The Rutan was re-adjusting to its oxygen-breathing form, water dripping from it. Sontar was disorientated.

'What is this?' Sontar snarled.

'Good evening, gentlemen. Welcome to my TARDIS. I've brought you here -'

'This was not part of the agreement,' the Rutan squeaked. 'We are alone here, wherever this is, this was not part of the agreement.'

'Where are my men?' Sontar roared.

The Doctor turned away for a moment, pulled the last few levers. The central column began rising and falling rhythmically. 'They are safe in your chambers. I have -'

Sontar pounced, leaping a good ten feet, pinning the Doctor to the console. His powerful bifurcated claw was grasping at the Doctor's throat, his finger and thumb were around his neck, the middle finger was crushing against his lips, chin and mouth.

'How dare you?' Sontar roared, filling the air with his oily breath.

'Sontaran!' the Rutan shrieked. 'That is a Time Lord! Do not kill the Time Lord!'

The Doctor was unable to open his mouth. He was pinned under Sontar, who must have weighed several tonnes even in Gallifreyan gravity.

'I am the leader of the most powerful race in the universe!' Sontar roared, trembling with rage. 'You will not treat me like some podling. I am not a pet for you to take out of its cage when you please.'

The Doctor tried to speak, but couldn't even draw breath.

Sontar's eyes were burning a furious red. They narrowed to tiny slits. 'You will pay for your insolence.'

The Sontaran snapped the Doctor's neck and then threw his broken body across the control room.

The Station was one of the Time Lords' secrets.

It sat right on the edge of Gallifrey's Constellation, in a perfect orbit around a red supergiant. There were a few barely inhabited worlds in this sector of space, but they were far from the normal trade routes and of little commercial interest. The area was notorious for shipwrecks and vanishments, and the charts would tell anyone consulting them that this was because of the particularly high concentration of asteroids, dust clouds and freak energy fields. The remains of once-powerful star cruisers passed silently by, powerless. Each of the ships was surrounded by a halo of metal fragments. Once a century or so, these dead ships would drift past older, less easily explained ruins. This part of the galaxy was a place that space pilots told stories about, not the sort of place they would ever visit, whatever payment you offered. Those that travelled out here had a habit of never coming back.

So no one ever saw the Station from the outside, had ever seen the dark cathedral-like shape, with a vast pyramidal tower emerging from the centre. no one had ever noticed that it, alone of all the ships of this graveyard in space, had escaped collision with asteroids and the other cosmic debris of the region. The pristine hull was dotted with spires and masts, fins and gutters. Some of the features might have been weapons emplacements, huge hangar bays or landing strips. Equally well they might not have been. Whatever angle it was viewed from, the Station appeared to be lurking in the shadows. It was very difficult to judge its size, but it was clearly the size of a city, if not a continent.

The interior of the Station was a maze of living quarters, workshops, armouries, engine rooms, storage holds and all the other rooms and features one would expect to find in a space station of its size. At some point in its history, the Station could have held a million people, maybe more, but if that had ever happened that had been a long, long time ago. Most of the time nowadays there was a skeleton crew, a handful of middle-ranking Time Lords, their servants and a small army of maintenance and service robots. It was a job that attracted the reclusive personality types.

Today the crew of the Station had swollen to three or four dozen. Most of these were Technicians, a few were members of the Watch. Half a dozen were Time Lords. They were all congregated within a couple of levels of the control deck. The Magistrate stepped from his TARDIS, out onto the main control area. Scientists and engineers in brown tabards were running tests and simulations, upgrading systems where they needed to. The Station had been built to last, though, and there was little work to be done. At the moment he alone knew the purpose of their presence here.

The other Time Lords were waiting for him by the control deck. This was a larger version of the standard TARDIS console, and shared the same hexagonal shape. But this was the size of a house, with three distinct levels leading up the sloped sides to the vast pillar in its centre. There were three Councillors, three specialists. The Magistrate had chosen them for their scientific knowledge, but also for their decisiveness. He needed people he could rely on.

He wasted no time with ceremony.

'The Doctor was right. The Matrix has located the source of the Effect far in the future. So far, in fact that it is difficult even for a Time Lord to comprehend.'

The timezone in which the Time Lords lived was around ten billion years after Event One, the creation of the universe. Ten with ten noughts after it. That was enough years to contain the creation of matter, the formation of stars and galaxies and planets, the rise and fall of many galactic civilisations. To all things there must come an end. The universe was no exception. All matter would eventually decay. Baryonic matter – anything with more mass than a proton – would break down into its component parts as its energy levels fell. This would be a very long process: the last proton would fizzle out in around one hundred thousand trillion, trillion, trillion years. Ten with thirty-one noughts after it.

'We have located the Source to within a few decades of Event Two, the end of the universe. It is far beyond the limits of our knowledge.'

The assembled Time Lords nodded, clearly still seeing this as an abstract scientific or philosophical question. The Matrix could model the universe, and use that model to make projections of the future, but even it could only see a few billion years into the future. The model was constantly being refined and updated, new observations were continually being made, but even Time Lord knowledge had to end somewhere. That point was clearly defined.

From its creation, the Universe had been expanding, forced outwards by the force of the Big Bang. Eventually, when the universe was a dozen or so times older than it was now, that impetus would run out, and the universe would begin to collapse back in on itself. At that point, time ended... at least as the Time Lords understood it. More correctly, time would be redefined in some unknowable way. Planets and stars and life would certainly still exist in the collapsing universe, but there would be no Time Lords to watch over them, and the laws of physics would have been subtly rewritten. Whatever this collapsing universe was like, it would slowly wind down, losing its energy to the forces of entropy.

Eventually, after an incomprehensible amount of time, the universe would be cold, lifeless, dead, and it would then collapse back into a single point.

Hedin was worried. 'The source of the Effect is out of our reach. No TARDIS can make such a journey.' He was right, of course. The Time Vortex petered out a little before the universe stopped expanding, marking the point beyond which no TARDIS could travel.

The Magistrate nodded. 'Our Infinity Chambers are barely able to discern the Source, even with the energies it is pouring out. It is like looking for a distant planet with an optical telescope.'

Lord Norval was rubbing his beard. 'But we can't travel there, can we? Even if we found a pathway, a TARDIS can travel – what? – no more than a few billion years between refuelling. It would take a billion such journeys – it would take us a hundred million years to get there.'

The Magistrate nodded. 'At the very least. Which is why the President has authorised the construction of a timegate. Essentially this will be a hole in spacetime, powered and controlled from Gallifrey. We will pilot this Station through the timegate, where it will be our base of operations.'

The other Time Lords were looking concerned. The Technicians and Guards had stopped working. They were sworn to protect time, and here they were contemplating punching a hole in it.

'There is a degree of risk in the journey,' the Magistrate conceded. 'There will be damage to spacetime – nothing that we can't retroactively repair. But we already know the dangers of leaving the Source unguarded.'

'The fleet will be flying blind,' Lord Quarduk noted.

'Indeed. And when we arrive in the far future, we will be all but cut off from Gallifrey. There will be a single link to the Eye of Harmony. Through it we will be able to communicate with the High Council and draw the energy we will need.'

Norval folded his arms. 'And we are to take control of the Source?'

The Magistrate nodded. 'Our first priority will be to establish an exclusion zone around the Source, to prevent other races from taking control.'

One of the Time Lords laughed. 'No other race could reach it, let alone harness it.'

'We do not know everything about our future,' Hedin cautioned.

'Races may well emerge in the interim with the necessary capabilities and technologies.'

'If another race reaches the Source before we do,' the Magistrate informed them solemnly, 'then Gallifrey – our entire universe – will be defenceless. We must make this journey, and we must succeed.'

Wycliff stirred a moment before it arrived.

There was a wheezing, groaning sound and a battered wardrobe materialised in the centre of the Doctor's room. The floorboards creaked a little under the new weight. After a short pause, the door opened, and Savar stepped out, pulling Larna behind him.

'Find the key,' he ordered calmly, releasing her.

Larna brushed her hair back into place with her hand, her eyes adjusting to the light. The control room of Savar's TARDIS had been dark. 'I still don't see what is so important about it.'

'All will become clear.'

'Why can't you just talk to the Council? Or the Doctor? If you know anything at all about the disturbance in spacetime then you should tell them. They might be able to stop it.'

Larna had reached the table and had found the bunch of keys. She held them in her hand, examined them. They were perfectly ordinary.

Savar snatched them from her. 'There is only one way that I can end this.'

'I might help you.' She tried to put a hint in her voice that the help would be psychological in nature.

'No.' He turned to her, his expression pained. 'No. You would try to prevent me from doing what I must.' He felt the keys, selected the one he wanted and discarded the rest.

He herded her back towards his TARDIS.

Thoughts swirled within the Rutan, formless thoughts, indecipherable to the lesser races. The Sontaran meat-warrior was hunched over the control station of the Doctor's time machine. It was unable to fathom the instruments, there was nothing in this creature's crude experience that had prepared him for this. Its animal mentality had become unstable, it was acting irrationally. But the Rutan was with the Host, it was infinite. The Sontarans were just individuals, and even the greatest amongst them was but one.

'You have committed murder. The murder of a Time Lord,' the Rutan stated, body tensing, adopting a combat form. 'It is a fact of nature that those that kill Time Lords themselves die. The Time Lords are very particular about ensuring that. By killing the Time Lord you have killed yourself.'

'Now I will kill you,' the Sontaran said inelegantly, bringing its ungainly body nearer the Rutan.

'The death of this Rutan will not help your cause. The Rutan are without number. Now you have killed a Time Lord, all of Gallifrey is your enemy. The Sontaran race is finished.' The Rutan paused, new concepts flushing through it. 'The Rutan race swears revenge for this dead Time Lord. We will ally ourselves with Gallifrey. You will be erased from history. You will never have existed.'

The Sontaran was within half a metre of the Rutan. Its fist was raised.

The Rutan unfurled a tentacle, whipped it around the Sontaran, and into the probic vent at the back of his neck. It found the orifice, forced its way in.

Sontar flailed, tried to reach behind itself with its unmalleable limbs.

The tentacle developed the muscles to lift the Sontaran from its feet.

Sontar struggled, but the tip of the tentacle was half a metre within its body, now, developing spines and barbs to keep itself there. To the Rutan, the Sontaran was a collection of electrical and temperature fields, concentrated in the torso. It began to drain the energy from the Sontaran's body, sucking it into itself. A satisfying method of execution. The Sontaran clearly felt pain during this procedure, that was clear from the form of its face, with its bulging eyes and the screeching wideness of its mouth.

'Your corpse will be a peace offering to the Time Lords,' the Rutan told Sontar. 'All the secrets of the Sontaran Empire are mine. The electrical patterns of your meat-brain, those things that you assert to be your thoughts and memories will be absorbed into the Rutan. That will be our prize. The Sontaran race will be a race of slaves, or of cattle. You have lost. You *are* lost.'

It was drinking the Sontaran's thoughts now.

One memory was foremost. Sontar had stood in the laboratories as the scientists – the Rutan could remember each and every one of their names – had made their proposal. The War had been running badly for centuries. His clones had fought bravely, they were numberless, tactical geniuses, but they were losing. The propaganda broadcasts still told of magnificent victories, but even the least perceptive foot soldier must have noticed by now that the magnificent victories were taking place closer and closer to home. The Rutan fleets were now less than fifty light years from the Throneworld.

(The Rutan remembered this time from the race memory.)

Every one of the trillion Sontarans had to eat, had to be kept warm. Most of the space aboard their warships were given over to providing food and water. The scientists had shown him a new clone. One without a digestive system or sex organs, one with easily synthesisable mineral solutions rather than blood. A stripped-down Sontaran, one that could be fed raw energy. They'd simplified the structure of the brain at the same time, streamlined much of the nervous system. Redundant features such as eyelids and fingernails had been removed. It would have no toes and only three fingers. This body would be easy to duplicate and maintain.

With heavy heart, Sontar had signed the order. From now on, every Sontaran would be like this. He had wept that night.

'You have lost so much,' the Rutan said.

The Rutan was unsure what to think, so it analysed its surroundings instead as it digested this new piece of information.

The column at the centre of the control console had stopped moving. There was a resonant chime, far below them.

'Stop!' a voice ordered.

No further analysis of the environment was needed. This was the Doctor. He was a powerful presence. There was much below the surface here, like an ice-ocean.

'You live!' the Rutan said.

The Doctor was at the edge of the room, close to where the Sontaran had thrown him. He was rubbing his neck, as if there was slight stiffness. 'It is very difficult to die inside the TARDIS while the engines are running. We exist in a state of grace, outside time as you would understand it.'

The Rutan twitched its tentacle around, holding up the Sontaran for the Doctor's inspection. 'Nevertheless, this ignorant, insolent creature attempted such a foul act. I have captured the creature that would have been your murderer. I will kill it!'

'No!' the Doctor said loudly. 'Let Sontar go.'

The Rutan retracted the tentacle, let the Sontaran fall to the floor.

'I understand. You wish to kill the creature yourself.' The Rutan had all but finished the Sontaran, which lay, dull and inert, at the Doctor's feet.

The Doctor held out its prehensile paw, helping the Sontaran to its feet. The Rutan saw its energy fields, knew that the Sontaran was weakened.

'Kill it!' the Rutan said.

'You don't understand, do you?' the Doctor asked. 'I couldn't kill Sontar in here, even if I wanted to. Now, I appreciate that bringing you here was a little unorthodox, but I wanted to show you something.'

He stepped over to the console, checking the controls.

'We've arrived.'

'Where?' the Sontaran grunted.

'Ten thousand years after your own time. You wanted to see your future. I've brought you here. This is what will happen, unless you change your ways.'

He was holding something in each paw: in one, the Rutan anti-matter Converter, in the other the Sontaran star-killing weapon.

'You said you did not know our future,' the Rutan noted.

'Indeed I don't. But I can guess what I'll see when I open that door. A spiral arm of dead suns and shattered worlds. The ruins of two mighty empires, now just a curiosity for archaeologists. My guess is that we won't see any Sontarans and Rutans. Your races will be long dead.'

Sontar drew out a long, hissing breath. 'Or a Sontaran galaxy, free from the stain of the non-Sontaran. A glorious empire, united under my rule.'

The Rutan remained silent.

'Perhaps that,' the Doctor conceded. 'Perhaps one under Rutan control. But what was the price of victory? Let's see, shall we?'

He moved round to another part of the console.

'Bear in mind that whatever we see is not fixed. The past cannot change, but the future is constantly in flux. It is never too late.'

He flicked a switch.

Shutters along one wall slid smoothly open, revealing a scanner screen. The display was a simple grey colour.

The Rutan waited, but the picture did not appear.

The Doctor was adjusting some of the controls.

'This is the future?' Sontar grunted.

'The Sontaran was at the console,' the Rutan stated. 'It may have altered the settings through its ignorance and incompetence and caused the malfunction of the scanner.'

The Doctor moved his head. 'No.'

He paused, then reached for another control. At the far end of the console room, a set of double doors swung open. Outside it was possible to see the same sea of grey nothingness. The Doctor walked slowly over to the threshold and perched there, gripping the door frame to stay inside.

The Rutan followed him over, the Sontaran trudging into place behind them. It gazed down, out past the Doctor. There was nothing there. The Rutan could not hear the consciousness, or sense energy patterns, it couldn't detect atomic forms.

Even in the darkest, most desolate corner of the universe there was more than this: virtual particles appearing and annihilating, a gas ion every square metre or so, the occasional photon. There was just the Grey, fixed for ever. It was the only Rutan, the only Rutan, the only Rutan. It felt panic form deep inside its body, it looked at the Time Lord, hoping for comforting words.

'There's nothing left,' the Doctor said quietly. 'No time, no space, no matter, no energy. The entire universe has gone.'

Chapter Seven
AD 100,000,000,000,000,000,000,000,000,000,000

The room was small, but it didn't need to be any larger.

It was an alcove, deep within the Citadel, a place few people ever visited. On the surface it resembled a hundred similar rooms dotted around the Capitol: three enamelled consoles, full of blinking lights and enigmatic displays, set at points facing the centre of the room, a couple of uncomfortable chairs, and a large view screen on the back wall. The lighting levels and gloomy decor would hardly encourage anyone to stay here longer that they had to. This room was situated by one of the great power conduits that ran through the lower half of the Citadel.

This deep down, the floor and walls throbbed with power from the Eye. Rassilon had captured the black hole, brought it to Gallifrey, imprisoned it beneath the Panopticon using unyielding equations and the strongest mathematics. For some reason lost to time, Rassilon had insisted that the black hole be called the Eye of Harmony. There was a brick-lined column, like a vast chimney stack, capped by the vast iron globe set in the centre of the floor of the Panopticon, a hundred storeys above, down to the Eye of Harmony, a thousand miles below. Secondary conduits and tunnels branched off at irregular intervals. A plan of the energy grid looked like a vast tree, the end of each twig representing an individual power point. Some branches were thick: those that powered the TARDISes, the Infinity Chambers, the Matrix and the other time travel equipment. The smaller branches powered the food machines, the hypocaust, lighting and the other items of domestic equipment.

An infinite amount of raw power blasted from the Eye, up the shaft, and was channelled along the conduits. The spare energy... well, actually, no one knew what happened to the spare energy. Perhaps it was just returned to the Eye of Harmony, perhaps it served some other purpose.

The Lord President and two minor noblemen huddled around one of the control panels. The President was staring into an eyeboard, using his authority to make all the necessary changes to the security codes. Only the President and a handful of the Council were authorised to make such changes. The two noblemen monitored his work, as their duties demanded.

Gradually the five-dimensional map of the timegate began sketching itself in on the display screen, tracing a line parallel to the Effect. As each stage of the journey was plotted, the power requirements were calculated. It would take almost all of the energy generated by the Black Hole to keep the timegate open.

There was an industrial-looking piece of machinery hanging from the ceiling. It was hexagonal, with a number of glass arrays and prisms stuck to the underside. As the President blinked in his authority codes and set up new power channels, the machine began humming, lights began fading up from within it. Within seconds, a column of energy began cascading down. The energy glittered and sparkled like a waterfall: golds and silvers and platinums glinting in the dim light of the room. Before this column reached the floor, though, it twisted into another dimension. Human eyes would have seen it abruptly cut off a foot or so from the floor. Gallifreyans were more sensitive to time, and saw it twist away like a tornado.

'Ergosphere at full phase,' the first nobleman announced.

'Time column stable,' the other confirmed.

The Magistrate came into existence. There was no distortion, no delay in the image despite the fact it was being transmitted from many light years away. It was as if the Magistrate was in the room, to the extent that the air moved around the image, and it radiated heat.

'Preparations here are complete,' the Magistrate informed his President. 'The crew have been briefed, our equipment is ready and the TARDISes have been stowed.'

The President acknowledged the news with a small smile. 'Good work, old friend.'

The Magistrate smirked at the expression. 'Is the Doctor there?'

The President shook his head.

'Doesn't he know about this mission?'

'We can't find the Doctor anywhere.'

The Magistrate digested the knowledge. 'If this mission should fail, then the Doctor will be Gallifrey's only hope.'

'The Peace Conference is due to resume at dawn, a few hours from now. No doubt he will resurface then.' The President leant forwards, conspiratorially. 'The Lady Larna is missing, too.' He straightened, beaming. 'Besides, your mission will not fail. Remember, Magistrate, that I have consulted the Matrix. This is to be a momentous time for Gallifrey.'

'You know the future?'

'Not all of it,' the President admitted. 'The Matrix merely shows me the pattern of what is to come, not the detail. But, Magistrate, soon you won't just know the future: soon you will walk amongst it.'

The Magistrate made a curt, almost military, nod. 'Is the timegate ready?' he asked.

'See for yourself.' He indicated the screen.

The Magistrate looked over his shoulder. The display was lurid, and anyone who knew about such things would be able to see that the flight plan was preposterous and the power requirements were absurd.

'It is,' the President confirmed.

The Magistrate hesitated, perhaps because he realised that he could see the Station in which he was standing on the display, a tiny mote surrounded by raging energies. The history of the universe was represented by a long, spiralling line running up the screen. The past was marked in blue, the present and known future in green, the unknown in red. At this scale, the blue could hardly be seen, the green didn't even register, and the red line accounted for over ninety-nine percent of the total length.

'Time moves in circles,' the President noted. It was an old Gallifreyan proverb, one that was literally and metaphorically true. The display showed the time spiral, the map of time. Usually, the Time Lords only concerned themselves with the first few hundred coils of the helix.

The Magistrate raised his head, his teeth bared in a smile. 'Activate the timegate.'

The President pressed the control.

The image of the Magistrate snapped out of existence and the energy column at the centre of the room brightened still further. The President turned his attention to the display screen. It showed the Station making its way steadily up the time spiral. He smiled. There was something beautiful, elegant, about the Station's progress.

The Magistrate screamed.

All around him, the crew were on their knees, screaming. The

TARDISes were screaming from their cradles. The Station itself was screaming. Bulkheads designed to sit safely at the heart of a supernova began buckling and distorting. He could hear the engines stepping up a level, then another level, automatically compensating for the stresses.

The Magistrate managed to pull himself to his feet by sheer force of will. It was like struggling against a hurricane force wind. It was Time, he realised, passing over them and through them at an incredible rate. Without the stasis haloes they would have been obliterated.

He hauled himself over to one of the seats, slumped into it. Ten feet from where he had been standing, but he felt like he'd run a marathon. He caught his breath.

There was something watching him. He could feel red eyes bearing down on him, staring at him, fixing him in place. All around and beyond the station were... shapes. The Magistrate tried looking into them, but couldn't interpret them. The image of the Station, reflected and distorted? He didn't know. Outside, reality was superimposing itself on whatever it was that existed here: ghost-like shapes flitted past the window. There were vast insects, bizarre mechanisms, even purely abstract shapes. Some were more human: angular-faced women in golden cloaks; a blue-skinned figure in an immaculate business suit; a man with a single bionic eye. The Magistrate saw himself with six faces, wearing a black tunic, head back, mouth in a cruel rictus. He heard mocking laughter. The universe had fallen to the darkness.

The Station continued to fall.

Dok-Tor had not said a word since they had left futurity.

The Time Lord was sitting in his chair, hands steepled, staring at the console. If he hadn't known better, Sontar might have thought that the steady rising and falling of the column at the centre of the console had lulled him into a hypnotic stupor. But Dok-Tor's silence and lack of movement weighed on Sontar's mind.

Sontar was tired. Sapped of his energy by the accursed Rutan, he knew that he was lucky to be alive. Perhaps it was only the same magic that had saved the Dok-Tor's life that sustained him now.

The Rutan sat in the opposite corner of the TARDIS control room, poised on its hind tentacles, apparently ready to pounce. After a war lasting millions of years, it was difficult for Sontar to feel anything but loathing for the Rutan and its kind. It had been many years since Sontar had come into physical contact with a Rutan. Neither side took prisoners any longer, and both sides had used diplomatic missions as cover for sabotage or assassination attempts. Hatred was like a trusty sword: he knew its weight and balance. It seemed the natural emotional reaction to have, hardwired into his nerves and sinews.

And had it all been for nothing? The universe was destined to end, Sontar knew that, but his scientists had told him that it would not be for untold trillions of years. Ten thousand years was nothing... a clawful of lifetimes compared with those that he had already endured.

Sontar shut off his eyes, and remembered the grey universe. Nothing but mist. Dok-Tor had stood over the console of his time machine, tried to interpret what its instruments told him, but there was nothing to interpret.

Nothing.

The Doctor had babbled about the lack of even the fundamental particles and forces, he had run tests and made observations designed to demonstrate that this was not a local problem. But after an hour of experiments, he had not changed his conclusion that the universe was gone, utterly.

How could that have happened? At first Sontar had suspected a trick, and so had the Rutan. This was a conjuring trick, designed to scare them. But Dok-tor had been scared, too. This wasn't the way that the future was supposed to be, this wasn't what is meant to happen, it was impossible. He said it over and over again, checking that it wasn't his time machine at fault, already knowing that it wasn't.

Had his people done it? Had the Rutans? Sontar imagined himself, in a younger clone body, ninety-nine centuries from now. The throne he sat on was the same, the courtiers were different, although all their faces were familiar. A triumvirate of scientists stood before him. They were telling him about the ultimate weapon, one based on simple principles, but with the ability to destroy vast tracts of time and space. The Rutan would already have such a weapon, his Spymasters were telling him.

A generation later, Sontar saw Rutan warships drifting over the Throneworld, crystal nests floating past the landmarks of his Palace, like lanterns against the darkness. Energy bolts streaking down, slamming into the ground, shattering the statues and palace walls, smashing through the defences. The gates have fallen. Rutan pour through the gaps in the walls, shock troops like giant jewelled crabs in their armoured battleforms.

Green blood in his eyes, his uniform torn, clawing into his thorax, Sontar drags his dying body over to the control, he operates the ultimate weapon. If his Sontarans are to die, then the universe will die. The ground is rocking from another nearby explosion.

He presses his claw against the button with his last ounce of strength. The countdown begins.

20
12
11
10
2
1
0

'A glorious victory,' he hisses. The universe dissolves into grey. He is the last to die.

Sontar reactivated his eyes.

He stood, still not used to the low gravity of the Time Lords' homeworld or their time ships. He took a few steps towards Dok-Tor. The Rutan turned slightly, suspiciously.

'Check your instruments again, Time Lord.'

Dok-Tor frowned. 'Why?'

'I... have reached a decision. I have not felt this desolate since the defeat at Hwyx.'

Dok-Tor looked puzzled, but followed the order.

'What am I looking for?' he asked.

'Has it changed?'

Dok-Tor shook his head.

Sontar sighed. 'I have just made a vow. If it is within my power, if it is ever within my power, I shall not let what we have just seen happen.'

Dok-Tor looked at him, clearly unsure how to react to the announcement. 'No?' he asked.

'No,' swore Sontar solemnly.

'Me neither.'

The central column was slowing down.

'We will be back on Gallifrey in the next few minutes. My people have detected a disturbance in spacetime. It's the only thing I can think of that could possibly have had this effect.' The Doctor stopped, stared up at the ceiling. 'Either the disturbance itself destroyed the universe, or the Time Lords' reaction to it did.'

There was very little that penetrated the dark of Savar's TARDIS, just that from the lights on the console and the soft glow from the scanner. Larna's eyes had adjusted enough to tell her that the decor of the control room was hard, military even. All steel handrails and sharp angles. Savar himself was somewhere in the darkness.

'I can help you,' she said. He needed someone to talk to, he needed someone who could get the right medical care for him.

'You changed,' she said. 'Do you know why you changed?'

She still wasn't sure how much Savar could "see". His eyes might be blind, but his telepathy and acute sensitivity to the time field seemed to compensate. He didn't know what she looked like, he'd not touched her – thankfully – the whole time they had been alone. So he almost certainly didn't know how long her hair was, or its colour. Unless he had simply been able to lift that information from her mind.

'Night fell,' a calm voice said from nearer than Larna would have guessed.

'It happens to you every night?'

'Of late.'

'Why?'

'Because my master demands it. There is a power drain from the Eye of Harmony,' he said, changing the subject. 'Why?'

Larna edged towards the console, locating herself in front of the controls for the main computer.

'What are you doing?' Savar asked her. He was on the opposite side of the console. She could see his face through the transparent central column. He was blind, how could he fly a TARDIS without seeing the controls? As Larna listened, she could hear the console whispering, she could see Savar carefully guiding his hands around the switches. The telepathic circuits had been adjusted, she realised. They were telling him everything he needed to know. TARDISes were symbiotically linked to their owners. Was this TARDIS as mad as Savar?

'I am trying to access information from the minutes of the High Council meetings,' she told him. 'There would have to be consent for such a diversion of power.'

'The power is being drained!' Savar insisted.

'No,' Larna corrected him firmly. 'it is being used by the High Council to power some device. Can't you see?'

'Is that meant to be a joke?' he snarled.

'No. No. Sorry.'

Savar was bent over his instruments. 'Show me.'

Larna pulled a few levers, and the display on the scanner changed. The pitch of the console's whispering changed, too. She assumed that he was being kept informed of the readings.

'This is the Citadel energy grid normally,' she adjusted the setting, 'and this is it now. Power has been channelled away to –' Larna checked another readout – 'a control room in the lower area of the Citadel, not far from the Council Chambers.'

'What are they powering?'

'An artificial wormhole, a tunnel that leads into the far future.' She reached down without looking, located the switches she needed, flicked them.

'How far?' he asked, looking straight at her.

Larna shrugged. 'Off the scale. I could check, but I just don't know where they could be heading. It's beyond the expansionary phase of the universe.'

Savar moved around the console, until he was at her side. Hurriedly, she pulled her hand away from the bank of switches.

'I know...' he said calmly. 'I know what they will find.'

The Doctor was busy preparing for landing.

no one on Gallifrey seemed to have noticed his absence. He patched himself into the Citadel's traffic control system with one hand, adjusted the TARDIS's course slightly with the other. Gallifrey was surrounded by force fields and transduction barriers, but there were plenty of chinks in the armour. It was easy enough to slip a TARDIS through if you knew the right tricks.

The console gave a bleep, and a ticker tape printer began reeling out a couple of inches of tape.

The Doctor watched it, fascinated. Until that moment, he hadn't even known that there was a printer there.

He tore off the slip and read it. It was from Larna.

'Ah... there's going to be a slight detour,' he announced to the Rutan and Sontar. 'I just need to nip out for a moment.' He recalculated the landing position, dialling the new co-ordinates in. He smiled at them, trying to reassure them.

The TARDIS landed, gently.

The Doctor kept the power circuits on, but locked off all the controls.

'Right,' he said cheerfully. 'Won't be long.'

He pulled the lever that opened the door and was outside before the aliens could react. Then he closed the door, locking it, slipping the key into his jacket pocket. The TARDIS had landed in a peculiar little room – almost a cupboard. This was deep within the Citadel, he could *feel* the hum of the power conduits. This wasn't far from the Council chambers. There was ancient equipment down here, some of the oldest time machines.

He had landed his TARDIS alongside another one. On their field trips to other planets, the Time Lords had quickly learnt to disguise their technology from prying eyes. Each time capsule had an array of defences, and this included the ability to transform its outer appearance into a native object. The systems had never been entirely reliable. The Doctor's own TARDIS was stuck in one form. This other one resembled a battered old wardrobe. It was unmistakably a TARDIS, though: place your hand on the side and you could sense that it was alive, or at the very least that there was a vast amount of power concealed behind its mundane outer shell.

Larna had sent her message from in there, but it was firmly locked. The Doctor bent down, examined the floor at the base of the door. There were footprints leading from the other TARDIS, industrial-looking boots, and a woman's bare feet. The Doctor crouched down. The boots had been striding, the woman had been dragged along behind, he could tell that by the scuff marks in the dust.

He heard footsteps. The Doctor hid himself in a niche in the wall behind the two TARDISes, but was careful to allow himself a view of proceedings.

It was the President, flanked by two Watchmen, with two very minor noblemen in Technicians' pinnies trailing after him.

'I shall monitor the arrival of the Station from the Council Chambers,' the President intoned. 'You will stay here and monitor the power flow.'

'Very good, Lord President,' the elder of the two replied.

The President swept away, with the guards.

The two Time Lords didn't return to their power room straight away. One of them looked right at the Doctor.

'What's that?'

The Doctor told himself not to flinch, but the message got lost somewhere and he flinched. But the other Time Lord hardly looked up. 'A couple of TARDISes,' he groaned.

'Here?'

'Oh yes, they often go wandering. Specially down here, near the Eye. Like moths to a flame.'

They stepped in, passing inches from the Doctor.

'Well, we can't leave them here, can we?'

'No.' He pulled back his glove to talk into his communicator.

'Transduction Control, this is Lord Kwep. Please transduct two time capsules to their cradles.'

'As you wish, my Lord.'

Within a couple of seconds, the surfaces of the TARDISes began to shimmer, and they faded away. They'd been teleported back up to their cradles, over a hundred storeys above. The Rutan and General Sontar were still in there. He'd have to get back to them. A more pressing problem was that the Doctor's hiding place had been severely compromised.

Luckily, the noblemen had turned away, and were shuffling back to the power room. Once he was sure they were out of earshot, the Doctor slipped out.

The corridors around here were a labyrinth, a real mess. Somehow, over the years, they'd escaped redecoration and rearrangement. This wasn't a place for ceremony, it was a workplace, and so the logic ran that everything had to be gloomy, functional.

Clearly the President was down here for a reason: it must be the Effect. What was all that about a Station? Perhaps, after due deliberation, the Council had made their projections, and they knew about the grey universe. They could have sent a team to investigate it. Perhaps not. He would have to warn them, but first he had to rescue Larna.

As if to emphasise that point, there were screams in the distance. A man and a woman screaming. The Doctor ran towards the sounds, feet pounding against the stone floor, turning the last corridor so fast that he nearly lost his balance.

The two nobles he had just seen were lying in the middle of the corridor, their blood staining the floor tiles. They'd been slashed with a long force blade. One had been stabbed through the hearts, the other had half his skull sliced away. Both were quite dead.

And although the Doctor was ashamed to think it, he was relieved that neither of them was Larna. She couldn't be far away.

He heard her scream, she was just around the corner. He dashed towards them, heedless of his own safety.

He was just in time to see a power room door slam down. Behind it he'd seen the control bank, a swish of grey cloak and a flash of white, the silk shirt of his that Larna had been wearing.

The Doctor slammed his fists against the shutters in frustration.

The Station didn't slow down, it simply arrived.

The crew pulled themselves to their feet. no one was injured. Now it was over, the Magistrate reflected, he could look back on it as an exhilarating ride. The images he had seen were simply dreams, things of no significance now that they had gone.

There was work to be done.

'Open the portholes,' he ordered. 'Prepare the defences. Our first priority is to seal off this time zone. Establish a communication channel with Gallifrey.'

The opaque screens dissolved back, letting them see the universe. At the same time, sensor arrays came on-line, scanning the universe. The Infinity Chamber in the central column lit up. The Time Lords formed a circle, looking up into the image of this dead universe.

Darkness. There were no stars, no galaxies, there was little matter or energy. Virtually nothing was left at all. In the Gallifreyan timezone, the universe was still warmed by the heat from the big bang. There was background radiation permeating the universe, at a practically constant three degrees Kelvin. That was only three degrees above absolute zero, but it seemed positively tropical compared with the temperature registering outside the Station now: 0.0000000000001 Kelvins. The instruments showed that there were stars here, but the hottest were barely over five Kelvin, cold enough instantly to turn water into ice, cold enough to freeze oxygen solid. Over the aeons that had passed since his time, matter had slowly evaporated, returned to its subatomic components. The largest star left was barely bigger than Gallifrey had been, and the vestigial planets that orbited them would be no larger than boulders. There was no light here, simply degrees of darkness.

It made their task easier. If it wasn't behind its stasis halo, then this Station would be burning bright against the heavens, like a match struck in the dark. The amount of energy it must be expelling, the Source should be incandescent. Of course, just as common as the embers of stars here were the black holes, formed as galaxies and clusters of galaxies had collapsed in on each other. The universe was tiny, now, and contracting further.

For the first time the Magistrate wondered what the people of the universe were doing on this day. There might still be life out here, huddled close to the last sources of energy. He wondered if the descendants of the Time Lords would be amongst their number. The planet Gallifrey itself would be gone, of course, its star long exhausted. The people of Gallifrey might have migrated to a new planet, or perhaps to an artificial environment of some kind. Gallifreyans had traditionally resisted the urge to transform into beings of pure intelligence – an option they considered rather gauche. When their new home wore out, they'd get themselves a new one. Onwards and onwards. Time Lord society had remained stable for millions of years, but that was nothing when compared to the projected life span of the universe. Perhaps some of the projections were correct, perhaps by this time the Time Lords would be long dead. But if Gallifrey could fall, then what hope for the lesser races? The Magistrate wondered if there was there any life here at all. Was sentience just a phase the universe went through?

No.

The Time Lords had achieved so much in mere millions of years, their science exceeded their imagination. What technologies must their descendants have at their disposal? Life would have found a way to leave this dying cosmos altogether.

The Magistrate looked down at this cold, dead vestige of a universe. He hoped so.

The madman holding Larna would be expecting the Doctor to come through the door. The Renegade had already demonstrated that he had expert knowledge of the Capitol's security systems. He knew that the thickest security doors could be over-ridden, and he'd be ready on the other side of the door, with that force knife of his. He'd be able to cut Larna's throat before the Doctor had got his foot through the door. The

Doctor checked his watch. Eight point nine bells. He'd been stood out here for ten minutes trying to work out his options.

But there just wasn't another way in.

The Doctor rested his palm on the door. It was pulsing with energy. There must be an active time column in there.

Even if he had time to get up to the TARDIS cradles, the Doctor knew that the power room was heavily shielded. He considered transduction, transmatation, teleporting... a whole load of other words used to describe essentially the same process, but none of them would work. Nothing got in or out of that room except through the open door. The Doctor, as a member of the High Council, had the authority. The Doctor hesitated. The Renegade had the knowledge somehow. So did that mean that the madman was a Councillor? Or that he had been a Councillor in the past? Or – and this was the prospect that worried the Doctor the most – that he was from the future?

Four bursts from the sonic screwdriver and the access panel to the door came loose. The Doctor lifted it down, tapped in his authorisation code. The door unlocked itself, perfectly silently. The Doctor took a deep breath, tugging the force knife out of his pocket. Larna had given it him in the refectory. He played with the dial and formed a metre-long u-type leaf blade. He weighed it in one hand, checked and then adjusted its balance, and then swung it experimentally. He was ready, but he didn't open the door, not yet. He would have to choose his moment carefully.

He heard Larna.

'The timegate is closing,' she said. 'The time vehicle, whatever it is, has come to rest.'

Even through a thick metal door, the Doctor could hear the fear in her voice. She was a hostage, trapped in a tiny room with a known killer. She'd have seen the Renegade kill those men, but she wouldn't have seen the Doctor hot on their heels. She didn't know that rescue was at hand.

'When?' a man's voice said. The Doctor recognised the voice from somewhere. He spent valuable seconds trying to place it.

'Within a few years of Event Two. It is difficult to say from here with any great certainty.'

'Keep the timegate open... do it!' The voice passed inches from the door. Which meant that he was on the other side of the room, now. Wasn't he?

'The end of the universe,' Larna said. *Left-hand side of the room.*

'What?' *He just moved back towards her.*

'Before, you told me that it was the end of the universe. You were right.' *Left-hand side of the room.*

'Yes. Good. You have done well.' *Right in front of the door.*

'What are you doing?' she asked. *Left-hand side.*

'I am preparing a phased energy pulse.' *He'd paused right in front of the door.* 'I am going to channel the energy from this column and direct it to the Station.' he said simply.

'The Station will be destroyed,' Larna objected.

'Yes. But the timegate will remain open. We will travel down it in my TARDIS.' *Right-hand side.*

There was no more time. The Doctor raised the sword in one hand, slapped the door control with the other and leapt through the door as it whooshed open.

He caught a flash of Larna to his left, the glittering of the time column to his front, but he spun to his right. The Renegade was standing over a control panel. His sword was drawn, but it was loose in his hand as he concentrated on operating the console. Not for long. The Renegade lunged, as the Doctor knew that he would. The Doctor blocked, then thrust.

The Renegade parried, trying to twist the blade out of the Doctor's hand using brute strength, but the Doctor had already begun his countermove, and the blades just glanced off each other, giving the Doctor time to straighten and look at his opponent properly for the first time.

The grey cloak the Renegade wore was rather luxurious. Underneath that, there seemed to be a spacesuit of some kind.

His face!

'Savar...' the Doctor gasped. He knew who this was... but this wasn't his current incarnation. This was his fourth regeneration, the one that had vanished, the one whose eyes had been taken. The angular cheekbones, the curly beard, it was unmistakably Savar. And his eyes were missing. It had taken the Doctor a moment to notice what was wrong. He had thought that the face was in shadow, but the eyes were shadow, there was nothing else there. The eyes were meant to be the windows to the soul – well, true enough, without them Savar looked incomplete, more like a skull than a face.

'Savar, it's me...'

But the sound of his voice merely gave Savar something to aim at. He had grabbed his sword in both hands and now swung it at the Doctor with all his strength. The Doctor half-fell, half-ducked to get out of its way. The blade swiped the air above him, carving a great scar in the stone wall.

The Doctor scrabbled, trying to gain footing.

Savar lifted the sword above his head and brought it down, but the Doctor was already out of the way. The blade gouged a hole six inches deep in the marble floor. The man's face was twisted, murderous.

But Savar... Savar was a noble man, an explorer, a scientist. He had been a friend of the Doctor's father. He'd been the Doctor's friend. After his return, they'd never shared the same relationship. Savar's condition had limited him, and rather like an elderly body with a debilitating illness, or encroaching senility, the young and healthy – and the Doctor was no exception – had avoided him, found him faintly distasteful. Unconsciously, perhaps, they were all scared that Savar's condition was contagious.

The Doctor was crouched now, sword in one hand. He pulled himself to his feet, swiping the blade ahead of him to give himself a little room.

Savar had returned to the console. The Doctor brought down his sword on the controls, making them explode.

Savar lashed out, and would have sliced the Doctor's arms off at the elbow if he hadn't let go of his sword and thrown himself back. He landed at Larna's feet, and she helped him up. He stood between her and Savar, although he knew that his body offered little protection against a forceblade. Her breathing was uneven, panicked. He could hardly blame her.

'We'll be all right,' he told her calmly.

Savar turned and began to advance, sword in front of him. The Doctor's blade was embedded in the console on the other side of the room, like the sword in the stone.

'The energy pulse is on a countdown,' she told him. 'He managed to get it going.'

He glanced over his shoulder. 'How long?'

She gave a helpless smile and shrugged.

Savar lurched at them, but they leapt out of the way – Larna towards the centre of the room, the Doctor to the edge.

'That was close,' the Doctor laughed, hoping that the edge of panic in his voice wasn't too obvious.

Savar swung around, taking the two strides towards him that he needed to.

He was blind. Savar couldn't see him, he was going on sound and... telepathy.

The Doctor stayed perfectly still and he reached into his mind. There was a point within him that... his breathing stopped. His hearts slowed. His mind emptied. The Doctor could still see, but only a blurred image.

Savar stopped in his tracks, unsure what had happened.

'Over here!' Larna called from her console. She knew. 'I'm just about to deactivate the energy pulse.'

Savar turned his back on the Doctor, and was about to take his first step towards Larna when the Doctor reached out, grabbing Savar's shoulder, and pulled down with all his might. Savar lost his balance, crashing to the floor.

The Doctor pulled himself over, pinning Savar down with his knee in his chest, his hand chopping Savar's wrist once, making him drop the sword.

'Doctor!' Larna shouted.

Savar still had a free hand and moved to grab at the Doctor's throat, but the Doctor had anticipated the move, and blocked it. Savar formed a fist and jabbed it hard into the Doctor's stomach. The Doctor gasped, eyes watering. Savar was rolling free, lifting the Doctor from the floor. His back arched, and the Doctor nearly toppled off.

And then something had grabbed Savar's free arm and pressed it to the floor.

Larna was alongside him, kneeling on Savar's wrist, one hand flat on his collarbone, keeping him pinned.

'Bitch!' Savar growled.

Larna grabbed the back of his head in one hand and then brought it hard down on the marble floor. The Doctor felt the body go limp.

The Doctor looked across at Larna and grinned breathlessly.

'Thank you for rescuing me,' he said.

'Thank you for rescuing *me*,' she replied.

They both got to their feet, a little awkwardly. They hugged. Larna was still shaking. Then she broke off, bent down over Savar, began a search of his robes.

'He had a key,' she explained. 'That's why he broke into the Archive Chamber, that's why he kidnapped Peltroc. The guards left it in your room.'

She found it, and handed it over.

'This is a TARDIS key,' the Doctor said, after a quick examination. He jabbed his thumb behind his shoulder. 'Savar's TARDIS. The wardrobe that was out there?'

'It can't be,' Larna said. 'We got the key from your room, and we went to your room in his TARDIS. He already had the key for that one.'

'In that case it must –' the Doctor glanced over to the console. 'You *did* switch off that energy pulse, didn't you?'

Larna's eyes widened. The two of them leapt at the console, flicking switches, working together to reroute the power circuits. Finally, the pitch of the time column changed.

'Close thing there,' the Doctor said, stepping away from the console and wiping his forehead with his handkerchief. He moved past Larna to examine Savar.

The crew of the Station had set up time buffers and early warning systems. Time travel to and from this timezone was impossible now, except for the narrow channel they were using to connect with Gallifrey.

With the defences in place, it was time to explore. The Infinity Chamber's observations were being hampered by the high concentrations of black holes and dark matter in the dying universe. The Magistrate had ordered that three TARDISes be sent out to map the dead universe. Lords Hemal, Quarduk and Norval were dispatched, each heading in a different direction. Information from their ships was relayed to the Station, where the Infinity Chamber began filling in the blanks in its model.

Hedin watched as the map began filling itself in. It was like picture restoration: scraping away the accumulated dust and dirt and soot from the candles to reveal the vibrant colours underneath.

The Magistrate hovered behind him, full of anticipation.

'Why so impatient?' Hedin asked.

'I can feel it,' the Magistrate told him. 'Power. Gallifrey is on the brink of a discovery that will put it... well, who knows where?'

Hedin could feel it, too. Time Lords felt the flow of time as the lesser races felt the air against their skin. 'But we are already by far the most powerful race in the universe. Isn't that powerful enough?'

The Magistrate shook his head, a smile on his face.

'A generation ago, the President thought as you did,' Hedin said.

The Magistrate raised an eyebrow. 'Really? I didn't think his ambitions stretched beyond devising new ceremonies and procedures.'

'He and I studied the Old Times together. The ROO texts, the legends of Rassilon and Omega.'

'Back then, Gallifreyans were more adventurous.'

Hedin's smile flickered. 'That's one way of looking at it, certainly.'

'Not one that you share?'

'No,' Hedin said, almost apologetically. 'For many years, I have thought that the best thing about Gallifrey being the supreme power in the universe is that no one else is. Imagine Gallifrey's might in the hands of the Daleks or the Faction Paradox. Better not to use the power than to use it unwisely.'

The Magistrate scowled. 'If Rassilon had thought as you do...'

An alarm buzzed.

It was an urgent signal from Lord Norval.

He had found the Source.

The Doctor was bent over Savar. Unconscious, the blind face still seemed troubled, enraged. As the Doctor watched, a shadow lifted, and it was the 'real' Savar again, the small, mild, man.

'It must be dawn,' Larna said, inexplicably.

Savar's eyes fluttered open. He was clearly disorientated, and this was hardly helped by the Doctor looming over him. So the Doctor leant a little closer.

'Where am I?'

'One of the power rooms,' Larna said from across the room.

'I didn't –?'

The Doctor nodded down at him. 'You most certainly did.' He held out the key. 'And it was all to do with this key. What's so important about it?'

'It opens the door of my TARDIS,' Savar said.

'Your original TARDIS? The one that was lost?'

'That's right.'

'I take it you found it again. Where?'

'There,' Savar said, turning his head as much as he could to indicate the power display.

The Doctor glanced at it and frowned, before returning his attention to Savar. 'Right at the end of time. It's a long way to travel. Why is it worth murdering and kidnapping for, hmm? What's in that TARDIS, Lord Savar?'

'A power beyond that of God,' he said.

Lord Norval's TARDIS was a plain white obelisk, spinning in space.

Inside its impossibly large control room was a three-sided central console. Beside it stood Norval, altering course every so often, checking that the TARDIS's scanners were still working at full efficiency and that the communication link with the Station was being maintained. He was a small man, in a collarless jade tunic. The Magistrate had chosen him because he'd run the odd errand for the High Council in his time: delivered messages, acted as an emissary. Chiefly he was an astronomer, though, quite at home in this strange, old universe. This was a place that he'd only read about in academic journals: a storybook land where time ran backwards and the stars were colder than ice.

The Source stood out from the dark background of this dead place. It was only a very few degrees above absolute zero, but it was amongst the hottest, most energetic things still in existence. Even the black holes, emitting nothing but Hawking radiation, counted as hot in this place. Apart from the temperature, there was also the shape. On the scope, each black hole looked like a tiny dot. This object resembled a dash. The TARDIS had automatically alerted him to its presence, and he'd changed course to get a closer look.

Still many light centuries away, the time field sensors had begun to go haywire as the Effect started registering. At that point, Norval knew for certain what he had suspected. Immediately, he had sent a signal to the Station, informing them that he had found the Source.

At this distance, even using Gallifreyan technology, it wasn't possible to get a very clear image of the object – there were just too many black holes and clouds of dark matter, all squeezing close together as the universe contracted. The Magistrate had suggested that he move his TARDIS to a point where he had a clearer view. Norval decided to keep his distance, and chose to lay in a set of co-ordinates that would place him around ten light years from the object. Even without accurate maps of the area, it had been relatively easy to find a suitable spot.

He opened the shutters of the scanner.

It dominated the screen even at this distance.

When confronted with the infinite – as the Time Lords were every day – it became banal, somehow, easy to imagine, impossible to *understand*. Norval's first impression was that the object looked like a knitting needle stuck in a black grape. The computers solemnly supplied the information that the object was a light year long and that the black hole had a diameter three times that of Gallifrey. But neither image helped him to comprehend it... even the Gallifreyan language lacked the vocabulary to bring home the sheer scale of what he was seeing.

Every system on the ship started whirring and chattering with new data. These findings were relayed on to the Station. It left Norval free to make his observations, to try to come to terms with the Needle. He was sure that nothing like it existed in any timezone known to Gallifrey. He conferred with the Magistrate, who checked the data with the Matrix itself.

The Magistrate's voice echoed around the console room from the various speakers.

'Lord Norval. The object is artificial. I repeat: someone built it.'

The Past
I of the Needle

'I have been a broken man for many years,' Savar began, 'but had no idea upon which wheel I had been broken. I had my dreams, brighter and more vivid than before, but upon waking, I couldn't remember anything more than flashes of colour, or a sense of movement. The truth was there, tantalising me. I felt that there was something watching me, red eyes in the sky, red eyes in the walls and floors and ceilings.

'The last ten days have been different. At night, I have... it's the breach in spacetime. It affects the mind. It has given you both nightmares, or waking dreams. The coming of night changes me now, transforms me into my past self, yet grants me my current memories. It turns me into something I am not, a twisted venomous version of myself. As I might have been. Why me? Because I was there at its creation. I have seen the face of God.

'Once, as an arrogant young man, I thought I could change the universe. A common belief amongst those just starting out in life. A few of my contemporaries thought as I did: your father, Hedin, your mentor, Lady Zurvana, even our beloved President... although he was merely a Chancellor back then. Come to think of it, that was before you were awarded your doctorate, so you wouldn't have called yourself the Doctor. No. Hedin was still a Hedin.

'Mid-day, in the Panopticon. The banners and sunlight were streaming. Was that before or after your wedding? What about the children? It was before the grandchild. Of course it was... you were much younger, standing at your father's side. You... you looked much as you do now. We played chess, I beat you, and you almost cried. no one had ever beaten you before. As we played, the adults discussed astronomy. You displayed your knowledge of the Chandrasekhar Limit. Just that morning you had been studying black holes. The others were impressed, and I cooed my own platitudes.

'But I was planning to do more than study black holes and learn their names.

'Two million years ago, Omega, Rassilon and the others took their starbreakers to Qqaba. Omega was lost, of course, but the others survived. The time energies infused them, made them into Time Lords. Rassilon captured the black hole, led it back through the streets of the Capitol in the greatest victory parade the universe had yet seen. Infinite power, time travel, incredible advances in science and technology, the banishment of all its enemies. Gallifrey had it all. But Omega was lost. Oh, the Time Lords never forgot him, they honoured his name. But Rassilon took most of the credit, and all of the spoils.

'I planned to do more than remember Omega: I planned to rescue him.

'Gallifrey has lost its way. For twenty thousand centuries we have squandered our great inheritance, we've been content to watch from our private utopia. We don't serve, but neither do we rule. Oh, you think I'm just another Morbius, intent on raising an army and conquering the universe, or a Marnal off on some impossible crusade. No. You think as I do, Doctor, although you won't admit it. You want the universe to change, and change begins at home. That's why you came back: you sense what is coming. Your father felt as we do, and so did the President back then. You think we are on the brink of a new golden age. I sense from her thoughts that Lady Larna agrees.

'It was simple enough. Remember what you told me about black holes, all those years ago? That's right: "nothing can escape a black hole". Well, you know now that isn't true. All you need to do is travel faster than light, although in practice the intense gravity warps hyperspace as it warps normal spacetime, so spaceships can't just fly faster than light to break a black star's hold.

'Yes... well done, Larna. They told me that you showed promise. A TARDIS. I was the one who would pilot my TARDIS into the black hole. I would rescue Omega, and I would bring him back to Gallifrey, where he would take his rightful place as Lord High President of the Time Lords. It would be so easy, and why had no one thought of it before?

'Oh yes, Doctor, your father knew of this. Did he approve? At first. But when it came to it, he merely stayed in his high tower. He watched, at least, as long as he could. Not even the Time Lords can see past the event horizon of a black hole. I passed through it in my TARDIS. He didn't see what happened to me after that, and I never saw what happened to him.

'After a time travelling through the darkness, I saw a doorway. It led into another universe, one with brighter colours and sweeter smells. It led into a garden. My TARDIS came to rest, and – suitably protected, of course – I stepped from him and onto the stonework of this gate that divided the two universes. All around me was black, except for the light pouring from that doorway. There were sights, and smells, but no sounds. I could see the birds in that alien sky, I could see a waterfall, but I couldn't hear them. I was about to place my foot over the threshold.

'I hesitated.

'And he was there. Ohm, ancient god of the Time Lords, chained to heaven as the legends told. I saw him, in the distance, and then closer, towering over me. He spoke to me, but I couldn't hear what he was saying, and he couldn't step over the threshold into our universe. He beckoned me forward, with one gloved hand. And then I knew that if I set foot in that place that I would be lost, and that it would mean the end of everything.

'He asked me what I wanted. He told me he could change the past, give me whatever I desired. He showed me my friend, dead two decades. He had died in a storm, his boat lost with all hands. Ohm showed me the boat returned to port. He showed me visions of how my past might have been had I been Astronomer Royal or had I left Gallifrey. Whatever I wanted, he said, as the past changed around me. All the mistakes of my youth, all my failed conquests both professional and personal. It could all change. Would I like to be a Prydonian rather than an Arcalian? Which title, honour or job would I wish? Would I rather be a woman than a man? It could all change, yet remain the same. His voice was a whisper. Just help him to leave this terrible place and a universe would be mine. Nothing was fixed, nothing. The past wasn't real, the present wasn't real, the future wasn't real.

'Fear filled my hearts at this prospect.

'"I am who I am!" I shouted.

'I fled. I stumbled back to my TARDIS, slammed closed the doors, flung myself at the controls. The flight from the black hole... all the way there, I had been fretting about my return. A journey such as mine had never been attempted before. Now, the technicalities didn't matter: I had to escape, or all would be lost.

'My TARDIS reached the event horizon without incident, but as we reached that final hurdle, we were attacked. The control room crackled with green lightning, I could feel the power seeping away, could sense the Time Vortex around my ship fading. I could feel the external shell of the TARDIS annihilating. I did what I could, I wrestled with the controls.

'My TARDIS screeched and shrieked as he tried to get free. Time and space... they are different things there. Matter and energy aren't as we know them. Finally, after an hour at the console, I broke free, or so I thought. I set the controls for a massive burst of speed, to get away from this terrible place. But I looked back, and I saw that the tiniest part of my TARDIS was still trapped in the black hole. I looked again, and I saw the hand of Ohm grasped there, pulling us towards the doorway.

'I panicked. I told the TARDIS to fly on, to leave. But this wasn't some cave, or the jaws of some sea creature, this was the event horizon of a black hole. There was no escape.

'An irresistible amount of power, trying to break free from an immovable force. A puzzle for the mathematicians! But no, Lady Larna, you are quite right. By definition, either there wasn't going to be enough power, or the event horizon would release me.

'There wasn't enough power.

'Oh, my TARDIS tried. He struggled, pulled, stretched out like toffee, pulled himself through more dimensions than we can conceive of. All the time I was clinging to the console. All the time, I knew that my TARDIS couldn't make it.

'There was only one course of action to me, I abandoned my dying ship, made for the escape unit. Behind me, I saw my TARDIS, his outer shell stretched and looped around itself, chameleon circuits reconfiguring and reconfiguring, trying to get away. But to no avail.

'Stretched thin, now, like a vast needle, a line that must have been a light year long, I saw the moment my TARDIS gave up the fight. He began falling, slipping into the black hole like a drowning sailor. I heard his telepathic cries for help, I heard him pleading: "Don't abandon me, don't leave me in this terrible darkness."

'As he fell, he tore a hole in time, like a fingernail down a blackboard. It was as if a hole had been ripped from the page of a book. I saw the pages behind ours, other times and spaces. Not parallel universes, but palimpsest universes. Reality is a slate, and history and memory and matter and time are just patterns of chalk on that reality. There is so much left unwritten, or just sketched in. A casual word, a glance down the wrong alleyway and... and everything could change. The Time

Lords hold such power, the power to destroy a planet or change a young girl's past. We devour time as a beetle chews up leaves or bacteria rots a corpse. That power scares me. Nothing is safe, nothing is sacred.

'But these observations were useless to me. I was alone. I was away from the black hole, but in a notorious area of space, with no power to enter the Vortex, not enough power even to call Gallifrey for help.

'I wrote the name of what I had seen on a piece of paper. OHM. The ancient name of the trapped God.

'I drifted, ice forming on the skin of my lifeboat. My food and water ran out, my air was growing stale. I have no idea how long I drifted. A hundred years? A thousand?

'They came while I slept, burning through the indestructible walls of my escape capsule. They were scavengers, they stepped into the darkness. They glinted, like emeralds and rubies, their legs were metal, jointed in all the wrong places, with glass spines embedded in them.

'An insect species, I thought. Their compound eyes watched me, swivelling in their sockets as they saw the technology that surrounded me.

'I told them my name, and where I was from. That interested them. They spoke to me. Asked me questions. I wondered if they were real, or were creatures from my dreams. I had long passed the point where I could make the distinction.

'Then they took my ship apart – their hands were like army knives, unscrewing and peeling back and sawing away the control panels, the power conduits, the computer core, the light fittings, the springs and mounts of my chair. They scraped away samples of the carpet, of the walls, of the fabric of my spacesuit. They passed it back behind them, into their ship, they did it without rest, relentlessly stripping the capsule of everything that could be taken.

'Then they started with me. They took some of my hair, my skin, my blood, extracted material from my glands, drained my spinal fluid. That wasn't enough for them. They stopped for a moment, communicated with each other in a chittering voice, like a man walking over broken bottles, and then they took my eyes. One held me down, without effort, and the other was over me, a hand over each eye, a needle-thin blade coming from its end finger. I felt the eyes slipping from their sockets, only the optic nerve holding them in place. Then I felt the nerves sliding out, like swords from a scabbard. I could still see. I felt the other one, the one who was holding me down, lean forward, I heard a sound like a buzzsaw.

'I heard them leave, welding the wall back into place behind them. It wasn't enough for them to let me die, they let me live. Despite that, I shouted after them. "Come back," I called. "Don't leave me!"

'But they had gone. Without my eyes, without life support, alone in space, I saw it all. I had time to think, and to dream.

'Nothing is real.'

Chapter Eight
Death of a Time Lord

The Doctor had stood, Larna at his side, as Savar had told his story. He'd listened to every one of the madman's words, speaking in a soft voice only to answer a direct question. It had been quite a contrast with Savar, who had strutted and paced around the room, the pitch of his voice rising and falling as he spat out the words. What this Savar lacked in physical presence and strength, he attempted to convey with venom.

The anger was as terrifying as it was fascinating. As Larna watched Savar's face contorting, as she analysed his sentence structure and posture, she realised that he was insane, by any of the accepted definitions. Of course that had been obvious from the actions of his other self: murder, kidnap, seemingly random destructive acts. This disturbed Larna, not for its violation of the criminal law, but the physical ones. Time Lords felt time flow through them, but more than that, they helped to shape and refine time and space around them. All sentient life did this, of course, their observations helping to resolve quantum events, bring the universe into its current form according to the four anthropic principles. But because of their unique powers and the scope of their technology, Time Lords did more than most races to affect the universe. Their victories in the Time Wars fought in the generations after Rassilon had helped to stabilise the cosmos, they had laid down the foundations of the modern, rationalistic universe. Would a mad Time Lord have the opposite effect? Would his insanity become contagious, affecting the past and the future like a virus?

When he had finished, Savar stood there panting like an animal, exhausted by his rants. The Doctor had glanced across to Larna, who had smiled nervously. The Doctor was an adept telepath, one of the most proficient that Larna had known, but Savar's powers seemed to be in a league of their own. She could feel his mind snarling at her. A further sign of his mental instability – that he couldn't even keep his thoughts to himself?

'The Effect can change the past?' The Doctor asked.

'Yes,' Savar replied calmly

There was a look in the Doctor's eyes, an intensity. These two men had a lot in common, Larna realised. Both had left the Capitol, seen the universe and been changed by the experience. Needless to say, the Doctor's experiences had been a great deal more enriching. Both were explorers, but Savar was dangerous, the things he had seen had been destructive, deathly.

'Changing the past is impossible,' Larna interjected. 'It's an alchemist's dream, like being able to reverse entropy or see the future.'

'The Time Lords of old could see the future,' the Doctor noted.

'It's a fairy story, unscientific rubbish.'

The Doctor looked over to her, flashing a quick smile. 'That's exactly what Rassilon said.'

'What would you do with the power to change the past?' Savar asked.

The Doctor looked away. 'We have to see the Council,' he told Larna quietly. 'We have to take Savar to them, give him a chance to argue his case.'

Larna couldn't believe what she had just heard. 'He killed Waym, he killed those other two Time Lords, kidnapped me and that guard...'

The Doctor nodded, brushing her face with the back of his hand. 'And he'll pay for his crimes,' he promised. 'But he holds the key to this, literally. This all started because of the damage his TARDIS caused to spacetime.'

'What are you saying there?' Savar asked from the other end of the room. All these years it had seemed that everyone bar a handful of people had been unsettled by Savar. All these years Larna had been disgusted by the others' dismissal of him, their taunts and quiet bullying. All these years, the bullies had been right: Savar *was* creepy, there *was* something sinister about him.

'We have to see the Council,' Savar agreed. 'You must convince them that I am right.'

'No!' the Doctor said softly. 'They will not listen. They will try to harness the Effect.'

Savar rubbed his chin. 'That must not be allowed to happen.'

'You've changed your tune,' Larna said. 'You wanted to rescue Omega, or Ohm, or whoever it is down there.'

'The blind Savar wants that,' the Doctor agreed. 'But you don't, do you?'

'My other self is a servant of Ohm. I sense that there is an evil at work. I want to seal off the future, prevent access. We can seal the breach in spacetime from here.'

'You haven't gone out of your way to persuade them,' Larna shouted back.

The Doctor stepped between them. 'No, no, he hasn't. Although to be fair, it would certainly take some explaining... According to his logic, the Council doesn't matter. The universe is going to end, so individual lives are of infinitesimal importance. That's not a philosophy that is going to win him many friends. We have to help him argue his case.'

'I agree,' said Savar thoughtfully. 'It is not too late to prevent this.'

Larna was angry again, just seeing the face, hearing the voice. 'Why do we have to listen to this madman?'

'I've seen the grey universe,' the Doctor explained urgently. 'There's nothing capable of that except the Effect.' There was a glimmer of terror in his eyes. If he couldn't persuade her, how could he hope to persuade the Council?

'But the Station is in the future now,' Larna said, pointing at the display screen. 'That's what will happen to the universe: it will run its course. The future you saw doesn't happen.'

'Have you understood nothing, child?' Savar asked her. 'While that Effect is active, nothing is fixed. The future with the Needle is one future, but not necessarily the one that we will enjoy. The Effect has the power to control every aspect of time and space, from the smallest particle to the Absolute. We have to warn the Council of this. We have to tell them of the omnipotent power of that place.'

'That is exactly what we mustn't do,' the Doctor warned. 'If we even mention the sheer power of this thing, we'll do nothing but encourage them to investigate it.'

'We are going to lie to the Council?' Larna said.

'To save the universe, yes. Come on.'

Norval's TARDIS hovered, its scanners beginning to capture beautiful images. The pictures and associated data were relayed to the Station, where the Time Lords and their computers analysed what they saw and prepared their reports.

Norval crossed his arms, studying the image on the scanner, letting his TARDIS fly itself. Except for its size the Needle seemed fairly straightforward. The Needle was a tube, like an immense length of drainpipe or a drinking straw. Gallifrey could have fit neatly down the hole in the centre. At one end, the Needle was stuck in the black hole, and this twisted its straight lines a little, and bathed it in hard radiation and gravitational distortion. All around that end of the Needle were waves of spacetime distortion: the Effect that they had detected from Gallifrey. These radiated out from the black hole like spray from a fountain.

The Needle was bone-white, smooth and immaculate. There were no craters, no irregularities. There had been impacts, inevitable encounters with asteroids, maybe even larger objects, but the Needle itself hadn't been damaged. Instead, rocks and ice had dashed themselves against the surface, forming dirty smudges that were barely visible from this distance.

The spectroscope had just come up with something interesting. Norval noticed it just before he heard the Magistrate's voice.

'Norval, fly a little closer.' The Magistrate read out a series of co-ordinates.

The TARDIS was already making the necessary course correction, its scanners homing in on the designated area.

Norval stared.

Impossibly – but not, by far, the most impossible thing about this artefact – a swathe of the surface at the end furthest from the black hole had once sustained a biosphere. It represented only a hundredth or so of the tube's surface, from this distance it was a speck. But even so, it was a huge area: a million times more habitable land than even a Dyson Sphere could provide. Enough room, perhaps, for the entire population of a galaxy. There must have been artificial suns here at some point, providing all the heat and light the population needed.

Like everything else in the universe, it was long dead now. The entire great stretch of the tube's surface was deep with thick snow and ice. This wasn't simply frozen water – although there was enough of that to have filled a hundred thousand oceans on Gallifrey – but also frozen oxygen and nitrogen. As the last energy of the universe had dissipated, the air had cooled and solidified, the sky had fallen, encasing the cities that had dotted this part of the surface. The tallest buildings were around ten miles high, and poked out from the snow.

Over the next few minutes, Norval identified at least a hundred settlements, one of which had been the size of a continent. The architecture was a mix of styles. Most of the buildings had been built from a white material, possibly a ceramic. It was clear, though, from the size and spacing of their doors and windows, that the people of this place had been humanoids of roughly Gallifreyan height, that they had needed roadways and arable fields.

Men like us, then, Norval thought. Had this been their last refuge? An ark where the last people of the universe had lived? If that was the case, then they hadn't made it to the end. Even the race capable of building this place hadn't been able to prevent their own extinction, as the universe collapsed and faded around them.

The end had been a long time coming: there were no bodies frozen in place, no evidence that buildings had been smashed by a tidal wave of snow. But neither was there any evidence of spaceports, or an evacuation effort.

'There are no roads between the cities,' he noted.

'No,' the Magistrate said, 'but the distances between the cities are so vast. They must have used transmats or aircraft.'

'Assuming that there was any contact between the cities at all,' Norval replied. 'There is no space debris, no satellite network, no artificial moons. It may have been the case that the cities just didn't know of each other's existence. Each city certainly has a distinct architectural style.'

Hedin's voice: 'It's difficult to say, but some of the buildings are a lot older than the others. This place could have been settled for a very long time... tens of millions of years at least. Spacefarers would have seen this place from many light years' distance, it must have dominated the heavens of a thousand worlds. Ships could have arrived quite independently of each other. This place is so large that their sensors might not have registered other life.' Civilisations larger and more mighty than most galaxies ever saw could have risen and fallen here, without ever encountering their neighbours.

'Are there any life signs?'

Norval checked. 'I am still some distance away, and the Effect is preventing a perfect view of the object, but if there is life down there then there isn't very much of it. Should I fly closer?'

There was a pause.

'Magistrate?'

'No. Best to be cautious.'

Savar strode through the Capitol, the Doctor at his side, the Lady Larna following. He sensed the fear of the Watchmen at the door to Temporal Monitoring as he approached and the Doctor negotiated their way in.

Temporal Monitoring echoed with the murmured words of those watching from the Gallery and the hum of the Infinity Chamber machinery. This was a public occasion, with crowds filling the galleries, cameras recording the momentous events for posterity. The Temporal Monitoring Main Chamber hadn't changed since his day. The Gallery was a hundred feet above the floor of the chamber, filled to rafters with the plebeian classes, baying and calling as if this were some theatrical production, with the Time Lords below them staring solemnly into space, as though it wasn't.

He looked around. 'Where are the Council?'

'The Council are here, just in the wrong place,' Larna told him quietly.

They were standing around the Chamber, looking down at an image of the object. It was being relayed from a TARDIS by the look of it. There were various sub-images: magnified details of features on the surface. Frozen cities. It looked like there was an ice age down there. Every planet must be like that in the far future, without suns to warm them. The Doctor broke away from them, striding towards the Councillors.

'What is the Doctor doing?' Savar asked.

'He has gone to talk to the Council. They haven't noticed him yet.'

'Lord Norval, how large is the Needle?' he heard the President ask.

'It is certainly large enough to qualify for the Bdo scale,' another voice – coming from a loudspeaker – announced. 'It is a tube, approximately one light year long, but barely fifty thousand kilometres in diameter. One end is embedded in the black hole. The timespace distortion Effect emanating from the intersection radiates in the visible and near-visible spectrum for a distance of a million parsecs.'

'Oh yes,' said the Doctor, announcing his presence, 'but as they say on Arrakis, "If you think that's big, you should see the sparrows".'

The assembled Time Lords began to turn his way.

'So the Doctor has finally decided to grace us with his presence,' Castellan Voran declared.

'Ah yes, and the Lady Larna has also shown her face,' Pendrel added. 'Synchronicity, I believe it is called.'

Savar fancied he could feel Larna's blushes. The President himself was stepping out from the group, the Doctor beside him, walking towards them. The Castellan was two paces behind them.

'Lord Savar,' the President declared, his voice weak with age. Savar bowed his head, as etiquette demanded.

'Lord President,' the Doctor told them. 'Gallifrey faces its greatest threat.'

'Yes, but also a great opportunity.' It was the Magistrate, standing at the President's side. He had thought that the Magistrate was in the far future.

His expression must have betrayed his confusion. 'That is a projection,' Larna prompted him, 'the real Magistrate is on the Station.'

Savar turned to this simulacrum Magistrate. 'Do you know what you have found?'

'Not yet,' the Magistrate conceded. 'It appears to be of Gallifreyan origin.'

'Indeed,' Savar whispered.

'Be very careful,' the Doctor said, addressing the Magistrate. 'That object is all that remains of a TARDIS that was damaged as it tried to break free of the black hole. It has torn holes in the spacetime continuum. Those holes have formed the Effect. There must also be collision of time energy from the TARDIS and anti-time from the collapsing universe, which means...' his voice trailed away. 'Well, I'm not sure about that bit.'

The President was beginning to piece it together. 'Your TARDIS?' he asked.

Savar nodded.

A number of the Councillors were muttering. Above all, Time Lords were sworn to protect the timelines, and this defied all those laws.

'This thing is an abomination,' one of the monks intoned.

'How has your TARDIS managed to break free now?' the Magistrate asked.

'That's simple enough,' Larna explained. 'Under the uncertainty principle, some of the particles from within the black hole will occasionally appear outside the event horizon. Over time every black hole evaporates. The black hole on that image is the same one that Savar flew his TARDIS into, but in the intervening aeons, it has shrunk a little. Less mass equals less gravitational pull. When Savar tried to get out originally he almost made it – in the far future, the black hole is easier to escape from.'

The Castellan was puzzled. 'What was your TARDIS doing in a black hole in the first place?'

'Savar was performing scientific observations into gravitation,' the Doctor said quickly. Savar felt the President's discomfort.

'But why couldn't these observations be made from Gallifrey?'

There were notes of concern from the gallery, and members of the Council.

'Because, Castellan,' Savar said levelly, 'sometimes to solve that which is unknown about the universe one has to look beyond the roof of the Capitol Dome.'

There were giggles from the gallery fodder.

'Not so, Lord, ah, Savar,' an elderly voice said. The Keeper of the Matrix stepped forwards. 'The Matrix is the repository of *all* knowledge. It contains all the mathematical axioms and scientific principles that govern the universe, and can apply them a great deal more efficiently than any one Gallifreyan. There are no mysteries to the Matrix.'

'There are limits to its knowledge,' Savar asserted. 'Perhaps your ambitions do not stretch beyond acquiring academic qualifications and meaningless ceremonial titles. Mine did.'

'And precisely what was your *ambition*?' the Castellan asked.

Savar smiled.

The Doctor grasped his arm. 'Savar, don't...' he warned.

Savar shook him away, raised his head, showed his face to the gallery for the first time. 'I was planning to rescue Omega himself!'

For a moment, those lining the galleries were unsure how to react.

Neither was the Castellan. 'Omega?' was all that he managed to say.

The Time Lords were returning their attention to the image in the Infinity Chamber. Savar could sense the turmoil as they tried to grasp what they were seeing, he revelled in the chaos that he had created in such an ordered place.

'Such was my arrogance that I thought I might liberate the greatest of our number from his eternal tomb.'

'So you have succeeded. After all this time, Omega has been found.' There was a tone of awe in the President's voice.

Lord Hedin pressed himself forwards. 'We must land, we must finish your great mission.'

'It is not Omega down there, but something infinitely more dangerous.' But they weren't listening to Savar's pleas.

The Doctor could feel them slipping away. He made yet another appeal. 'No. No. There is great danger here. Magistrate, you must stay away from the Needle –'

'You must destroy it!' roared Savar.

' – and return to Gallifrey.'

'Only the President can give such an order,' the Castellan reminded the Doctor disdainfully.

'President?' Savar begged.

The old man was calm. Savar felt his thoughts. The President had studied Omega, he had written a dozen books on the subject. His time in office had been dedicated to restoring Omega's reputation. This would be a culmination of his Presidency, standing down to allow the Restoration of Omega, his crowning as the first Lord High President since Rassilon himself.

'No!' Savar cried. 'No!'

'We should seize this opportunity,' the President breathed. 'Not only the Effect, but Omega himself!'

The Doctor had failed. The President was about to say it, he was about to allow this expedition to proceed. The Doctor was saying something, but Savar had no time to listen.

He reached into his robe, wrapped his hand around the force knife.

'No!' the Doctor shouted. Savar knew the words were directed at him, but they served no purpose.

Savar leapt, his hand clenched over the dagger. He telepathed his President's feelings, as he had for all his victims. He felt the fear running up the spine, the coldness in the hearts as they quickened. The increased heartsrate only made his target still easier to find. The eyes he didn't have were wide with terror. But did not allow the emotions to cloud what must be done.

He brought the dagger down, plunging it through the ribcage. With a metal blade you'd strike up, to avoid a glancing blow off a rib. With a force knife there was no need for such subtlety. It passed through the bone like air.

The President fell forwards, warm blood spilling over his cream robes and the ceremonial Sash of Rassilon he wore. The Doctor was pulling Savar away, grabbing him from behind. All around, people were breaking ranks, calling for the Watch and for the physicians. The Chamber was full of clattering footsteps.

It said something about Gallifrey that the President's personal physician was at the scene almost a full minute before the Watchmen. Surgeon Grutnoll knelt at his President's side, opening up his medical bag. The President himself wore an old body, and might not have the strength to regenerate.

'Why?' the Doctor asked Savar.

Savar was grinning. 'Be calm, Doctor, just a blow to the primary heart. Nothing that an hour with a surgeon won't cure. But it'll leave something of a power vacuum. No decisions will be made, and our purposes will have been served.'

The Doctor looked up at the circle of Time Lords that was beginning to form around them. 'Neat,' he concluded curtly.

'Thank you. Show me the key to my TARDIS.'

The Doctor did so, finding it in his jacket pocket.

'Use it wisely.'

Half a dozen of the Watch had pushed their way to the front of the crowd. Now they separated the Doctor and Savar. Savar offered no resistance, indeed he was very calm as one guard strapped the restrainer on his wrists, the others frisked him for weapons. His knife was already lying on the marble floor, covered in the President's blood. This time he wasn't carrying a spare.

As Savar was led away, the Doctor knelt at the President's side. The old man looked up at him, a little disappointed. The Doctor leant over, much to the irritation of the physician working on the stab wound.

'If you have to be here, help remove this Sash,' Grutnoll harrumphed.

It was heavier than it looked, but easy enough to lift over the President's head. It was a great segmented thing, and it resembled the carapace of an armadillo, only it was made from a material that seemed to be half-gold, half-leather. The Doctor held it in his hands as he bent over the President. The blood was already beginning to dry out.

'So,' the old man whispered. 'Isn't this what you always wanted?'

The Doctor was rather taken aback. He held up the Sash. 'This?'

'*Change*,' the President explained. His voice was so weak. As Savar had said, a blow to the primary heart was not the most serious of injuries, not with all the medical and scientific techniques at the Time Lords' disposal. But the President's body was so old, so weak.

The Doctor considered his response carefully. 'No. This is a backwards step, this is looking to the past.'

'Omega was the greatest of all the Gallifreyans, the records are very clear on that.'

The Doctor had read every one of the President's papers on the subject, he'd helped Hedin with his biography and he had his own special insight into the man.

'Omega would have been a tyrant,' the Doctor declared. 'He wouldn't just be welcomed on Gallifrey, he'd be lauded, paraded, crowned President. Do you really think that people like Voran and Pendrel would want to stop a man who has crushed stars in his hand, a man who stood side by side with Rassilon as the Capitol fell?'

'Isn't that what you always say you want the Council to do? Intervene?'

He lent over the President. 'I want the Time Lords to help others to reach their potential, I want them to spread peace and knowledge. I don't want them to conquer the universe.'

'No!' the President snapped. 'There is another reason you wanted the Magistrate to stay away from the Needle. Tell me!'

'I can't.'

'I am the President of Gallifrey.'

'I'm sorry, Lord President, but I can't tell you.'

'Very well.' The President lifted his hand. 'Castellan Voran. I place you in charge of this situation.'

The Castellan licked his lips. 'Such an elevation is against all custom, Lord President.'

The Doctor smiled, sympathising. The promotion was something of a poisoned chalice in the circumstances.

'That is not so: the President has the right to name his successor. You, Castellan.'

'Gallifrey needs strong leadership at this time,' the Magistrate shouted.

'This could very well be the decision that leads to the destruction of Gall–' the Doctor stopped in mid-sentence.

'How?' the Magistrate asked.

The Doctor could see the Castellan out of the corner of his eye, talking to one of the Technicians. Somehow the Doctor doubted that he

173

had much longer to make his case. 'You have to trust me,' the Doctor said. 'I know a little about what's down there and –'

'Doctor?' the Magistrate asked.

'Can you hear me?'

Both the Doctor and the Magistrate turned to the Castellan.

'You've cut the sound link.'

'I have muted the Doctor's words, yes. Doctor, you are a dangerous influence. The President's wishes were very clear. Lord Norval is to prepare for landing on the surface of the Needle.'

The Magistrate loomed over the hologram table. Temporal Monitoring was represented on it, the tiny councillors resembling tiny dolls, or chess pieces. He could see the Doctor gesticulating, but he couldn't hear him. Behind the Doctor, a small circle of Councillors and monks were running through a rather abridged version of The Ceremony of Temporary Investiture, hurrying to ordain the Castellan.

'No,' the Magistrate said. 'Not before I hear what the Doctor has to say.'

The tiny hologram of the Doctor ran forwards, stood right in front of the Magistrate's hologram. But no words came out.

Instead: 'Lord Norval, this is the Castellan, invoking Presidential authority. Land your TARDIS, please.'

'No!' the Magistrate shouted. But he could tell from his displays that the Station's voice link had been cut, too. Gallifrey was talking directly to Norval.

'As you wish,' Norval said. He had no idea of events on Gallifrey.

'Castellan, I must be allowed to speak with Lord Norval. I have operational command here. This Station might be needed as back up.' But the Castellan was ignoring him.

'Energy burst from the surface of the Needle!' shouted one of the Technicians.

The Magistrate hurried over to the main display.

'Heading for Norval's TARDIS?' the Magistrate called.

'I'm just trying to track it. There we are.'

Norval's TARDIS began arcing towards the Needle, but the strange light was far below.

The main screen switched to an overview of the scene. Lord Norval's TARDIS was zooming in on a point on the surface of the Needle. The tiny pinprick of green light was millions of miles away, heading away from Norval.

'A ball of energy, ten feet in diameter, travelling at just under the speed of light.'

'A natural phenomenon?' Hedin asked.

The Magistrate shook his head. 'I don't think so.'

Hedin nodded. 'Analysing composition now.'

The Magistrate watched the tactical display. The ball was slow as lightning, but there was something mesmerising about it. On the other side of the Needle, Norval's TARDIS was beginning its descent.

'It's just light,' Hedin concluded. 'Possibly a signal flare of some kind. Limited sentience, perhaps. It could be a probe of some kind?'

'A weapon?' the Magistrate asked.

'Possibly.' There was no concern in the Technician's voice. Why would there be?

'Locate its point of origin,' the Magistrate suggested. Hedin nodded.

Alarms started ringing all over the console deck.

'What is it?' the Magistrate asked calmly.

'Lord Norval's TARDIS just crossed a detection beam.'

'Didn't he see it?'

'It was a passive sensor. Now we know where to look we can see that there is blanket coverage of the Needle. Someone knows that he is there.'

They heard the Castellan's voice. 'Norval, change course on a random vector.'

The TARDIS vanished momentarily.

And rematerialised right in the path of the energy ball.

'Don't worry,' the Castellan said. 'It's just light. It will pass straight through you.'

'It might temporarily blind the scanners and cause slight damage to the outer plasmic shell,' Hedin warned. 'It might be as well to drop to full defence mode.'

Norval nodded. 'Five seconds. Four, three, two, one.'

The ball of energy hit the TARDIS. It punctured the forcefield. It went straight through the secondary force field. When Norval's TARDIS automatically made an emergency jump five seconds into the future to avoid the impact, the ball of energy followed it. Finally it blew a hole in the outer plasmic shell.

The Magistrate's screen faded out.

'What's happening?' he asked.

He turned to the main viewer, which was showing an external view of Norval's TARDIS. Green energy raged through the gap in the outer shell, eating through it like acid, making the hole larger and larger.

'The dimensional barrier might be breached,' Hedin warned sharply. 'The infinite interior dimensions might start to pour out.'

But there was no need to worry about the eventuality. The green fire was destroying the interior just as effectively as the exterior.

'A self-sustaining chain reaction,' the Magistrate noted.

There was a final flash of light, and then the TARDIS had gone.

There was silence on the bridge of the Station.

There was uproar in the Temporal Monitoring Room.

'Clear the public galleries!' one of the ushers was calling.

Larna watched the Councillors, and she was as dumbstruck as they were.

The Castellan was staring down at the image. 'How is this possible?' he asked. 'How is this possible? Re-establish the voice links.'

The Doctor stared at him. 'I told you, Castellan, *anything* is possible now. Someone down there on the Needle used the Effect against us.'

'No,' said Larna.

They all turned to her.

'If they had control of the Effect, then they wouldn't need to use anything so crude. They could have just wiped Norval from the timestream.'

'We have run an analysis of the energy ball,' the Magistrate announced. 'It was a concoction of energies that seems to have been custom-made to destroy a TARDIS.'

'But it was launched *before* they detected Norval,' Larna objected.

'Only from our perspective,' the Doctor noted under his breath.

'In any event, there is no such weapon,' the Castellan snapped.

'Not yet, Castellan,' the Doctor said. 'But there will be plenty of time to develop such technology. Fellow Councillors, it will only be a matter of time before whoever fired that weapon discovers the existence of the Station.'

The Magistrate rubbed his beard. 'The Doctor is right. We can't defend against it... if they have control of the Effect, then not even Gallifrey is safe.'

'They don't have control of the Effect,' Larna repeated. 'If they had, they wouldn't need to use anything else.'

'That's only a guess,' the Doctor warned her.

'I have located the source of the energy ball,' Hedin announced. 'A structure on the surface of the Needle. We are not close enough to run a full scan, but there are energy sources there, and traces of sentience.'

The Castellan was nodding, almost distractedly. 'We must destroy it.'

'What?' the Doctor shouted. 'Destroy them before we have even found out who they are?'

'They have killed a Time Lord,' Hedin noted. 'There is no greater crime. They fired without provocation.'

'How would we destroy them?' another Councillor asked.

'A directed blackstar,' the Magistrate suggested.

'The blackstar was devised to crack open Dyson Spheres. Using it on the Needle will annihilate an area a billion kilometres in diameter.'

'A tiny speck on the surface.'

'An area hundreds of times larger than the surface of Gallifrey,' the Doctor objected, 'an area large enough to support trillions of lifeforms.'

Voran held up his hand. 'I am not suggesting that we use a blackstar. There are *other* options.'

The Magistrate and the Doctor both turned to face him.

'You can't mean...'

'In the face of ultimate force, we would be justified in using the ultimate countermeasure. Show me it.'

The image in the Infinity Chamber shifted. Now it showed an apparently empty starfield. The picture panned slowly across, until a barren ice planet filled the screen. There didn't seem to be anything else there, until a patch of blackness appeared in the bottom half of the screen. Looking closely, it was possible to discern a disc, the light sliding from the omniscate on its top surface. It passed behind the ice planet, and it became apparent that the disc was larger than the world it was passing.

'Prime it,' Voran ordered. 'We must be ready to use it.'

'Once again the glorious past raises its head,' the Doctor said archly. 'Even during the Vampire Wars we never had to resort to the –'

'They fired first,' Voran snapped, cutting him off. 'What is done is done.'

'Not any more,' the Doctor whispered.

But the Councillors were already moving into new positions, like dancers preparing for a new act. The Doctor was left alone with Larna in the middle of the floor.

He grabbed her. 'How do we stop them?' he asked.

She bit her lip. 'They'll need the Great Key, they'll need to reconfigure the phased energy conduits, they'll need to establish a spacetime vector –'

'That isn't what I asked,' the Doctor snapped.

'I'm thinking,' she shouted back. 'Power room. They'll need to channel the energy beam through the timegate.'

'Shut down the gate and they can't fire?'

'Right!'

'Come on!'

No one noticed them leave.

They hurried out of Temporal Monitoring and past a couple of gossiping Time Lord historians in the antechamber. They broke into a run, cutting across a number of quadrangles and atriums to reach the main staircase. The Doctor led the way, pounding down the steps three at a time. Larna lagged a little, until the Doctor grabbed her hand and pulled her along behind him.

They swept down the main staircase, passing small groups of Watchmen and Technicians. No one challenged them as they carried on down the staircase to the power room level. They were alone down here, alone apart from the bodies of the two men that Savar had killed.

The power room door was still open, the floor was still littered with the debris from his swordfight with Savar. That had only been a quarter of an hour ago, the Doctor realised, and his body hadn't quite finished with the adrenaline that it had produced back then. The column of time energy coruscated in the middle of the room, pouring like a waterfall down a well.

Larna had already found her place at the control panel. The Doctor joined her. He needed both hands, so he pulled the Sash over his head. They didn't need to speak. Remove the safety interlocks. Done. Activate an eyeboard. Done. Access the power control systems. Done.

The Doctor stared into the retinal scanner. This wasn't as straightforward as altering a couple of settings, as it had been when he'd used the eyeboard on the Castellan's desk. This required total immersion. The soft blue glow filled his vision, like the sky. The sense of movement and freedom in three dimensions felt like flying.

One of the Castellan's aides hurried into Main Temporal Monitoring with the case that contained the Great Key. The Castellan was at one of the consoles, surrounded by Technicians who were prompting him. He, and he alone, as Acting-President, had the authority to do this.

He placed the case reverentially on the console, opened it up. Just looking at the Key, it was difficult to imagine that this was one of the most powerful artefacts in the universe. In times of great emergency, it allowed the President of the Time Lords to unlock some of the Time Lords' self-imposed restrictions, it allowed them to break their own rules. The Gallifreyans had weapons and techniques at their disposal that could never be used lightly.

The Castellan took the Key from the case, slotted it neatly into its allotted place on his console. He turned the Key, then placed his eye over the eyeboard.

'They've got the Great Key!' the Doctor called.

The datascape around him had just changed beyond all recognition. It had been like a clear sky before, and now there was a vast storm cloud there, and he was floating towards it.

'They will try to configure a conduit,' Larna told him. Although she was standing a foot away from him, her voice seemed to come from a million miles away, or from a dream.

The sky was churning.

The Doctor was still squinting into the scanner. 'I'll try to stop it.'

'There's someone trying to stop me,' the Castellan whispered.

The Technicians merely murmured.

'Well,' he demanded, 'what do I do?'

'You are the only man with the necessary authority,' Pendrel assured him.

The Castellan began altering the settings, saw the conduit forming. But there was still someone in here trying to block his every move. Sad blue eyes.

'It's the Doctor!' the Castellan yelled. He checked the readout. 'He has to be in the Power Room. Send the Watch down there.

* * *

'He's seen me,' the Doctor sighed.

'Don't worry, you're slowing him down.'

'He's got the Key, it's too powerful.' The sky was black now, the tip of a tornado swirling down and down. The Doctor knew not to get too close. But how could he stop it forming?

The Castellan's eyes appeared in the air in front of him. 'Give up, Doctor, there is no way that you can win.'

The Doctor stared back. 'I have to. You'll destroy us all.'

'I am the President of the Time Lords, with the full backing of the Council, and the Great Key itself at my disposal.'

The conduit was almost fully formed.

The Castellan kept staring at it, and the harder he stared, the more solid the conduit became.

The conduit snapped into place. Power began flowing down it. The hum of the machinery in the power room changed pitch.

'He's done it,' Larna cried. 'All he needs to do now is calculate the spacetime vector.'

'Which console is he using?' the Doctor asked, without taking his eyes away from the scanner.

'I –'

'Hurry!' he ordered.

He could hear her moving around. 'Console Five, Main Temporal Monitoring.'

The Doctor gave the eyeboard a single command.

The spacetime vector equations began resolving themselves. The Castellan watched the datascape as mathematics of crystalline clarity began to appear.

The Castellan smiled. The Doctor had a prowess at this sort of thing, but he had been beaten. He could see the panic in the Doctor's eyes.

The Castellan's console beeped.

'What is that noise?' he asked.

The Technicians weren't sure.

'Tell me!' he commanded, unable to move his head without breaking the connection.

'It's... look away! Look away!'

The Castellan scowled. 'The equation is nearly ready.'

He looked into the datascape, saw the new power configurations in place, saw the co-ordinates fading up as the answer appeared.

There was a flash of light so powerful it felt almost solid. It shot up through the eyeboard, shutting down every safety feature as it came. The light pierced the Castellan's eyes, lunged down his optic nerve.

The Castellan lurched back from the console, clutching his face, crying out load. The Technicians moved to catch him. He couldn't see. He swore he could smell burning.

'Finish it!' he ordered, rubbing his eyes. 'Finish it! Someone take over!'

'Only you have the authority,' one of the Technicians reminded him.

The pitch of the humming began winding down, and almost immediately the column began to fade a little. Like iron in a fire it would be a little while before it had cooled down completely.

'You did it,' Larna exclaimed. 'The timegate is shutting down. They won't be able to launch the blackstars or anything else, not now.'

The Doctor leant back, catching his breath.

'How?' she asked.

'He blinked first.'

As the eyeboard retracted, the Doctor stood and took a step towards the time column. Larna had also worked her way around her console, now she was between him and the column of energy. Together they watched as the power began to bleed away.

Larna clasped the Doctor's hand. 'They'll have to work all day to get that running again.'

'Well done,' he said.

The door chimed. Someone was trying to get in.

'I... need to get past you,' he said.

'Wait,' Larna said, moving to block him.

The Doctor hesitated.

'I know what you're planning,' she said.

The Doctor bit his lip.

There was a banging at the door. 'Doctor! This is Constable Sapro! Open this door!'

She glanced over her shoulder. 'You are planning to be the last thing through the timegate before it shuts down. You're going to the far future, because you want control of the Effect for yourself. You want to change the past.'

The Doctor didn't reply.

'Take me with you.'

'No.'

'Why not?'

'Well, look at you... you're not even wearing shoes.'

She glowered at him.

'It will be too dangerous.' He paused. 'You won't be in any trouble here. You can say that I forced you to help me. Larna, I haven't much time.' He could hear the power levels dropping. Behind Larna, the energy column was fading a little. It was only a matter of moments before the timegate powered down.

She moved closer to him, filling his field of vision. Behind her the column was diminishing more and more as every second went past. 'Doctor, I'm not stupid,'

He took her hand, held it to his hearts. 'I never said that you were, I –'

'I know what you want to do. You know I can't let you.'

The Doctor caught his breath. 'You can't stop me,' he said.

'I only have to delay you,' she replied. 'Just a few more seconds. You'll thank me, Doctor.'

'I'm sorry,' he said.

'I –' Larna glanced down, saw the blood on her waistcoat. In the Doctor's hand was the force knife, hilt deep just below her left breast.

'A single blow to the primary heart,' the Doctor explained, lowering her tenderly to the floor. 'The guards will be through that door in a moment, it'll only take a surgeon an hour to fix you up. But you'll have to take it easy for that time. And that's only as long as I need. It's for the best: they'll think that I was forcing you to help me. I'm so very sorry.'

Right on schedule, the iron door began to reverberate as staser blast after staser blast began slamming home.

Larna shook a little, the shock was beginning to hit her nervous system. 'Very neat,' she said. 'No loose ends, no complications. You always win, don't you, Doctor?'

'No, no. Not always. If there was another way...'

Larna smiled. Then she twisted her torso around to the left. The force blade sliced through her spinal column, found her right heart. She pulled herself to her full height, despite the damage to her spine, bringing the blade up through the heart. The action was enough to kill her.

Horrified, the Doctor tried to establish a telepathic link. He needed to trigger her regeneration. But all he found was Larna blocking his way again.

'I want to save you,' he said, bending over her.

'Well,' she said, 'you can't have everything that you want.'

She kissed him, then fell back. The Doctor tried to steady her, and ended up lowering her to the floor.

He stood over Larna's body, watched the dark stain spread over her crisp white shirt. Her face and fingers were already becoming grey. But her hair was just as vivid a blonde as before, her eyes were just as blue. The Doctor didn't know what to do. He was clutching the knife that had killed her. He didn't know what to do.

The door was buckling. It would only be another few moments before the guards were through. There was blood all over his hands, all over the Sash.

Larna was right, he'd already made his choice.

He stood, the knife still in his hand.

He leapt forwards, into the energy column.

Part Three
The Opposite of Matter

Chapter Nine
Thresholds

The Doctor fell.

It was like plunging into a lake, that same sense of not knowing which way up he was, and having something alarming wash over his skin, filling his ears and forcing him to screw his eyes shut for a moment. There was the same sense of inexorable movement as he was dragged down. He plunged further and further, and the water was much colder and deeper than he was expecting. His mind was giving him advice that would have saved his life if he had been underwater. Every instinct screamed at him to hurl himself upwards, break the surface, fill his lungs, pull off the Sash, take off his coat. Their weight is making you sink. But it was only the arcane power of the Sash that was preventing him from being torn apart by the time energies. It was his lifejacket, not a millstone.

By the time the Doctor had opened his eyes, he realised, he had already travelled beyond any future known to the Time Lords. All around him, the swirling walls of the Time Vortex were an almost comforting pattern, even if they did seem to form the sides of a bottomless well. But waves of colour and sound were streaking up past him, with no pattern to them, at least no pattern he could decipher.

He let himself fall further. Not that he could stop it now, of course. He started to see things. Were they there, or were they simply tricks of the mind? One of the most fundamental philosophical questions, one that not even the Matrix had solved: what is reality?

Memories of years long gone, thoughts of family and childhood. He remembered his father and mother. He remembered a trek in the mountains, and what he found while sheltering from a storm in an ancient cave.

He saw himself falling. There was someone with him... a woman... professional-looking with a generous mouth, wearing a tailored suit and baggy coat... heavily pregnant, with long legs, high cheekbones and ruffled black hair... a teenager, blonde streaks in her ginger hair and Rupert Bear trousers... a wiry young woman with blue eyes and fair hair...

He saw Larna, lying drowned in a black tarn, her skin like moonlight on the water. No, not drowned. There was a knife wound, washed clean. She looked so peaceful floating there, and so young. Her slender body was almost androgynous, and it seemed symbolic, a representation of everything that he had lost over the years.

He let go of the knife, which crumbled to dust.

Larna faded away, and time continued to wash over him.

He turned his mind outwards, tried to imagine the universe beyond that of his own head. All the stars of his own time would have reddened and died, new stars would have sprung up in their place. But just as city streets retain their shape over the centuries, the galaxies would survive in something like their current form. There would be change, of course. Giant galaxies, such as Gallifrey's, would exert gravitational pull over their satellite galaxies, and draw them inexorably in. It was a process so slow that the civilisations rising and falling there wouldn't even notice it happen. In the Doctor's timezone, the Sagittarius Galaxy had already been absorbed. Perhaps – he was in the realms of speculation now – the fate of the giant galaxies was to be absorbed into ever larger groups of stars, the galactic groups merging into vast clusters, the clusters into ultraclusters, the ultraclusters into just one vast monogalaxy.

There was a definite moment when the Doctor realised that he had changed direction. The universe had stopped expanding, the energy of the Big Bang finally spent. The cosmos drifted onwards for a little while, then began collapsing, much faster than it had expanded. It began to feel a little cold, too, like being caught in an autumn breeze, but that sensation must have been purely psychological.

There were red eyes, watching him.

And then he was standing on the deck of the Station, catching his breath.

The power room was an almost identical copy of the one he had left. But it felt emptier. There was something here, all around him. Evil. What else could have compelled him to kill Larna? For the first time, he allowed himself to think about her death, to examine his emotions and state of mind. It shocked the Doctor to realise that he felt nothing other than numb. Larna was part of the past, and the past didn't change. She was gone, and no amount of introspection would change that.

He knew then that nothing from without had influenced him, that he'd taken the knife himself and made the choice all for himself.

The door slid open, revealing the Magistrate and a couple of Watchmen. The Doctor dusted down his jacket, straightened his scarf.

'Hello there,' he said, trying to sound cheerful.

The Magistrate grabbed him by the lapels and slammed him against the nearest bulkhead, fixing him with dark eyes.

'You've killed us,' he shouted, making the Doctor wince. 'You've cut off our power, left us stranded here. It will be hours before Gallifrey can re-establish the link.'

'At least a day,' the Doctor said. The Magistrate slammed him against the wall again and then let go of him, let him slide down the wall, turned his back on him.

'If I hadn't done it, you'd be dead,' the Doctor called after him.

'Without power we *are* dead.'

'You've still got battery power.'

'For an hour, perhaps an hour and a half.'

The Doctor beamed. 'Then why not use what power you have to capture one of the local black holes and use that as an energy source? It's not as though there's a shortage of them around here.'

The Magistrate stopped in his tracks, hesitating. Finally he nodded to one of the Watchmen, who hurried off to the control deck to organise it.

'There you go. What would you do without me?'

'Spare me, Doctor, I am not in the mood. A Time Lord has died, we face an enemy of unknown origins and powers, one capable of destroying a TARDIS. By killing our power and cutting off our links with the Council and the Matrix, you are hardly helping matters.'

'The High Council were planning to attack the Needle. If they had done that, there's no telling what would have happened. We *might* have wiped out whatever is down there, but there was no guarantee of it. Whatever's down there could be in control of the Effect, and if that's the case then I have just prevented a war that Gallifrey couldn't possibly have won.'

'If they are in control of the Effect then they may destroy us anyway.'

'I don't think they are. They clearly have access to technology in advance of our own, though, and this Station has to be considered at risk.'

There was a mechanical *thunk* all around them, and the lights flickered, before returning to their previous brilliance. 'My crew have harnessed a local black hole,' the Magistrate informed him.

'Good. Good.' The Doctor looked around, unsure what to do. 'I have to get across there. Down to the Needle.'

'Lord Norval was killed trying to land,' the Magistrate reminded him.

'Yes...' the Doctor said, his voice trailing away.

'And you won't be?'

'No...'

'They have detector beams, cross them and they launch a retroactive attack – hit you *before* they detect you. It's impossible to get down there.'

'No. No.' The Doctor paced the room, tapping his lip. 'No.'

'If I might make an observation: saying that doesn't make it true.'

'This close to the end, the parallel universes are beginning to converge, aren't they?'

'Those that survived this long.'

'Right. Now... in our time, the parallel universes keep a nice safe distance from each other. We can use a TARDIS to travel sideways in time, but it's hazardous.' The Doctor had begun to make complicated gestures in the air to explain his theory. 'What if I were to transmat myself *around* the defences, via an alternate universe, one where the defences don't exist? The beauty is that I could convert myself into a state of quantum uncertainty, and then I'd *have* to arrive, because the only way the events could be resolved would be for someone down there to observe me.'

'Or if you tripped the defence grid.'

'I'd be down there already. They'd have to change the past to erase me, but by doing that they'd set up a paradox, one part of which would involve me down there. So I'd get through in some form.'

The Magistrate was shaking his head.

'Well, have you got a better idea?' the Doctor asked.

'That's hardly an idea at all. It's ludicrous.'

'It's quantum mechanics: of course it's ludicrous. I'll get a transmat bracelet. Next thing you know, I'll be down there.'

A lion-face stared at the Doctor, its head cocked. It had a thick red mane, its face was lighter. Its eyes were coal-black, but there was a glimmer of intelligence there. There was a moment of contact, of mutual respect.

The creature was on top of the Doctor, pinning him down. It had bowled him over the moment he had arrived, even before he had found his footing on the broken, uneven ground. The Doctor was on his back now, able to look right into the eyes of the creature. He felt hot breath on his neck and melting snow creeping into his coat. He forced his head around... and then whatever it was on top of him roared and leapt away, intent on something else. The Doctor pulled himself up, congratulating himself on reaching the surface of the Needle. Then he was slammed back to the ground by another of the things.

The Doctor could hear another of the beasts roaring, its voice echoing around this arena. This one was pinning him down with powerful forearms... it wasn't a quadruped, then. The Doctor twisted to try to get a better look, but the creature reared over him, and snarled. He thought better of moving. He didn't recognise the creature, but there had been plenty of time for entirely new species to develop. This one wasn't as novel as it might be. It had the head of a lion, but the body looked like a cross between a kangaroo and a gorilla. It might have been a hybrid, the Doctor supposed. It let out a roar.

Its ears pricked and it looked away from him for the first time. The pressure on his chest eased. Then the creature had gone. The Doctor scrambled to his feet. The other creature, the first to attack him, had also vanished.

'Where did they...?'

It was dark here, and cold, but nothing like as dark and cold as the rest of the dead universe. He buttoned up his coat and tucked his scarf in. The bitterest winter wind Outside on Gallifrey was warmer than this. At first he thought that he had materialised in a courtyard or a cloister, but then he saw the splintered beams around the edges of the ceiling and seen that this room had – until recently – been covered by a roof. He was walking on smashed slates. It had been a large room, a ballroom perhaps, or a meeting hall. The walls were sheer redbrick cliffs three or four storeys high. The sky here was featureless, black objects on a black background.

The light came from dull lamps fixed at intervals around the walls. Electric lamps by the look of them, but barely 20-watt bulbs. There was *some* warmth here, but it was very bitter. There were at least a dozen exits along each wall. Which didn't really help.

There were three men standing around him.

Two behind him, one in front. They wore outfits that resembled the *shinobi shozoku* of the Japanese ninja: loose – even baggy – sleeves and leggings, a tighter fit around the shoulders, waist and cuffs, a wide belt and flat-soled boots. There had been patterns embroidered into the material once, but now they had washed out into a grey sameness. They all wore glistening cloaks made from a rubbery-looking substance.

All three were male, all three were in late middle age. Broad-chested types. Old soldiers. They had guns and a few other pieces of military equipment slotted and clipped into their belts. The Doctor tensed.

'Greetings, Doctor,' the one in front of him said. The accent was unfamiliar, but full of sadness.

'You know my name?' he asked.

The one at his right moved towards him. He was taller than the first. 'We must leave here. The Maltraffi must have roared, as the rest of the pride are coming, they will arrive in a few minutes.'

'Those lion creatures are called Maltraffi?'

'They have learnt not to fight us,' the third one, whose skin was a little darker, stated, 'as we will always drive them away.'

The Doctor wondered if there was a message there for him. 'Yes, I was just wondering why they ran off so fast. I mean, they are so much larger and more agile than a man, they had all those claws and teeth.'

'Yes,' the tallest one replied.

'And you are the people that killed Norval?'

'Did we?' asked the dark-skinned one.

'You destroyed his TARDIS as it came into land.'

'All who try to come here must die,' said the first one, and the way he said it, you'd think that he was making a conciliatory gesture.

The Doctor hesitated, taking time to choose his next words carefully.

'That does not include you,' the first one said quickly.

'Of course not,' the tallest reaffirmed.

The Doctor smiled helplessly.

'Gordel,' said the dark-skinned man,

'Willhuff,' said the tallest man.

'Pallant,' said the first man.

'Er...'

'You were about to ask our names.' A statement, not a question.

'Yes,' the Doctor admitted.

'We do not have much use for names around here,' Willhuff said sonorously.

They had moved into a murky corridor, glowing with the same faint light. The Doctor affected a casual glance as they passed one fitting.

'These are Thompson Lamps,' Pallant informed him. 'They are everlasting.'

'Old-fashioned tungsten-filament bulbs?' the Doctor asked. 'Surely in a hundred trillion trillion trillion trillion years someone could have come up with something better?'

It occurred to the Doctor that they might be mind readers. They had that annoying habit that psychics had of answering questions before he'd asked them. He framed the thought, 'Are you a psychic?' and aimed it at the first one.

Pallant didn't even glance his way.

Perhaps he was a psychic liar. He framed a slanderous, inflammatory and anatomically precise insult and directed it at Willhuff. He didn't even blink.

'We are here now. This is Helios.'

'Er... yes, good,' said the Doctor, a little embarrassed.

There was one point of illumination: a small bonfire in the middle of the room. There was a column of smoke, with ashes lazily ascending it. The orange flames were comforting, hypnotic. There was another man here, an older man with a large wooden staff, which he used to poke the fire. He was wearing the same loose-fitting garments as his colleagues, and had a neat white beard.

It was tempting to let his eye be drawn towards this old man and the fire, but instead the Doctor took the time to look around the room. It was a rather forbidding place, and the gloom made it difficult to come to any firm conclusions. This had been a colossal dome, indeed it retained most of the structure. The uppermost part of the roof had cracked and fallen away, like a boiled egg tapped with a spoon. Wear and tear had done the trick, though, not enemy action or a natural disaster. The room was full of shelving and racking, all stacked to the point of overloading. And all around were statues and fragments of statues: men in full armour, women draped in marble cloth, horses and lions and eagles and bears.

'This room contains artefacts from the planet Earth,' the old man said.

'It's a library?' the Doctor said. 'Or a museum. An art gallery! Although not a very well-maintained one.' He paused, looking over to his hosts. 'If you don't mind me mentioning it.'

They didn't seem to. 'You will join us for mushrooms,' Pallant said.

'Our priorities are different here,' Willhuff told him, almost apologetically.

The other men were taking their places around the fire. Helios had been frying mushrooms on a metal tray. The Doctor sat, realising at the last moment that his seat was just a pile of great big leather-bound books. The spines had come away, the leather was faded. There were other, smaller, books lying around. He picked one up, opening it to the title page.

'*O Time Your Pyramids*,' he read. 'The lost novel of Borges. I thought I had the only copies of this.' He bent over, picked up three more volumes. '*Alice's Adventures in Wonderland*, *The Time Ships*, *Slaughterhouse-Five*.'

The others barely acknowledged him, content to nibble at their mushrooms.

The Doctor looked around, saw their shadows flickering over the walls of the dome, and all the artefacts here. 'This is the last of Earth? Preserved here?'

'There seems to have been flooding,' Pallant admitted, a little embarrassed. 'Many of the books were damaged beyond repair.' He held up one. The complete works of Milton – the title was picked out in gold leaf on the cover. The pages, however, were crinkled and mashed into each other.

'They are in a terrible state,' the Doctor tutted.

Pallant tossed the book onto the fire despite the Doctor's gasped attempt to catch it. The Doctor looked down, watched the fire consume each page in turn, watched the ashes float up and out towards the ceiling. *Comus*, *Paradise Lost*, *Samson Agonistes*, *Areopagitica*, all Milton's Latin poems and State letters. All gone because the Doctor anticipated that Pallant was going to throw the book to his left, and he actually threw it to his right.

'We have no other use for them,' Willhuff said, almost apologetically. 'There is so little time remaining, now. Little time for reading.'

Gordel passed over a small bowl of the mushrooms to the Doctor. 'You will enjoy these, although you will think that they are a little too sweet at first.'

The fire had been started with broken-up furniture, fuelled with some of the largest books. The Doctor bit into a mushroom, and wondered what treasures had already been lost to the flames. At the same time, there were more pressing concerns. He had to see a man about a God.

'Yes, these are sweet, you're right. The taste grows on you, though.' He held up one of the books. 'Do you read these before you burn them?'

'We are the last ones. Even the immortals are long gone now,' Pallant said, not answering the question. He'd sparked off a whole new set for the Doctor, though.

'You are the only life remaining in the entire universe?'

'Perhaps, perhaps not. A few pride of Maltraffi survive, the mushrooms survive. There may still be other forms of sentience which we will never make contact with. Beings of dark matter, abstractions, that sort of thing. There may even be other people here, but we will never meet them, and that is all that matters.'

'It is impossible to die here, at least until the final end,' Willhuff added.

'Yes, of course... I was just going to ask what the Maltraffi eat, but this is a TARDIS, everything here exists in a state of temporal grace. That's why the collection here survived the proton decay that's affected the rest of the universe.'

The Doctor picked up another, newer book. This one was handwritten. A diary. He slipped it into his pocket to read later. Not very good manners, but his hosts weren't being very forthcoming, and time was drawing short. The Doctor looked up at the sliver of the night's sky visible through the gap in the roof. Total blackness, all its possibilities and potential mined and exhausted.

Helios looked up from his bowl of mushrooms for the first time. 'The Librarinth is a vast place, containing the greatest artefacts from many thousands of civilisations. We thought we would bring you here because Earth is a world for which you have great affection.'

Willhuff was reaching down and searching through a cloth sack at his side. The contents of the bag rattled, clinked, rustled. What was in there, the Doctor wondered, plunder from the rooms they'd visited? If they really were the last people left alive then it was hardly stealing, was it?

'Isn't there a room like this for Gallifrey?' the Doctor joked.

'We found this.' He handed the Doctor a small pocket book.

He examined it before opening it. It was bound in reptile hide of some kind, with an omniscate embossed on the cover. He flicked it open.

'A book of prophecy,' Willhuff explained. 'The Other Scrolls.'

'Surely all the prophecies are used up by now?' the Doctor said lightly. 'This is as much use as last year's calendar.'

'It talks about the future of Gallifrey and your people,' Pallant told him.

'Well,' the Doctor said, gently closing the book. 'I don't think I should look at it.'

The men were silent.

'You're showing me this for a reason?' The Doctor opened it up again, flicked to a page near the end, some superstition preventing him from reading the very last page. He glanced down and read a sentence at random.

He slammed the book shut, suddenly pale.

'By your logic, it has already happened,' Gordel assured him.

'It won't happen that way.' The Doctor threw the book into the fire, where it hissed and crackled. 'It may be in your past, but it is still in my future. I have free will, I can prevent it from happening that way.'

'I am sure that you won't.'

'You certainly *seem* very sure.'

'There are few records about the library itself,' Willhuff said, changing tack again.

'No records? You mean of where everyone went? Is there no indication of when this place was abandoned?' The Doctor paused. 'Who built this place? Your ancestors?'

'God,' said Willhuff reverently.

The Doctor almost choked on his mushrooms.

Pallant was holding out his hands. 'There are the various monuments, we mustn't forget them. The House of God has travelled through other universes in its time. Many races have come to the Librarinth over the ages. It has been our sacred duty to prevent the unworthy from finding Him. All the evidence suggests that there have been many wars fought, that many millions have died. Now, as the universes finally converge into a single, final, end, we know that we have fulfilled our vows.'

'Amen,' said Gordel.

The Doctor had seen this sort of thing on a number of worlds, places that suffered some terrible catastrophe: meteor strikes, atomic war… anything that could make a civilisation collapse, leave a tiny population eking out a living in the ruins, unable to comprehend their surroundings or their ancestors.

'All praise to the Lord,' Willhuff said.

Helios gestured around. 'The legends tell us that God is here, behind one of these doors. Of course we don't know which one.'

'I imagine that if God lived anywhere, then it would probably be somewhere like this,' the Doctor conceded thoughtfully, munching a mushroom. This sort of society often incorporated the remnants of their technology and 'race memories' of their past into elaborate religions and legends.

'Yes, the graveyards on the southern side of the building,' Pallant whispered. 'I remember going to them once. There are clues on the tombstones.'

'We mustn't forget the time you found my grave,' Helios said matter-of-factly.

'How is that possible?' the Doctor asked.

'Who is to say? Every morning we wake and find ourselves here, we remember where to find the mushrooms, which room we are in, where the Maltraffi lie in wait for us. What other way is there?'

'You have an admirable philosophy. Discover each day anew.'

Pallant looked at the Doctor, smiling. 'We are Gallifreyan/Human hybrids, the Children of Kasterborous. Before the Curse, we pursued interventionist policies designed to promote harmony in the known galaxies, and ushered a new age of universal peace. We failed in our mission: this is our punishment.'

The Doctor's eyes widened.

'That is Willhuff's theory,' Helios added. 'I think I like it best, even though it probably isn't true. It relies on apocryphal sources and a great deal of speculation on his part. Gordel's theory is equally outlandish. I incline to the view that we are from the Accidentally Left Behind When Everyone Else Transcended This Reality Interest Group. It would certainly explain our obsession with finding God.'

'I think that Helios is Merlin,' said Willhuff.

Gordel looked wearily at the others. 'We are clearly the super-evolved survivors of the Thal race, fleeing the penultimate destruction of Skaro that sparked off the Final Dalek War.'

'You don't have the slightest idea who you are or where you came from, do you?' the Doctor asked, exasperated.

'Where is my diary?' said Pallant suddenly.

'Your diary will turn up shortly,' Gordel said, looking pointedly at the Doctor.

Willhuff and Gordel had begun to write in notebooks, ones almost identical to the one the Doctor had found.

The Doctor shrugged, feigning ignorance. 'Would anyone mind if I stretched my legs? I just want to look around this room. Who knows, Pallant's diary might be over there. Anyone else coming?' None of them answered. 'You've probably seen it already,' the Doctor concluded, getting up.

The four men sat around their fire, Helios and Pallant finishing off the mushrooms, the other two writing their diaries. The Doctor stepped away, carefully over the broken ground, and found a spot between two shelves, just under one of the electric lamps.

When he was sure no one was able to see him, the Doctor tugged Pallant's diary from his pocket. He flicked through, starting about three-quarters of the way in. It was mainly maps, a rather appealing symbol of a Maltraffi's face presumably marking out the territories of the various prides. They did read the books, or at least Pallant did. The pages were dotted with quotes, and some even had glued-in pages ripped from various volumes. There was one page taken from a dictionary of architectural terms, showing various forms of door, a copy of the periodic table, a couple of pictures of women. Just reading a few pages, the Doctor discovered information about where to find water and mushrooms, a very specific list of things it would be inadvisable to try, and an almost childish title page: 'This book belongs to Pallant'.

The first section was a straightforward autobiography. Too straightforward. Why did Pallant have to give his mother's name, the names of his brothers and sisters? The Doctor couldn't think of a reason why Pallant would need to make a note of such banalities. Any other generation might have written for posterity, but there wasn't a posterity any more, there was only fifteen years of future left. Who was he writing this for?

Were they all amnesiacs?

That could be it... 'Every morning we wake up and find ourselves here', that's what Pallant had said. So he'd check in his diary, and find out who he was. If they all had problems with their memories that might explain their rather odd behaviour and conversation techniques.

It would explain why they were trying to piece together their pasts from the scraps of knowledge they uncovered while looking for fuel. Perhaps the Effect was affecting them in some way. Writing a diary like this would be a very good way to cope with time distortion and reality shifts.

No. There was something wrong with the theory. These diary entries were meticulous, almost obsessive, in their details. Here: the account of his arrival. Times, descriptions of the Maltraffi, exactly which books he had picked up. Exact word for word quotes, and how Pallant felt. The person that had written this hadn't got anything wrong with his memory.

The Doctor paused and re-read the last paragraph on the current page. It described how Pallant had lost the diary, how the Doctor had enjoyed the mushrooms and how he'd gone off to be by himself.

The Doctor stared back over towards the fire, where the four men were still about their tasks. When had Pallant had time to write this?

He wet his finger and turned the page.

The Time Lords attacked the Librarinth without warning, defeating us. There was nothing we could do that could be done, our every move was anticipated and counter-anticipated. Two of their kind moved through our ranks as if we were not there.

He turned the page.

Helios was gone, Willhuff was seriously wounded, though he was restored by the golden light. The Magistrate and his fleet were gone, as was our god. What good had come of this day?

Now that was rather odd.

A diary from the future? But no... the Doctor instinctively knew that these people weren't time travellers. They... he fished around for the answer. Had someone already written the script, and they were just players?

The Doctor gave up and checked today's diary entry.

'Of course!' he whispered.

'Of course!' he exclaimed. 'You remember the future. Only the future, not the past. How odd. Oh, I found your diary by the way.' He threw it at Pallant, bowling a real googly, but Pallant knew where the book would end up, and he caught it easily. The Doctor grimaced. The following conversation might well be a little awkward.

'It is a curse,' Willhuff said glumly.

'I don't know. It's useful, really. It saved me a lot of time when I was trying to work out what was going on: I just flicked to the next page and saw the answer. You get to win the lottery every week and back every winning horse, it's great if you're playing cards, all your guesses are correct, you only need buy insurance in years when you know you'll need it, no nasty shocks around the next corner or an unexpected bill, you get to avoid all the traffic jams… well, here you get to avoid the Maltraffic jams, you'll know straight away whether you'll hit it off with a new friend.' The Doctor hesitated. 'But you'll know how every love affair ends before it even starts and the punchline to every joke you hear, you'll know what you're getting for your birthday, you've heard every song you'll ever hear already, you remember growing old but not your childhood friends, you couldn't read an Agatha Christie novel because you'll know how and why the butler did it, there are no pleasant surprises. And when you look at someone you'll know how they die.'

'The past is a mystery to us, as the future is to you.'

'But the past has happened, hasn't it, that's the difference.'

'It must appear odd from your perspective, but your predicament is more odd. At least we have a record of the past. You hurtle blindly into the future.'

'And I wouldn't have it any other way. So you cope by writing your diary… but you do it the night before. "Tuesday: Tomorrow I'm off to the zoo, and I'm writing this because by the time I get back I'll have forgotten I've been."'

'Our memories are like yours, they merely face in the opposite direction. We are not infallible… something might happen tomorrow that slips our mind, but we all have vivid memories of events a decade from now.'

'There's the slight difference that if you lose your keys, all you'd have to do is remember where you're going to find them and go there first… but I suppose you'd say the same about me, that all I'd have do is remember where I left them. It's still a logical absurdity. What if you told me that…'

'The future has happened. We'd tell you the correct answer: thirty-five.'

'If you'd let me finish. What if I were to ask you to tell which number I was thinking of? You've just said what it would be. Fine. In that case I say something different. I'd say... thirty-five.'

The Doctor hesitated. He'd not said 'thirty-five', he'd said a different word, and then before that, they'd said it, so he'd said a different number, so they'd said it. It was an endless sequence, like trying to name the biggest number, or working out whether the chicken came before the egg. He could understand what was happening, but the answer remained just one step out of reach. It was a simple question with an infinite answer.

'The past is as malleable as the future. We see the future, we do not affect it. It might seem paradoxical to you, but as a time traveller you must understand something of the complex nature of the universe. There have been occasions on your travels when you have seen the past unfurling around you, just as you remember reading would happen. Time is relative.'

'The observed past does not change,' the Doctor objected. 'That is one of the fundamentals of time theory.'

'You have free will,' Willhuff assured him, 'in the past, the present and the future. Nothing is fixed, nothing that can be remembered can't be forgotten.'

'But how can you say that I've got free will when you know what my actions will be?'

'We will stop you.'

'Doing what? Ah, but of course. You know why I am here. You know that I'm looking for the doors, and you'll try to stop me.'

'You will fail. From our perspective you already have.'

'You've read a few pages ahead, is that it? Life's just a book that you can flick through. Well, I may rewrite the history books yet, you know.'

'We have our sacred duty. This is a place of great power, and there are those in the universes that would have that power for themselves.'

'So you kill anyone that comes here, like poor Norval. And you knew where his TARDIS would end up when it made that random jump. You fired your weapon even before your target arrived. No wonder the Maltraffi steer clear of you.' He sat looking at their faces, watching them in the firelight.

Willhuff pointed to the back of the room. 'You spend the whole night in that corner, in a self-induced coma.'

'We bring you closer to the fire in the morning,' Pallant said.

'Then, just as you are regaining consciousness, your colleagues come down and rescue you.'

Helios smiled. 'Wander off if you want, we already know that you don't reach the Door, and exactly how you spend the night.'

'You'll not try to stop me?' The Doctor was already pacing away from them, his mind juggling the various possibilities. Lying in that corner asleep? That didn't sound like him at all. It had always been the same, since his very earliest days: if someone told him to do something, he would do the exact opposite. Keep Off the Grass; You Mustn't Go Down There; Please Don't Violate the Laws of Physics. But these people had seen the future, they were telling him what had already happened. There was another way, he knew that, there was a way to escape them. But the Doctor found that he was marching purposefully towards the very corner that Willhuff had indicated. This part of the room had the same sort of fascination something always had when it was forbidden: Don't Look There; Try Not to Think About That.

He was about to turn on his heel and stride off in completely the opposite direction when a thought stuck him in place.

'What if the *solution* is in that corner?' he whispered to himself.

He set off towards it with new vigour.

He was meant to lie down in this corner... he did so.

No solution presented itself.

His shoulders sagged. It was cold down here. He pictured himself there, lying down, just as the old warriors had foreseen.

He rolled over, peeked at them. They were all still sitting around the fire. They'd glance up from time to time, checking that he was still there.

Of course!

They only *thought* they saw him here. Actually he'd sneaked off, fooled them. All he had to do was fashion a dummy of some kind, something that would deceive them from this distance, in a room that was pretty murky anyway.

Except that Pallant said that they'd come over and moved him in the morning.

The fact that they saw the future was confusing him. He needed to take a step back. Picture the scene as an observer would. A bird's eye view. He ran through a number of permutations, but the best he could hope for was that they were lying, trying to change his course of action. Why would they want to? If he did escape, they would know that they didn't succeed. Was it a self-fulfilling prophecy? They would demoralise him so much that he would give up even trying? Well, one of the features of a self-fulfilling prophecy is that it comes true, whatever the underhand methods used.

He'd fooled them somehow, and he'd been in two places at once.

He remembered his trick with the Sontarans and the Rutans – his stomach dropping as he also realised that he'd completely forgotten about the Conference, he had left the two leaders stuck together in his TARDIS. There was nothing he could do about that now. First things first. He'd been in two places at once then. Of course he'd used his TARDIS, and there were no time machines around here.

So what did he have to hand?

He emptied his pockets: a ball of string, sonic screwdriver, the transmat bracelet, his copy of *Four Quartets*, a bag of Monster Munch, a bottle of iodine and the Rutan Converter.

It was an eclectic set of items, and it took him a full ten seconds to work out how he would do it.

Helios had stood, making a half-hearted effort to stretch. The old man had glanced over at the Doctor's sleeping form, and then picked his way across the rubble towards one of the archways.

The Doctor had seen it all from his vantage point, standing in the shadows on the other side of the room. So far, the plan was working. Now he had to follow the old man.

He slipped from the room, careful not to disturb the others. Helios was a fair few seconds ahead of him, and the bricklined corridors here were labyrinthine, but the Doctor could hear the old man's boots squelching along the wet flagstones. He followed the sound, trying all the time to gain on them. There wasn't day or night here, just night. Perhaps the Needle People slept when they wanted to.

The sounds of footfalls had stopped. There was a whirring, grinding sound. Then the Doctor heard Helios moving again. He couldn't be more than a dozen yards from him. It sounded like a heavy door pulling itself open.

The Doctor peeked around the corner. There was an doorway, and a light pouring from it that would have been faint anywhere else, but which was almost blinding here. The Doctor edged forwards, looked through. It was a small room, almost a crypt. Helios was nowhere to be seen, but there was plenty of other things to occupy the Doctor's attention. This was a shrine to the universe, the most precious items carefully preserved in their own display cabinets and caskets. A rather battered segment of the Key to Time; a semi-organic helmet; the much-coveted Crown of the Fifth Galaxy; a blue-gold ovoid with a flower growing from it... there were many other objects, some of which the Doctor recognised, some of which he couldn't put a name to. Objects of power in their time, but their time had long past. These were relics now, nothing more. There was also a backlit computer panel mounted to the wall. It seemed nondescript, but might bear further examination.

There were wet footprints on the marble floor, and they led straight from the door through one of the walls. The Doctor smiled, tracing the steps until he found the secret door. Once you knew the door was there, locating the small pedal switch that opened it was a doddle. It parted gracefully and silently, revealing yet another corridor.

This part of the building was a little warmer, a little lighter and a lot better maintained than the rest. The walls hadn't fallen to damp or disrepair, the musty smell wasn't quite as pronounced. There was a faint hum in the air, electricity or energy of some kind.

The far end of the corridor opened up into a large chamber. The Doctor hesitated at the entrance. The room was well-lit, and dominated by a set of great double doors. They were set into the floor, like a bomb bay, or the way into a Kansas storm shelter. These were an immaculate white, like porcelain. There was a keyhole and two handles, set slightly apart from each other. Helios was here, as the Doctor assumed he must have been, knelt facing the back wall, supporting himself awkwardly on his stave. He was mouthing some prayer, or invocation. When he had finished, carefully, ritualistically, Helios stood and walked over to the doors, examining them.

The Doctor shifted forward to get a better look, his shoe dragging against the dry marble. Helios looked up, surprised by the noise.

'I know you are here, Doctor,' Helios said calmly. 'I see the future, remember?'

'And the past,' the Doctor noted, stepping into the room. 'You reacted *after* I scraped my boot just then, not before.' He stopped in his tracks. 'And that also suggests that your knowledge of the future is not perfect, or you wouldn't have been surprised.'

Helios smiled, more than a hint of warmth there. 'You always were too clever for your own good. Alone amongst those here, I see the past as well as the future, but I have only snatches of memory of either.'

'The worst of both worlds.'

'Indeed. I have no idea, for example, how you managed to get past the others, or trick us into thinking you were asleep all night.'

The Doctor walked over to the doors, talking to disguise the fact that he was getting a good look at the lock, the handles. 'I was very, very clever, and I'm itching to tell you how I did it, but if I ever do, then you might remember what I say and you'll be able to warn them. Perhaps even retroactively.'

The doors had faint roundels on them, worn smooth by the ages.

'Now you want to open these doors.' It wasn't a question.

'I thought I might,' the Doctor admitted lightly.

'In all the millennia that we have been here, very few have reached this far. But you cannot be allowed to gaze upon the face of God.'

The Doctor smirked. 'God? He's behind these doors, is he? Odd, that, because when we were talking about Him earlier, I distinctly remember Pallant saying that he didn't know which door God was behind. Funny thing is, you've known all along where the gates are, all about the secret route to them. You've kept that information from the others, though, haven't you?'

'The temptation might prove too great for even the most devout of His servants,' Helios said easily.

'But the temptation is not too great for you?'

The lined face clouded over. 'No! I have resisted temptation for many millennia, I know that I resist until the end.'

'So you've never tried to open the door?'

'No! Of course I was tempted, but I resisted.'

'Not been tempted even the once?' the Doctor tutted, reaching into his jacket pocket. 'What if I were to tell you that these aren't the gates of heaven, just the doors to a damaged TARDIS belonging to a man named Savar? What if I told you that I had the key to this door?' He held the key up, let it glint in the soft light.

Helios gave a faint smile, held out a closed hand. 'I'd tell you that I know, that the door is unlocked anyway, and –' he opened his hand, revealing an identical key.

'You know the truth, but still you won't open the door?'

'I know what I have been told, but I have faith. I believe that my God is behind those doors, awaiting me.'

'So why not open the doors?'

'What?'

'Why resist? What are you so worried about?'

'I...'

'Go on. If you're that sure, then...'

'What if I were to open the gates –'

'Yes?'

'What if I were to open the gates and God was *not* behind them? What if there was no God, after a hundred thousand centuries of waiting? As long as those doors remain closed, there is always a possibility. Open that door, and the possibility might evaporate.'

'Schroedinger's God,' the Doctor chuckled, slotting Savar's key into the lock. 'A very cruel thought experiment, I've always thought, one for the imaginary animal rights campaigners. Imagine locking a cat up in a box and trying to poison it. Time to let your god out for a stretch and a chance to use his litter tray, I reckon.'

'You cannot be allowed to open the doors,' Helios shouted, brandishing his stave.

The Doctor turned the key, unconcerned. He reached for the handle.

The stave parted the air in front of the Doctor's hand, then it swept back, until its tip was hovering an inch from his face.

The Doctor fell back, his hand slapping down onto the ground for support.

'Almost made it,' he concluded.

Helios turned away, tapping the doors with his staff. 'Whatever is beyond the doors, it is a power that no man should possess.'

'The universe of anti-matter,' the Doctor explained as he got to his feet. 'A spacetime continuum like ours, equal but opposite, reached via a singularity. Normally, if I'd opened the doors, the two universes would have come into contact. There would have been annihilation.' He held up a small cylinder. 'But this is a Rutan device that converts anti-matter into matter and vice versa. It will stabilise the gateway. I know what I face, Helios, and I'm not afraid of it.'

Helios shook his head. 'You don't know. You don't have the slightest idea. If you did you would run away from here, screaming, cowering.'

The Doctor studied the old man's face.

'I know you,' he realised.

'Yes,' Helios said simply. 'As I know you.'

'Do you remember what happened? Why you are here?'

'Not all of it,' Helios admitted. 'But I think that is for the best. I remember my wife and my family. I remember names and times. I know that I came to the Needle to continue my father's work... I can say no more.'

'If you know me, you know why I have to open these doors,' the Doctor said.

Helios caught the Doctor's arm, stared deep into his eyes. 'There will come a day when all is lost.'

The sincerity in his voice alarmed the Doctor. 'Today?'

'No. What you face now, the universe will survive. But you have already taken your first steps on...' he stopped himself. 'You have seen glimpses of what is to come. You read the scrolls, you've seen the enemy. Step through those doors, and that future is set in place.'

'The future can't be fixed,' the Doctor said firmly. 'There's always hope, there is always a way out. Forewarned is forearmed.'

'I can't say any more,' Helios insisted.

'Then step out the way,' the Doctor suggested, reaching for the handle again. 'I know what I'm doing. If there is a power here, it can be harnessed, used to our advantage.'

This time Helios didn't stop him.

'You knew,' the old man said quietly. 'Remember that as the universe falls around you. You knew what you were doing, it was your choice. I have lost everything now, everything but my faith. I tried.' Helios straightened. 'I saw the future, I knew that I was destined to fail to convince you. But I tried.'

He turned, and walked from the room.

The Doctor hesitated, but only for a moment. The doors were humming, he could hear whispering around him. Meticulously, he placed the Rutan Converter at the top of the doorway, slotted the key into the lock and stood back as the doors slid smoothly open.

A column of fire burst between the open doors, throwing him to one side. A column of flames rose up to the ceiling. The heat was intense, and the Doctor backed away a little before it started to singe him.

There was someone within the flames.

'I have come here for you,' the Doctor said. 'I know who you are.'

'And who is that?' a voice asked calmly from the fire.

The Doctor straightened. 'You are one of the greatest of all our race, you are Omega.'

There was laughter, but not the booming, mocking laughter the Doctor had been expecting. A woman's laugh.

'You don't know a hart from a hind.'

She stepped forward from the centre of the flame to its edges. Fire flickered up between her toes and around her long legs, reaching up as far as her navel. She was backlit by the flames, and there were amber shadows over her body. Blonde hair cascaded over her shoulders, covering her. Her lips were red, her eyes were blue.

And for a fleeting moment she was a smaller, fuller, woman with short, dark hair, green eyes, freckles on her shoulders and a birthmark on her ankle.

Blonde again, she smiled down at him,

'You are here already,' the Doctor said, laughing, hardly daring to believe it. He stepped towards the fire, hot air blasting over him. 'I came here for you. I was going to ask him –'

'I know.'

She held out her hand.

'He has been expecting you.'

Together they stepped into the flame.

Chapter Ten
A King of Infinite Space

The Doctor stepped through the garden, the woman at his side.

He had got used to the cold of the Librarinth, and how musty the air had been, and the darkness. Only now did he realise how few colours there had been at the end of the universe. The world had been sepia, drained of colour and light. His new surroundings were dazzling, the fresh air blew against his face. It was difficult taking it all in at once.

It was a warm spring day here, light was streaming through the trees. They were walking hand in hand along the banks of a stream, on even, weedless, grass. The stream ran through a carefully ordered garden, where every tree, statue and flower had apparently conformed to some vast design. The flower beds, statues and pathways were all spotlessly neat, although there was no sign of any gardeners. There was music like birdsong in the air.

The Doctor flexed his anti-proton fingers, tapped his lips with them.

'An anti-matter body feels exactly the same as one made of matter,' she assured him.

'This body is much like my old one,' the Doctor agreed. 'Whereas you, on the other hand...'

She was wearing a loose-flowing gown in ivory silk and lace, with bare shoulders, gathered at the waist by a wide belt. Her long blonde hair was held up by a gold clasp, and swept down to the small of her back. She wore a necklace of white flowers, and held a feather fan. She was his height, a little taller as her feet were bare and he was wearing shoes.

She smiled. 'I regenerated.'

'Only Time Lords regenerate when they die,' the Doctor objected. 'The Gallifreyans of old avoided the problem by never dying.'

'It came as a surprise to me, too,' she said, laughter in her voice. 'I was born a Gallifreyan, but I've lived long enough that I may just have evolved beyond that.'

The Doctor looked over at her, unsure about her. If it *was* her. 'How did you end up here?' he asked.

'Omega brought me here. He has made this his domain.'

At that moment, they turned a corner and, ahead of them, massive, was Omega's castle. It was the size of a mountain, as dark as a stormcloud. It appeared to have been piled there, layers of buttresses and battlements upon layers. The walls were either sheer rock faces or solid blocks of stone. Some of the turrets and towers defied gravity, tapering or seeming to hover.

The Doctor bristled, sensing the power radiating from the place.

'You knew Omega before you knew me,' the Doctor said.

'A long time before. A very long time ago.'

'You were his wife,' the Doctor murmured.

'I am two million years old. Do you know what that means?'

One corner of his mouth lifted, the start of a smile. 'I should wish you happy birthday?'

She stopped, facing him, angry. 'It means that I was born knowing the future, and that I was a young woman at the time of the Curse. It means that I saw the starbreakers leave for Qqaba, and the Time Lords return. I remember the Darkness. I've lived in palaces and on the streets. I've lived amongst two hundred generations of Time Lords. I've seen so many of my friends and lovers grow old and die around me. I've seen mountain ranges rise and fall. I've lived long enough to see even Gallifrey change. If I hadn't changed in that time, then I wouldn't have lived my life, I'd have wasted it.'

'Oceans of water under the bridge,' the Doctor said thoughtfully. 'My theory of evolution is that it's not what you are, it's what you do with it.'

'I did what I could,' she replied.

They had stopped by a small pool.

'We have some privacy out here,' she said quietly.

'Shall we sit down?' the Doctor offered, taking off his jacket and laying it down on the grass, worried for her immaculate white gown. She knelt, then sat there, stretching out one leg, tucking the other underneath it. She batted herself with her fan. The Doctor knelt behind her, so that she had her back to him, and that his chest almost touched her shoulderblades. He steadied himself, not quite touching her leg. He looked over her and down into the pool. The water was so clear you could see right to the bottom.

'There should be fish in there,' the Doctor observed.

And there were a dozen rainbow streaks in the water. The Doctor looked up, delighted. She looked back over her shoulder at him and he grinned back.

He looked at her face, the first time he'd had a proper chance to do so. It was almost too beautiful: oval, framed with golden-blonde hair. She had deep red lips, a perfectly proportioned nose, blue eyes.

She turned back to the water, watching the fish darting from one side of the pool to the other, leaving the Doctor to look at her broad shoulders and thin neck. Her skin was so pale. He reached out, touched an almost alabaster left cheek with his left hand.

'I thought I'd lost you,' he told her.

She stroked his wrist. His hand was drawing fingertip circles on the side of her head. She kissed the base of his thumb. She lifted her right arm, bent it back so that her hand could reach the back of his head. She drew a line up his neck to his hair, toyed with his short hair. All the time they were drawing closer together.

'I didn't think –' he began.

Her thoughts. A single point of contact at her temple and they were sharing thoughts and memories. The Doctor closed his eyes. This was her, there was no possible cause to doubt that now. She had lived so much longer than him, lived at his Family home for countless generations. She had tutored his grandfather and his father. She had been there at his birth. She had nursed him, taught him, danced with him, loved him, borne his children.

She had let go of his hand. 'You were always there.'

'I knew that I'd find you.'

The Doctor remembered the night that he had been too late, saw it as she had. The Watch marching through the courtyard of their home, rounding up the children and the House guests. The Capitol was burning on the horizon, and even from here it was almost possible to hear the mobs in the Panopticon. Her eyes were full of tears as the Watch searched the bedchambers for her daughter-in-law, read out the charge that the family had been consorting with aliens. And she couldn't say anything as they dragged her away, or they might find out her secret, they'd know that not all the Womb-Born had died, that some had merely been hiding amongst the general population for all these hundreds of centuries.

She shifted herself around until they were knelt facing each other.

Her daisy-chain necklace had come unravelled and was about to fall away. Her hand was flat against the small of his back, steadying them both. He was holding onto her shoulder, skin against skin.

'I'll never leave you again,' the Doctor promised. 'Whatever I have to do, I'll never leave you.'

Even this early in the morning, the market was bustling.

Captain Raimor didn't pretend to understand the full complexities of the Low Town economy. Produce and other items were brought to the market by traders from all over Gallifrey and hawked here. There was an ancient currency, the treazant coin, but mostly goods and services were exchanged. Fish from the subterranean sea were exchanged for silvertree wood or nails for the fishermen's u-boats. That was a simple case, and the system was a great deal more elaborate than that, with strict rules about the basis of contract, the value of goods, that sort of thing.

The market was Outside, right on the edges of Low Town, not even in the shadow of the Capitol Dome. Sunlight streamed over the place, picking out the brightly coloured wares and the rich patterns of the merchants' robes. It was noisy, too, bartering voices merging in with the whine of horse drawn gravcarts, the clump of feet, the clattering of crates of goods being loaded and unloaded. There was bunting out today, and an air of excitement. One word over and over again. 'Omega.'

Raimor and Peltroc made their way through the aisles of the market area, the crowds instinctively parting in front of them to let members of the Chancellery Watch through. Raimor's expert eye could spot everything from pickpockets to gangster bosses amongst those present, but the best thing about the criminal fraternity was that its members understood the rules. The people here knew that the Watchmen weren't interested in them and their dealings, they only came down here on Time Lord business. No one was stupid enough to try to pick a fight, not when a hundred Watchmen could transmat in at a moment's notice. The grossest offenders disappeared into the woodwork for a minute or two, knowing that there were still a few things that the Watch couldn't turn a blind eye to. But the lower criminals like the palliards and twachylles didn't even move from their patches.

'Unashamed,' Peltroc muttered.

'They don't bother us in the Capitol, Constable, and so we don't bother them down here. If a Time Lord were to come down to pay a visit, and found himself in trouble, then... who are we to judge our elders and betters?'

There had been efforts in the distant past to clean up Low Town, purge it of criminals, but all such actions had been doomed to failure. The authorities had removed some gangland boss only to find his rivals taking over his interests, his territory and his assets, growing stronger as a result. It was a chaotic system, one that neither the Watch nor the High Council really understood.

'Best to adopt a code of non-interference, like the High Council, isn't that right, Peltroc?'

'Is there going to be a place for us in the new regime, do you think?'

'New regime?' Raimor scowled.

'*Omega*,' Peltroc said. 'There's talk that the President is planning to abdicate in his favour. I can't see Omega standing by while others rule Gallifrey.'

'Yes, well, perhaps the Watch don't share the general population's relish.'

'Passed the Omega Memorial on the way down here,' Peltroc said. 'There were crowds gathering.'

'There were people praying and laying tributes in the Panopticon last night. The Council weren't sure whether we should be arresting them or joining in.'

'You know, though, don't you?'

'I've been with the Watch for nearly nine hundred years, Constable. Plenty of time to read the regimental histories. I know my duty.'

'You'll try to carry it out?'

Raimor just looked over at Peltroc.

'You'd kill Omega?' Peltroc repeated.

Raimor nodded. 'Rassilon gave us express orders, and Rassilon had his reasons. He knew that for all their power, for all their knowledge, his Time Lords aren't perfect. He realised who the enemy really is.'

'The Watch was here before the Time Lords, and the Watch will be here long after the Time Lords have gone,' Peltroc said, quoting the first line of their oath of office.

'That's right.'

'Isn't the Doctor one of the Four Names, too?'

'He is. But Rassilon was very clear that the Doctor should only be killed when he –' Raimor paused, then reached out and grabbed one of the passers-by by the collar of his jacket. His target was a small man in a patched-up tunic. 'And where do you think you're going?'

The man had the same myopic look and twitching expression he always had. 'Captain Raimor, sir. Just on my way through the market, sir. Strictly tekram business only, yeah? Your new body suits you, Captain. Little young around the edges for my tastes, but – eep!' Raimor yanked him off his feet, placing him down between himself and Peltroc.

'Who's this, Captain?' Peltroc said, getting into the spirit of things by bending over the little man.

'This is Grote,' Raimor told him. 'Remember how I said the Lower class keep themselves to themselves? Well, this is one of the exceptions. He's a forger, I caught him once with a number of keys to the Capitol.'

'Aw, Captain. That was three hundred years ago!' Grote objected whinily. 'It's not as though I used them or anything.'

'Oh, I remember you telling me about him once,' Peltroc said. Accidentally or not, the lad had picked up on Grote's particular brand of paranoia.

Grote blinked. 'I'm known to the Watch?' he said slowly.

'*Everyone* knows about you up there, Grote,' Raimor told him. 'When tutors want to scare their pupils they say, "Don't do that or you'll end up like Grote."'

'Wait... the *Timeys* know about me?'

'Time... Lords,' Peltroc corrected slowly. 'They don't like that word you just said. It doesn't show the proper respect they say. Only Groteys use that sort of language, the Time Lords say.'

Raimor allowed himself a smirk. Peltroc would have to be careful not to overegg the pudding, but by the look on his face, at least one of Grote's hearts had just stopped beating.

'But...' Grote began, unable to think of the second word for an instant or two. 'But surely the Time Lords have got better things to be doing today? What with the aliens and the Doctor and Omega. People down here are excited enough by the idea that Omega's coming back... it must be a party up there.' He jabbed his finger upwards to indicate the Dome.

'Funny you should mention the Doctor,' Raimor said softly. 'Tell me what you know.'

'Well, he's vanished, hasn't he? That was on the Public Record.'

'People don't just vanish.'

'Yeah, I know, he's gone to ground. Hiding.'

'Is that what he's doing?'

'Well, isn't he?'

'You tell me, Grote. You know the Doctor, don't you?'

'*Everyone* knows the Doctor.' Grote objected. 'You know the Doctor. Makes you a suspect, does it?'

'The last person to use that line of reasoning was an accomplice of the Doctor,' Peltroc said.

'She ended up dead, stabbed through the hearts,' Raimor added. 'She's not the only one who's ended up that way in the last couple of days.'

'I think that he knows where the Doctor is,' Peltroc said, with a surprising air of menace. 'Shall we use the mind probe on him?'

Grote tried to back away. 'Hey, you know, no need for that. He doesn't come down here as often as he used to. I haven't seen him for years.'

Raimor glared at Grote, made him jump again.

'I haven't,' Grote insisted. 'He's probably jumped into that TARDIS of his and left Gallifrey again.'

'All the TARDISes have been accounted for, Grote.' Raimor sighed. 'Run along. If you see the Doctor, you find a way to tell me, OK?'

Grote was absurdly grateful, bowing and scraping as he backed away from the two Watchmen. He merged into the crowd and vanished.

'The Doctor's not here, is he?' Peltroc said.

'No. And even if he were, he's not the murderer.'

'So why did the Acting-President send us down here looking for him?'

'It's all politics, Peltroc.' They found a bare stall, and rested there for a while. Raimor took his helmet off, scratched his head. He looked up at the Dome, looming over Low Town, glinting like ivory in the sunlight. 'They've got infinite power in there,' he said. 'They can do just about anything, go anywhere, know everything. Most aliens must think that they are gods. They don't realise that all that power, all those options... it's as limiting as having no options at all.'

Peltroc snorted. 'That sounds like the sort of line the elite would come up with to keep the rest of the population happy with their lot.'

'Perhaps. But why do you think they spend all their time performing rituals and ceremonies, why do they spend so much time plotting against each other and awarding each other honorary degrees? Because when you live for ever and can do anything you want, you might as well do nothing at all.'

* * *

The two Watchmen leaning against a market stall faded from the cracked glass. For a moment it was a mirror once more, showing nothing more than a vast form hunched forward in his throne. It was a monster, it must not be faced. A new image began to form, bright sunlight banishing the golden glint of metal and dissolving the red glow of his eyes.

A man and a woman, walking in a garden. He was a little over average height, with a long face and closely cropped hair. He wore a baggy silk shirt and tan, narrow-cut trousers. A blue woollen jacket was draped over his arm. He was wearing Argyle socks, with no shoes. Her hair was loose. He recognised the flowing white dress, noting that the wide belt she usually wore with it was missing.

They were walking briskly, businesslike, along the main path leading to the castle. It would be a matter of minutes before they reached the drawbridge. The man wore a serious expression. Behind them was nothing, nothing at all. If either of them were to turn their heads, then the garden would be there for them to observe. But otherwise... it... didn't exist except as a thought, but this was all there was here: his mind, and who was to say that it was real and who was to say that... he could not... The throne room began to dissolve, fade into nothing as he began to think the unthinkable.

He reasserted his thoughts, concentrated on the new arrival.
This was the Doctor, here in the universe of anti-matter. He was staring up at the castle, clearly impressed by the architecture, the ramparts and battlements, the solid stone of the walls. But it was a castle of the mind, it had only existed for an instant before he'd turned the corner, it would cease to exist as the Doctor and his wife crossed the threshold.

'Are you the only one here?' The Doctor asked. His voice was soft, he swallowed his words.

Her voice was clear, like music. 'Yes. Apart from Omega, of course.'

'He's keeping you here against your will.'

She smiled. 'I'm not his prisoner. He intervened to rescue me. I was right on the brink of death in the matter universe. When he brought me here he converted me into anti-matter, repaired the damage. His will sustains me. It's the reason that I can never leave.'

'We'll find a way,' the Doctor promised.

Omega laughed, leaned towards the mirror. If anyone in the universe could make good that promise it was the Doctor. But first things first.

The Doctor was thinking aloud. 'So he brought you here. That means that Omega can affect our universe.'

'The breach in spacetime caused by Savar's TARDIS allows him to observe, and a degree of influence.'

'How long have you been here?'

'When we dream, it's only for a second or two at a time. We can have dreams that seem to last for ever but they all take place in a single second.'

'Not strictly true,' the Doctor corrected her, 'the rapid eye movement phase of sleep in which dreams occur can last up to an hour and a half a night.'

'But you understand what I mean?' she said, mock-exasperated. 'You understand that I have no way of telling whether I have been here for a day or a thousand years.'

'Has Omega changed since you knew him?'

'He's not mad.'

'That isn't what I asked.'

She hesitated, aware of the eyes upon her. 'He's been trapped here all this time.'

'That's not what I asked.'

'No. No, he hasn't changed.'

'He still loves you?'

A hand, trapped in its gauntlet, reached out to the mirror, tried to touch her face behind the glass. 'That isn't why he brought me here.'

'No?'

'He brought me here because of you. You have the only thing that he wants. Freedom.'

'I don't understand why he's trapped at all. If he's got the power to create all this, he must be able to whip up an escape route.'

'No.'

The Doctor stopped. 'Oh come *on*, if the Rutans can convert matter into anti-matter then I'm sure that Omega can.'

'It isn't as simple as that. This universe only exists because he wills it. Without his consciousness it would cease to exist.'

'So he can't leave because he just can't take that last step, a part of him has to stay behind.'

'That's right,' she said. 'I don't understand why he would want to leave. It's a beautiful place. He's a god here.'

The Doctor looked up. 'He wants to go because the sky is wrong.'

She looked up, and as soon as she did, she frowned. 'I never noticed that before.'

Omega sighed. The sky here was impossibly blue and the clouds looked as though they had been daubed on with poster paint and a thick brush. It wasn't the colours, it was the shape. It looked as if the sky and the clouds had been painted onto the inside surface of a vast dome, one that seemed to curve and fall beyond the horizon. It didn't feel like the outside at all.

'There's sunlight, but no sun,' the Doctor said.

Omega knew that. The light streamed down, but it wasn't coming from anywhere, and the shadows were confused, lying at different angles at different places.

'This place is created from his thoughts, and after all this time, he's forgotten what the sky looks like,' the Doctor said. 'And that's why he needs to escape. For all his power, he's impotent.'

No, Omega thought. No. That wasn't it. In any act of creation, there is always frustrated ambition. The most perfect sculptures and portraits and poems are not quite what the artist imagined. Sometimes the faults are minor, occasionally they are even beneficial, forming unintended meanings, new purpose or clarity. More often, though, the perfect form remains trapped in the mind. Even here, where his thoughts and dreams were all that there was.

Omega remembered the sky. He remembered the sun on his face, the clouds drifting past. But he couldn't recreate it.

He closed his eyes, head slumping forwards. When he returned his gaze to the mirror, the image was that of the matter universe. It was an office, a bright, airy place. It overlooked a vast statue of a young man, his space helmet tucked under his arm. It was a man with a stony face full of hope, just about to forge a glorious future that he would not be part of.

Castellan Voran was uncomfortable in his chair as the Great Panopticon Bell struck Four Bells.

He was merely the Acting-President, and had felt it in poor taste to take up residence in the Presidential Chambers, especially as his tenure should only have lasted a couple of hours. But that had been this morning, and now Surgeon Grutnoll was advising that the President should get at least another day's rest. It had been a minor wound, but the President had worn his current body for over a millennium. The stabbing wasn't enough to justify complete bodily regeneration. The Castellan just wished that the President had picked a better time to be stabbed, that was all.

From this office he could look out over the Panopticon, and see the people gathering at the foot of the Statue of Omega. Ask them why they were doing it and they probably couldn't answer. Omega was returning, and the people needed a way to express and explore their feelings about that. The Castellan wondered if he'd be out of a job. When Omega returned, there was no doubt that he'd be given a place on the Supreme Council. He'd almost certainly be elected President – which College would stand against him? Would Omega sweep away the old structures or would he try to work within them?

So this was 'change', this was what the Doctor had been going on about all these years. The possibility of gain, the probability of loss.

As Acting-President, Voran could consult the Matrix, but he couldn't connect his mind directly to it. He had to list the problems himself and find his own solutions.

The most important thing was to rescue Omega, and to do that, Gallifrey would have to find a way to re-establish the link with the future and then to defeat the inhabitants of the Needle. Restoring contact with the Station was simply a technical matter, and the science teams were confident that they would succeed by nightfall.

A way to get past the defences of the Needle existed, the Castellan was sure of that, but it was a matter of finding that way. The Time Lords had fought wars before, and a number of times those wars had been waged and won against opponents a great deal more powerful than themselves. But this was the first time since Marnal's day that such a show of force had proved necessary, and the key to victory had always been preparation. The Time Lords had always been careful to collect intelligence reports. They'd never allowed themselves to fight without knowing their enemy. That had been Marnal's Error.

However, there weren't many enemies who could survive being hit by a blackstar, and there were plenty of other tricks up Gallifrey's sleeve.

The Castellan only hoped that the Doctor hadn't doomed the Time Lords to extinction. With the timegate closed, there was no way of knowing what was happening in the far future. The Station's batteries must surely have run down by now. The Magistrate was a resourceful man, and would have found a way to preserve his crew, the Castellan was sure of that. But they would be defenceless out there on their own. With a full day to prepare and the Effect at their control, whoever was on the surface of the Needle would have the Station at their mercy. If that was the case, they could locate the Station's planet of origin, and launch an attack of their own, hours before the blackstar could be launched.

The man who had stabbed the President, Lord Savar, was in custody, but was saying nothing sane, merely his usual rants and raves.

The source of all Gallifrey's problems, the Doctor, had vanished, leaving behind an almost-full city Morgue. A Technician called Waym. A pair of minor noblemen working in the power rooms and the Lady Larna. The Technician had been the member of a powerful eastern family. His Senior Cousin had come over from Olyesti by rail, arriving in full mourning dress with her retinue of servants and robots. The Castellan had met her at the terminus and gone to the morgue with her, seen them all lying there, ceremonial clothes draped over the faces of the three Time Lords. Waym's face was uncovered, as befitted his status. His Senior Cousin conducted a short ritual and then her assistants had placed the corpse in an iron coffin. They would take the body home and bury it, which was the custom in the east. Out of respect, the Castellan had got someone from his office to arrange all the necessary permits in advance. The Cousin had perhaps spoken a dozen words in the whole hour she had been in the Capitol.

The three Time Lords were being matriculated now, their minds being processed so that they would join the vast collective consciousness of the Matrix. When Larna's mind emerged from the datascape, perhaps it would prove possible to solve the mystery of the Doctor's disappearance. Constable Sapro's report into the affair was sitting on Voran's desk half-read. The Doctor had left the Temporal Monitoring room with the Lady Larna during the investiture. He had deactivated the timegate and sabotaged the power links. Larna had been stabbed, presumably because she had refused to co-operate with his plan. The Watchmen had broken down the door, but the Doctor had gone. Sapro offered no explanation as to where he might have gone. His men were continuing their search of the catacombs, ventilation ducts and sewers.

Voran's secretary, Pendrel, came bustling through the door.

'Couldn't you knock?' the Castellan asked irately, holding up the sheaves of Sapro's report.

'Apologies, Acting-President. It's rather urgent, sir.'

'Have you noticed, Pendrel, that everything seems to be urgent this morning?'

'The Sontaran delegation want to talk to you, sir, they say that their leader has been kidnapped.'

They walked over the drawbridge, into Omega's fortress. The moat was dry, covered in grass.

Inside was a long corridor, lit by burning torches. The ceiling was low, the floor was bare flagstones. There were no doorways leading off, just a set of double doors a hundred yards or so in front of them.

'Fascinating decor,' the Doctor noted, his words not even echoing from the masonry.

'Omega maintains only what he needs here.'

The Doctor jabbed his thumb back over his shoulder. 'That garden is hardly functional.'

'That is his gift to me, he grants me the power to tend it.'

The double doors at the end of the corridor swung open as they reached them.

They stepped into the throne room together. The room was triangular, with a simple vaulted ceiling. The door they had just come through was at one point of the triangle. The throne itself was on a raised dais opposite. It was a vast upholstered thing, with a high back and vast arms, but it reminded the Doctor of an armchair more than anything else.

There were darkened archways leading off in all directions. A fulllength mirror sat by the throne. The only other feature was a vast fireplace, with a roaring fire.

The Doctor watched the flames dancing in the hearth, as fascinated as a moth might have been. He wanted to reach out, let the fire lick his hand.

'The source of his power,' she told him.

'A fire?'

She shook her head, smiling. 'That's how he chooses to represent the singularity. It gives him control over the physical laws in this universe.'

They stepped over to it, and the Doctor looked into the flames. When a certain type of black hole formed, all the matter and energy it contained collapsed in on itself, the immense gravitation condensing and condensing the material until it reached infinite density. That condition repealed some of the fundamental laws of quantum mechanics, breaking down the ordinary distinctions between matter and energy, space and time. Instead of 'normality', there was just quantum... well, at the point a singularity formed, words couldn't hope to explain what was going on. Theoretically it allowed anything to emerge, anything to happen. A state of singularity was how the universe had been created, and this is how it would end. Usually, the fact that all such singularities were locked away safely behind event horizons kept them from affecting the universe. Trapped behind the event horizon himself, Omega had found a way to bring the theory into practice, a way of harnessing the power of the singularity. He had shaped it to his will.

'I imagine that it will also let him channel anti-matter through the Effect to give him an practically inexhaustible supply of energy in our universe.'

'That's more your field than mine,' she replied.

'It's evil,' the Doctor told her. 'Can't you hear it whispering? A sound like a lullaby?'

'DOCTOR.'

The voice seemed to come from all around, as if it was being relayed by a loudspeaker system. Despite that, the Doctor could sense that the source of the voice was to his right, emerging from one of the archways nearest the throne.

Anyone who had been to the Panopticon would have recognised the man who stepped out, although most would have been surprised by his sheer size. He was over seven feet tall, and broad with it. His huge muscular shoulders and a beard that curled down his chest only emphasised that this was an ogre of a man.

He wore a purple cloak that reached to the floor, hissing as it was dragged over the flagstones. Was there a hint of a limp there? The Doctor couldn't be sure, it might just be the weight of the golden armour. He wore a helmet, one that was almost fitted to his skull, encasing the back of his head, covering his hair. Great ram's horns sprang from the temples, curled behind his ears, sweeping back around until their tips faced forwards and upwards. The Doctor wasn't sure whether the horns were part of the helmet or not.

He dragged himself past them, not even stopping to look at his guests. Instead he climbed the three steps of the dais and took his place on the throne, hands clasping the arms of the chair.

'Lord Omega,' she said. 'This is the Doctor.'

'Yes. Leave us,' he commanded. 'Dress for dinner.'

She bowed, and left through one of the archways.

'Am I all right as I am?' the Doctor asked, indicating his coat with his hand. 'I didn't realise we were going to be quite so formal. The invitation didn't say black tie.' He looked up at Omega, whose purple cloak was spilling over the edges of the throne. 'Or fancy dress.'

'Would you like a drink?' Omega asked.

The Doctor shook his head. 'No thanks... a chair if you have one, I've travelled quite a long way to get here and I've not sat down for a while.'

A small wooden chair appeared behind him.

'Thanks.' The Doctor sat, realising that it made him appear even smaller and less significant compared to the giant on his throne on his dais. He stood, began pacing around the room. He examined the mirror, peering into it. Apart from seeing himself, he saw stars and planets.

'A window out over the universe of matter,' Omega explained.

The Doctor pursed his lips. 'That's what I call a looking glass.' He looked around again, aware that Omega was staring at him. 'Nice place you have here,' he concluded. 'So you saw how I got past the Needle People?'

'It was simple enough. When matter is transmitted, a duplicate is created at the destination and the original is destroyed. You rigged your transmat bracelet so that the original was not destroyed. That body is in a self-induced coma.'

'Clever, wasn't I?' the Doctor said lightly. 'So you can look out over the real universe. What about this place?'

'This is my domain. I see everything here, I know everything here, I control everything here.'

'Including your wife?'

'She is bathing, preparing herself. Wearing nothing but that new body of hers.' He leered. 'Would you like to see her?'

The Doctor turned away from the mirror. 'Would I like to see her? No,' he said matter-of-factly. Instead he looked into the fire, watched it flare up.

'"No"? Perhaps you mean "not like this". She would never know. You could touch her, take her thoughts, and she wouldn't know.'

The flames were calmer now, almost hypnotic. 'Is that what you have done?' the Doctor muttered. 'Is that why you brought her here?'

Omega's laugh filled the room. 'I have other priorities. Her heart belongs to you, for the moment. She is a fascinating woman.'

The Doctor turned. 'You are jealous of us? You want her for yourself?'

'If I wanted her, Doctor, make no mistake I could have her. And she has no feelings for me now, if she ever did.' The Doctor looked Omega in the eye for the first time. The ancient Time Lord's face was lined, his red eyes surrounded by shadow. It was as if he hadn't slept for a million years, and borne the weight of creation on his shoulders all that time. 'We talk, that is all. She has told me of Gallifrey, the Time Lords, her dead children, the countless millennia that she has lived through while I ruled… this. She has a rather unique perspective on the history of our planet.'

The Doctor had been walking towards the throne as Omega spoke. Now he stepped onto the dais. 'She has seen the best and worst of what our people have to offer.'

'Your people, Doctor.'

The Doctor took another step up, looked Omega in the eye. 'You're a Gallifreyan, Omega. You're more than that. You must have been hit by the time energies when Qqaba went nova. You must have taken the full force of the explosion. My bet is that you understand Time a great deal better than your average Time Lord.'

Omega laughed, the sound originating all around the room. 'You may be right.'

'And existing outside your native universe must also have given you – what was your phrase? – a "unique perspective".'

The red eyes narrowed. 'I have seen the past and future change. I have seen a universe where there was no Rassilon, and the Time Lords were gods thanks to me. I have seen a universe where Rassilon still rules Gallifrey from deep within the Matrix. Another where he was a woman, and my lover.'

'Parallel universes?'

'Such places exist, but this was our universe, riddled with paradox and contradiction likes weevils in a biscuit.'

The Doctor drew back a little. 'I know a number of seafarers who prefer their biscuits with weevils. It adds to the taste, and weevils are a very good source of protein, or so I'm told.'

Omega was ignoring him. 'In all of those realities, in every version of history I am trapped here. Sometimes by treachery, sometimes by design, once even through choice. There are an infinity of choices, an infinite number of Doctors. Yet I am all the Omegas, I am the only one.'

'So you've searched all those different realities looking for a way to escape, and never found the answer?'

'I have the answer.'

'The breach in spacetime? The Effect.'

'I have used it to observe the universe of matter. As it grows, so do my powers there.'

'But they are still very limited. And I rather think that the Effect is out of your control now. When Savar's TARDIS fell into the black hole, you tried to use it to escape, you tried to power it up using the anti-matter here. But it didn't work for some reason, it just triggered the Effect. You might have lit the blue touch paper, but now the anti-matter-matter reactions have spread far faster and further than you were expecting.'

Omega's face was a mask of rage. 'True, but this is not a bad thing, it allows me control over events.'

'Including events in the past?'

'Indeed.'

'You can't change the past, it's impossible.'

'Shall I bring back Larna, make it so she never died?' Omega paused. 'Make it so that you never killed her?'

The Doctor straightened. 'Yes.'

'As you wish.'

The image in the mirror became cloudy, and then began to resolve.

The door to the Castellan's office slid open, and the Lady Larna walked in, escorted by a member of the Watch.

The young woman had changed back into high-collared dayrobes. Her hair was tied back. It was formal clothing, but not her robes of office. She refused to sit, forcing Acting-President Voran to stand as well. What she wore was a message, one that Voran had no difficulty in decoding: she was quite prepared to lose rank and status as a result of her actions, but she would not recant them.

'Lady Larna,' Voran said, hoping to convey a patronising tone.

She gave a small nod. 'I am not sorry for my actions, and demand my right as a Time Lord to stand before a full Tribunal to justify them.'

Voran smiled, and decided to sit down after all.

'After all this is over, Lady Larna, I sincerely hope that there is enough of Gallifrey left to hold a judicial review.' He made a show of looking through Constable Sapro's report. 'It says here that when he entered the power room, you were clearly trying to prevent the Doctor from jumping into the time column.'

Larna grimaced. 'If that idiot hadn't pulled me away, I'd have managed to stop him.'

Voran chuckled. 'Perhaps. In view of the current crisis, we will have to delay your trial. You demonstrated a great deal of guile and technical expertise in helping the Doctor to sabotage the power room. We need those talents to undo the damage. I'm going to second you to the restoration team. Dismissed.'

Voran's secretary, Pendrel, came bustling through the door, pushing his way past Larna.

'Couldn't you knock?' the Castellan asked irately, holding up the sheaves of Sapro's report.

'Apologies, Acting-President. It's rather urgent, sir.'

'Have you noticed, Pendrel, that everything seems to be urgent this morning?'

'The Sontaran delegation want to talk to you, sir, they say that their leader has been kidnapped.'

The Doctor watched Larna leave the Castellan's office. The image in the mirror began fading away, replacing itself with the Doctor's own, haunted face.

'Thank you,' he said.

'She is a beautiful young woman.'

'Yes,' the Doctor said, faintly embarrassed.

He remembered her lying on the mosaic floor of the power room, her blood spilling over the tiles, the knife that had killed her in his hand. He looked over at Omega, and thought of his wife, thought of her portrait in his rooms and her pendant around Larna's neck. The Doctor had made his choice, discarding – murdering – Larna. He had climbed over her dead body to get here, he had abandoned her and Gallifrey and the Sontarans and Rutans, all because of the power here.

'You still feel guilt, do you?' Omega said.

'Of course I do,' the Doctor insisted. 'Whatever I have done to redeem myself since, I still stabbed her.'

Omega frowned. 'But now there was no crime. You are feeling guilty about a crime that you didn't commit.'

'I committed it.'

'Not any more. It never happened.'

'And it's as easy as that?'

'Yes.'

'It seems like cheating, somehow,' the Doctor noted, remembering that he had taken Larna's hand, started to dance, shared thoughts and intimacies with her.

'Just different rules.'

She had returned, wearing a green dress that wouldn't have been out of place at a medieval banquet on Earth. It had a full skirt and an embroidered bodice, with a tight waistband. Her hair had been carefully arranged around a pearl tiara.

'Dinner is served,' she announced.

The Doctor walked over to her, took her arm.

'Are you all right?' she asked.

'Are you all right?' he repeated. She gave a careful nod.

The Doctor looked up and the throne room had become a banqueting chamber, dominated by a large triangular oak table. There was a high-backed chair at each point of the table, and three full place settings had been laid. Beyond the other archway was the clanking of pots, the rattling of cutlery, the hissing of pans. The kitchens. And the room had always been like this, he remembered. They'd walked in and the table had always been there, and Omega had always been seated with his back to the fire. The flames glinted from the metal armour and framed his vast body. An effect, of course, that was fully intentional.

The Doctor stepped back into the room, pulled a chair back for his companion, then took the remaining one for himself. He glanced down. The cutlery was all of the finest silver, lovingly engraved with various designs familiar from ancient Gallifrey. Each of the three diners had enough of it in front of them to open a shop: laid out in front of his plate, for example, was a teaspoon, tablespoon, coffee spoon, soup spoon, cake spoon and a serving spoon, along with a few others with more arcane function. There were equivalent numbers of knives and forks.

He looked up. Omega was already munching at a leg of… something. Chicken, probably.

'What will you have, Doctor?' he asked, the meat visible in his mouth as he spoke.

'I've not seen the menu,' he replied.

'You can have anything. Anything at all.'

'Anything at all?' the Doctor repeated softly.

Omega nodded.

'Not meat. I'm a vegetarian.'

'Whatever you eat, Doctor, no animal will die. Your meal will be the product of my mind.'

The Doctor snapped a smile. 'It's the principle.'

'What principle? That you don't eat imaginary animals? Feast yourself on minotaur steak and dragon scale soup.'

'When I meet unicorns, Lord Omega, the very last thing that I want to do is turn them into burgers. It would be like… well, you wouldn't serve roast Gallifreyan, would you? Even imaginary Gallifreyan.'

'No? I could do so…' He paused, a wide smile on his lips. Then he laughed, the half-chewed remains of an imaginary chicken spluttering out over his part of the table.

The Doctor shuddered. 'Could I see the menu, please?'

Omega grunted his disapproval, but with a flourish of his gauntlet a slim volume appeared on the Doctor's side plate.

The Doctor grinned, and picked the book up. 'Ta.'

'What will you have?' Omega asked his wife as the Doctor busied himself. She selected a vegetable soup and a glass of a particular type of Gallifreyan sweet wine. It duly appeared in front of her. She selected the appropriate spoon, and began to eat.

The Doctor opened the menu in the middle. The pages were thin, almost tissue paper, like the pages of his mother's old Bible. He had to wet his finger to turn them. He flicked through a few starters.

'Well, Doctor?'

'Perfectly well, thank you, Lord Omega.' He closed the menu and then opened it up. Once again it seemed to open in the middle. This time it was halfway through listing all the Main Courses, in tiny writing. This page listed three dozen variations of beef dishes. He rifled through the book, a dozen pages at a time, but never seemed to approach the end. Finally, he slammed it shut.

'The best thing about books,' the Doctor confided to his fellow diners, 'is that you can always tell when you're getting to the end. No matter how tricky the situation the hero's in, you hold the book in your hand and think, "Hang on, I'm two hundred and twenty-nine pages in, with only another fifty-one to go. It started slow, but it's building to a climax." This menu, though, with every single detail spelled out for you on an infinite number of pages is just dull. Where's the fun if everything's possible?'

Omega glowered at him.

'I'll just have a glass of water, please.' It appeared in front of him. 'And the bill.'

'You're my guest.'

The Doctor sipped at his water. 'Tanstaafl. There ain't no such thing as a free lunch. We both know that I was brought here for a reason. If we could get down to business.'

Omega placed his drumstick on his plate, where it dissolved.

'I want to cross back to the universe of matter.'

'Well,' the Doctor said, taking a deep breath, 'you can't have everything that you want.'

Omega rumbled, the castle shaking a little.

'There's no use rumbling,' the Doctor said scathingly. 'It's not possible. Your consciousness is needed to maintain this universe you've created, without you all order will end. But you're a part of this universe. You can't leave without destroying yourself. You've been here for two million years, an infinite amount of power at your disposal, and you've not worked out a way around that problem. I'm very flattered that you think that I'll work out a way over dinner, but... sometimes there just isn't a solution.'

'You are very perceptive,' Omega growled.

'Well, yes,' the Doctor agreed. 'Now, the solution seems obvious: get another consciousness in to take the burden from you. He maintains the universe while you make your escape. That's the deal you offered Savar – to be a god here in this infinite gilded cage. But Savar didn't like the terms, and all you managed to do was make him especially sensitive to the ravages of the Effect. I take it that you are behind his transformations?'

Omega nodded.

'So you started fishing around the universe, looking for another candidate. A Time Lord on the brink of death, someone with nothing to lose. You'd answer their prayers, not only give them life, but eternal life.'

The Doctor glanced across the table, smiled across at his wife. 'But our mutual friend here refused.'

'No,' she said softly. 'No, I didn't.'

Omega's laughter filled the room again.

The Doctor looked around, a little disconcerted.

'Tell him,' he commanded.

'I was killed,' she said calmly. 'A bullet in the back of the head. Not enough of my brain survived to initiate or control the regenerative process. I would have died. Omega was watching me, he removed me from spacetime, the instant before my death. I materialised on a vast expanse of grey sand, naked and alone. I thought it was the afterlife, and in a way it was.'

'After a while, I made myself known to her, made her comfortable.'

'I'm sure you did,' the Doctor said. 'After all, you had so much to gain if she accepted the terms of your offer.'

'Listen to him, Doctor. He saved my life.'

'For a reason,' he replied. 'He wanted his freedom in return. If Omega simply wanted to save you, he could have manipulated the timelines, made it so the bullet missed. I was testing you out on that one before, and you proved you could bring Larna back to life without having to bring her here.'

'Perfectly correct.'

'But your little scheme didn't work, did it? Why not? Her consciousness should have been enough. That's been bothering me. Is that why you brought me here? To find out why it didn't work?'

'You are not here to *provide* the answer, Doctor. You *are* the answer.'

The Doctor pursed his lips. tapping them with his finger. 'Are you absolutely sure you're asking the right question?'

Omega leant back in the chair. 'I shattered one set of chains only to discover another. My body was destroyed. Only my... soul survived. Only that part of me which is me still exists. There is nothing of me that can return to the universe of matter. Not without... help.'

'Omega needs a consciousness here to maintain the universe as he leaves,' she explained, 'I could fulfil that role. But at the moment there's nowhere for him to go. He needs a body for his soul to take over. He can't create one from scratch, for the same reason he can't leave the universe of anti-matter.'

'My body's already taken,' the Doctor said, palm over his chest. 'By me.'

'You have a spare.' Omega pointed at the cracked mirror. The Doctor saw himself, asleep on the floor of the Librarinth.

'A Time Lord body, in the universe of matter, right on top of the Effect itself. I could transfer myself into that, resume my place in the universe. A situation so perfect it is almost contrived.'

'By whom?' the Doctor asked.

Omega chuckled.

'You will remain here, in a universe where you are a god, with the woman you love and thought you'd lost for ever. You can shape this place, populate it, at will. You will have everything, all that you want. Literally your wildest dreams. Everything but the power to return to the universe of matter.'

The Doctor stood, grabbing the edge of the table. 'And what makes you think that I'll agree to all this? Why would I let a god loose in the universe, particularly one with a grudge against the Time Lords?'

'I wouldn't be a god there, a naked singularity cannot exist in the real universe. I don't want to be a god there. Before I was a god, I was a man, and I long for that again. It is the only thing my powers cannot grant me here.'

The Doctor smiled, not fooled by Omega's pained expression. He turned away from Omega, paced towards the fire. 'You came from an age when Gallifrey ruled by the sword, when it used its great powers to dominate others. As President you will be given full access to the Matrix, the Great Key, the Demat Gun, the Magnetron, the blackstars... not to mention a whole arsenal of weapons that only the President knows about. And you're one of the Gallifreyan Elders, one of the true immortals. You would be President for ever. Singularity or not, even as a man there would be nothing to stop you. Nothing. So I'm afraid I couldn't possibly allow you to go back.'

Omega gave a small smile, barely noticeable.

'Whatever makes you think you have a choice?'

Chapter Eleven
Speak of the Devil

A burst of blue light splashed over the ramparts of the Station, the only light in the dark universe. Moments later, there was a distant roar, like a crashing wave or a rumble of thunder. The entire structure of spacetime was churning and boiling like a cauldron, and the Station rocked with it, but the stasis halo held.

The six crewmen stood at their posts around the Station's console. They'd got used to the shifting floor beneath them many hours ago and, as the Station rocked, they rocked with it. The Station wasn't sustaining any damage, and they'd concluded that this wasn't an attack directed at them, simply a side-effect of the increasing size of the breach in spacetime. Since contact with Gallifrey had been lost, the crack had widened, and space and time around it had strained to accommodate the growth. Sudden, violent bursts of energy were only the most obvious effects. After almost a day in the dead universe, the crew of the Station had analysed the anti-matter/matter annihilations that caused the breach, they had begun to be able to predict the Effect's behaviour.

A few of the less sensitive monitors were still aimed at the Needle, and Lords Hemal and Quarduk had brought their TARDISes around to surround the object. At a very, very safe distance, of course. Those remaining in the Station were calm. They were waiting now, sure that they could sit out the storm. They were waiting to see if the inhabitants of the Needle would react to their presence, waiting for the disturbances to subside, waiting for Gallifrey to restore the timegate.

They had spent the day building up a composite map of the habitable area of the Needle, collecting as much intelligence as their instruments allowed. Hedin had been on duty the whole time. The Technicians were operating a rota system: five hours on, five hours off. Even the Magistrate had needed rest, although - like the other crewmen who had tried - he had found it impossible to sleep. He sat in his armchair, sipping at his wine, admiring the older man's stamina. Hedin was still there, patiently plotting points and comparing the results of observations with the computer predictions, showing few signs of fatigue.

'We have it, now, I think,' Hedin announced. 'Complete topography, with a full analysis of energy flow.' The Technicians at the other stations were nodding.

The Magistrate placed his glass on the side table and returned to the console, climbing back up the steps to take his place in the centre of the control deck. Kinxoc, the youthful Technician who at been at the post, stepped down.

'Show me,' the Magistrate commanded.

A holographic representation of the Needle appeared in the column in the centre of the console. All six people operating the controls stared into it. It was surrounded by fine yellow lines.

'The defence perimeter envelops the whole Needle,' Hedin began, 'with the energy projectors mounted every few million kilometres along the length of the Needle. There is a greater concentration in the habitable zones.'

The image rapidly zoomed in to the area that had supported a biosphere.

'Here there is very little activity. Plenty of evidence of extensive life in the distant past, almost no life or energy signs now. But there is a small fusion generator... here –' (another zoom) – 'and this is the crucial area.'

It was a roughly pyramidal structure, several miles high, in a state of serious disrepair.

'There are life signs down there. It also coincides with a major nexus of the information infrastructure. I suspect that the entire defence system is run from a complex in that area.'

'Lifesigns? Have you located the Doctor?' The Magistrate stared into the image as if he might see him there.

Hedin gave a quivering smile. 'I cannot say. Hold on –'

There was a bright flash of light, running from one end of the Needle to the other. The entire structure rocked visibly. The Needle was so large that any force capable of doing that was truly awesome.

The lights had begun to flicker. The Magistrate looked around. 'Are we under attack?' he asked.

Technician Apa was grinning. 'No, no. Just the opposite.'

There was a wheezing groaning sound, and a featureless white obelisk slowly faded into existence in the corner of the control deck. Before the process was complete, the door had slid open and half a dozen Time Lords and members of the Watch began to pour out, fanning around the room. They all carried medical cases. Three coffin-like medical caskets floated out after them on a raft of antigravity.

At the front of the group was the Lady Larna, in a cranberry work tunic.

The Magistrate smiled. She'd seen him, and made her way towards him. He joined her halfway down the steps of the console.

'You have power here,' she said.

The Magistrate nodded.

'Your link to the Eye was cut, we feared the worst.'

Hedin had shuffled around to meet them. 'The Doctor came up with a solution.'

'He made it,' she said nodding. She'd known, and had never doubted him. 'Where is he now?'

The Magistrate swept his arm to indicate the central column and the hologram of the Needle.

Larna nodded again, businesslike. She knew just as well as the Magistrate that the Doctor could look after himself. 'We haven't much time.'

She unclipped a small box from her cuff and slotted it into the nearest control panel. Instantly, the image of the Castellan appeared. It fizzed for a second. The Magistrate frowned. Technology as simple as a temporal imaging system shouldn't fail. He looked back over to Larna, who had her finger on one of the controls and a grimace on her face.

'He's planning to remove it from spacetime, he's been itching to do it all night. Talk to him.'

The Magistrate nodded. She released the control.

'– to them. See to it, Pendrel.'

'I can hear you now, Castellan,' the Magistrate announced.

The tall hologram turned around, clearly pleased that the link was open again. 'I'm still the Acting-President, Magistrate. It is good to see you. We feared that you had been destroyed. Our counter-measure is primed and ready for launch'.

'The situation here has stabilised. Hold your fire.'

Voran was clearly annoyed. 'A pre-emptive strike might –'

'The Doctor is down there,' the Magistrate insisted.

'Right now, Magistrate, that statement is more likely to make we want to –' The Castellan sighed, a little melodramatically. 'If you are sure...'

The Magistrate was nominally still talking to the Castellan, but he turned to Larna. 'The Doctor managed to reach the surface of the Needle, but we don't know what has happened to him since. We've now got detailed maps of the Needle, including its defences.'

The Castellan was nodding. 'You seem to have the situation under control there. Good. There are a number of matters that demand my attention here on Gallifrey. We will continue to monitor your situation, and of course you may have any men or resources that you feel are necessary. I will send reinforcements to you, Magistrate, but I'm afraid that Lady Larna must now return to the Capitol.'

The young woman gave an almost imperceptible shake of her head.

The Magistrate stepped between them. 'The Lady Larna's expertise is needed here, Castellan. We need to form a plan of action.'

Voran sighed. 'Very well. I want that plan from you within the hour. I'm keeping our other option on standby, Magistrate, and I want the Station and the remaining TARDISes to go to Demat configuration. The situation there still endangers Gallifrey, don't forget that. That's it, Pendrel. Thank you.'

The image of the Castellan was gone.

'Thank you,' Larna said. 'What's the Doctor planning?'

'I was rather hoping that you would tell me that.'

'He wouldn't tell me.' There was disappointment on her young face. 'But there's power down there. I don't think he wants it for himself, but it's such a temptation.'

The Magistrate pointed out a section of console. 'Thanks to Lord Hedin, we know that the Doctor managed to reach the surface, we even know roughly where he is.'

She was already moving towards the instruments. 'I'll see if I can pinpoint him.'

'I haven't been able to,' Hedin said, shaking his head.

Larna smiled down at him. 'Lord Hedin, you are clearly on the brink of exhaustion,' she whispered, 'and it has probably been a while since you have created an Infinity Chamber model, rather than just manipulated one.'

'Besides,' the Magistrate began, impressed by her lack of modesty, 'you should find it much easier to locate his telepathic traces.'

Larna blushed, and both Hedin and the Magistrate chuckled.

He hadn't slept for many weeks.

Savar's dual existence robbed him of sleep, of dreams.

His other self, the blind one, had no sense of the loss. It fuelled his insanity, served his purpose. His dark master was returning. This Savar sensed it, he had to prevent it at all costs.

He could sense the powers of evil and darkness drawing closer. Not just the trapped god. He was merely the first. His defeat might ward off what was to follow, though, delay the inevitable.

There had been a time when Savar had doubted the existence of evil, seen it as a construction of an ordered society or of that society's elite. Darkness then had simply been the absence of the light. But not any more. *He* was evil, or a part of him was, at least. He knew that as night fell, a version of him emerged with dark hearts. He could feel that evil within him now, locked into his blood, his marrow, his DNA. But was that evil within everyone or just him? If it remained locked away, then was that just the same as it not being there at all?

He had a waking dream of the future, he saw candlelit tunnels, the very oldest parts of the Citadel. The place this would be decided. He had to be there, he had to call on the darkness within him.

His mind reached into the lock of his cell. It found the tumblers and bolts, drew them around, slid them apart.

The door clicked open.

Larna rubbed her eye, watched another panning shot of the Needle's surface move across the display. She tapped a search sequence into the computer.

The console gave a soft chime.

'I've found him,' she announced.

The Doctor's bio-signature was registering at the edge of the structure that Hedin had located. There were other life forms there, too. Now she knew where to look, Larna began increasing the resolution of the scan.

The Magistrate was stepping up the console to stare into the central column. The display was zooming in at dizzying speed towards the structure. It focused in on a dome, then the scanners penetrated even that. 'Already?' he asked.

'Hedin was closer than he realised.' But she could tell that the Magistrate didn't accept her explanation, that he was truly impressed.

The display in front of her was resolving into a sharp picture.

Larna gasped.

The Magistrate stared into the column, looking at the same image: the Doctor lying slumped on a pile of bricks.

'Is he alive?' she asked.

'He's in a deep coma,' Hedin reported. 'Four humanoids in the same chamber.' The picture switched, showing three sleeping men in dark clothes. A fourth sat on guard, watching over them.

'Are those the Needle People?' asked one of the Technicians. 'I was expecting... you know... something bigger.'

'What do we do?' she asked.

The Magistrate looked at the image of the Doctor for a moment.

'Come with me,' he ordered. 'Lord Hedin, report our findings to the Council.'

Voran stared down into the Infinity Chamber.

From here he had a perfect view of the Station and the two TARDISes as they moved into their attack positions around the Needle. They were the only four objects with any energy or light to them in the dead universe.

The ranks around him were depleted, and no one seemed entirely sure where they should be standing, except the monks who kept their distance.

Hedin – an image of Hedin – stood at his side. 'As you see, Acting-President, we have taken up a defensive position.' The Chamber image moved silently down to the Needle, until they were inside one of the buildings.

'Activity is centred here,' Hedin reported. 'This is where we have located the Doctor. The Magistrate plans to take his TARDIS down there and –'

Voran felt a familiar tug at his sleeve.

'What is it, Pendrel? It had better be important.' Voran turned, to be confronted by Pendrel and, behind him, one of the Sontarans.

'This is Chief of Staff Grol. He wishes to speak to the leader of the Time Lords on a matter of the greatest importance.'

The Acting-President snorted. He'd forgotten all about the aliens.

They could rot for all he cared, but he was shrewd enough not to say that out loud. It was squat, and wore the same space armour as the creatures he'd seen on the Public Record Video. It smelt of diesel oil.

Voran turned to Hedin. 'Please bear with us, my Lord.' Hedin bowed respectfully.

'Where is Dok-Tor, the leader?' the Sontaran barked. His bloated head and piggy face did not go well together, the wispy moustache simply adding to the impression that this was something less than human.

'I am the Lord Voran, Acting-President of the High Council of the Time Lords.' He didn't think it advisable to mention that the man in charge of the negotiations was a fugitive and a murderer.

The Sontaran grunted. 'You will suffice. We have lost contact with our leader.'

'He is very busy in Conference,' Voran said delicately. He hesitated. 'A private session with the Doctor and the Rutan ambassador.'

Behind Grol, the image in the Infinity Chamber flared up. Voran leant around the Sontaran to get a better look. The Needle was crackling now with energy.

'Hedin, what is that?' he asked.

'A surge in energy from the breach in spacetime, Acting-President. It falls within our predicted model.'

The alien gave the same grunt as before. He stepped back between Voran and the Infinity Chamber. 'You are lying, you are a dishonourable creature.'

Voran was rather taken aback. 'How dare you! I am the leader of the High Council of the Time Lords.'

'Your title means nothing to me. Show me General Sontar.'

Voran scowled. 'Oh, go away, would you? I'm far too busy.'

The Sontaran jabbed his claw towards Voran. 'You have taken the supreme leader of our race hostage. That is an act of war. Our delegation will return to the fathership. If you do not present Sontar to us within one hour, we shall be forced to take military action. We are acting within our rights under Intergalactic Law.'

'You are declaring war against Gallifrey?' Voran said, still straining to see around Grol. 'That is ludicrous.'

Grol strode past him, towards the exit.

Pendrel looked over at Voran expectantly.

'What?' the Acting-President asked, shrugging apologetically at an impatient Hedin.

'You will have to authorise the use of the time scoop to return the Sontarans to their fleet,' Pendrel explained.

'Fine, fine. Good riddance to them. See to it,' Voran said, waving his hand. 'I'm sorry, Lord Hedin. You were saying?'

Idly, Larna wondered what Vrayto would make of the Uncertainty Suit.

Her maid would have approved of the fact that it covered every inch of her body except for her face and her hands, but at the same time she would have been shocked by how thin that covering was. It was a matt black skin, stretched taut over every curve and joint of her body like a silk stocking. Putting the garment on had been an unpleasant experience – she'd placed a patch on her hip and it had quickly spread over her like a mould. Now it was on, it was dry, and surprisingly warm.

Larna was in the Magistrate's TARDIS, in the nearest guest quarters to the console room. Modesty had prevented her from changing in the presence of the Magistrate.

She looked in the mirror, and was surprised. Vrayto would definitely approve. Rather than drawing attention to it, the Suit made her body a void, a black shape that you almost instinctively looked away from.

Which was the whole point.

She tied her hair back. Once that was done, she was ready to return to the console room and the Magistrate.

He was also in a Suit. Larna found it impossible to look at him, so instead she concentrated on what he was doing. He was bent over one of the medical units that her team had brought here from Gallifrey. It was a metal casket that bore a disturbing similarity to a coffin. Only the pulsing of soft light from within the box and the two symbols on its lid gave away its true purpose. The Magistrate was using a small tool to stabilise the anti-gravity field that held the coffin aloft.

He pulled himself up, and Larna giggled when he looked straight past her.

'Are you ready?' he asked, taking his place at the console. 'You know what we must do?'

She took a deep breath and nodded. 'We fly in, via a parallel universe, the method that the Doctor used, and then rescue him.'

He handed her a small palm-dispenser. It fitted neatly in her hand, sticking there.

'It contains four Z-caps,' he explained, holding one of his own up. 'Discs the size of a coin that stop the flow of time over a limited area. Press one anywhere on a person's body and they will be immobilised.' He slotted the disc back into place, ready for use. 'Once we have secured the Doctor and timelocked the Needle People, we will locate the Needle's control centre and disable the defence systems.'

Larna's expression must have betrayed her feelings, because the Magistrate smiled.

'There's no risk,' she said, 'I know that.'

Now his smile was wider. 'There's a risk,' he chuckled. 'We are going to be risking our lives. And our actions down there – actions that the Acting-President does not know about, and which he hasn't authorised – might well provoke a war between the people on the Needle and the Time Lords.'

She caught her breath, then laughed, suddenly liberated. 'I understand, and I'm ready. When do we leave?'

The Magistrate pulled a lever, and the door swung open. 'We arrived while you were changing.'

He strode through the door, and the first of the Needle People was on his back, unconscious, before she'd followed him out. She wondered what the strange crumpling noise was, only to see the Magistrate standing over the slumped body of an old man in loose black clothes. There was a Z-cap on the man's forehead.

The floor was littered with rubble. There was broken ground beneath her feet, a cracked dome above her head. She glanced back and saw that the TARDIS had disguised itself as a block of fallen masonry.

The Magistrate was already advancing towards the fire in the centre of the room. Larna – her training finally asserting itself – helped him by pulling in close behind him, advancing with him, watching his back. In the image of this room that they had seen from the Station, the Doctor had been lying unconscious by the fire. Three Needle People had been asleep there. The fourth had been on guard, nearer the edge of the room. He was the one that the Magistrate had just immobilised.

The light quality here was poor, but her eyes quickly adjusted to it. She hadn't been ready for the cold, and the Suit was no help. She had to rub her hands together and speed up her metabolic rate.

The Doctor was there, prone on the floor, seemingly in a deep coma. The three Needle People were around him, asleep.

She stepped over to the Doctor, and she could hear the medical unit following close behind her.

The three Needle People were stirring. She could imagine the Magistrate edging round them, invisible now in his Suit and the darkness. The best she could do was stay in plain sight, distract them while he got into position. This way she could also tend to the Doctor.

'Halt!' a voice commanded behind her, to her left.

'Good evening,' she said, not looking up. Instead, she knelt at the Doctor's side. As she had thought, he was in some sort of healing trance. There were no signs of external injuries.

'Stand up.'

She didn't. They were moving to surround her. The oldest one held a stave, a six-foot wooden pole. The others had guns of some kind.

'Where's Pallant?' one of them asked. A hand knocked at the lid of the medical unit. 'This is some sort of mobile intensive care unit?'

Larna rose to her feet, folded one hand in front of the other. 'It's only a medical unit,' she said.

'Hands apart!' one of them shouted.

Another, the eldest one, the one with the stave, was pulling back, disappearing into the shadows. An odd time to leave the room.

Two of them remaining. Larna smiled, and began walking towards the nearest. She had just seen the Magistrate in the shadows. The eldest man was making his escape, the Magistrate was following him.

'Halt or I fire!' the man she was approaching called.

Larna continued to walk towards him. She was between them both now.

'I don't know what to do...' he shouted across to his comrade helplessly.

'Helios, what do we do?' the other one cried pitifully, obviously appealing to the old man who had deserted them.

Larna hesitated.

They both opened fire. The guns were energy pulse weapons of some kind, firing off sparse bursts of light and a chirping sound. At this range, they couldn't possibly miss.

The Suit kicked in, and suddenly Larna was standing a little to the left of where they were aiming, and so they missed her. A simple application of Heisenberg's Uncertainty Principle, linked with really rather primitive time travel technology. The Suit monitored the future, and arranged for it and its wearer to be elsewhere when anything hostile was due to hit it.

But the energy had to go somewhere. Two energy bolts. The first came from in front of her, streaked past her head, she heard a crack and a muffled explosion as in slammed into the back wall. The other bolt came from behind her. It spat past her at about chest height, travelling in a perfectly straight line. A fraction of a second before it happened, she realised it was going to hit the man in front of her.

His chest burst, and he fell back, his legs and arms flapping irrelevantly. Larna tried to shout a warning, but it had already happened, he was being thrown back by the force. The man behind her was panicking, firing again and again at her. Other blasts started blowing chunks from the walls and shelves.

Larna was unscathed as she strode towards the wounded man, the shots simply bounced from the medical unit. There was, however, the danger that a stray shot could hit the Doctor.

Larna reached the wounded man, knelt beside him. There was a nasty, sucking wound where the man's chest should be. She slipped a Z-cap from her palm. He was still alive, looking at her with pleading, terrified eyes. She smiled down at him, pressed the Z-cap to his forehead. He froze, the wound had stopped moving. A stable condition, as a physician might have put it.

The old man with the stave had fled, the wounded man was frozen, the night Watchman was frozen. There was one remaining, the gunman. He'd hardly moved, he was still standing by the fire, not very far from the Doctor or the medical unit. He was still firing at her, but he seemed to understand the hopelessness of doing so: the shots were less frequent now. Thankfully, it hadn't occurred to the gunman that he might take the Doctor hostage. His only tactic was to unclip his cloak, letting it drop to the ground, freeing up his arms a little more.

Larna strode towards him. He shot twice, both bolts going wide. When she was two feet away he swung the gun at her, trying to club her with it. He missed. There was a metal plate by his chair. Larna bent down and picked it up, allowing him time to miss her once again shooting from point blank range, this time blowing a great hole in the floor. She swung the plate at him, connecting with the side of his head. Dazed, he lost his footing.

He managed another shot. It hit the plate, knocking it out of Larna's hand, hurting her. She yelped, clutching her wrist. She went cold as she realised that he had dislodged the Z-cap dispenser, and it was on the floor somewhere, in amongst the debris.

The Suit fizzed.

No, this wasn't happening...

She held out her arm, saw it beginning to resolve. He'd damaged the Suit, managed to catch it out. In moments she would be facing an armed man, a trained soldier, wearing nothing but a body stocking.

A glint caught her eye. One of the Z-caps, picked out by the firelight, just out of reach.

She stood her ground as her Suit's power faded, let the gunman assess her: see where she was, that she was just a woman.

The Suit had seconds of life left. He raised his gun. They were three feet apart, standing over the Doctor.

Larna reached out, grabbed his wrist with one hand and twisted it. He squealed, dropping the pistol. He balled his fist, but she rolled out of the way and he punched solid marble, almost certainly breaking his hand. Despite that, the man lurched for her, throwing all his weight behind a punch that was destined to miss. Larna side-stepped, recovered the Z-cap from where she had seen it and pressed the disc onto his forehead. He fell over, almost comically, frozen in position but still subject to gravity.

Larna took a deep breath and knelt down to examine the Doctor, feeling for his pulses. He was warm – warmer than she was. He was in a deep coma. She checked his breathing, his neck and his chest. He didn't show any obvious signs of injury. She put her arm around his waist, grabbing his hip, placing his arm over her shoulder and hoisted him up.

He made a low moaning noise.

'You're safe,' she told him. They were fully upright now. The medical unit had moved around in front of them, its lid was open, it was tipping itself up on its end to allow him in. Larna took a step forward, bringing the Doctor with her. He dropped into the casket. The lid was already sliding shut.

It was cold. She remembered that the last of the Needle People to fall had discarded his cloak. She found it, draped it over her shoulders. As she had suspected, it was very warm. The material was a good insulator, and it felt as if it contained heating elements, like an electric blanket.

She'd forgotten about the Magistrate. He had gone up after the last one, the older man with the staff. After that he would start looking for the room where the defence controls were. Larna had seen which door they had used. She hurried after them, through and along a short, dimly lit corridor. There was silence... no, she could hear someone moving around. This was the first time she'd ever done this, the first time that she'd ever walked down a corridor without knowing what was at the other end. She'd spent her entire life in the perfectly regulated environment of the Capitol, she knew every room and alcove. Here... here there could be a room full of the lion things that she'd seen from the Station, or defence robots that didn't show up on scans.

Twenty yards along was a brick archway. The sound was coming from that room. Larna tensed, peeking around the corner.

'Come in, my dear, it's all over.' The Magistrate was at a backlit control panel. The old man was slumped in one corner, bruises over his face and a Z-cap stuffed in his mouth. The walls of this small room were inset with ledges and alcoves, these were packed with various ancient-looking artefacts from any number of planets.

The Magistrate noticed that her Suit wasn't working. 'Trouble?'

'I got them all, the Doctor's safe in the medical unit.'

He returned to the controls. 'Do you have your computer?'

She took her place beside him, unclipped the terminal from her belt, placed it over an interface socket, and dialled the activator. Gallifreyan equipment was generally able to decipher other technology, and this was no exception. The unreadable text on the display rapidly resolved into Gallifreyan script.

'It's advanced,' she said. 'Normally I'd just link it up to the Matrix, but if we do that, there's a chance that the Needle People could infiltrate.'

'They've all been dealt with,' the Magistrate reminded her.

'The ones we know about, and we don't know how smart their computers are.'

He nodded thoughtfully.

Even just using portable equipment, the alien computer couldn't keep its secrets.

The Magistrate peered at the display. 'This controls the defences for the whole Needle,' he said disbelievingly. 'Well, Hedin predicted that this was where we would find the control system.'

She adjusted a few of the dials. 'This is the only controller. The entire defence system is automated, channelled through this box.'

'Sensible enough when there's a small population here,' he said coolly. 'It would be prudent to leave back-ups hidden around the place, but they'll need priming and programming. Can you reroute all defences through that box?'

She nodded, tapping the control that did it.

'Defence grid now controlled from here. All defensive systems dropping to standby mode.'

'Good. May I?' The Magistrate moved her aside and then took a stubby black tube from his belt. He pointed it at the wall panel, which cracked, then burst into a shower of sparks.

'That should help us,' he said. He took her computer from her.

'We should get the Doctor back to the Station. Go back to the TARDIS and get him inside. I'll finish up here.' He handed her the TARDIS key.

'I don't want to go alone –' Larna began, but swallowed the words before the Magistrate heard her.

He smiled, trying to put her at ease. 'Take this,' he suggested, handing over the weapon he had used to destroy the control panel. 'You won't need it, but if it makes you feel safer…'

The gun was heavier than it looked. Larna checked she was able to find the trigger and then clipped it to her belt.

The build-up of energy around the Needle was reaching a climax. Bolts, like lightning, began flickering across the surface. They caused no damage, or noise. Silently, they surged along the length of the Needle, radiating outward.

Something was happening.

Something was coming.

The Magistrate was on his knees, gasping for breath. The flagstones were wet, cold water was seeping through the skin of his Suit.

'Will you serve me?' a calm voice asked.

'Never!' the Magistrate spat, facing his attacker.

The red eyes boring down on him grew brighter, the Magistrate heard himself yelping, and couldn't help but look away.

'I have watched you, I have seen all your lives. I know what you have been and what you will be. You do not deserve an end like this. Serve me!'

'No,' the Magistrate said, summoning as much dignity as he could. 'So be it.'

With a wave of a hand, the Magistrate vanished.

The ground was shaking at irregular intervals as Larna reached the room with the fire, the one where the Doctor was safe in his medical unit. It sounded as if there was vast machinery beneath her, like the engines of a vast ocean-going liner. Machinery that was spasmodically grinding down to a halt. The sounds were mechanical, echoing, distant.

She walked towards the fire, the only point of heat in the room, the only source of light apart from weak lamps mounted on the walls and a soft blue halo around the medical unit. The firelight was enough to define the outlines of the shelves, and the shapes of the items stacked on them, but it wasn't enough to tell what the items were.

The only sound was the heartbeat thump of the medical unit's generator. She knelt to check the readout. It told her that the Doctor was in a deep coma, with no signs of physical injury.

Larna held up the TARDIS key.

There was a noise from the back of the room. A rustling, clattering noise.

She was on her feet in an instant, head down, poised for an attack.

The three unconscious Needle People would be where she had left them. She picked her way across the rubble to check each one of them in turn. The first was holding out his hands as if he was trying to ward her off. Some instinct prevented Larna from getting too close. She told herself not to be so foolish: the Z-cap was still plainly visible on his forehead.

The second man wasn't going anywhere, the Z-cap was saving his life. There was a hole in his chest, a wound made even more vile by the fact that it wasn't moving, that the blood was held in pace by the stasis field. Larna wondered who these people were, what they were called. On the Station, she had scanned the area for life signs. There were a number of groups of hunting carnivores, but very little else in the way of life. Although they couldn't completely rule out the possibility that there were other inhabitants, they hadn't found any other Needle People anywhere. Did they feel as lonely, as isolated as Larna felt here? She knew that she had a Station and a planet to return to. This ruin was all that these people had.

Where was the third one?

She turned, trying to reorientate herself. He had been by one of the three doors, but which one? Whatever direction it was into the shadows. She steeled herself, allowed her pupils to dilate to improve her vision. The way was clear: the people had cleared a route through the debris to the door. Beneath the rubble was a beautiful marble floor. When there had been sunlight here, it must have been possible to see beautiful gold-green veins there, but such subtleties were a thing of the past in this deadening darkness.

There was another clattering. Coming from the direction she was heading. Larna took a deep breath, but didn't stop.

The last one was standing where he should, the Z-cap stuck firm to his head where the Magistrate had put it. He was the last one *here*, she corrected herself. There was the other one, the oldest, frozen to the floor of the control room. This one was darker than the others. He looked calm, confident. Again, something prevented her from getting too close. She was six feet away. Even from here, even in the darkness, she could see that his metabolic processes were in stasis. He wasn't breathing: his chest wasn't rising, his nostrils were perfectly still. Even the most skilled gymnast would not be able to hold that one-legged pose naturally, not without some tremble of muscles, some slip of his foot.

He was in stasis, so why was she so afraid of him?

She told herself to stop being so foolish and took a step closer.

His clothes were worn, faded. The cuffs were frayed. They'd been beautiful once: ornate embroidery over the finest cottons and silks. The rubbery cloak he wore looked newer, as though it had been broken out of stores only a few years ago.

She took another step, and now they were inches apart.

His face was kind. This was an honourable warrior, not some vicious fighter.

She reached out, stroked his face. She was still afraid of him. This man was a statue, held in place by the same processes that stopped yesterday being today, or page two hundred and thirty-seven of a book from being page two hundred and thirty-eight.

She was a Time Lord of Gallifrey, she had graduated top of her year. And now she was here on an alien artefact, trillions of years from home, in charge of the situation, entrusted with the life of a member of the

High Council. This was where she had always wanted to be, and now she was letting her irrational fears conquer her.

Larna smiled, and closed her eyes. She was at one with the universe. Her isolation was liberation. This is how she always hoped it would feel. There was danger here, there was uncertainty, but there were real choices and opportunities. She didn't know what would happen next, or what she would see when she opened her eyes.

Something brushed against her hand.

Her eyes and mouth snapped wide open. There was a small sound, not even a yelp. Larna realised that she had made it.

There was a trail of dust over the man's face and shoulder. It had been dust and plaster from the ceiling.

She started breathing, brought her body's production of adrenaline back to something like its normal levels.

Calm again, she turned her back on the frozen warrior, back to the fire at the centre of the room. The medical unit was still there, solid as a standing stone.

She was just in time to see it topple onto the fire.

It crushed the light out of the fire, sending a cloud of cinders billowing in all directions. The room was suddenly dark, but Larna was already striding across it, certain of where she was heading. Its antigravs had failed, all its power had gone.

'Doctor!' she shouted. He'd be all right in there, protected by the unit's casing for a little while. She couldn't say how long.

Pain! She'd caught her leg on something. A metal beam. She stopped, reached down to assess the extent of the injury. When her hand came up sticky with her own blood, she felt as if it had infected her, as though the particles of rusty metal were growing inside her body like bacteria.

She was dizzy, she had to sit down. Some part of her brain guided her safely down to the floor.

It saved her life.

The medical unit burst open in a shower of shrapnel. The heat of the flames must have generated pressure enough to –

'Doctor!' she shouted again. She was on her feet, her wounded leg forgotten.

The remains of the medical unit were twisting and curling in the heat of the flames.

Larna stood at a safe distance, knowing that if the Doctor was still in there that he would be dead. Her only hope was that he had somehow been removed. She made her way forward, but the heat was intense.

There was clattering behind her. Larna tugged the Magistrate's gun from her belt and held it up like a torch.

'Who's there?' she asked.

The shadows were moving. A glimpse of a head here, a limb there, all around her. She was casting some of them herself, but not all of them. Not all of them. There was someone else here.

It was the Doctor.

He stumbled out of the shadows, steadying himself on the side of a shelving unit.

'Doctor,' she said softly. 'It's me.'

He stood properly, straightening his back, staring around, a little wildly.

The room shook, the brickwork beginning to grind against itself. Trails of dust and plaster hissed down.

'Great power... unleashed. We have to get to safety.'

For a moment she wondered if he'd become another Savar, driven mad by what he had seen.

She took his hand. He looked down at first, unsure, but then looked her in the eye and broke into a tight, uncertain, smile. He looked her up and down, as if he barely knew her. Finally, he lurched forwards, hugging her, almost squeezing the breath out of her, planting kisses on her face.

'Larna,' he said, 'Larna, Larna.'

She rested her head on his shoulder, unsure who was supporting who. 'I thought you'd gone,' she said.

The Doctor shrugged her off his shoulder and began looking around for an exit. 'We have to hurry, the anti-matter/matter annihilations are increasing.' As if to emphasise the point, the ground shook once more. 'The breach in spacetime is growing wider.'

He had seen the TARDIS and started to stride towards it. Larna caught his arm.

'Slow down. Doctor, look, you'll have to explain what's going on.' She indicated a pile of books, hoping that he'd sit down for a moment.

'Sorry. Yes,' he began, but carried on towards the time machine. 'I'll explain on the way.'

He reached the door, ran his hand across it.

Larna opened it with the key, and they stepped over the threshold.

kicked her with his other foot. She dropped the gun, and he caught it with one hand.

He lifted her, carried her over to the lever.

'THROW THE SWITCH,' he commanded, dropping her onto it. She felt it shift beneath her back, and she scraped down it.

Omega had stepped out of the way.

Larna scrabbled around for the lever, tried pulling it back down, then up again, then down. It was too late.

Behind her, the aperture was closing, the column of energy was fading.

Voran was staring into the Infinity Chamber.

The two remaining TARDISes and the Station hovered in their positions at points around the Needle. The energy still crackled from the surface of the artefact, it seemed to have intensified.

'Lord Hedin, has there been any contact with the Magistrate or the Lady Larna since they departed?'

'No, Acting-President,' Hedin admitted, 'Our sensors suggest that the defensive grid has been deactivated. There was also a suggestion of a TARDIS launch, but the breach in spacetime is now interfering with our sensors.'

Voran steepled his fingers and drummed them together. 'Worrying, worrying.'

'We could send down another TARDIS?'

'And risk another loss? No. Stand by for further instructions.'

Pendrel hurried over. 'A communication from the Sontaran fathership, sir. It is Chief of Staff Grol once again.'

Voran shook his head. 'I suppose I'll have to talk to them.'

The squat form of the Sontaran Chief of Staff appeared in front of him, rezzing and fizzing as the two technologies came to an arrangement.

'Acting-President,' the rasping voice began, 'you have had your chance. You have not presented Sontar to us. In full knowledge of the Supreme Sontariat, I formally announce that the Sontaran Empire is now at war with the Time Lords of Gallifrey.'

'You can declare war all you like, it still doesn't mean I know where your General Sontar is.'

Grol's eyes narrowed. 'You have violated every principle of Galactic

The console room was warm and dry compared with the surface of the Needle People. The Doctor was stepping over to the console. Larna trailed after him, having to rub her wounded leg as she moved. 'We have to wait for the Magistrate.'

The Doctor didn't react, instead he started flicking switches and pulling levers, seemingly at random.

'There's no time. We must get back to Gallifrey.'

'No!' Larna shouted, but it was too late: the Doctor had thrown the dematerialisation switch. The central column began rising and falling rhythmically, and Larna could feel the power surging into the vast time engines beneath them.

The Doctor was hunched over the instruments, checking and rechecking the course he'd laid in. 'We'll travel directly down the timegate,' he explained. 'It's a long journey, a couple of hours at least.'

He turned to her, looked at her properly for the first time since she'd rescued him. He smiled, a little awkwardly.

'Your leg is in quite a state,' he said. He began rummaging through his pockets. 'I've got some iodine here, I think.'

'Tell me what's happening,' she asked as he came over. 'Why have we abandoned the Magistrate? What about Omega?'

He knelt down, peeled away the part of her Suit around her leg wound. He had found a small bottle and soaked his handkerchief with its contents. Now he pressed it to the wound, made her wince.

'Sorry,' he said.

'What happened?' she said, softly. 'Savar said there was great power down there, but that –'

The Doctor placed a finger to her lip. She caught his wrist.

'Tell me!' she insisted.

'I crossed the threshold,' he said. 'I passed into another universe. Antimatter, regulated by a naked singularity.'

She let go of his wrist. Instead of returning it to his side, he stroked her cheekbone with his fingers and traced a course around her ear, before bringing it back.

'The boundary between the universes of matter and anti-matter is a source of infinite, self-sustaining power. A sentient being can harness that power by using the singularity, and bring theories into fact. It literally allows you to do anything you can imagine – uncouple matter and energy, resolve paradoxes, redraft the laws of mathematics and physics.'

'Including finding a solutions for the Agathon Equations? Allowing whoever controls it to control the past?'

'Yes. Just like Savar said. Omniscience ad omnipotence.'

She gasped a laugh. 'Why come back?'

'All that power comes from harnessing the singularity, and that's safe behind the event horizon of the black hole, shut off from the rest of the universe, like nature intended. It can only exist in the universe of anti-matter.'

'It –' Larna began. The Doctor stared into her eyes. 'Might it be possible to –'

His lip curled into a smile. '– to have a naked singularity in this universe?' he finished for her.

'It ought to be possible,' she said. 'We'd need to find a way to evaporate a black hole to expose the quantum foam at the core. We'd then have to find a way to control the energies that were released. First of all, we'd have to harness a black hole.'

The Doctor smiled. 'Or to go somewhere where there's already a captured black hole waiting for us.'

Larna hesitated. 'The Eye of Harmony.'

The Doctor shrugged. 'A rather melodramatic name, but yes. The black hole that Rassilon brought to Gallifrey.'

Larna looked over at the central column, rising and falling. She bit her lip. 'It would make us into gods.'

'Would you want that power?' he asked. He was testing her, she realised.

'Isn't that what you always say you want the Council to do? Intervene?' The Doctor lent over her, brushed her face with his hand. Larna let him. 'You want the Time Lords to help others to reach their potential, you want to spread peace and knowledge. You don't want to conquer the universe.'

'What do *you* want?' he asked.

She laughed. 'It doesn't matter what I want.'

His hand moved down her neck to the pendant at her collar. He toyed with the blue gem for a moment. Larna looked down at his face.

'Of course it matters,' he said. 'It matters more than anything.'

'What do you want me to say?' she asked quietly. 'It's fantasy.'

'It's power,' he said, sliding his hand over her shoulder, baring it. 'You know how to take it. What would you want with it?'

Larna swallowed. 'You're testing me.'

'Don't you want me to test you?' He was working at her shoulder, massaging away some of the stiffness.

'The High Council won't let us evaporate the Eye of Harmony,' she laughed. 'It's the source of power for all of Gallifrey. And it's not *ours*.'

'They might want it back,' the Doctor conceded, leaning closer.

'Think about what you're saying: civil war on Gallifrey, infinite firepower on both sides. They would have no choice but to use timewar against us.' She shuddered. The Time Wars in Gallifrey's past were a nightmare of contradiction, paradox and death. After the war, the Time Lords had been forced to seal off whole areas of time and space that had become damaged beyond repair.

'*I'd* use timewar against them. I'd use it first, if necessary.'

'Do you think that's what created the grey universe?' she asked, trying to ignore his attention. 'A Time Lord civil war?'

'It's not the only way it could have happened, but it certainly could have happened that way.'

'And you're prepared to risk it?'

'Are you? I would need your help, your expertise.'

She tensed. 'You're not the Doctor, are you?'

'No.' He leant in, nuzzled the side of her neck.

'You're Omega. You've taken control of the Doctor somehow, crossed back into this universe. What have you done with him?'

'The same thing I did with the Magistrate, put him out of harm's way.'

He kissed her cheek. She pushed him away.

'You are evil,' she stated, preparing to stand.

He held her shoulder, didn't let her up. 'How? I have given the Doctor what he desires the most. I have ended an injustice, made things as they should have been.' He leant back in again. 'Without the singularity I am one man. With it, we would be gods. Do you really think anything could stop us? You could have anything you want. More than that: you could have everything you want. It wouldn't be tyranny, not one drop of blood need be spilt, the universe would willingly submit to you. Is that evil?'

'Would you submit to me?'

'Is that what you want?' he asked, releasing his grip on her shoulder. 'Without the singularity, I'm powerless to prevent it.'

'You're just a man?' Larna felt the weight of the Magistrate's gun on her belt. 'Mortal?'

He smiled, held out his hand. 'I'm just a man. It's your choice, Larna. What do you want?'

Chapter Twelve
Infinity and Beyond

Hand below hand, hand below hand, Savar climbs down the brick power shaft towards the centre of Gallifrey and the Eye of Harmony.

The pointing has worn over the millennia, there are plenty of holds for his hands and feet. The mortar crumbles as his fingers brush against it. Behind him is a column of energy, blasting up from the Eye. It's pure white, thick as a tree trunk. It pulses slightly, it hums like a monastic chant.

The source of this energy, and so much more besides is calling to him, or so he believes. Is that his mind, or some Time Lord instinct? The intense gravity of the black hole warps space and time around it, and he can feel that distortion as a lesser creature might sense a bright light or a hot flame. Even here, still far from his destination, his skin tingles.

All the time, the dark Savar inside him strains, writhes, trying to get out. It wants to reach the Eye at all costs, too. That scares him a little, the thought that he might be collaborating with *that*, or even that they might share common purpose.

He understands the paradox, he knows the lunacy of the thought, but he must reach the Eye before the other Savar, he must get there first.

Savar continues his descent.

Lightning flashed over the magic garden, the distant thunder waking the Doctor.

The night air was cool against his skin, but not too cool. The ankle-deep grass was as soft as any mattress. She was fast asleep besides him, at the base of a great apple tree, the smell of her hair mixing with that of the blossom. He could feel her swelling with every breath, and the throb of her single heart. There wasn't a moon in the sky, but there was auroral light, as if it were nearly dawn. But there would be no morning here, not until he willed it.

The Doctor got up, gently so as not to disturb her, and stood over her for a moment. She was at peace, only a little curled up, her head resting serenely in the palm of her hand. Her long, curved body was a pale grey in the no-Moonlight, her blonde hair looked white. He looked at her and knew that he couldn't imagine life without her.

They had been here, together, since the universe had begun.

He knew that this was a prison. He knew that he had been placed here by a being called Omega. The Doctor knew that he wasn't meant to have that knowledge, that Omega hadn't wanted him to know. What the Doctor didn't understand was why Omega had kept that information from him. Why would Omega have thought that he would ever want to escape?

Restless, Larna had made her way back to the control room.

The decor of the Magistrate's TARDIS was sepulchral throughout; narrow corridors with coal-black walls leading to dark, crypt-like bedchambers or cavernous libraries and laboratories. The control room was no exception: a gloomy, intimate space, panelled with ebony, bereft of furniture apart from a single, severe, high-backed chair. The only things by way of decoration were gleaming mechanisms mounted to the walls that may have been vital machinery or mere sculpture. Here, the familiar humming of the TARDIS took on a brooding, sinister note.

Larna took a place at the console itself. The central column was rising and falling like a piston. Far beneath her feet, she could hear the lullaby grinding of the time engines. The lights and displays on the console winked and flashed in their arcane sequences. The time path plotter pulsed, but still wasn't giving any indication of their arrival time. The journey was out of the hands of the TARDIS or its pilot. They were essentially falling through the hole in time rather than flying. There was no indication that their course had varied even slightly from the mathematically perfect, pre-set, preordained course calculated by the Matrix. There wasn't a hint that any of the innumerable safety features that the TARDIS bristled with were failing to operate. Despite that, Larna could sense the unease of the TARDIS, and she shared it.

The return trip to Gallifrey had been straightforward; a far more pleasant experience than the outward trip, with its visions and hallucinations. Despite her long day, despite her aching muscles and headache, Larna had been unable to sleep. Part of it was excitement, her not wanting to miss a moment of this adventure. But mostly it was fear of having another nightmare and of feeling herself die again. The last few nights it had been so real. Drowned in an icy lake, stabbed through the heart by the man that she loved... she had woken each time, desperately surprised and grateful to be alive.

There was a whirring and clicking from the console. She moved around in time to see a display slapping into place. It would only be another ten minutes before they arrived. Arrival point was confirmed as being far below the Citadel.

He would need to know.

She stepped down from the console dais and walked from the control room. The master bedroom was nearby, the door was open.

Larna walked in, expecting him to be asleep there, where she had left him. The bed was empty, except for the white cotton sheets laid curled and twisted at the foot of the four-poster and the pillows at broken angles to the headboard.

She turned as he emerged from the shadows behind her, doing up the last button of a high-collared black jacket, hiding the crisp white shirt beneath. He didn't have his – the Doctor's – glasses on. Was that vanity, or an indication that he didn't need them?

He picked up pair of leather gloves, but after a moment it seemed he had decided against wearing them. 'Those are the Magistrate's clothes,' she chided him.

'You took the ones I had been wearing,' the Doctor's voice reminded her lightly.

'I'm sorry,' she began, looking down at the cashmere jacket, feeling a twinge of guilt.

'Oh, don't worry,' he said, his arm snaking around her waist. 'They suit you much better than me.'

She looked at his new outfit. The clothes were severe, neat, and this man in the Doctor's body didn't look like the Doctor at all. 'Yours are also fitting,' she said.

He kissed her cheek. 'Barefoot again,' he noted, a little coldly.

'You know your shoes don't –' she began. 'How did you know about before? You have his body, do you have the Doctor's memories as well?'

His mouth curled. 'No. The breach in spacetime allowed me to observe the matter universe, and I had special interest in the Doctor.'

'You watched us?' Larna asked, her hand instinctively rising to cover her chest.

'I observed much of the universe,' he said. 'I saw the three suns of the

Sigimund Galaxy aligning to form the Aurora Arctialis, I saw the spinning of leptons, the formation of gemstones, the birth of kings, the preparation of great banquets.' He paused. 'I saw it, but I was condemned not to touch nor smell nor taste it...' he looked around the small, dark room as if it was the summit of the highest mountain, glorying in every detail. For the briefest moment, he was the Doctor again.

'We'll be landing in about ten minutes,' she said.

He nodded, as if he had already known.

'Do we need to prepare?

'No.' He laid the gloves down on the bed.

The garden was monochrome with a pastel wash.

The tree was darker, almost black. The Doctor looked up admiringly at it, and then decided to climb it. Balancing was easy, he found a branch that was easily thick enough for him to perch on it and for it to support his weight.

From this vantage point, the Doctor could see the plan of the hedgerows and flower beds, straight lines and perfect order for almost as far as the eye could see. On the horizon, though, he could see that the garden was surrounded by a high stone wall. Outside the walls was moorland, flat and empty. Beyond that was the sea, it was just possible to see it glinting and hear it crashing. The night's sky above them was full of stars arranged in unfamiliar constellations.

This wasn't a prison, and he didn't want to leave.

The Doctor ran his hands along the rough, ancient bark of the tree trunk. How long it had stood, what history it had seen, how many other lovers had fallen into blissful sleep in its evening shade?

He knew that the answer was none.

This tree had stood for less than a day, if it stood at all. This was a figment of his imagination. All the signs of weathering, any initials he found carved in the bark, or branches that had snapped off in winter storms were simply put there by his unconscious mind to convince him that this was real. For some reason, the thought made him uneasy, and he decided to climb down from the tree.

Who was to say that it was any different anywhere else? The past didn't exist, only the memory of the past. Perhaps the past was necessitated by the present, and not vice versa.

It was only the first night, but a number of centuries had already preceded it.

If time was an illusion, then what did that make a Time Lord?

No... the past existed, it was real, he'd been there, his own past and other people's.

He looked down at the woman sleeping far below him. She had been part of him for generations before his birth. She'd taught his father and his father and his father. She'd helped to raise him, she'd been his tutor, his friend, his first love, his wife, the mother of his children, she had been everything to him in the past. She had always been there, she wasn't just a whim, a fictional construct.

But how would he know if she was?

There was a rumble of thunder far away, over the sea.

Either she had always been there, or the past was changing, renewing itself. If he woke up tomorrow and she had never been there, would he still remember her? He looked down at her again, suddenly full of the thought that he should be with her for every moment that he possibly could be just in case she vanished, never to be seen or mentioned again.

He scowled, although there was no one to see it. This was nonsense, sophistry. The Doctor knew exactly who he was, who he'd always been. He was a Time Lord, from the Noble House of Lungbarrow on the planet Gallifrey. He had been born of the Loom, son of the greatest explorer of his age and a human woman, Annalise... no... his mother's name had been Penelope. He knew his father's name, at least: his father's name *wasn't* Ulysses, and he was a professor at Berkeley.

His own name escaped him for the moment, but he knew that he had one.

Lightning flashed overhead, unbidden, marking out the silhouette of the fortress like a signal flare.

It was a cathedral, kilometres across.

Light streamed from stained glass windows set in the limestone ceiling, walls and floors. It was a vast circular vault, a web of buttresses and supporting ribs. Close to, the arcs and parabolas appeared to be straight lines, as flat as the surface of a planet. Each roof beam was wide enough for an army to walk along, although no army would ever be allowed this far.

It was impossible architecture, of course. The inside of the chamber was far larger than the outside. The floors and walls eschered into one another and out along the power conduits and great arched portals. The light wasn't sunlight. Gravity was a local phenomenon, governed by whims rather than law. Look too closely and it was all too possible to see that the room was held together by optical illusions and false perspective.

But no one who came down here ever spent long looking at the architecture because hanging, aberrant and isolated in the mathematical centre of the vault, was the Eye of Harmony itself.

The black hole was encased in an iron globe ten kilometres in diameter. The dark metal was pitted and cratered with age, there were streaks of rust running along it, like dry river beds. It was suspended in its own gravity, apparently motionless. The power radiating from it was palpable, compelling.

At the top of the globe was a tiny aperture, and from that poured all the energy that Gallifrey needed, and so much more besides.

Savar stepped down into the vault, found his footing on the stonework.

He scurried down to a higher level, knowing where the TARDIS would arrive, and that it was imminent. The wheezing, groaning sound filled the air, echoing around the chamber. Savar was in place to see it arrive. hidden at a higher vantage point. The air swirled and parted like the curtains of a magician's cabinet. The TARDIS stood where it hadn't before. In this sanctuary of sanctuaries there was no need for camouflage, and the time capsule retained its natural form, that of a bone-white obelisk.

A panel in the front slid open, and two figures emerged.

The first wore the Doctor's clothes, but the waist-length blonde hair and the graceful movements were those of the Lady Larna. The second figure wore the Doctor's body, but it was not him either. Savar could sense its red eyes and true form. The trapped god, unbound and here, at the fount of all Gallifrey.

Savar reached for the force knife he'd recovered from his room. Clutching it in his hand, he began edging down.

'Explain the principle to me,' the Doctor's voice asked.

'You don't know?' Larna replied. There was no anxiety, no hint of coercion. She was the trapped god's willing servant.

'Rassilon's plan was simply to use the supernova as fuel. It would have supplied Gallifrey for many centuries. After that... I imagine we would have detonated another star. There is hardly a shortage.'

After a moment's silence, she continued. 'The Eye of Harmony is a rotating black hole. As it spins, it distorts space and time around it. The area affected, the ergosphere, is concentrated around the equator.'

'This globe contains both the black hole and the ergosphere?'

'That is correct. Otherwise we would have been destroyed by gravitational forces and radiation. Although in theory it is possible to escape from the ergosphere, anything within it would break up – part of it sucked down into the black hole, part of it flung out in the direction of rotation. But the part that escaped would be accelerated by the distortion of spacetime, like a slingshot. The black hole is so powerful that a tiny amount of energy can be amplified to near infinite levels.'

He pointed to the column of light pouring from the hole in the globe.

'That's right,' she said. 'The inside surface of the globe is mirrored. Rassilon shone a lamp through that hole, just for a second or so. Since then, the light has bounced from the ergosphere to the mirrored surface and back, gaining energy every time it re-emerges from the ergosphere. That ray of light now provides the fuel for all of Gallifrey.'

He laughed. 'Ingenious. Magic.'

'Superradiant scattering,' she corrected him primly, 'allowed for by all the laws of physics.'

'And at the heart of the black hole is the singularity, the point where those laws break down.'

'The point where physics allows a certain latitude,' she replied, quoting one of her tutors. 'But the universe is careful to hide such a dangerous place. Between us and the singularity is a cloud of radioactive matter; then a region of massive spacetime distortion; then an event horizon – a gateway that will let us in but not let us return; finally a stellar mass or more of matter that becomes steadily more solid until, at the core, it has reached infinity density.'

'I am Omega. Nothing is hidden from me.'

From his vantage point, Savar smiled.

As the thunder caught up, the Doctor peered over the garden to the castle.

The trees and the hedges and the sky were whispering to him. 'What's the matter, what's the matter, what's the matter?'

'What's the matter?' his wife asked, stirring and looking up at him.

The leaves were rustling. All around him, they were crinkling, shrivelling, falling.

'Omega,' the Doctor whispered, sitting at her side.

She shivered, drawing her gown over her shoulders. 'He's gone,' she told him. 'He left us in peace here.'

'No.' He stared at her face. 'No. No. No.'

The Doctor looked over at the castle. There were lights on in there.

The wind was whipping up the newly autumnal leaves. The rosebuds died on their stems, the grapes wrinkled on their vine.

'Come on!' the Doctor shouted, standing, starting to run towards the castle. She was right behind him.

A cold night wind drifted over as they ran through the garden.

The leaves were shrinking, desiccated, coming off the branches in droves. The stream was running dry, the imaginary fish flapping uselessly in the parched mud. The Doctor stopped when he saw them, willed them away. He stared up at the sky. The stars were winking out, one by one. The air was thick with autumn leaves and particles of dust. The lawns beneath their feet were sprinkled with sand now.

Lightning flashed around the fortress, lingering for longer than was natural.

'Come on,' she urged.

He picked up his pace.

Omega stepped up to an observation pulpit, located a small control panel and flipped it open. He began keying in a series of code sequences, rewiring the ancient circuits with the Doctor's sonic screwdriver. He had already surrounded their section of the chamber with a stasis halo. Now he was drawing a new power grid, preparing to implement it.

Larna leant over to get a better look at what he was doing. 'Would you like me to check your work?' she asked softly.

'That will not be necessary,' he replied, shifting a little, blocking her view.

'These are complicated equations, I could –'

'No,' he replied firmly.

He touched a control, and the panel closed itself up. 'I'm done here. Throw that switch, would you?' He pointed over to a large lever on her right.

Larna hesitated. 'Are you sure this is the right thing to do?'

'Throw the switch.'

Larna shook her head.

He moved towards her. 'Do it,' he commanded. He grabbed Larna's wrist in one hand, and before she could prevent it he'd grabbed her other wrist, too. He pushed her back, pinning her to the console, then slowly turned his hands, twisting her wrists, hurting her. She broke from the grip and lashed out at him, her hand balling into a fist as it did so. Larna had always been strong: the strongest of her Cousins, the strongest of her classmates.

She hit him hard, right in the face, and he went down.

Larna examined the control panel Omega had been working at and checked the new settings. He was planning to close the aperture. If the energy was sealed in the containment globe, it would increase exponentially, the pressures would pent up and before long the globe would explode. The singularity at the core of the black hole would be exposed, but the energy released would certainly destroy the Capitol Dome, it might enough to destroy Gallifrey.

Larna reached forward to disable the controls.

A hand grabbed her from behind, an arm was around her throat, pulling her away from the controls. She tried pushing him away, but he was too strong for her. She bent her knee, trying to wriggle free, but that didn't work either. He punched her hard in the stomach. She sank to her knees. Omega strode towards the lever.

Larna looked around for a way to stop him.

She still had the Magistrate's gun. She could feel it on her hip. Although that was the Doctor's body, it wasn't the Doctor. She mustn't think of it as the Doctor, mustn't let her memories stop her from destroying the body. Larna reached round, felt the warm metal. Her fingers wrapped around it, finding the trigger. Omega was holding out his hand to grab the lever.

She raised the gun. There was no time to aim it.

The Doctor – *Omega* – dived out the way as she squeezed the trigger. The end of the device opened up and glowed, an energy bolt sizzled out. It shot off into the depths of the chamber, with little effect.

Omega was down on her before she could fire the second shot. He stood on her wrist, already hurt in the fight with the Needle People. He

Law.'

'We *enforce* those laws, Grol. We wrote most of them.'

'That gives you the right to break them at will?'

'Chief of Staff, we have misplaced your leader, and I'm terribly sorry about that, but what would you have us do?'

'We could check the last place we saw him,' Pendrel suggested.

Voran scowled. 'Has anyone actually checked the xenodochia?'

There were a few muttered comments from the monks behind him.

'Now you must face the retribution of the Sontaran race for the terrible crime you have committed,' Grol growled. 'Vengeance will be swift and massive, and the universe will long sing of the day when –'

Voran yawned. 'Do what you will, Chief of Staff, we are currently dealing with a situation that –'

'Acting-President,' a voice behind him interrupted.

'Shut up, Pendrel. I'm sorry about that, Grol. As I say, a situation that requires our full attention, one that is a little more important than looking for some lost alien.'

'Acting-President,' Pendrel insisted.

He turned away from the Sontaran to see Pendrel. The ridiculous man was virtually tugging at his robes. 'This had better be important.'

'It is, Acting-President. It's the transduction barriers. They've been switched off.'

'What? On whose authority? Turn them back on, you idiot.'

Another aide came over to one side. 'There is no power going to the transduction systems or to the quantum forcefields.'

One of the Technicians was frantically squinting into his eyeboard. 'Total power drain on all systems. We're losing them all, one by one.'

'Gallifrey is utterly defenceless,' Pendrel concluded.

Grol's face was set is a long, lipless smile. Then his eyes narrowed, stared straight at the Acting-President.

'Admiral Krax, you are authorised to commence the attack,' the Sontaran said, his image fading away.

The Sontaran fleet had held its position since its arrival. Now, as one, their spectronic drives fired.

The fleet maintained its double arrowhead formation, their weapons systems coming on-line. They were quickly at battle speed. For the last few days, the strategy computers had been analysing Gallifrey. Bomber units were already streaking ahead of the main fleets, torpedoes had already been loaded into their tubes. The energy weapons had been charging up for days.

Behind them, the Rutan fleet was also powering up.

The Sontaran strategy computers had predicted this, but had concluded that the Rutan computers would not be expecting the Sontarans to attack Gallifrey itself. Caught unprepared for vital seconds by the Sontarans' audacity, the Rutan strategists would realise that there were two possibilities: either the Gallifreyans would swiftly annihilate the Sontarans, or the Sontarans had a secret weapon powerful enough to punch its way through technology a million years more advanced than the Rutans' own. Neither option favoured Rutan intervention.

The sudden power loss was unexpected, but a sign of providence, a sign that the war gods favoured the Sontaran.

As predicted, the Rutan ships let the Sontaran fleet power forwards, monitoring it closely.

The bridge of a Sontaran ship is a womblike space, suffused with red light, power cabling and umbilicals.

Admiral Krax sat at its heart, a hundred pilots and warriors at their stations around him. He couldn't see them, his eyes were covered by blinkers that gave him independent displays of fleet and enemy strength.

Fighter and bomber units were streaking ahead, already in the Gallifreyan atmosphere. The combined firepower of the fleet could shatter the planet into rubble. How long could the Capitol survive such an assault?

Gallifrey stood before them, defenceless. There wouldn't be another chance like this.

'Fire,' he ordered.

The Doctor saw it in the mirror.

'Gallifrey...' he said, his voice trailing off. He concentrated, felt the breach in spacetime shift. But he couldn't control the Effect.

The first missiles were detonating on the planet's surface.

'Gallifrey will be destroyed,' she told him.

'The Capitol Dome is indestructible.'

'But Gallifrey itself isn't,' she insisted. 'And Omega is loose.'

The Doctor stared into the mirror. 'That is where I came from once, but not any more. I come from here, now. I belong here with you. He can't hurt us, here. He made me a god.'

The picture shifted. There was a familiar young woman, with ash blonde hair. She was crying, in pain. His wife placed a hand on his shoulder. 'Larna?'

He nodded.

'She's beautiful.'

The Doctor nodded again, a little embarrassed. 'Look at her, though. She isn't you, she never could be. She's from *there*, and you're perfect, you're everything.'

'You could stop Omega.'

'I know.'

'You are the only other being in creation in control of a singularity. You are the only thing that can stop him.'

The Doctor nodded.

'You can go back, now. Omega was trapped here, but now that he's exposed a singularity in the universe of matter, you can use it as a doorway. It's a clear way home.'

'This is home,' the Doctor insisted. 'You are all that I want. I've left that place behind, with all its squabbling and imperfections and unrequited love and decay and...' His voice trailed off as he gazed into the mirror and saw a man in his body pinning Larna down, as he saw her mouth screaming at him for help. 'You are perfect, you are all that I want. If Omega had offered me the choice between this and that, then I would have chosen this.'

'You must go back.'

'I can't,' he said. 'My will keeps you alive. You're a figment of my imagination. If I leave, you will die. I can't leave you. I can let this end.'

Perfect red lips smiled, a little uncertainly. 'Everything ends. You know that, you know that it's how it's meant to be.'

She kissed him.

Omega was all over Larna. She could feel his breath on her face. Hot, ammoniac, like a bull's. He was pinning her down, she could feel his strength on hers. Larna had always been strong, but she wasn't anything compared to this. She could feel her muscles clench and strain against this creature, but it was as if they belonged to someone else. Her strength just wasn't relevant.

'Omega!' a familiar voice called from behind her.

Omega released his grip, turned to face the new arrival.

Framed in the entrance to the pulpit was Savar. The one who could see. The force knife in his hand was a broadsword, longer than he was tall.

'I have waited a thousand years for this moment,' Savar said, advancing.

'Have you, now?'

'He's got a gun,' Larna shouted over.

Omega levelled the Magistrate's weapon, but Savar was already bringing his sword up. He sliced the gun in half.

Savar raised the sword.

Omega's eyes flashed red.

A shadow fell over Savar, and when it lifted there was another Savar. A blind man in grey robes.

'Master,' Savar answered, lowering himself to his knees. 'I offer myself to you. A body in this universe of matter. I have waited a thousand years to make such a sacrifice.'

'You're just an hour too late,' he observed. He held his hand to his chest. 'I have a body, now.'

The blind man hesitated.

'Savar,' Larna called. 'Remember me? It's Larna.'

'Master...' Savar said helplessly.

'He's going to kill you,' Larna warned him. 'He's going to kill you unless you kill him.'

Savar was hunched up, he didn't seem to be listening.

'He's been using you, but now he doesn't need you any more. Kill him!'

Savar leapt forwards, swinging the sword, bringing it down hard on Omega's shoulder. The blade connected with Omega's neck, half-severing it. His head lolled.

Larna pulled herself out of the way.

The second blow sliced the left femur, the third chopped a kneecap. Omega slipped over.

'I am your god,' the Doctor's voice rasped, blood and spit in his mouth. He held out his hand. 'Bow down.'

Savar brought the sword down on his shoulder, and the arm flopped back. All part of the same movement, the blade swept up, cutting his nose and cheek.

He swung the broadsword straight at Omega's head.

Omega caught it in one hand, tugged it from Savar's grasp and tossed it over the edge of the pulpit.

'There is only one future.'

He gave a great shout, an animalistic roar from deep inside him. When he had finished he stood there uninjured, his broken bones mended, the blood gone from his wounds.

'There is only Omega.'

He waved his hand, and Savar evaporated. The blind man's cloak tottered back, slapping into the ground in front of Larna.

She slumped.

Omega bent over her. 'You know,' he said, 'I really see why the Doctor has his companions. Doing all this is really much better with an audience.'

'You turned him,' she said. 'You transformed him into the blind Savar, the alternate one.'

'Not just Savar.'

She could hear screaming. Men howling, like wolves. Agonised sounds that started like words.

Larna looked up at him. Omega had his back to her, he was staring up at the containment globe. The iron was bubbling, blistering, disintegrating. At its heart was a chink of *something*. The singularity.

'Night has fallen on Gallifrey. Can't you feel it? Oh, don't worry, my dear. You're protected, here in the stasis halo. But out there, they've all transformed. Voran, Pendrel, all of them. They're blind and alone, desperate. Without the power of the Eye to protect them, without Rassilon watching over them, hear what they've become. Hear what they are *really*.'

A man crying. A choir screaming in harmony. Strangulated calls and guttural, primeval noises. Explosions, shattering masonry, falling statues, burning flesh. All of the sounds echoed down from the Citadel, filtered through the thick limestone walls.

Larna pulled herself up, stood eye to eye with him.

'With the power of the singularity, you'll be able to do anything, have anything. Is this really what you *want*?'

The Doctor's face smiled down at her.

'Yes.'

He stepped off the edge of the pulpit, fell towards the singularity, grasped it, became god.

As the power flowed through him, Omega shed the Doctor's skin. He became a vast, hunched creature like a bull or a warthog. The armour that surrounded him was built from solid plates of metal, the sort of cladding usually only seen on battleships. He had ram's horns, a beard that curled down his breastplate. His right hand burned with the singularity where he had touched it. He was no longer a man, no longer an animal... no, he was a force of nature like a hurricane or a forest fire.

Men can't fight the hurricane.

Omega saw that it was good.

There was a slow clapping from behind him.

He turned. The Doctor was there, mocking him with applause.

'Apotheosis,' the Doctor said. 'The merging of your physical body and the power of the singularity. Congratulations.'

Omega's eyes flashed red, he willed the Doctor's destruction, invoked the fundamental powers of the universe to annihilate him.

The Doctor yawned, held up his right hand. Flame flickered around it. 'Snap,' he said calmly. 'I've got a singularity of my own. Let me show you something.'

They were standing on grey, devastated ground. A desolate place, the sky full of fog, and gravel and tektites underfoot.

'Where are we?' Omega demanded.

'A planet in the seventh galaxy which died in nuclear fire. The twelfth world of its star system. It is centuries since that war and the radiation levels have fallen. The sky is still black, the oceans and lakes are still frozen.' The Doctor paused. 'This is Skaro.'

They began to walk on the broken, blackened soil.

'Is there anything living here?' Omega asked.

The Doctor drew a deep breath. 'A fifth of the population died in the initial attack. Toxic gases, waste and biological agents filled the air as the cities burned. Every piece of asbestos, every drop of toxic waste. Another fifth of the population died, because there were no adequate surviving medical services to stop them from dying. Immense amounts of particle matter quickly accumulated in the upper atmosphere, obscuring the sun. Water supplies froze, food would not grow. Another fifth of the population died. And, as the long winter ended, a year later, the situation became worse. Every animal larger than an insect had already died. With no predators to hold them in check, insect life swarmed across the planet. The corpses were beginning to defrost. Epidemics and pandemics spread with nothing to stop them. What could survive here, what would want to survive?'

Omega's eyes narrowed. 'The Time Lords could have prevented this. With our powers, we could prevent this from happening here and on the million planets where the same pattern was repeated, over and over. Or we could simply remove this from history, excise it.'

The Doctor pursed his lips, apparently impressed. 'So you can destroy it?'

'Gladly.' Omega waved his glove, and the planet's star went nova, obliterating the dead planet in an instant. They watched the destruction from a safe vantage point in a neighbouring star system.

The Doctor gave a quiet, satisfied smile.

'Now bring it back.'

Omega grunted, but with another wave of the hand, the planet was back in place.

'Destroy it,' the Doctor repeated.

As the planet blew itself apart once again, he turned to the Doctor.

'What is this meant to prove? All this proves is that we have the power of the gods.'

'You're nothing,' the Doctor said finally.

'You will not deny me. I am everything!' Omega shouted.

'You're both,' the Doctor snapped, silencing him. 'Destroying and undestroying planets with the merest thought.'

'What I can do to one planet I can do a thousandfold. I live in infinity, Doctor, not in some narrow universe where only one thing can happen. Now you can kill and let live. We can make the universe dance to our every whim, to all our whims.'

The Doctor smiled sympathetically. 'Of course we can.'

'You doubt me?' Omega snarled.

The Doctor gave a tiny shake of his head. 'Oh no. I pity you.'

'You are not worthy of godhood.'

'No, it's not that. What's the point of controlling a universe without meaning, where nothing of any consequence ever happens? Why shed tears when someone dies if they can be brought back, why cheer on your favourite team when if they lose they can also win? I don't want to be a god.'

'You are weak.'

The Doctor shook his head. 'Answer me this, Omega: what's the opposite of matter?'

'Anti-matter,' Omega replied instantly.

'Wrong, wrong, wrong. The opposite of matter is "doesn't matter".' The Doctor sighed. 'That's what we've created – a universe where everything is nothing. A universe where nothing matters. Of course you can rewrite history, but you shouldn't. As long as you have these great powers, nothing is real.'

'I am god, Doctor, I define reality. I am all.'

'Of course you are, of course you do, of course you are,' the Doctor said, smirking.

Omega roared and raised his hand.

The Doctor smiled. 'Even if you could kill me, you'd only get bored sooner or later and bring me back. You're trapped. You're trapped by your omnipotence, just as you were trapped in the anti-matter universe.'

'That is not true,' Omega insisted. But for all his omniscience and omnipotence he couldn't say why.

'Because you will it?'

Omega felt the galaxies within him. He felt the stars and planets in his mouth and his eyes, time and space flowing through him like blood. 'I am infinite. I am everything.'

The Doctor raised his head. 'Is that all you are? Infinity? Is there nothing more than *you*?'

Omega faltered. 'You are right.'

There was silence for a moment.

'Is this all that I am?' Omega asked, looking down at his hands. 'Is this it? My moment of triumph? I have dreamt of this moment for more nights than the Time Lords have ever dreamt. To be a god! To be *the* god!'

The Doctor grinned. 'I knew you'd see sense. You can still be a man, Omega. Before you were a god you were a great man. Become that again. Come back to Gallifrey and resume your place there.'

Omega gave the same, small, flickering grin. '"Think'st thou that I who saw the face of God and tasted the eternal joys of heaven am not tormented with ten thousand hells in being deprived of everlasting bliss"?'

The Doctor tapped his lips. Quoting Mephistopheles wasn't always the sign of a stable mind.

'Faking a real life?' Omega spat. 'Such a life would be just as much a sham as being a hollow god.'

He paused, looked around. 'Nothing is real now, nothing has meaning.'

He stepped away from the doorway, a tear in his eye.

'You have destroyed all my hopes, you have condemned me to a meaningless existence.'

'Not meaningless!' the Doctor shouted. 'You must find new meaning in your life, yes, but no life is meaningless.'

'There is only one freedom left to me.'

The Doctor grabbed Omega's arm. 'There's no need to take your own life.'

He smiled down. 'Not just my own life. This universe is lost, this universe has no meaning. Time to end it.'

Outside, the dead stars and planets began vanishing. Time and space began to wind down.

'You can't destroy the whole universe,' the Doctor gasped from the doorway.

'And why not?'

The Doctor shrugged. 'Well, for one thing, where would you live afterwards?'

'There will be no afterwards,' he said quietly. 'There will be no before. This universe will never have existed. There will have been no torment, no betrayal by friends and lovers. No disappointments or disease, no wars. No one will ever have died or lost a loved one. It will be a simpler place, a better place.'

The Doctor remembered the garden, and the beautiful woman with moon-white skin. 'Everything ends,' he said softly.

'Indeed.'

The Doctor took a deep breath. 'You're right, perhaps it's time to end it.'

Omega gave a grim smile. 'You were a worthy opponent, Doctor.'

'Thanks. Shake on it?' The Doctor held out his hand.

Omega clasped it.

'One last thing,' the Doctor noted. 'Ever wondered what would happen if a singularity came into direct contact with an anti-singularity?' He squeezed Omega's right hand very tight.

* * *

Everything ended.

Larna watched as the aperture opened, as the column of energy burst forth once more. To her side were the smoking remains of Savar's cloak. Around her the screaming and bombardment had stopped.

In front of her was the Doctor's body, naked and inert. It was pale, but his chest was rising and falling, ever so slowly, his breath was condensing in the cold air.

She bent over him, taking her jacket off, covering him up. 'Doctor?'

His eyes flickered open. 'Larna?'

It was him, she knew it. 'Where's Omega?'

'I don't know,' he said weakly, pulling himself into a sitting position. 'Banished. Sealed away. Dead. I don't know. His singularity came into contact with my anti-singularity. I don't know what happened after that... there's no such thing as an anti-singularity, I made it up, so there's no theory to account for what happened next.'

'And you?'

'I... I think I might have just saved the entire universe from destruction.'

Larna helped him into his jacket.

The Doctor smiled, a little uncertainly. 'Thank you, Larna,' he said finally.

Larna laughed lightly, and kissed him. 'Thank *you*, Doctor.'

Epilogue
So This is Victory

Sunlight poured through the cracks in the Capitol Dome, like a liberating army.

High above, maintenance teams had been working around the clock to repair the damage, and this would be the last sunrise that the Capitol would ever see. Golden sunlight picked out the vivid colours of the roof terraces, the intricate mahoganies of the Citadel walls, the golds and silvers and marbles of the clocks and monuments. It made the walkways and computer towers gleam. This was the home of the most powerful race in the cosmos, this was the capital city of the universe. A day since the defeat of Omega and the events of the previous week seemed like a distant nightmare. The rubble had been cleared, the damage from the riots and the bombardments had been cleaned away, the dead had been interred. Life was returning to normal.

The chimes of the Clock Tower rang out over the hexangles of the Eastern side of the Citadel. The Time Lords and Technicians began to emerge from their quarters and glide smoothly to their work and their leisure. Lord Henspring and Lady Gehammer passed each other by the living fountain, three members of the Watch marched past, on their way to lay a wreath at the Monument to Lost Explorers. A small group of students stood around discussing the cultivation of roses and chess endgames. Deep within the Citadel, the TARDISes sat in their cradles, surrounded by humming machinery, as they had done for hundreds of thousands of years.

Constable Peltroc hoisted the phased trion burster up against the keyhole, Captain Raimor keyed the firing sequence. A small group of Watchmen stood around, trying to hold back the Sontarans. Half a dozen Councillors stood nervously on the other side of the room. Technically, they were still at war with the Sontaran Empire, although the Sontarans had been markedly less hostile since the restoration of the transduction barriers.

'Hey, hey,' said the Doctor, bustling in, 'careful with that TARDIS, it's a family heirloom.'

Acting-President Voran waved his hand, and the two guards lowered the burster, grumbling a little.

'Open this capsule up, Doctor, we've waited long enough.'

The Doctor gave an uncertain smile, fishing the key from his coat pocket. He opened the door, then he stepped back to see what would emerge.

For a moment there was no movement. Then General Sontar stepped over the threshold. The Doctor had left him a broken man, violated and drained by the Rutan. The creature that emerged now was entirely different. It looked like Sontar, but with little of the ancient creature's brooding menace.

The Doctor acknowledged the Sontaran leader's arrival, but was more concerned with what was behind him. The soft, gelatinous glow of the Rutan was becoming visible.

The other Sontarans tensed. But Sontar shook his head.

The Doctor gasped.

'We thought you would have killed each other,' the Acting-President informed him.

'I killed the Rutan,' Sontar said. 'It killed me.'

'Over and over, again and again,' the Rutan echoed. 'Within the confines of your time machine, the final death is not possible. Within minutes our enemy lived once more, whatever horrors we had inflicted. A fascinating technology.'

Sontar edged forwards. 'After a while, we realised the futility of our actions. Our thoughts turned to escape. We did not co-operate in these attempts, but each learned from the other's failures. The console was locked off, and resisted all attempts to reactivate it. There were no other exits.'

The Rutan flared brighter. 'It soon became clear that escape was impossible. We meditated on our fate – to be confined for ever with the deadliest of our enemies, in the certain knowledge that whatever our hopes, whatever our achievements, that we were doomed. The universe would fall to the Grey.'

'It was then that we realised how much we shared, how insignificant our differences were. We talked. Events have transpired as you planned, Doctor. Alone, unable to fight or escape, we reached an accommodation.'

The other Sontarans shifted in place, but none dared to contradict their emperor.

'Thank you, Doctor. Your wisdom has shown us the path to peace.'

'Thank you,' Sontar repeated. 'An unorthodox method, but more effective than a thousand years of peace conferences. You tricked us into thinking you were a fool, with nothing to say. All the time, you had your plot. Chain us together and leave us to find our own peace. You are a brave and cunning man.' He slapped the Doctor on the back.

'Well,' mumbled the Doctor as he regained his footing, 'it was nothing.'

'We will signal our fleets, and signal the immediate cessation of hostilities.'

'Is it really as easy as that?' Voran asked. 'Your entire economies have been geared for war for thousands of years. War is in your blood.'

'Blood can change,' the Rutan said.

'Both our races are capable of rapid adaptation,' Sontar explained. 'As the Time Lords know, clone races are easily controlled, easily guided. The Sontaran clone banks can be re-engineered, the Rutan Host can suppress the creation of certain of the more hostile forms.'

'Swords into ploughshares?' asked the Doctor.

Sontar nodded. 'Exactly that.'

'Our races pride ourselves on our obedience, our single-mindedness. Now we are united in peace.'

'Just like that?' the Doctor asked.

'Just so. There will be the largest demobilisation in the history of the universe, massive restructuring of the forms of our empires. But these are mere details.'

'I wish you well.'

Sontar smiled and held out its claw, and the Doctor shook it. The Rutan unfurled a tentacle, which the Doctor squeezed.

Finally, General Sontar turned to the Rutan and offered it its claw. The Rutan grew a three-fingered hand and shook it.

'The war is over,' Sontar said. 'Thanks to the Doctor. The Time Lords, of course, will man the checkpoints, guard the buffer zones around our territories. With Gallifrey maintaining the peace –'

The Doctor held up his hand. 'No, no, no. Not our style at all. We'll be happy to advise you, but we're not going to watch over you. This peace is your responsibility, no one's going to enforce it for you.'

'I understand,' the Rutan agreed.

Sontar was nodding thoughtfully. 'We must return home, and begin our work.'

The Watchmen snapped to attention.

Voran nodded, pleased. 'Good. Good,' he said, as the Sontarans formed ranks behind their leader and the Rutan delegate and began marching from the room.

For a moment there was silence, the Doctor and Voran alone together.

'Well,' the Doctor said.

Voran paused. 'And there is work to be done here. There will be a Council meeting at Eight Bells to discuss the aftermath of this affair. Your attendance will, of course, be expected.' He swept from the room.

The Doctor closed the TARDIS door and put the key back in his pocket. He patted its side.

'Well done, old girl,' he said.

The Doctor knocked on Larna's door. Her maid, Vrayto, opened it.

'Councillor...' she said, curtseying.

Behind her, the Doctor caught a glimpse of Larna. She turned, a broad smile on her face. The Doctor stepped past the maid and down into the room. He knew what the quarters in this part of the Citadel were like – this wasn't too far from his own room. The main difference was the lack of clutter – the shelves hadn't been filled, let alone packed to bursting. There were no pictures on the walls, and only a handful of ornaments and trophies lying around. There were a few crates full of things though.

Larna was looking over a large sheaf of paper. Astronomical diagrams by the look of them – reports from the Astronomy Bureau. She was wearing a neat collarless jacket and tight trousers in Prydonian scarlet and orange. Her hair was loose, down her back.

'You've been a Time Lord for a little while now,' he said. 'You really should have found the time to unpack.' He rummaged in the crate and pulled out a psychology textbook.

'I'm packing up.'

He laid the book down.

'I got a new job. I got what I wanted.'

There were plenty of vacancies now, as the Time Lords shuffled around to fill the gaps left by the deaths and disappearances. Rumours were circulating about the possible new appointments to the High

Council. Voran would no doubt be rewarding his cronies like Pendrel. But every promotion caused a further vacancy to form, more duties and titles to spread amongst the Time Lord aristocracy.

To avoid thinking about what he wanted to think about, the Doctor racked his brains, tried to imagine what they'd have given Larna. 'Head of research somewhere? Something practical?'

She nodded. 'The breach in spacetime caused a lot of damage. I've been appointed leader of the group that will clear up the mess left by the Effect. We'll be locating and neutralising the after effects.'

The Doctor opened his mouth and waved his hands helplessly. 'Well done,' he said finally. 'That's quite a responsibility.'

'Well, most of the other candidates are dead or –'

The Doctor pulled back. 'No need to be modest. It's a high honour. You wouldn't get the job if you couldn't do it.'

'There will be a lot of fieldwork,' she said. 'I'll be away from Gallifrey for most of the time, leading a team of specialists. It's just what I've always wanted. The chance to travel, to leave the Capitol. There will even be contact with other timefarers.'

'You could be away for some time.'

'The Matrix estimates that it will take around two thousand years.'

The Doctor's smile flickered. 'That *is* a long time,' he mumbled.

She looked over at him, a little sadly. 'Yes.'

The Doctor stood. 'I... don't want to hold up your packing. I've always hated goodbyes. Good luck.'

Larna leant over and kissed him on the cheek. 'Thank you,' she said.

There had been one candle for every year.

The Doctor snuffed out the last between his thumb and forefinger. The room was dark, the smell of wax heavy in the air, reminding him of a church. It must have been the smoke that was making his eyes water. He stepped from the room. The door closed, and – anticipating its owner's mood – locked and bolted itself. And then there was nothing behind it. The Doctor slumped against the wall for a moment.

So this was victory.

Lord Norval, Savar and a couple of dozen others dead, the Magistrate lost. Larna leaving. Omega... whatever. Broken. His wife gone. Voran Acting-President, Pendrel as Castellan. Hedin back in the Endless Library, rewriting his biography of Omega from the beginning. Nothing had changed, because nothing ever changed on Gallifrey except over geological timescales. Nothing was better, nothing was worse. The Sontarans and the Rutans could change, it seemed, but not his own people.

He looked over at her portrait, remembered the day he had painted it. She'd been standing in the atrium of the family home, in that dress of hers that she had found somewhere. As she had stood there, she'd told him, ever so calmly, that a miracle had taken place. She was pregnant. He remembered how he had felt – that combination of elation and trepidation. The knowledge that there was a future, a sense of destiny, of inevitability. Things would never be the same again. He'd never look to the past, he'd told himself, only to the future.

The Doctor moved away from the wall, towards his favourite chair. Wycliff trotted out of his box to join him, brushing against his legs. He stroked the cat's head, deciding that he wouldn't sit down after all.

The Doctor could feel the key to his TARDIS in his trouser pocket, warm against his leg. He took it out, held it up.

The first time he had left Gallifrey, it had been for a short hop across the Constellation, to his parents' summer house. He'd stared up into the dark night's sky, seen all the moving points of light. 'Not stars,' his mother had told him. 'Ships. Those ships don't travel on the sea, those are ships that travel in space and time.' He had wanted to ask where they were going, and who was in them, but he hadn't. When he got back, he'd asked his tutors and looked in books and the video archive, but the answer remained elusive. He'd read about the stars and the planets, and all the people that lived out in the universe, and all about their histories and their sciences. He thought up a lot of questions, and not all the answers were in the books that had been written so far or on the Public Record Video.

To find the answers, he would have to go looking for them. He'd have to leave Gallifrey, get out there, out into the universe. Who knew where the future lay? Who wanted to know?

The Doctor smiled.